The
Price of Trust

By
Amanda Stephan

The Price of Trust

©2011 by
Amanda Stephan

Cover Design: Linda Boulanger
www.TellTaleBookCovers.weebly.com/
Interior Layout: Amanda Stephan
www.BooksByAmanda.com

Published by: TreasureLine Publishing
www.TreasureLinePublishing.com

ISBN: 978-1-61752-109-6

Also available in eBook publication

The following is a work of fiction. Names, characters, places, and incidents are fictitious or used fictitiously. Any resemblance to real persons, living or dead, to factual events or to businesses is coincidental and unintentional.

Printed in the United States of America
1. Fiction / Romance / Contemporary   2. Fiction / Religious

I would like to dedicate this book to my family,
Who always believed in me and thought I could,
To my loving husband who told me I should,
And to God, because without Him, I am nothing.

Chapter One

One more mile. Please, Lord, take me just one more mile, Carly prayed, trying to coax the wheezing junker to the next town. Without realizing it, she was rocking back and forth to encourage the old car to keep up the speed.

It wasn't working. Going slower and slower, she was afraid that she was going to stall and didn't stop praying until she reached the dingy service station that was next to the ramp. The car stalled as she pulled into a parking space.

Thank you so much, Lord. Thank you so much. She prayed with a sigh of relief. *Now will you please take me to where you want me to go? I don't know anyone, and I have to be careful with the little money I've got left. Please let me know what you want me to do*, she prayed under her breath as she got out of the wreck that belonged to her.

A man in dirty overalls came out, wiping his hands on an old grease rag.

"Excuse me, but I noticed your car. Is there anything I can do for you?" he asked, looking her up and down warily.

She was used to stares. Especially in little towns like this one. Newcomers were rare, and most places she'd been, they didn't trust new people right away but looked at them with suspicion. She gave him her best smile and decided to be as friendly as possible.

"Well, I'm not so sure what you can do to fix that old junk, but maybe you could point me to the nearest place to find something to eat, and then I'll decide what to do with it. Will it be okay where it's at for now?"

"Yeah, it'll be okay there for now. But you'll have to take care of it later. The owner doesn't like people just leaving their stuff lying around. There's a diner across the street," the mechanic said, turning around and walking back into the garage.

Nice fellow. Not talkative, but not rude. That was a change

from the last place she'd been. She'd been to so many she was a little tired of new places. She wished and prayed that maybe she could stay here longer than the last place. She wanted to belong somewhere. Stop running. Just stay and be happy. But it didn't seem likely to happen any time soon. She sighed.

"Thanks," she called after him. She turned, and crossed the street to the diner. Taking a deep breath, she pushed open the door and walked in. Everyone turned to stare at her.

Whew! What a way to make people nervous! She smiled bravely and seated herself at the counter.

"May I help ya?" a waitress asked with a drawl.

"Well, I'd like a bowl of soup and water please. And could you tell me if there's a junkyard around here? I've got a donation for them," she said, smiling sardonically.

The waitress proved to be more talkative and friendly than the mechanic.

"Well, we've got two junkyards, but they're run by the same family, so you won't get much from them. They're pretty stingy when it comes to paying for junk cars. Or anything for that matter. You new in town?" the waitress asked while pouring her water.

It always made her nervous when people asked questions. They always wanted to know more than she could, or would, tell them.

"Yeah, I just arrived. Do you know of anyone that's looking for some help?" she asked, trying to curb the waitress's curiosity.

"Hey there, Sandy! Could I have another cup of coffee over here, or are you going to jaw away the day and let your customers die of thirst?" a man in a booth called out good-naturedly, waving his coffee cup in the air.

"Aw, come on George, I'll get to ya! When have I ever let ya down?" Sandy answered. George guffawed in return. "I'm not too sure about any jobs around here. Are you lookin' for anything special?" Sandy called to her while pouring George's coffee. Carly turned red. "George, ya know anyone that's lookin' for some help?" Sandy asked loud enough for everyone to hear.

George smirked. "Well, depends on what she's looking for. I

hear them junkyard people are looking for someone to work in their 'office.'"

"I wouldn't send her to those people! They're mean! They just ain't right. In fact..." Sandy trailed off as the door swung open and the diner bell tinkled. A bulky man walked in. Carly looked at him as he came in and sat two stools down from her. He was big with black hair, a belly that hung over his waistband, scruff on his chin, and a mean hard look in his eyes.

"Sandy!" the new man barked needlessly. A silence had fallen over the diner as soon as he had walked in. Carly noticed that a few customers were leaving, quickly paying their bills and leaving their tips strewn on their tables.

God had blessed Carly with an uncanny ability to figure people out, and most of the time, she could tell if they were to be trusted, if they were honest, or if she should stay away from them. Sometimes she made a mistake, but it wasn't very often.

She didn't trust or like this man sitting by her at all, so she quickly ate her soup, hoping that he would continue to ignore her.

"Yes, Bob. May I help ya?" Sandy asked very quietly and not as friendly as she had been with the other customers. Carly could tell that many people were afraid of this man.

"Give me my usual." And that was it. No please. No thank you. Nothing. Just rudeness. Without looking at her, he asked, "Is that your piece of junk sitting at my garage?"

Carly assumed, correctly, that he was talking to her.

"Yes, sir. I was just going to get in touch with the junkyard, and I'll have it taken off your property," Carly stammered, turning red.

"Well then you'll be talking to me, seeing as I'm the owner of the junkyard." He sneered meanly. "What do ya want?" he asked as Sandy brought his food, and he began to eat noisily.

Lord, please help me, she prayed silently, disgusted with this man and his manners. "Well, how much will you give me for it?" she asked with a brave smile.

"I'll give ya fifty bucks and that's it," he said, dribbling food out of the corners of his mouth.

Repulsed, Carly replied, "That's fine. Thank you. I just have to get my stuff out of it."

He looked at her for the first time. "If you mean the radio or anything that is part of the car, you better leave it," he warned, his eyes hard and menacing.

"No, I just meant my clothes and stuff like that," Carly stuttered.

"You're new in town, aren't ya? I would have recognized that hair anywhere," he said, laughing at Carly's red hair.

Carly had always been a little oversensitive about her hair. The kids in her schools had always made fun of it, and this man making fun of her didn't endear him to her either. She held her head higher and gave him a defiant look. She wasn't going to let this guy get the best of her.

"I'll go empty my car right now," Carly answered, leaving her money on the counter for Sandy to pick up. He laughed at her as she walked out the door.

Dear Lord, I know that you love that man in there, and I think it's a good thing that you do. I just can't imagine anyone else doing it! she prayed indignantly. *I need your help again, Lord. I hope you're not getting tired of helping me so much. I need a job, and a place to sleep. Somewhere Ian won't find me. Will you please lead me where you want me to go?*

After both her parents had died, God was the only one she had to take care of her. And she had to admit, he always did a good job of it. He always answered her and showed her the way. She had no reason to think that this time would be any different.

As she was getting her old, ratty bags out of the car, she heard a cough behind her. She turned to find George from the diner standing a bit aimlessly on the curb by her car.

"Sandy said you were looking for work around here. I think you might try the hardware store. They're getting on in age and could use some help. And, uh, watch out for Bob back there. He's really not a nice guy. You stay away from him and his two sons.

4

You hear?" He walked away before Carly had time to say anything.

"Thanks," she called after him. She closed the door to her car sadly. It felt like a chapter of her life was closing. She knew it was only a car, and it was silly to feel sad about a car dying, but it was the last thing that was really hers, except for her two suitcases with all her clothes and toiletries.

Lord, you've never let me down before, so please give me the courage to go on. This is where you have placed me, and I ask you to please give me strength and the nerve I'm gonna need, she prayed as she saw Bob walking toward her, grinning.

"Maybe I've offered you too much for that junk. I think I'll change my mind. Naw. I suppose it's worth fifty bucks for scrap." He laughed raucously as he threw a fifty-dollar bill at her. She stooped to pick it up off the ground and started to walk away. "You should meet my boys. One of 'em is bound to like ya. Let us know if you get lonely!" Once more, rude, loud laughter erupted behind her. She kept walking, acting as if she hadn't heard him.

She strolled down the sidewalk, looking for the hardware store. Walking in, she left her suitcases near the front door and went to the counter where an older gentleman was bent over working on some receipts.

Pausing to study him for a moment, she decided rather quickly that he was someone she would like working for.

His mess, bushy white hair reminded her of a picture she had seen once of Albert Einstein, and the gold-rimmed bifocals that were almost slipping off the end of his nose completed the effect. The mustache he sported was not exactly like Mr. Einstein's, but she liked it anyway. However, what drew her to him the most was that he reminded her of an old friend she had known in church long ago.

Nostalgia and memories of days long gone threatened to bring tears to her eyes.

Swallowing the lump in her throat, she said pleasantly, "Hi, I'm new in town, and I heard that you might be able to use some help?"

"Well, as a matter of fact, I am looking for some help. What can you do?" he asked, looking at her worn suitcases. She hesitated.

"Well, I'm pretty good at accounting, data entry, making change, stocking shelves, shoveling out barns, babysitting, farm work, cleaning houses, you name it. I can learn anything you want me to if you'll just give me a chance," she gushed out finally, turning red. She was afraid that he would think she wouldn't be right for the job. She had had to learn so many things, that she was sure that she really could learn anything.

The man looked at her for a moment. Then he came around from behind the counter and held out his hand to her.

"My name is Samuel, but the town folk just call me Sam."

"Carly. Carly Adams," she answered, turning red as she gave her mother's last name instead of her own. She shook his hand and felt that he knew she hadn't told him the truth. She hated to fib.

"Carly Adams," he repeated, as if trying it out. "Hmm. Well, I've always been partial to the name 'Red' myself. Would you mind if I called you Red instead?" he asked, with a twinkle in his eye.

Red. She used to hate that nickname, but somehow, this old man made it all right. He didn't mean it as a cruelty to her. Instinct told her that she could trust him.

She chuckled. "Yes, that would be fine."

"I can't pay you too much, this being a small town and all, but I'll do my best. If you need a place to stay"—he nodded toward her suitcases—"there's a room upstairs with a small bathroom the manager used before he left you could have. That way you wouldn't have to pay for a place to live, and I could feel easier about the pay. Would that suit you?" he asked, looking at her above his glasses.

"That would be wonderful! Thank you so much!" She felt like crying, she was so happy. God was so good to her. He always provided for her needs. Even when she didn't understand or when people failed her, she knew she could really trust God to take care of her.

"Here. I'll show you the way upstairs so you can put your things away and get settled a bit," Sam said, taking a suitcase while she took the other.

He led her up the stairs at the back of the store and opened the door to a tiny apartment at the end of the hallway. Sam placed her suitcase on the floor beside the door and showed her around.

"It's not much, but it is a place to stay. Here's the bathroom." He opened a small door to the tiny bathroom that had a sink, toilet, tub, and nothing else. "Here's the kitchen, refrigerator, stove. That's a table that you pull down from the wall, and here's the bed," he said pointing to an older couch that pulled out to a sleeper bed. It was small, but extremely clean and well cared for. "My wife came in here and cleaned up after the manager left, so there shouldn't be any surprises." He laughed.

"Thank you so much, Mister..." She trailed off, not sure what to call him.

"Please just call me Sam. That's all. Just Sam. My wife's name is Sue. You'll meet her later when she comes in to see me around four. It's a habit she's always had. She always comes, and she's never late. Well, I'll leave you be for now. You unpack, take care of your things, relax. Whatever. But we do ask that you don't smoke or drink in here. We're Christians, and we don't think that would be right for us to allow that while you're here," he said, turning to go back downstairs.

"You're Christians?" Carly asked, delighted.

He turned back to her, surprised. "Yes, we are. Why?"

"I am too. Where do you go to church?" she asked, smiling.

"Well, we go to the little church down the road here. Got a real good pastor that preaches right out of the Good Book. It just doesn't get any better than that. We'd love to have you come with us tomorrow if you'd like," he invited.

"I'd love to!" Carly said with an eager shake of his hand.

Chapter Two

"Momma, Momma! Don't leave me, Momma! I want to go with you! Please take me with you," the child screamed in agony, holding her hands out as if trying to catch hold of something or someone.

Carly woke up with a start, soaked in sweat. The dream again. She'd been having it a lot lately, and she couldn't seem to stop it. She always felt so depressed afterwards. But it was always like that when she was running and scared. So she did the only thing she knew to do. She prayed.

Good morning, Lord. Please help me be all that you want me to be today. Please help me be a blessing to someone else, even if I don't feel like it. Help me to know that you have a purpose and a plan for me, and continue to lead me. Thank you for answering all my prayers and still loving me when I let you down. Please don't let Ian find me. Amen.

Carly got ready in just a short time. She didn't have many clothes, and she wore the best she had. She walked down to the church on the corner and went inside. She found a seat in the back row and tried to relax, averting her eyes from all the people coming in.

It wasn't a big church, and it wasn't fancy, but that suited her. She felt awkward and took up a hymnal to look at the songs when Sam and Sue walked over to her.

"Good morning, Red," Sam said, smiling at her. "This is my wife, Sue. You were upstairs when she came in yesterday afternoon, and we didn't want to disturb you. Sue, this is my new shop assistant, Red."

Sue, a gentle-looking, good-natured woman, shook Carly's hand.

"It's nice to have you here with us this morning, but I'm pretty sure you have a different name than 'Red.' I hope Sam doesn't offend you." She looked at him fondly. "He's always finding nicknames for the people we know, and some people are particular about it. You just never mind him when he calls you Red. I've always wanted red hair, but God didn't see fit to give it to me. I say, your hair color is beautiful. Strawberry-blond always was my favorite. Do you like it?" Sue put Carly at her ease right away with her carefree manners.

"It's nice to meet you. Sam doesn't bother me a bit about calling me Red; now, if he meant it meanly, then I would have a problem." Carly laughed agreeably. "But I don't understand why you would want red hair when your hair is such a pretty brown."

"Clairol," Sue whispered, smiling before she introduced Carly to some other folk that had come up to meet her and make her feel welcome.

The service was wonderful. She hadn't been in a good church service for weeks, it seemed. She was more comfortable here than she had expected. The people were friendly and kind, and the preacher taught "right from the Good Book" as Sam would say.

These were dangerous feelings, and she knew she shouldn't be thinking about being comfortable. If Ian found her, she would just have to leave again, and the less people she knew and liked, the easier it would be.

She slipped out the back door of the church as the preacher was saying the closing prayer. She had to be careful, she admonished herself as she walked to her apartment.

She looked into the windows of the shops in town as she walked past, thinking about all that she had left behind her. Ian had been her big mistake, but God had used that mistake to help her trust him and lean on him for her every need, not Ian.

She was lost in her own thoughts when she heard someone calling her. She turned around to see Sam and Sue.

"Red! Wait!" Sam called, puffing. "We were wondering if you'd like to come on over to our place for dinner this afternoon, but you left so fast."

"Oh, well, um," Carly stuttered, trying to think of a reason not to go.

Sue interrupted her. "Oh come on now, we know you're new in town, and we're pretty sure that you're gonna need some food in ya. Put some meat on your bones. We'd really like to have you over," she said gently.

Carly couldn't refuse. She was hungry, and she really liked these people, but she knew that it was risky to accept. Ian always found her, and she had no reason to believe that this time it would be any different. But the promise of food tempted her, and she allowed them to persuade her to join them. She enjoyed the walk to their house, filled with chatter from Sue, occasionally interrupted by Sam.

"Is there anything I can do to help you, Sue?" Carly asked, following her into the kitchen, leaving Sam to read the afternoon paper in peace. "Just point me in the direction, and I'll be as much help as possible."

"Well, there isn't much left to do. I hope you're hungry. I've had to cook for boys, had four of my own, so I always cook for an army. I just can't seem to cook less." She rolled her eyes emphatically. "You could make some tea for us, while we wait if you wouldn't mind."

"I haven't had a home-cooked meal in a really long time." Carly busied herself with the teakettle.

"Roast chicken on Sundays. That's what Sam likes," Sue said, preparing a salad. "Tell me a bit about yourself, Red. You know, I haven't been told your real name yet. What is it?"

Carly turned scarlet. *Here come the questions*, she thought.

"Well, my name is Carly," she said, omitting the fake last name. "I'm twenty-four, and both my parents are dead. My mom died when I was just eight, and my dad passed away three years ago. I don't have any brothers or sisters, so I'm on my own. I was saved when I was young, so I've got the Lord, and I'm trusting on him to help me every day," she finished simply.

"You poor, poor child," Sue said gently. "To have nothing. You're certainly brave. Do you have a special fella?" she asked, turning away and allowing Carly to turn red privately.

"No," she answered shortly, pouring hot water over the tea bags into the cups.

"I don't believe it! Why not? I'm sure there are lots of boys that would like to get to know you. In fact, I did hear some handsome young bachelors in the church asking Sam who ya were." Sue smiled knowingly. "You know, we could arrange something if you'd like. I'd love to ask a few of the young people over here to meet you. We could have a church social. It would be nice. Them Baird boys are your age, and quite handsome, too. Oh, well, Todd, the younger one, has a girlfriend. She was the pretty girl with curly blond hair, and that was Todd sitting beside her, two rows in front of us. Seem to be pretty serious about each other. I wouldn't be a bit surprised to hear that he popped the question. But his older brother, Joe, now he's a fine fella. There are quite a few young girls trying to catch his eye," Sue said, putting the chicken on the middle of the table.

"Carly, would you please go and call Sam? Dinner's just about ready and it always takes him a little while to wash up."

Thankful that the conversation was interrupted, Carly left the room to call Sam.

Dinner was delicious, and the uncomfortable conversation seemed to be dropped. It was while Carly was helping Sue with the dishes that she started to talk about a church social to Sam.

"Sam, what would you think about having a few young people over this way to meet Carly? It wouldn't need to be a big deal, just a few people for her to meet. We could have some dessert—"

"Sue. Why don't we ask Red what she thinks?" Sam interrupted. "I don't mind it if she wants to, but she may not be obliged to. She may just want God to take care of things in his own way." Sam winked at Carly.

"Oh pooh. It would be lots of fun." Sue flipped the dishcloth at him. "Carly, what do you think? Would you like to meet some of the other young people?" She asked hopefully, looking at the red-faced girl.

"You know, it sure is nice of you to want to take on so much trouble for my sake, but honestly, I'd really rather not. I...I just don't think I'd like that right now," she answered, trying to be as gentle as she could.

"Honey, why ever not? I think you'd really enjoy yourself, and I'm sure that Joe Baird would like to meet you." Sue was obviously disappointed.

"Sue, maybe she'd like that later. Don't worry her to death," Sam said, sipping some coffee, looking over the top edge of the paper.

Carly felt terrible. She felt as though she'd hurt her feelings and wished that she could take it back.

"Do you remember asking me if I had a boyfriend, Sue?" she said, trying to ease her disappointment.

Sue nodded quietly, watching her.

"Well, I did have a boyfriend a while back. In fact we were engaged to be married, but things didn't work out, and I broke it off." She hoped that Sue would be comforted, but unquestioning.

"Oh, that's too bad. I wish it hadn't gone off for you. Was this before your dad passed away?" she asked, fascinated.

"Sue, just let her be now. Don't be prying into her business," Sam said, seeing Carly's discomfort.

"All right, Sam. I'll stop. I'm sorry, Carly. But you just remember that anytime you want to talk, you just come on over here, and we'll have us a nice little chat. And don't forget the social either. We can have it anytime you want," Sue said, hoping that she would tell her more in spite of Sam.

They passed a peaceful time together after the kitchen was cleaned up, and Carly was thankful for the invitation to stay all day. The subject of her past wasn't mentioned again, and they walked back to church for the night services in sociable silence.

Carly looked over at Sam and Sue. They were so perfect together. Holding hands, smiling at each other, just enjoying each other's company.

"How long have you been married?" she asked, unable to curb

her curiosity.

"It'll be forty-four years this November," Sam replied, smiling down at his wife.

"And it's been a wonderful marriage, right, Sam?" Sue winked up at him.

"Yes, it's been good. Real good. I wouldn't change a thing. Not even our bad times."

"Bad times?" Carly was surprised. They seemed so happy that she had a hard time believing they had faced rough spots.

"Oh yes. We've had some pretty hard things to deal with, but when we said our vows, we meant them. We've lost many sleepless nights because of that verse that says not to let the sun go down on your wrath, but we were too stubborn to relent. There have been ruts, everyone deals with that. Marriage is a job, but the trick is not to let anyone except God between you, and to put God first. All the troubles and problems seem to fade away into nothing when we just let go and let God deal with whatever the situation was at the time," Sue gushed.

"Sue's right. The best thing we've found, we've got to be honest with each other and with ourselves. Sometimes that was the hardest thing to deal with. But, then, it wasn't too hard. Sue's the closest thing to perfect this side of Montana." Sam gave her an affectionate hug.

"One day, you'll see, Carly. You'll find your best friend. Maybe you and your old fiancé can work things out, and you'll get married after all." Sue was hopeful.

"Fiancé? I didn't know you were getting married," Sam, who hadn't listened to their conversation earlier, said in astonishment.

"No. I'm not getting married, we're not going to get back together, and I know he isn't my best friend," Carly replied with a vigorous shake of her head.

"Well, I'm glad that Joe Baird has a chance then. He needs some happiness, and I'm positive that he would just adore you. Here we are. Hi, Helen!" Sue called, walking abruptly away to talk to her friend.

"You'll have to forgive Sue. She loves a good romance, and if there aren't any around, she doesn't mind setting things up her own way. Give her no mind. She doesn't mean anything by it. After you," Sam said, holding open the door for her.

She didn't reply, just gave him a pretty smile and walked past him into the church. She found the same seat open in the back and made herself comfortable.

There weren't as many people there at night services as there were in the morning. She was surprised to see quite a few young people though, and she could pick out the girl that Sue had described to her that day. She was very pretty, small, and talking animatedly to the nice-looking guy next to her. He seemed to hang onto her every word. This was obviously Todd.

She was happy for the couple but a bit cheerless for herself. If she had stayed with Ian, she would have been married right now, but that was out of the question. That wasn't what God had wanted for her. She didn't regret breaking things off with him, but she still yearned for affection and a place to belong. She was young, but she felt so old. She couldn't be carefree like she used to be. She had to watch her every move and action.

As she sat there occupied with her thoughts, she didn't realize that she was the subject of conversation between Sam and a few of the young men of the church.

Chapter Three

Her first month at work was not very eventful. She learned very quickly to please Sam. He was patient with her and trusted her completely. She stocked and dusted shelves, worked the counter, answered minor questions of some of the customers, and assisted Sam wherever and whenever he needed help. She sought things to do. If she saw something that needed attention, she tried to fix it. If there was dirt on the floor brought in by muddy shoes, she swept it up. She liked to please people, especially those that she liked and liked her in return. Sam and Sue were some of those people.

She was in the back of the shop sweeping up one day when she heard the bell over the door tinkling.

"Hello? Sam? Anyone here?" a voice called.

Carly set her broom against the wall and went to see if she could help. She saw a young man standing next to the counter and recognized him from church as the younger Baird boy, Todd.

"May I help you?" she asked, feeling a little nervous and self-conscious, her face turning red. He looked at her with some surprise.

"Well, Sam," he drawled, a smirk playing at his lips, "you sure look different this morning. Sue been doing something new to your coffee?"

His manner set her at ease immediately. She smiled and replied, "Yeah, I told her there was something wrong with the cream. I usually only use a teaspoon, and I think she's been giving me a bit more." His baritone laughter filled the air.

He held out his hand. "My name is Todd Baird. We've seen you at church, but you take off before we have a chance to make you welcome."

"Carly Adams, and I felt pretty comfortable almost as soon as I walked in. Is there something you need?"

"Well, I don't know if you'll be able to help me, but Pop sent me into town to see if Sam could replace this fuel line for his tractor." He held out a tube for her to see.

"Honestly, I don't know where Sam is. Oh wait. It's four o'clock. I bet he's gone to see Sue. He said that he might surprise her today by going to see her instead of her coming here." She was babbling, but she couldn't stop. She shook her head, hoping to clear it so she wouldn't sound so stupid and idiotic. "I'm sorry. I wish I could help you, but I have no idea. Let me call him."

"No, don't bother him. I'll just step on by his house." He stopped and turned around, the door held open slightly. "So, Carly, right? You're not from around here, are you." She was on the defensive immediately.

"Nope."

"Well, it's good to have you around. I hope you like it here." And he walked out the door.

Sam and Todd walked back into the store together a little later, laughing. She involuntarily looked up from her sweeping to see Todd looking at her, a thoughtful expression on his face. Sam seemed to have whatever he needed, and Todd finally left with a friendly wave to Carly.

"Sorry, Sam. I feel so stupid. I wouldn't have even known what that thing was if he hadn't told me. I'm not a lot of help."

"Red, you did fine. I don't usually have too many of those in stock, and it's not something we have a lot of demand for. We can't have perfection. You'd make me look bad," he joked, smiling at her.

She couldn't help but smile back, resolving to know a lot more about her job. She couldn't stand mediocrity.

The next day, she paid more attention to the merchandise she was putting on the shelves. She read the box and listened attentively to Sam while he helped other customers. She was friendly to everyone that came in, as well as helpful to Sam.

The bell rang about four o'clock, and Sue walked in.

"Hi, Sue. Sam's in the office ordering some stuff. Did you have a good day?" Carly asked, going over her receipts.

"Yes, I've had a pretty good day today. Just did some sewing, cleaning, baking, and talking, which I think must be the most important thing. I dearly love a good talk with a good friend. I heard that you met Todd Baird yesterday afternoon." She smiled meaningfully. "He's pretty handsome, but not nearly as handsome as his brother."

Carly didn't have time to comment as Sam came out and rescued her.

"Howdy, sweetie," Sam said, kissing Sue and giving her a hug. They walked into the office, leaving Carly alone.

As Carly continued over her receipts, she noticed a big black truck drive slowly by the store. Instinctively, she stepped back beside the wall. She continued to watch out the window as the truck passed by twice more. The third time, it stopped in front of the store. Carly almost ran to the office in a panic as a brawny man came into the store.

"Sam, could you please see to the customer? I don't feel very well," she said breathlessly. Without waiting for a reply, she took two stairs at a time to her apartment, praying the entire way.

Oh please, Lord, don't let it be anyone from Ian. I'm not ready to leave yet! Please, Lord; please, Lord, she couldn't concentrate on any words that would make sense as she paced back and forth in the small apartment. She almost screamed as someone knocked on her door. She stood staring at the door, her feet refusing to move toward the offending piece of wood. The knock came again a little louder this time.

"Carly? Can I come in?" called Sue, her voice muffled a little.

"You can come in," she choked out, turning away to hide her face.

"Are you all right? You're pale as a ghost, and you're crying!

What's wrong? What is the matter?" Sue asked anxiously turning Carly to face her.

It was hopeless trying to answer. Sue seemed to understand, and put her arms around her, drew her close, and patted her back.

"Shh. There now. Shh. Do you want some tea?" she asked as she comforted the distraught girl. She seated Carly on the sofabed and looked for something for her to drink. Finding no tea, she poured her some water in a glass and sat next to her and waited silently for the barrage of tears to end.

"I'm sorry," Carly said, sipping some water and trying to control herself. "Do you know that man who came into the store?"

"Is that what scared you so?" Sue asked in wonder. "That was just Bob Pruit's son Billy. I think he came in here looking for you. I know that there have been a lot of people talking about you, and he was probably just curious."

"Oh," was all she could say, feeling immensely foolish. She tried to smile, but fresh tears gushed out. Tears of relief and shame. "I'm sorry. I don't mean to blubber like a cry baby," she finally said after the tears subsided.

"You just go ahead and have your little cry out. I may have had four boys, but I do remember what it was like to be scared, lonely, and just plain miserable. Did you think it was someone else?" she asked, looking directly into Carly's face.

"Yes," she said quietly. "I thought my ex-fiancé sent him to find me," she blurted out.

"It's okay. I think I understand now. You don't want this ex-fiancé to find you, right?"

Carly nodded silently, wiping her eyes.

"Well, then, you go ahead and wipe your eyes, take care of yourself, and come on back down. This Billy isn't going to hurt you. Come on now. He's not anything to be afraid of," Sue said, giving her another hug before leaving the apartment.

About ten minutes later, Carly was back downstairs, feeling foolish but hoping that Billy was gone. Except for slight redness around her eyes, Sue couldn't even tell she had been crying.

"Carly!" Sue called her over.

Billy was still there.

Just my luck, she thought, a plastic smile pasted on her face. Billy Pruit looked just like his father. Big and sweaty.

Maybe he won't be as rude as his dad, Carly thought. Billy looked her up and down, making her uncomfortable.

"Hey, you're the girl Dad was telling us about. My brother been over here yet? He really likes redheads; I've never been one to like them too much, but you're not too bad," he said, looking admiringly at her figure. "You're kinda cute. I'm Billy Pruit. Maybe you'd want to go out sometime?"

Not if I'm alive, Carly thought. She felt the best thing to do would to be to answer straight forward so there could be no mistake.

"I'm not interested in dating anyone right now, thanks though." She tried to turn away, but his raucous laughter stopped her.

"Dad said you were a real piece of work. He wasn't kidding. No really. Let's go out tonight." He leered at her, making her skin crawl.

He was definitely on the do-not-trust list.

"I'm sorry; I can't. I've got other stuff to do," she answered with a steady stare, her fake smile gone.

This guy gives me the creeps, she thought. Doubting he'd leave her alone if she acted scared of him, she returned his leer with a glare.

"Mmm, feisty. I like that. Say what you want, but you'll change your mind." He sneered at her and walked out of the store, loose change jangling in his baggy pants.

"Yuck," she couldn't help saying, a shiver shaking her frame. She looked at Sam and Sue. "Are they all like that?"

"I'm afraid so. You be careful with them Pruits. They're mean," Sam replied. "Whenever they're in here, you just let me wait on them, okay? Don't talk to them too much; they have a way of twisting people's words. Not too many folk around here pay 'em much mind, but some do. I was real proud of the way you handled him. Smart to not act like you're scared, makes 'em meaner when people are afraid of 'em."

"I may not have *acted* scared, but I'm really terrified," Carly replied, watching Billy pull out and squeal his tires.

Should I leave now? she wondered. Mentally calculating her tiny hoard of money, she realized she'd have to buckle down and stay a little while longer.

With one last shiver, she went back to clean up before the store closed.

"Ian Lane, please," a man in a dark suit spoke into a cell phone. He was seated in his car in front of the coin laundry, watching the store in his rearview mirror.

"Ian here," a strong voice crackled through the receiver.

"We were right. It's her. Do you want us to bring her back?" A man opened the door and slid into the leather seat next to him.

Silence. Then, "No, let her get comfortable. I'll come up to surprise her this time. Keep an eye on her, but don't let her know you're there. Call me back if anything happens. And don't let her run again; I'm tired of paying you two idiots." Ian hung up.

"What a jerk," the man replied and put his cell phone in his pocket. "I don't understand why he wants her so bad. I don't think she's very pretty."

"She's pretty, but not as pretty as that secretary he's got right now. She's gorgeous! I'd like to have her as my secretary." They sniggered and continued to watch the hardware store.

Chapter Four

The following month was average for Carly. Billy Pruit almost left her alone, which she was glad of, and she was learning the store better. Most of the people were friendly to her. There were a few that were rude, but not too many. Sam seemed to always be around to help her with the mean-spirited people. But rude people included, it was a pretty good start. She was starting to really like this little town.

Wednesdays and Sundays were her favorite days. Carly had grown up going to church every Sunday morning, evening, and every Wednesday. She didn't know what she would do without going to church. It wasn't that she felt that going was her ticket to heaven or earning her some extra credit with God; it was that she really and truly loved going. She loved the singing, the reading, the music, but mostly, she just loved the Lord. He had helped her through some pretty rough times.

Her father had told her once before he died that when he went to church, he tried to put all his thoughts of the past week away, his pain, his sorrow, everything, and just sit and learn at the feet of Jesus. It was refreshing to him and prepared him for the rest of the week. At the time, Carly hadn't understood how he could feel that way with all the pain he was going through, but now, being alone, hurt, and scared, she understood everything better. It was like the Lord had used all those bad experiences to draw her closer to him, and to get her to trust him for every need she had. The last three years had seen her grow closer to God every day, and she was thankful for each hard experience she'd endured.

Wednesday evening, she walked down the street to the church, enjoying the weather. Birds were singing, the breeze was blowing, and leaves were changing colors. It was her favorite time of the year. Fall. The time when the plants take their break and go to sleep. Apple picking, pumpkin pies, spiced cider, all the good things that go hand in hand with autumn.

Her thoughts were disturbed by a noisy Camaro slowing down next to her. She looked over and saw Billy Pruit in the passenger seat, staring at her with a smirk. He said something to the driver, and they both laughed and drove past.

The walk didn't seem as pleasant anymore, so she quickened her pace to the church as the car turned around to come back. She reached the steps as the car stopped in the church parking lot. She tried to act unconcerned and unafraid as she struggled to keep her pace even going up the steps. If she ran, they'd know that they bothered her. Then they wouldn't leave her alone.

She didn't notice Todd, his girlfriend, and a couple of other people out on the steps, and would have walked right past them if they hadn't spoken to her.

"Excuse me," the blond girl called.

Carly turned. "Yes?" She tried to smile, but she could only see the Camaro out of the corner of her eye.

"My name is Kelly Martin. Are they bothering you?" she asked, noticing Carly's anxiety.

"Hi, I'm Carly Adams; it's nice to meet you. Yes, they're making me a little nervous. I've already met Billy Pruit, but I haven't met the driver. I don't think I want to," she said, looking over at the car again.

"Would you like me to ask them to leave you alone?" a deep, husky voice asked beside her. She turned to see a handsome young man about twenty-five or twenty-six leaning on the railing.

Take that back. He was better than handsome. *Lots* better. Tall, broad shouldered, coffee colored eyes, thick, wavy brown hair, killer smile. She stared at him for a moment, unable to tear her eyes away.

"No, I'm afraid that if I act scared, Billy won't leave me alone, and I don't want to make things worse. But thank you, I appreciate your concern." She smiled, her face turning bright pink. She hoped he wasn't able to read her thoughts as she forced herself to look at the blond girl that had spoken to her first.

"Todd, let's go in so they can't stare at her anymore. If they want to see her, they'll have to come inside," Kelly said, taking Carly by the arm and leading her into the church. "Would you like to sit with us? We usually sit together, and we'd like for you to join us."

"Thank you, I'd like that." Carly smiled, relieved to be inside and away from the piercing eyes of Billy Pruit. "Who was the driver?"

"Well, that was Randy Pruit's car, so I'd have to say it was Billy's little brother, Randy. Not a nice group of people there. Would you like me to introduce you to some of my friends?" Kelly asked, smiling. She was a likable girl. Blond hair, brown eyes, and friendly. Carly was comfortable with her right away.

"I don't want to be a bother. No, I'll be all right," she protested as Kelly led her to the group of young people that had been on the steps when she walked up.

"You're not a bother! I'd love to introduce you! You need some good friends to help you look out for the Pruit people. This is Mark, Christy, Paul, Angie, Meg, Todd...he's my boyfriend," she whispered. "Greg is over there, and this is my cousin, David. Oh and there's Jeff coming inside right now."

Carly shook hands with them, and although they were all pretty friendly, she found herself looking for the tall man she had seen outside on the steps. Disappointed, she turned her attention to the people in front of her. They didn't have much time to talk as the pianist started playing, and they were asked to open the hymnbooks to page twenty-four.

The group found their seats toward the front and opened their books. Carly was a little ill at ease being in front of so many people, but she endeavored to be comfortable. She was near the end of the long pew, with Kelly to her left. No one was next to her on her right, which was nearest the aisle. She began to unwind with the singing and enjoy the service when a movement caught her eye. She turned to see the tall man who had spoken to her outside take a hymnal and stand next to her.

It was impossible to be comfortable now.

Maybe he'll go away after the singing, she thought to herself.

He was so handsome he made singing for her out of the question. It sounded like she was squeaking. Even Kelly noticed. She looked over at Carly, her eyes twinkling. Carly wasn't sure, but she thought she saw Kelly nudge Todd and felt her face grow warm.

The singing over, she leaned forward to put her hymnal away. The man next to her did as well, and she caught a smell of some very nice cologne. This was pure torture. She could hardly pay attention to the sermon, so she tried to pray.

Lord, please help me. This guy is getting all my attention, and I don't want to like him, or be attracted to him. It'll just make everything worse.

Maybe you won't have to leave again, a small voice in the back of her mind whispered. She pushed the thought away. *Please help me pay attention*, she prayed silently. She paid such hard attention, that when the preacher started to pray, she forgot to close her eyes.

After service was over, the man turned to her and introduced himself.

"Hi. My name's Joe Baird. That's Todd, my little brother, and that's his better half." He smiled at Todd and Kelly as he shook her hand.

Carly avoided his gaze as she stammered a barely audible, "Nice to meet you." Turning red, she pulled her hand away as soon as she could.

"Are you from around here?"

"No, I just got here. Bye," she called over her shoulder and quickly walked away, leaving a very amused young man behind her.

"Carly," he called, following after her. She turned around, a pensive look on her face.

"Could I walk you to the store?"

She smiled weakly her heart fluttering. *That wouldn't be very good,* she thought. "I can manage, thanks though." She turned around hastily and walked out of the church.

Carly began to walk back to the apartment as fast as she could without running, not carefree and joyful as she had been before church.

What was going on? Was she allowing herself to think too much of this little town? Or just the people in it. She blushed as she remembered how her heart had sped up as Joe had sat next to her.

You're just being silly, she said to herself. *You got yourself into trouble last time you allowed your feelings dictate what you should do. He's probably just another Ian, and I don't want to know anything about him. I just want to be left alone.*

Deep inside, she knew he wasn't like Ian and that she did want to know him better. She would like him more than she felt was safe.

Maybe she already did.

She walked along deep in her thoughts, not knowing that he walked a little ways behind her to keep an eye out for Billy or Randy Pruit.

She didn't sleep well that night and came downstairs looking tired. Sam and Sue were standing in the office sharing some coffee and some turnovers.

"Carly! Come in, sweetie, and have an apple turnover," Sue called cheerily. "You look tired. Didn't you sleep well?"

"Good morning. I slept all right," she replied, taking a bite of a crusty turnover. "They're delicious!" Sue was touted as the best cook in the county, and Carly enjoyed it whenever she brought in extra little treats for Sam and her. Taking another bite of the delectable treat, she listened as they chatted about their upcoming day, and she gave a wistful smile.

Carly didn't really know what grandparents were like, not having known her real ones, but she imagined them to be just like Sam and Sue, and she was growing very fond of them.

"Did you have a good time in church last night?" Sam asked

with a wink. Carly tried not to blush.

"Yes, I did. I love to hear the pianist. My mother used to play," she answered, trying not to notice the amusement in Sam's face. He knew she was trying to skirt the real issue. Joe Baird.

"Well, it sure was nice to see them young folk take you under their wing like they did. That Kelly Martin is something else, isn't she? She's always been so friendly, and that Todd almost worships the ground she walks on. They were made for each other. I tell you, I'm surprised he hasn't popped the question yet," Sue said dreamily. "I just love weddings, and we haven't had one in the church in so long. I kind of miss them." She sighed.

"Sue, I do believe that you're an incurable romantic." Carly laughed, sipping her coffee.

"Well, it's so rewarding to see two young people that really love each other get married and serve the Lord together. I just think that they have what it takes to make it last a lifetime like marriages are supposed to. Sam," Sue turned to him, abruptly changing the subject, "Are you going to give Carly any days off? Or are you just going to work her like an ole mule?"

Sam looked thoughtfully at Carly, rubbing his chin. "You know, we haven't really discussed the days off, have we, Red?"

Carly tried not to grimace. Her mind flew to her tiny hoard of bills, and she couldn't help but wonder how she would save enough to run again if she needed to.

"I don't need any. I've already got Sundays off, and we close so early in the evening, I'm fine. Really. Don't worry about it."

She would need the money if she had to leave again. She was saving as much as she could now, but her little horde of bills didn't seem to be growing any bigger.

"Oh, but surely you'd like to see the town and meet new friends," Sue suggested, putting an arm around her shoulders. "You know, there are some pretty good yard sales I've seen this morning already. Do you like yard sales?" she asked hopefully.

"Yes, I do," Carly answered. She had to like yard sales. That was the only place she could get "new" clothes that she could afford. She didn't even go into clothing stores anymore. She remembered how Ian would take her shopping anywhere she wanted and he would buy her loads of clothes, shoes, jackets, purses. Anything she wanted, he would buy for her. At first, Carly thought that was wonderful, until she started noticing that if he bought her something, it wasn't really for her. It was really for him. He would tell her what she could or couldn't wear, who she could or couldn't talk to; it was like he owned her. She wouldn't have minded it so much if he would have given her just a little freedom. But if she went out without him knowing where she went, or with whom, he'd get so angry that she'd be scared out of her wits. But that was only in the beginning of their relationship. Things had gotten progressively worse.

"Well, what do you think?" Sue asked excitedly, squeezing her arm.

Carly had been so lost in her own thoughts that she hadn't heard a word they had said.

"I'm sorry, what did you say?" she stammered.

"You don't have to take a full day off, just a half day, and you could go with me to a few yard sales this morning, we could have lunch, and afterwards, I'll bring you back here. What do you think? Doesn't that sound like fun?" Sue looked so excited that Carly couldn't resist.

"If it's okay with Sam, but if he needs me this morning, I'll stay here. I don't mind." Carly added with a hopeful glance at Sam.

"Oh you girls with your shopping." He laughed as Sue flung her arms around his neck and kissed him. "How can I say no now? I shouldn't need much help this morning. It's Thursday, and people don't usually come in until afternoon anyway. Y'all go on and have fun," he said shooing them out of the office.

"Thank you, dear. We'll be back around one. Love you!" Sue called to Sam as Carly went upstairs for her money.

She looked at her small roll of bills and sighed, her expression grim. She didn't trust banks anymore. She'd made that mistake the first time she'd run away from Ian. Now, she kept all her money with her, tucked away in a safe place. Taking a couple of bills out, she put them in her pocket, sent up a prayer and stashed the rest away.

Carly and Sue passed an enjoyable morning together. They were getting pretty close, and Carly thought of Sue as a dear friend. They walked to the yard sales that Sue had wanted to visit, talking companionably.

"Now is the end of the yard sale season, so if you find something that you want or need, you should get it. It'll be a while before anymore come out. Oh look at this vase!" Sue exclaimed, holding up an attractive crystal vase. Carly smiled and went to look at the clothes.

She really needed some jeans, skirts, or dresses. When she had left Houston, she had only taken the things that she had bought with her own money. Once, when she had gone back to her apartment after going shopping, Ian was waiting for her, angry that she'd gone out without his knowing it and bought something she didn't ask him about. She'd gotten aggravated with him, and told him that he acted like a two-year-old. He had slapped her so hard that he bloodied her nose and knocked her to the floor. That's when she had begun to see what he was really like. She'd been scared. Still was.

"Hello there, Penny!" Sue's voice broke into Carly's thoughts, and she looked up. "Come meet my friend!"

"Penny, this is Carly. She's new around here, and she works for Sam at the shop. She's been such good help too, she didn't even want a day off, but I finally talked her into a half day. Carly, this is Penny Baird. Joe and Todd's mother."

Penny shook her hand warmly, her brown eyes twinkling. "Hello, Carly. It's nice to meet you. Do you like our little town?"

Carly smiled. "Yes, ma'am, I do. It's one of the nicest towns I've been in."

While the other two women were talking, Carly studied Penny.

She was in her mid to late fifties, still very pretty, brown hair like her two boys, but not as dark. There was a little gray at her temples, and she had laugh lines about her mouth and eyes. Carly could see a little bit of Joe's features in her face, but Todd seemed to take more after his mother. He looked just like her.

"I hear that you had a little bit of excitement last night on your way to church, Carly," Penny said. Sue looked surprised. Carly hadn't told her about Billy, not wanting to worry her.

She smiled soothingly at her friend. "Nothing much. Billy and his brother just drove past a couple of times, that's all."

Sue wasn't convinced. "Carly, maybe you shouldn't be alone in that apartment anymore. I'd never forgive myself if something happened to you. I don't really think they'd try to hurt you or anything, but I do think that they would try to bother you as much as possible. I'll have to talk to Sam about it."

"Oh no, really. It's okay. I'll be all right. I don't even think they know that I live above the store. I'll let you know if there's any trouble. I can handle it. Really. It's all right." Carly tried to calm Sue's fears.

"You know, I do believe Kelly has really taken a liking to you. That's all she talked about after church last night. She's a good girl that one. I'm glad Todd picked her. There are a lot of girls out there that just aren't worth anything. I wouldn't want him to be sorry for his choice later on, if you know what I mean." Penny and Sue continued talking about girls, boys, choices, and possible marriages while Carly looked around. She paid for her items, a pair of jeans, a skirt, and a denim dress, and they all parted company.

"Penny is such a good mother and a good friend too. She and Tom really tried to raise those boys right. There just doesn't seem to be very many young men these days that want to serve the Lord like those two. They're a good catch for any young woman," Sue said, looking knowingly toward Carly. "I noticed that you and Joe were introduced after all. I told you that he'd like you."

"No, he was just being friendly. Kelly had me sitting beside her, and he needed somewhere to sit," Carly protested, her face turning hot.

"Well, honey, if that's what you want to believe, then you go ahead and believe it. So what did you buy back there?" Sue asked, changing the subject. They talked about Carly's purchases and visited four more yard sales. Carly found some things that she had needed and bought them, and they walked on to the diner for lunch.

There they met Penny again, and they all sat down for a pleasant lunch together, laughing like they were old friends.

"Well, hi, there again," Sandy said, coming over to take their orders. She looked at Carly. "Did you find a job okay?"

"Yes, I did, thank you. I work over there at the hardware store for Sam," Carly replied, smiling.

"I'm mighty glad to hear it. I was worried about you with that Bob Pruit sitting so close to you. What would you like to eat?"

"Just the vegetable soup, and a water," Carly answered. The other two women ordered, and Sandy left. They were about to resume their conversation when Penny groaned and rolled her eyes.

"Don't look now, but the Pruits just walked in. Well, we must be in for a treat," she said wryly. "Maybe they won't notice us if we keep our heads down and talk amongst ourselves."

They kept their heads low and talked quietly, but their plan didn't work. They were spotted at once, and the Pruits sauntered up to their table.

"Hey, Red. You shirking your work and leaving poor Sam all alone? Sue, Penny," Bob Pruit said slowly, nodding his head in their direction.

"Red, how you doin'? It's been a while, sugar. So when are you and me gonna go out?" Billy asked, leaning on Carly's end of the table.

"Mr. Pruit. Billy. How's the car holding up?" Carly replied, looking fearlessly up at them.

"That was her car, Pops? Well, I wouldn't have guessed it. She looks fancier than that ole heap," said the younger son. "We scrapped it this morning before coming into town. We didn't find much in it except a picture of some guy. You want it back?" He grinned at her suggestively.

Billy laughed. "Yeah, Randy, we'll give it back to her, but she's gotta come over to get it."

"You found a picture? How odd. It must not be mine," Carly replied, trying to seem unconcerned. Sandy brought them their food, and the Pruit's had to move out of the way, but they were in no mood to leave them alone.

"Sorry, Red. Nice try. I'm sure this picture is yours, seeing as how you're in it. I'm pretty sure you'd like the changes we made to it. The man looks very interesting now, and well, I'm sure you can figure out the rest." Billy laughed contemptuously. "I'll come pick you up for dinner tonight, and if we have a good time, I'll give you the picture back. Deal?" He leaned closer to her, but she didn't shrink away. She was mad.

"You know what, I don't want the stupid picture back, I don't care what you've done to it, and I'm not going out with you, so you can stop asking. My answer isn't going to change," Carly said through gritted teeth.

"Anyway," Penny interjected, seeing Billy turn red with anger. "She's coming out to my house tonight for dinner, and we won't have any problems. If we do, I'm sure Tom, Joe, and Todd will take care of anything that needs settling. Now please excuse us. We'd like to finish our lunch in peace."

The Pruit's laughed and acted like they thought it was funny, but they did leave the diner, squealing their tires and giving obscene gestures to them through the window. The ladies didn't say a word for a little while, as Sue was clearly upset, and Carly fought back tears. She didn't want to eat. She just wanted to leave the diner, find a hole to crawl into, and hide.

"Carly, you're invited to our house for dinner tonight. Will you please come be our guest?" Penny asked quietly, patting her hand. "We'll ask Kelly to be there as well so you won't feel so out of place with just me and the men. We'd really like to have you out."

"Thank you, but I'd hate to be the cause of something. I appreciate you stepping in for me like you did though. That was very kind," Carly choked out miserably.

"Ha! They wouldn't dare start any trouble. We've had run-ins with them before, and I think they're pretty scared of us. We Bairds don't back down from a confrontation, whatever it is. I was going to ask you anyway, but Billy kind of helped me along. Really. I won't take no for an answer." Penny smiled kindly.

"Thanks. I'd like that," Carly answered truthfully, smiling. She thought of Joe involuntarily and pushed the thought away.

"I'll have the boys come into town to pick you up around five thirty, all right? Now, what were we talking about before we were so rudely interrupted?"

Sue was true to her word. She had Carly back at the store promptly at one o'clock, and not a minute sooner.

"Well, did you girls have a good time today?" asked Sam, giving Sue a kiss on the cheek.

"Yes, we did, thank you for letting me have a half day. Did you need my help today, or was it pretty slow?" Carly asked, walking toward the back so she could take her things up to the apartment.

"Nope. It was pretty slow like I said. Just the preacher and a farmer or two."

She heard Sue telling him about the Pruit adventures when she returned a few minutes later.

"They were so rude, weren't they, Carly? But she stood right up to them and didn't back down. Billy's bothering her about a date again. But I don't think he'll be back after what she told him. Well, I've got to go start dinner. You let Carly out right on time tonight, you hear? She's going to have dinner with the Bairds," she called out as she left to go home.

"You had another run in with the Pruits I hear. I can't understand why they're so persistent. Usually when a pretty girl says no like you did the first time, the fella just tucks his tail in and hides from her from then on. Huh. You be careful now, and let me know if you need any help," he said as he walked to the office.

The rest of the day was uneventful, but the closer time got to five-thirty, the worse she felt. She kept dropping things, couldn't answer the phone right, and kept knocking things off the shelf that she was trying to stock. Sam came out of the office at five and closed the store.

"You go on up now and change for your dinner. How are you getting out to the Bairds' place? It's way too far to walk."

"Penny said that she would send the boys to come and get me," Carly answered, still stocking the shelf. Truth was, she was just as scared of the Bairds as she was of the Pruits, but for entirely different reasons.

"Come on now, you get along upstairs. That stuff can wait until tomorrow. Scat!" Sam said, pushing the broom toward her.

Carly reluctantly got up and trudged upstairs.

Why did I agree to this? Things will just get worse if I make new friends, she thought morosely as she got ready. Being alone for so long made the temptation too great to resist. She couldn't ignore the yearning to belong somewhere and for these people, the Baird's as well as Sam and Sue, to like her and accept her. She changed into a fresh shirt, brushed her hair until it shone, and waited nervously for Joe and Todd to arrive.

"Red! Your ride's here!" Sam called up the stairs.

She slipped through the door and closed it silently behind her, her heart galloping like a herd of wild mustangs.

Please, Lord. Help me tonight. I don't really want to do this. I'm scared. But, whatever your will is, please let it be done tonight.

Sam and Joe were talking quietly at the front door when Carly walked in. She heard her name and Billy's, but they fell silent when they saw her come into the room.

"Hi, Carly." Joe smiled. "You ready to go? Todd and Kelly are in the truck waiting. Night, Sam." He held the door open for her.

"Hi," she said quietly, not looking up as she slipped past him, catching a smell of his cologne. Joe opened the passenger door for her so she could slide in behind Todd, and he climbed in beside her.

"Hey, Carly. How are you today?" Kelly asked, turning so she could talk to her. Todd started the truck and backed out of the parking spot.

"I'm doing pretty good. How about you?" Joe's arm brushed against hers, and her heart sped up. She had made up her mind not to pay him too much attention, but it was going to be very difficult.

"It's your turn to pay," Todd said good-naturedly to Joe as he pulled into a gas station. Joe groaned and rolled his eyes at Carly, and she couldn't help but laugh. He grinned and got out of the truck.

As Joe was filling the tank, Todd got out to clean the windows, leaving the two girls alone to talk. Todd had a sneaking suspicion that Joe was interested in Carly, and he wanted to give the girls time to get acquainted. Maybe Kelly could encourage her to show Joe a little extra attention.

"Well, Joe, what do you think?" Todd asked walking with him toward the gas station.

"I think it's gonna rain tomorrow," Joe answered, looking up at the dark clouds. He knew what Todd wanted to know, and he wasn't going to give him any information.

"You know what I mean. Do you like her?"

"Well, you don't beat around the bush, do you? Yes. Kelly's a wonderful girl, and I hope she can put up with you."

"Thanks. That's a load off my mind," Todd said, punching him in the arm. They walked in silence to the drink coolers. Todd picked out two sodas while Joe looked inside with a thoughtful expression.

"Which do you think Carly would like? A Mountain Dew or tea?" he asked, rubbing his chin.

Todd groaned and smacked his forehead with his palm. "Not the 'tea test.' I can't believe you use tea to see if you're compatible with a girl. You are so bizarre. You know, you could just try talking to her. It's worked really well for me and Kelly." Joe grabbed him and put him in a headlock, tousling his hair as they walked back to the truck.

They opened the doors to find the two girls giggling

hysterically. They had obviously found something to talk about.

"Joe, I don't think it's such a good idea to leave these two women alone together. Evidently they enjoy having us gone." Todd winked as he started the truck and drove toward the Baird's residence.

Joe grinned, looking at Carly. "What are you two laughing about?" They giggled harder. Humor lit her eyes up like fireworks, and he couldn't take his eyes off her. She was beautiful. He had the irresistible urge to grab her in his arms and hug her.

"Here, have something to drink," Todd said, handing a soda to Kelly.

"Thanks." She giggled. "Carly was just giving me her rendition of the Pruits. She has Billy down pat; it's hilarious. Carly, you have to show them."

"Oh yeah. I bought you something to drink too, but I wasn't sure which you would like. Mountain Dew or tea?" Joe said, holding them both out to Carly.

"You didn't have to do that," she said softly, smiling up at him. "Which would you rather have?"

"Nope. You have to pick first," he said, grinning. She was softening toward him, and he wanted to keep it that way.

"Um, I'd like the tea if you don't mind," she said, hoping it was the right answer. He grinned and handed her the tea. "Thank you. I appreciate it."

Todd groaned and looked up at the ceiling with exasperation.

"What? Did I pick the wrong one?" Carly asked, worried. She looked up at Joe. "Did I pick the wrong one? You can have it if you want it. I'm sorry."

Todd moaned, rolling his eyes. "No. You definitely picked the right one."

"That's your favorite, isn't it? I'm sorry; I'll give it to you. Minus a little swallow," she said, looking up at him with her eyes wide and sad, a playful pout upon her ruby lips.

"No, you picked the right one. Are you going to show us your Billy Pruit enactment?" he asked, his eyes warm and dark as they roamed over her face.

"Not until you tell me the truth. Which is your favorite? Mountain Dew or tea?" she said teasingly.

He laughed. "I plead the fifth."

"That's not fair! You haven't incriminated yourself. Yet." She punched his arm lightly. He grabbed his arm where she had punched him and rubbed it with a smile. He was enjoying himself immensely.

"I have nothing to say. I'm sorry to disappoint you."

She punched him harder this time and smiled with satisfaction at his "ow."

"Todd, will you give me an answer?"

"Oh no, you can't go asking people who have inside information!" Joe cried in mock indignation.

"Excuse me, sir, but I believe you already pled the fifth. You have the right to remain silent now. I gave you a chance, buddy." She waved her hand at him. He tried to grab it. "Todd, which is Joe's favorite drink, Mountain Dew or tea?"

Todd laughed. "He'll beat me up if I answer you!"

"If he tries, you just come and talk to me, and I'll take care of business!" Carly responded, giggling. "Don't you dare beat him up, or I won't talk to you anymore." she added, grinning at Joe.

"You don't talk to me now, so what do I have to lose?" Another punch to the arm.

"Then I guess you wouldn't have to worry about entertaining me anymore. Todd, which is it?" Kelly was laughing hysterically at their antics, and Todd was enjoying himself just as much.

"Well now, what's it worth to you? You know, even witnesses have to have something to gain by their testimony."

"Let me see," Kelly interjected, "you won't have me talking to you if you don't give an answer? How's that, Carly?"

Carly clapped her hands with glee. "Wonderful! You ready to talk now?"

"Joe, they've got me in a corner. I'm sorry, but I've gotta talk," Todd apologized, and Joe groaned, leaning back against the seat.

"All right, all right. You win. I knew we should have never gotten these two together. Go ahead, spill the beans." Joe sighed.

"His favorite drink is…hey look! Isn't that the Pruit car?" Todd announced, trying to get out of the situation.

"Todd," Kelly warned. "Spill it."

"Tea," he answered dejectedly, hanging his head in shame. "I'm sorry, brother. Will you ever be able to forgive me?"

Joe smiled at Carly. "Nope."

"I knew it. I feel terrible. Here, take the tea. I'll have the Mountain Dew," she said, trying to hand him the half full bottle and take his. He pushed her hand away laughing at her.

"You already drank almost all of it! Anyway, it's too late. We're here. Ha!" he said as Todd pulled into the driveway.

Carly was surprised. It seemed like just a couple of minutes, when in fact, it was closer to thirty. She looked at the beautiful two-story farmhouse.

She could easily see the old house on a Christmas card. White siding hugged its frame, a bow window in the front, wrap-around porch with white, wicker rockers that were set off by red geraniums lining the pebble walkway. More geraniums were planted around an old lamppost and lights shaped like candles burned in the windows, completing the picture, making it perfect.

"You live here?" Carly asked breathlessly, looking at Joe as he helped her out of the truck.

"Yep. You surprised that two country farmers could live in such a nice house? You snob!" He laughed and jumped out of the way as another playful punch was aimed at his stomach.

"No, I'm not surprised; it's just so beautiful. This whole place is fantastic!" She breathed deeply as she gazed around her, turning to take it all in. "I didn't know you had horses!"

Joe watched her. She was like a little kid in a candy store. It was almost like she'd never seen a farm, let alone been on one. The more he watched her, the more entranced he became. He wanted to know so much about her, just be with her. It had been a long time since a girl had made him feel that way.

Carly looked at him and gave him a beautiful smile. He was hooked.

"Thank you for bringing me here. Wherever I go, I'll always remember it, just like this," she said. "This is the most beautiful place I've ever seen."

Joe walked her into the house, puzzling over her last statement. Was she planning on leaving? Did she think that she wouldn't ever be invited here again? He'd have to find out.

"Carly, hi there! Come on in and make yourself at home. This is my husband, Tom," Penny introduced her to a well-built man that was sitting in an oversized chair, reading a newspaper. He put the paper down on the floor and got up to shake her hand.

"Carly, it's nice to meet you. Thanks for coming on by for dinner. I see the boys delivered you two safely enough. Hi, Kelly," he said, giving her a pinch on the arm. "I haven't seen you in so long, I thought for sure you two must have broken up," he said, winking at her.

"Pop! Don't be giving her any ideas!" Todd said, putting his arm around her shoulders. Kelly laughed. It was plain to see that they were very used to her being there and enjoyed her company.

Carly was struck by an intense sense of sadness by the playful banter. She hadn't had a family in so long, that she had forgotten how they could act with each other. She missed her parents dearly.

"Mom, how long till dinner?" Joe called, seeing Carly's sadness and wanting to do something to make her smile again.

"Oh, about a half-hour."

"Is there anything I can do to help, Mrs. Baird?" Carly asked, running her hands up and down her arms as she came to stand near her.

"Oh no, everything's just about complete. Just finishing up these carrots, and we'll be done. Did you have a good trip out here? I hope Todd didn't scare you too much with his driving," Penny asked, rolling her eyes.

"We had a fun time," Carly answered quietly with a faint smile.

"Mom, I'd like to go show Carly the horses, if you don't mind.

We won't be long. Just call us when you need us, okay?" Joe said as he steered her out the door, not giving her a chance to resist.

Penny watched them walk toward the barn. She hadn't seen Joe try so hard to please a girl in a long time. She watched them until Todd and Kelly came into the kitchen and broke into her thoughts.

"Well, Mom, what do you think of her?" Todd asked, helping himself to some freshly cut carrots.

Embarrassed that her younger son had caught her spying, she blustered around the kitchen with more ferocity than normal.

"Todd William, stay out of those carrots! They're for dinner!" Penny pushed him away from the food. "And what do you mean, 'what do I think of her'? I don't know anything about her."

Todd munched on the carrots, not in the least perturbed by her rebuke. "Well, Joe seems to like her pretty well, doesn't he, Kell?"

"He did act different with her. Usually he's so reserved and distant but not with her. It's like they connected or something," Kelly answered.

"Oh yeah. They connected. She passed the tea test," Todd said, a sly grin spreading across his handsome face.

Penny frowned, confused. "The tea test? What on earth do you mean?"

"Let's just say she gained some major points with him, and she doesn't even know it. He bought two drinks and offered her first pick. She picked the tea, and he took the Mountain Dew."

"I don't see what that has to do with anything." Penny obviously didn't see the importance of what Todd was telling her.

"Exactly. Now he knows that they have something in common, something to build on, and something to talk about and remember."

"I just hope he's more careful than the last time. I don't want him to get hurt again."

Kelly was quick to soothe Penny's fears. "I don't think she's like that. She seems lost and lonely. I really kind of pity her."

Penny sighed. "I just wish we knew more about her." Her mother's heart was troubled for her son.

Chapter Five

Joe and Carly were at the corral, watching the horses. Standing on the lower rung of the gate, she clicked her tongue to get their attention.

"Here," he handed her some sugar cubes. "Don't give the big gray mare too many. She's got a sweet tooth and won't let any of the others have any. She's not a horse, but really just a big pig." He scratched her ear gently as she nickered at him. "This one is mine. Her name is Ashes."

"She's gorgeous," Carly breathed. She gave her a few sugar cubes and rubbed her between her ears. "How long have you had her?"

"I bought her on my twentieth birthday," he answered.

"And how old are you now?" she asked mischievously, her eyes twinkling. She glanced sideways at him, and he looked back at her, grinning.

"Oh no. I don't answer any more questions until you answer some of mine."

"I never said I would answer any questions." She flipped her hair over her shoulder with a mysterious smile.

"I answered yours, and now you have to answer some for me."

"Only on the condition that if I think it's too personal, I don't have to answer it. Agreed?" Carly held out her hand to shake. Joe took her hand.

"Agreed."

Carly pulled her hand away, blushed, and turned back to the horses.

"Where do you come from?"

"From my parents. Next."

"You smart aleck. You know what I mean," he retorted, pinching her ear.

"Ow! Well, you made it sound as if I came from another

planet, and I just wanted you to know that I am an earthling," she retorted, rubbing her ear. "I'm from Houston, Texas. That was my last real home." She really liked teasing him. She sensed that she had some sort of affect on him and she flaunted it.

"What do you mean 'real last home'?" he questioned.

"That's where my dad and I lived."

"What happened to your dad?"

Her sad, wistful smile twisted his heart. "He died about three years ago."

Joe took her hand and squeezed it sympathetically. "I'm sorry. I didn't mean to make you feel bad."

"No, it's okay. I'm dealing with it." She turned to look at him. He still held her hand. She began to pull it back, and he let it go grudgingly.

"I mean it. I'm sorry that you lost him. How old were you?"

"I was twenty-one. Speaking of age, I believe I answered quite a few of your questions, and you still have to tell me how old you are," Carly said casually, trying to lighten the conversation.

"I'm twenty-six."

"That's too bad." She jumped down from her perch and started walking toward the house.

"What's too bad?" he demanded, following her.

"*It's* too bad." She walked faster.

"What is? What do you mean?" Carly started running to the house and jumped up onto the porch, taking Joe by surprise.

"I meant that it was too bad that you're so old. You were pretty easy to beat to the house you know." She laughed, opened the door, and walked into the kitchen, leaving a speechless Joe staring after her.

Dinner was about ready, and Kelly was setting the table. Carly washed at the sink and set to work helping her. Kelly smiled at her with eyebrows raised. Carly winked and smiled back.

"Time for dinner, boys!" Penny called everyone in. "Better wash up, I won't have any dirty people at my dinner table!" She smacked Tom with her towel as he walked past her. He swatted back at her as she went back into the kitchen.

"You better find your seats before they get back in here, or it'll just be one big hassle. Thank you for helping me set the table; it's wonderful to have kitchen help. Besides eating, that is. I have all the eaters, but not many helpers," she said, smiling as Kelly and Carly sat down next to each other.

Todd sat at one end of the table next to Kelly, Tom sat with Penny at the other end, and Joe, the last to sit, was kitty-corner to Carly. After they were all seated, Tom asked the blessing on the meal, and they helped themselves. Carly sat back to watch how they did things at their table, not wanting to make any mistakes.

"Girl, you better help yourself if you want any dinner tonight!" Todd called, piling a huge helping of mashed potatoes onto his plate.

"My goodness, Todd! Are you going to save any for the rest of us?" Kelly looked incredulously at his mounding plate.

"What?" he asked innocently, a smile playing on his lips.

Carly couldn't help but laugh at the look on his face. It was a very enjoyable dinner. They told stories of growing up on the farm that kept them all rolling with laughter. The talk turned to their guests near the end of dinner.

"So, Carly, where are you from?" asked Tom politely.

Joe groaned, rolling his eyes. "Don't ask her that one."

Carly laughed, "I only give smart-aleck remarks to smart-alecks. I moved to Houston with my dad when I was twelve."

"Where's your mother, honey?" Penny asked, concerned.

"My mom died of cancer when I was eight, and Dad raised me on his own. Boy, those years were rough!" Carly sighed. "But God was good to us and gave Dad lots of wisdom." End of speech.

"Then what?" Kelly asked curiously.

"Well, he died a few years later." Carly said, looking at Joe. "When I was twenty-one."

"How old are you now?" asked Penny.

"Twenty-four. I just had a birthday last month."

"What have you been doing for the last few years?" Tom

asked.

"Well, I was engaged, broke it off, and I've been traveling for the past two years. That's pretty much it," Carly answered hurriedly. She couldn't resist a quick glance at Joe. He didn't change perceptively, but his eyes were darker, and the smile seemed to have faded a little.

"Broke it off? You're not engaged anymore?" Kelly asked.

Joe looked at Carly steadily as she answered. "No, that was one of the worst mistakes of my life, and I'm glad it's over." She couldn't look up. Joe breathed again.

"Anyone for dessert?" Penny asked awkwardly, breaking the silence. "Fresh apple pie!"

Penny served the most delicious pie Carly had ever eaten. Lots of cinnamon and nutmeg, it was wonderful.

Carly leaned back in her chair and patted her belly. "Wow. I hope I can be that good of a cook one day. Right now my specialty seems to be macaroni and cheese."

"Mom, thanks for dinner. We're doing the clean-up, right, Joe?" Todd said with a twinkle in his eye, making Carly wonder if it were a set up.

"Yep. We sure are. You girls mind?" Joe answered, looking at Carly.

"Sounds good to us," Kelly answered for her. Now she was sure it was a trap. She smiled.

"Oh no, I couldn't have you do that. It's all right; I can do it," Penny protested as Joe and Todd led her and Tom out of the kitchen.

"Come on, darlin'," Tom said with a fake drawl. "Seems like they want to do this for us. The least we could do is oblige."

"I'll put the dishes away," Todd volunteered, making a gesture at Kelly.

"I'll dry," Kelly stuttered hurriedly, knowing what Todd wanted.

"That leaves washing and rinsing. Which will you have?" Joe smiled at Carly. "Your choice."

"Oh no. Don't even go there! I'm not making any more choices. I made the wrong one last time. You be a man and figure out which one you want, and I'll do the other," Carly gave him an impish grin and started to clean off the table.

"Cat," he muttered and jumped out of the way as Carly tried to swat him with the dishcloth. "All right. I'll wash; you rinse. You have to be so difficult." He sighed heavily, running the dishwater.

They formed an assembly line as Joe washed, Carly rinsed and stacked, Kelly dried, and Todd put away. They all harassed Joe for being so slow and talked animatedly to one another.

During a moment when Joe was scrubbing at a particularly stubborn piece of burnt on food, Carly started to tap her foot impatiently.

"Hey now, take your time and don't rush me." He laughed. "I've got the hardest job here."

"Whine, whine, whine," Carly said quietly, rolling her eyes at Kelly, who was laughing with delight.

"What? What did you say?" Joe asked archly. "I know you weren't talking about me. I never whine."

"Hmm?" Carly asked innocently. "Was there something you needed? I couldn't understand. There was too much whining going on."

Todd laughed and shot Joe a look. "I know you're not going to let her get away with that one, brother. You've got to have a comeback."

"Uh huh. She's going to give me a bad name." Joe smirked and splashed Carly with dishwater.

"Oh, that's just not nice!" Carly cried, jumping back. "You brat! All over my shirt! I see how you are," she said, nodding her head.

"Watch out," she whispered to Kelly as she grabbed the sprayer and aimed it at Joe.

"You wouldn't dare!" he said in astonishment. She squirted him liberally, making Todd and Kelly laugh hysterically.

"I think she dared, Joe," Kelly gasped, grabbing her side.

Joe stared at her in amazement. "You're going down, oh yeah."

He splashed her with a cup full of dishwater, while Carly squirted in retaliation.

Penny and Tom came into the kitchen to see what all the commotion was about. Penny gasped. "Oh my goodness! What a mess!" She stared at her sopping floor, her wet son, and her wet guest.

They hung their heads in shame. Joe poked Carly in the side and made her yelp in surprise. Todd and Kelly started to giggle. Soon they were all giggling, Penny and Tom included. Carly poked Joe back, and he slipped and fell flat on the floor.

"I'm sorry," Carly managed to wheeze out between laughs. "Here, let me help you up; I'm so sorry." Carly reached down to help him up. He took her hand and pulled her down with him.

"Now I'll help you up," Joe said gleefully, getting carefully to his feet and holding out his hand to help her.

Penny laughed. "I'm so glad that you all wanted to help clean up the kitchen so much. It needed a good mopping!"

"We'll finish up in here, Todd. You two just go ahead and do what you wanted to do," Joe said, grinning wickedly at Carly.

"Are you sure? You're no match for her, you know. I could stay and be your support." Todd ducked as some soap flew at him. He left, pulling Kelly after him and Joe and Carly finished their cleaning up without further incident.

"I hope your mother isn't mad," Carly worried as she soaked up the water with the mop Penny had provided. "I really don't want her to be afraid to ask me over again."

"Mom? She isn't mad. Or won't be as long as we clean up," Joe watched her mop.

Carly looked up and caught him looking at her. She colored. "What?"

"You missed a spot." He pointed to the floor. She raised her mop.

"Where? I don't see anything. Where?" Joe laughed at her bewildered look. She glared at him. "You're lucky, you know that."

"What do you mean I'm lucky?"

"That I have a good sense of humor."

He grinned. "I know I'm lucky." Carly blushed. "I like it when you blush like that you know." Carly reddened even more, but was pleased by the compliment.

"Are you two done yet?" Todd and Kelly walked into the kitchen. "We've still got to take these two home, and it'll be getting late. Some of us have to work for a living," he teased as Kelly punched his arm.

"Carly and I work just as hard as you two. We've got to make people happy, not just animals," Kelly protested, acting insulted. She worked at the local bed and breakfast that her uncle and aunt owned, and knew what it was like to have to deal with rude people every day.

"Carly, I'd like to see them two do what we have to do in a day."

"No, I don't think you would," Carly replied, winking. "I think it would be too ugly. They couldn't handle it."

"Oh really? I think we've got ourselves a wager coming on," Joe retorted. "What do you think, Mom? Do you think these two city-slickers here could outwork us two handsome, appealing, strong farm boys?" He flexed his muscular arms, as much to make her laugh as to gain her admiration.

Kelly gagged while Carly sat in a chair and pulled her legs up to her chin. Joe looked at her in wonder.

"It's just getting really deep in here."

They all laughed. Joe pretended to be injured. "You cut me to the quick, little lady. I'll never be the same," he said, grabbing at his chest and hanging his head in defeat.

"Don't get me involved with your little dispute. I'm staying neutral," Penny said good naturedly. "But you better get. They've got to go to work in the morning."

"Thank you for dinner, Mrs. Baird. It was wonderful," Carly said, giving Penny a hug.

"Thank you for coming. I really enjoyed myself. Especially the mopping! You come on back another time. You're always welcome." Penny smiled kindly. "Take care of yourself."

"Well darlin', looks like Joe's got himself a little bit of spice," Tom said as the young people were walking out to the truck. He put his arms around her and drew her close.

"Yes, I do believe she'll keep him on his toes. I just hope he's careful." Penny sighed.

"He knows what he's doing. He's got a good head on his shoulders." Tom kissed her forehead. "Let's go watch a movie."

They dropped Kelly off first. and then proceeded to drive Carly to her place. The town was dark and looked lonesome.

"You can just drop me off here, and I'll walk around to the back. I don't like to go in the front during the night."

"We'll take you back there," Joe said before Todd could answer. "I wouldn't feel right just dropping you off like that."

"I'll be all right; I can handle it. I wouldn't want you big strong farm boys getting lost in the dark alley. You might get scared," Carly teased.

"Joe, I think we should just kick her out here and make her walk all by herself!" Todd retorted, slowing the truck down.

"Just park in the front, and I'll walk to the back. I don't think the garbage has run, and there's an awful lot of boxes and trash back there. I really don't think the truck will fit," Carly said nervously, her stomach in knots.

"Go ahead and park. I'll walk her back," Joe directed Todd. "Don't fuss about it either. You're going to have a chaperone to make sure you're okay."

"Yes, Daddy," Carly said in a little girl tone, but she was touched by his thoughtfulness. "Thanks for driving me home, Todd," she called as she got out of the truck.

"You're welcome, and thanks for coming out for dinner. I know Kelly really enjoyed your company. We'll have to do it again sometime," he called back before Joe shut the door.

He followed Carly to the door in the back and waited patiently as she got out her keys and unlocked the door. She turned to face him. She was self-conscious and wasn't sure what she should do. She didn't need to worry.

"Thanks for coming out to dinner. I had fun," Joe said, shaking her hand. She was very much relieved.

"Thanks for putting up with me," Carly said quickly. "It was very nice of you all to make me feel so welcome. Tell your parents I said thanks."

"There wasn't anything to put up with. I'm glad to have gotten to know you a little bit, and I'd like to get to know you more," he said meaningfully.

"Joe, at the risk of looking like a complete fool, I just have to let you know that I might not stay here long. I'll probably be leaving soon," Carly gushed out, looking down at the ground, feeling stupid.

"Going? Where? Why do you want to leave?" he asked, surprised.

"I don't want to leave. I have to," she spoke so quietly that he had to lean down to hear her words.

"I don't get it. If you don't want to leave, then don't," he said simply.

"Joe, you're very kind to make me feel so welcome, and I really appreciate it, but…"

"Do you think the only reason I'm nice to you is to make you feel welcome?" he interrupted, lifting her chin to make her look at him. "I am interested in getting to know you better."

Carly was stunned.

"Okay, now I think you're on drugs," she whispered awkwardly. Joe laughed and let her go.

"Don't think about leaving yet. There's just no sense in it, and you've no reason to go," Joe said, hoping to make her believe him. "Go on in and turn on your light so I know you're okay. All right?"

"All right. Good-bye." And she was gone.

Joe walked to the front of the store, got back in the truck, and watched the upstairs window. There it was.

"Okay, Todd. We can go now," he said, trying to get a glimpse of Carly. He was hoping she would look out to wave. She didn't.

"I think we should stay here for a little while," Todd said. He looked over at Joe with a strange look on his face. "While you were so long in the back," eyebrows raised, "two guys in a black BMW drove past and parked a little ways down."

"So? What's wrong with that?"

"Well, first is the type of car. It was really expensive and definitely not from around here. Next, they never got out of the car, and when they saw me, they backed up and drove away. I sat here, still waiting for you by the way, and they drove by again. Don't you think that's weird?"

"I still don't see the big deal. What are you getting at?" Joe was a little annoyed by Todd's cloak-and-dagger behavior. "Just tell me what you're thinking."

"They seemed to be watching the hardware store," Todd said meaningfully with a nod of his head.

"Why would they be watching the hardware store?" Joe asked uneasily.

"There they go again!" Todd exclaimed, looking in the rearview mirror. Joe turned around and watched the car drive slowly past them, turn right at the next corner, and disappear. He looked up at Carly's window, thankful the light was out. Todd looked at him. "What do you want to do?"

Joe was silent. He was thinking of Carly's statement about having to leave soon and wondered if she was in trouble.

"Let's follow them," he urged. Todd started the truck, backed out, and followed the same direction the mysterious car had gone.

"What do you think is going on?" he asked Joe quietly.

"I don't know. They probably weren't even interested in the store, and we're going on a wild goose chase," he said, frowning. "I don't see them. Hurry up."

Todd knew that he was worried about Carly and didn't take his curtness as rudeness. He was worried for her too. He had hoped that Joe would like her and that she would bring him some happiness. It had been too long since Joe had taken an interest in anyone outside their family, and he wanted him to be happy. Like he and Kelly were. They were like-minded, they both loved to tease, especially each other, they just seemed so right for each other. Todd kept driving.

"I don't see them anywhere," Todd said after the third time going around the block. They stopped at the blinking red light and waited. "What do you think, Joe?"

"I haven't seen them. I think if they were watching the store, they're gone now. Let's go home," he said, still looking out the windows. Todd drove them home.

After Carly went up to her room, she turned on her light as Joe had asked, waited for a few minutes, then turned it off again. She went to her window to look out. They were still there. After a moment, they drove away.

Dear Lord, I've gotten myself into trouble. She sat on her sofa bed and started to pray out loud. Sometimes praying out loud made her less lonely.

"Can you please help me again? Joe Baird says he's interested in me. I didn't mean for this to happen; we just hit it off right away. The last thing I wanted was this. Lord, I really like this guy, but I'm afraid Ian will find me. Please let me know what you want me to do and give me the strength to do it. Even if you want me to leave. Please be with Joe. Take care of him and bless him."

Carly went to the tiny bathroom, brushed her teeth, changed into her pajamas, and lay down. But she didn't sleep for a long time. Her mind was full of memories, old and new, and she couldn't chase them away. Finally she drifted off to a fitful sleep.

"We'd better call the boss," the passenger in the BMW said to the driver. "He ain't gonna like it that she's got a boyfriend hanging around. Maybe he'll come up here sooner, and we can get away from Hicksville."

The driver pulled into a parking space and turned off the car.

"I'll do it as soon as I'm in my room," he growled. "You were supposed to watch and make sure no one was around, and yet you couldn't even figure out that someone was sitting in that dumpy truck. You can't do anything right." They both stopped talking as they walked past the night receptionist sitting at the desk, knitting.

"How was I supposed to know the kid stayed in there? I can't see too well in the dark," the little one whined as soon as they were past her.

"Shut up and go to your room," the other snarled as he let himself into his own cozy room and shut the door. He sat on the bed, dreading to make the phone call.

Well, here goes, he thought as he dialed.

"Ian Lane here," was the almost instantaneous answer.

"Ian, this is Steve. We're just checking in," Steve answered lamely.

"Well good." He almost sounded cheerful. "I was wondering how my baby's doing out there all by herself. How is she? Still beautiful?" He laughed gleefully. "She's about ready to come home, right?"

"Well, uh," Steve cleared his throat. "Not exactly."

"What do you mean 'not exactly'?" he snarled. "Did you lose her again?"

"No, no, we didn't lose her. We still have her, and we're keeping an eye on her, but uh, I think she's got a boyfriend." He grimaced and waited for him to explode.

Quiet. Then, "What are you doing about it? You're doing something. I know you are. Because if you aren't," Ian threatened, "you won't want to come back. You will have no job. You will have no life. No one gets near my girl. She's mine, and I won't share her with anyone, you got that?"

"Yeah, I got it, but I don't really know how to keep her away from this guy without her running again," Steve complained. "I don't know what you want me to do."

"Call her. Let her see you watching her. She'll remember that she belongs to me, and she'll push this guy away and you won't have to. You can figure out the rest." Ian hung up.

I hate him, Steve thought, dropping the handset back into the cradle and leaning his head on his hand in exasperation.

Chapter Six

The next morning, Carly came to work with her mind made up. She had decided to make Joe understand. She had to convince him that he really didn't like her, and that it wasn't going to work out anyway. That it was better for both of them if they just stopped now. She just didn't know if she would be able to go through with it.

Sam came in with a curious glance at Carly. She knew that he would want to hear all about it, and she decided to tell him the whole truth. About their dinner, that is. Not about her resolve to break it off before it began, or about Ian, but she did want to let Sam know that she truly did have fun.

"Well, Red? How was it?" he asked before he even went to the office to put away his lunch. He placed both arms on the countertop and leaned forward so he wouldn't miss a word.

"I take it you mean the dinner?" she asked innocently.

"Yep, and take your time to tell me everything. I have strict instructions from Sue that I better not leave any part out." Carly smiled. She told him everything, even of their little mishap on the kitchen floor, and had Sam chuckling within five minutes.

The phone rang and interrupted her story.

"S&S Hardware. May I help you?" Carly answered.

No response.

"Hello? S&S Hardware. May I help you?" she repeated. She could hear someone breathing, but they wouldn't say anything. "Hello? Hello?" Finally they hung up.

"Do you get a lot of prank phone calls, Sam?" she asked, brows furrowed.

"Can't say that I do," he said. "Probably Billy Pruit trying to aggravate you. Go on with your story."

Carly continued but not with as much mirth as before. She was wondering if it could have been Billy after all. She made up her mind that it must have been and gave Sam her attention again.

Half an hour later, the phone rang again.

"S&S Hardware. May I help you?" she asked into the phone. Again no answer. "Hello? Billy? Is this you? If it is, grow up!" she hollered and hung up.

Sam came to the front. "Another prank?" he asked. She nodded, her face pale.

"I'm sure it's nothing to worry about. Here's a customer." And Sam went back to inventory the shelves.

A short, ugly man wearing an expensive double-breasted suit walked in. Carly didn't recognize him from town.

"May I help you?" she asked, warily giving him a slight smile.

"I need nails," he barked rudely. He kept staring at her, and it unnerved her. She showed him to the nails.

"Here you go," she said as politely as she could and hurried away.

She was sweeping the front of the store when he finally came back to the counter fifteen minutes later.

"Are you ready?" She put the broom down and went to check him out. He put one box of nails on the counter silently and stared at her. Carly rushed to get this ugly man out of the store. He was making her extremely nervous. "That's three fifty please."

He wordlessly handed her a fifty. She gave him change and went back to sweeping, but he just stood there for a few seconds longer, watching her work.

"Is there anything else you need or want?" she asked guardedly, gripping the broom handle just in case she needed to defend herself.

"Nope," he said, sneering at her. It made her skin crawl. This guy was a real creep.

Sam came to the front after he left.

"Did you know that guy?" Carly asked, watching him walk across the street.

"Nope. But judging from the way he was toward you, I'd have to say he was a relative of Billy Pruit's!" Sam laughed.

Carly saw Joe's truck drive by. She'd thought that he might come by today, and she was apprehensive.

"Sam, may I take a break?" she asked, hoping he didn't see Joe drive by. She couldn't see him right now, and it would look odd to Sam if she didn't talk to him.

"Sure. Have fun," he said off-handedly. He hadn't seen Joe. Carly almost ran upstairs, the bell tinkling behind her as she closed her door silently.

"Hey there, Sam!" Joe called, looking around. "Where's Carly?"

"Just missed her. I just let her go on break," Sam replied. "I hear you had a good dinner last night."

"Yes, I had a great time," he said, disappointed. "How long will she be on break?"

"I usually give her about fifteen minutes. You're welcome to wait here, if you're wanting to. She usually comes back early. How do your parents like her?"

"Well, I guess they like her all right. We really haven't talked about her much. You know what, I'll try back later before you close. I've got some other things to do as well. Will you please tell her I was looking for her?" Joe said distractedly, hoping he could catch her in town if he left right away.

"Yep, bye," answered Sam.

Carly watched to make sure he was gone before she came back down.

"You just missed Joe, Red," Sam called over his shoulder. He was inventorying again. Carly came over to help him. "He said he'd try back before we closed."

"Oh, okay," Carly mumbled. She didn't know how she was going to avoid him, but she was going to give it her best effort.

Joe stopped at the little hotel Kelly worked at as receptionist and all around assistant. She was at the front desk when he walked in.

"Joe!" she said, a happy smile brightened her face. "Wow, this is a surprise. What brings you to town this afternoon?"

"Hi, Kelly. Has Todd called you yet?"

"No, the phones have been pretty busy. Why? Did he need something?"

"I need to ask you a few questions. I'm not sure if you can give me any answers, but maybe you could help me out."

Kelly was intrigued. "Sure. I'll see what I can do. What do you need?"

"Last night Todd and I saw a BMW in town, and we were wondering if the owners were staying here?" Joe asked quietly, looking around to make sure no one was listening.

"BMW. Hmm. Let me look, just a minute," she answered. The phone rang, and she picked it up. "Bailey Bed and Breakfast. May I help you? Oh hi, Todd. Joe's already here. I was just going to look when you called. All right, I'll tell him. See you later." She turned her back toward Joe and said quietly, "I love you too." She hung up the receiver and went to the filing cabinet, her face pink.

"Here we go," she said, coming back to the desk with a manila folder. "We have two people with BMWs staying here. Do you know the license plate number?"

"No, I didn't get a glimpse of it." Joe stopped as a customer came to the desk to complain of not enough towels.

"I'll send some right up, sir," Kelly answered, smiling. The man turned and walked away gruffly.

"He's been grumpy since he arrived." Kelly shook her head and sighed. "I just can't seem to make him happy with anything."

"Can you tell me where the people that own the BMWs are from?" Joe was whispering now.

"One is from South Dakota, and the other is a rental from Billings. I'd guess they rented it from the airport. Is there anything else?" Kelly answered quickly and efficiently.

"Did you check them in?" Joe asked.

"Yes, one was tall and thin, and the other man was short and really ugly. They were both very well dressed. You know, the city-slicker type. The tall, thin man bossed the other one around a lot, and they both had Southern accents."

"Do they have any particular habits that you noticed?" Joe was getting excited now.

"Well, when one is in, the other is out. The tall, thin man is a photographer, I think. He carries a camera bag with him everywhere he goes. I don't really think the short, ugly one does anything but sightsee. He never takes anything with him. That's about all I know," Kelly said apologetically. "Todd asked me to let you know that your mom needs some bread and cheese from the store."

"Thanks, Kelly. I appreciate it. Have a good night," he called, going toward the door. Changing his mind, he turned and walked back to her. "Would you do something for me?" he asked, thoughtfully.

"Sure. What is it?" Kelly was interested. Joe never needed anyone to do anything for him.

"Would you talk to Carly? Kind of buddy up with her and keep her company a little bit? I don't trust"—he hesitated—"Billy. She's all alone over at that store, and she's vulnerable. Would you mind?"

"Of course I will! I think she's just great! Especially how she keeps you on your toes." Kelly grinned mischievously.

Joe just smiled and walked out. He drove back to the hardware store, hoping to see Carly.

"Hey, Sam. Carly off break yet?" Joe called as he walked inside.

"Oh yeah. She's back, but you won't find her here. Sue called and needed her help at the house for a while. I told her you came in earlier," Sam said, peering over his gold-rimmed glasses. "Carly's been jumpy as a cat today. She couldn't seem to settle down and was real nervous like."

"Jumpy? Why would she be jumpy?" Joe puzzled. "We had a great dinner, and I thought she enjoyed herself."

"I know she enjoyed herself, 'cause she told me all about it. Her face positively lit up like a candle talking about it. I don't know why she's so jumpy today. There have been a few crank calls, but I don't see why a few pranks would work somebody up like that."

Joe's curiosity was piqued. "Phone calls? What kind of phone calls?"

"Oh there were about four prank phone calls that she answered today. They didn't say anything, they would just breathe, and then after awhile, they'd hang up. I think it's just Billy tormenting her."

"Did you answer any of them?"

"Yes, I did. But when I answered someone would say, 'Sorry, wrong number' and hang up. Carly quit answering the phone, and they stopped after I started to answer. You leaving?" Sam asked as Joe started toward the door.

"Yeah, I've still got to get some bread and cheese from the store for Mom. Have a good evening, Sam," Joe called over his shoulder.

He was sure now that someone was purposely bothering Carly, and he suspected those two men had a part in it.

Chapter Seven

Carly was successful in avoiding Joe, Kelly, and Todd the following couple of weeks.

She didn't answer the store phone on the pretense that she was afraid it was a prank call. She was always out when Joe or Kelly came in, and she was purposely late for church and left early before anyone could stop her.

One such Sunday afternoon, Joe left his seat as soon as the services were over and almost ran outside, looking for Carly. She was nowhere to be seen. Frustrated, he turned to find Angie standing behind him.

"Hi, Joe. What are you looking for?" she asked, batting her eyes.

He wasn't in the mood.

"I was looking for Carly. Excuse me," he tried to pass her, but she stepped in his way.

"I don't know why all the guys seem to like her. I find her pretty boring and uninteresting myself. You can't be too careful with people like her, you know."

Joe's brow glowering, he turned his attention to her, wishing he could swat her away like a pesky fly. "What do you mean, 'people like her'?"

"Well, no one knows anything about her." She stepped a little closer to him and lay her hand on his arm. Forcing himself to be nice, he stepped away, making her to lose her grip. "Billy likes her pretty well, and that should tell you enough. I heard that she's running from the law. It could be true you know. She doesn't talk to anybody. She just stays in her dumpy little apartment all the time or hangs around Sam and Sue. Don't get me wrong, they're nice people and all, but she doesn't have any friends."

"You know, I find that amazing. I find her extremely interesting and very pretty, and I'm certain she's got quite a few friends that are worth having." He walked back inside to join Todd and Kelly, leaving a fuming Angie behind.

"I didn't see Carly here today," Kelly said, worried.

"She was here. She sat in the back again and left right before church ended." Joe grabbed his coat and swung it over his shoulders.

"Why didn't she sit by us?" Kelly wondered, more than a little hurt. "Do you think she's mad? It's been a while."

"No, I think she doesn't want to see me." Taking his keys out of his pocket, he headed toward the door.

"What do you mean? I thought you two got along great that Thursday night!" Kelly was talking to Joe's back, so she turned to Todd. "Did something happen?" He just shrugged his shoulders and followed Joe, Kelly tagging behind.

"What are you doing, Joe? Where are you going?" Todd asked, putting his hand out to stop him.

"I'm going to go to the hardware store, break down her door, and make her talk to me," he said through gritted teeth, striding down the aisle.

"I don't think that's a good idea." Todd restrained him. "Let's go outside."

They noticed Angie watching them angrily, but Joe didn't care. He tried to shake off Todd's hand, but he held on. Kelly put her hand on his other arm and whispered, "Do you think she was jealous that Angie sat next to you last week?"

"I don't know; she won't see me or talk to me. Every time I go near her, she runs the other way. I don't know what's going on," he said as they walked to the truck.

"Joe, I think you should leave her alone," Todd said quietly. Joe looked at him crossly. "No, I think you should think about this before you do anything."

"Why?"

"Do you want her to trust you?"

"Yes." He paused. "But I don't want her to leave either."

"Why would she go anywhere?" Kelly asked, looking at Todd.

He gave a slight shake of his head.

"She wouldn't tell me." Joe rubbed his forehead, and leaned on the truck. "She said that maybe it wasn't good for us to get to know each other, and that she might have to leave."

"Do you think you might have scared her?" Todd asked, looking at him thoughtfully.

"No. I didn't scare her. She was comfortable with me, and I think she liked being with me."

"I did too. That's why I'm surprised at this change of heart so quickly," Todd said, bemused.

"I don't think she had a change of heart." Kelly defended her friend. "I think it's just what Joe said. She told Joe that maybe it's not good for them to get to know each other better. That sounds like she's scared to me."

"Yes, that's what it sounds like to me too. Now we need to know what she's afraid of. Maybe it could be those two guys we saw," answered Todd. "Joe, I think you should leave her be for now. Let her think about things. We'll pray for her if you want us to."

"Two guys? What two guys?" asked Kelly, her eyes wide.

Todd took her hand. "I'll tell you about it later."

"All right. I'll leave her alone for a little while, but not too long. I'm going home. I'll see you both later." Joe got into the truck and drove away slowly.

"Todd, do you think he's afraid of Carly doing the same thing Amy did?" Kelly asked anxiously.

"Maybe. But I don't think that's what's bothering Carly. I think she's really scared about something. I don't think it would be a bad idea for you and her to be really good friends." He looked down at her and gave her hand an affectionate squeeze.

"I agree. I'll see what I can do." She smiled up at him. "Maybe if she felt that she had friends here, she could tell us what's bothering her."

Later that night, Penny woke up. A light was on in the kitchen. She squinted at the clock. One-thirty.

What in the world... she wondered. Draping her robe over her shoulders and sliding her feet into her slippers, she went to investigate.

"Joe! What are you doing up at this hour?" she asked, pulling out a chair and sitting down across the table from him, yawning.

"I'm eating some of your delicious pie," he answered between mouthfuls. Penny looked at him. She could always tell when something was bothering her boys. It showed up in their appetites.

"Do you want to talk about it?" she asked, propping her chin up with her hands. Joe chewed slowly and carefully, weighing his options. He looked up at Penny and gave her a miserable grimace.

"Mom, what do you think of Carly?" He was curious, as neither Tom nor Penny had talked about her while he was around.

"Well, I think she's a nice girl," Penny answered evasively.

"Yeah," Joe said, before taking another huge bite of pie. Penny waited.

"You know, there are other girls out there. She's not the only one in town. What about Angie? She likes you." Penny knew that she wasn't telling Joe what he wanted to hear, but she wanted to know how much he was interested in Carly.

"Angie? I'm not interested in Angie," he answered with a frown.

"Why not? She's cute, friendly; she goes to church." She could tell she was starting to exasperate him.

"Mom, Angie isn't my type. She's got a mean spirit, and I don't want to be around someone like that." The scene after church flashed in his mind. "I'm interested in Carly."

There it was. He'd said it. Penny smiled knowingly. "I know. I knew that the first time I saw you around her. If you're interested, what's the problem?"

"I thought the night she was here that she liked me too, but now she acts like I've got the plague. I don't know. Maybe I misinterpreted something," he said glumly, pushing his plate away.

"Huh. I'm shocked. I thought she liked you pretty good too. Maybe you should just give her some room, and she'll let you know in time." Penny smiled. "She's not been here very long. Are you sure you like her? You don't know much about her."

"I know. That's the weird part. After Amy, I didn't think I could ever be interested in anyone again. I thought Amy was perfect. I'd rate every woman I met with her, and they just never came close. Then I gave up and decided God just didn't want me to have a wife. So I was fine with that. Then I met Carly, and somehow we fit. It's almost like home; you know where it is, and you're happy when you're there. Carly was like that. I could be myself with her, and she'd laugh. It wasn't like that with Amy. She was always trying to change me to fit what she thought I should be like. I didn't see it until she left, but looking back, I can see it all pretty clearly now. And you know the weirdest part?"

Enthralled, Penny shook her head.

"I'm glad Amy left. I am so thankful God didn't allow me to make the biggest mistake of my life. I'm glad we didn't get married. Amy doesn't hold a candle to Carly." Joe sat back in his chair and looked at his mother. "It was pretty hard on you too, wasn't it?" he asked softly.

"Amy treating you like that? Yes. It was hard, and it's made it a little harder to trust anyone else too. Joe, I'm glad that you like Carly. I like her too, just do your poor mom a favor and be careful. Don't forget to ask for God's will to be done. No matter what, okay? I'm going to bed." She stood up, put his plate in the sink, and went to bed.

Joe watched her leave then prayed fervently for God to take care of the whole situation and that his will would be done—even if it meant that he would lose Carly like he'd lost Amy.

Carly was at the counter the next morning checking out a

customer when Kelly walked in and waited patiently for her to finish up.

"Carly, are you mad at me? I haven't seen you in a while," Kelly asked, concerned.

She looked at her sheepishly. "Mad? At you? No way. I've just been running late a little bit, that's all." Carly looked down at her nails and started to pick at them.

Kelly studied her. "Good. I was wondering if you would want to have lunch with me today at the diner?" She had her cornered.

After a few seconds of silent battle, and just enough time for Kelly to think she was going to refuse, Carly finally smiled. "Yes. I'd like that. Thank you."

Excited, Kelly clapped her hands in glee. "What time is your lunch? Mine is at one."

"That's fine. Sam's pretty good at letting me go whenever I need to." She blushed, remembering all the times she'd taken off because Joe was coming in.

"All right. It's all settled then. I'll see you at the diner at one! Bye!" Kelly waved as she walked out the door.

As soon as the door closed, panic struck Carly. What if Kelly had set her up? What if Joe was there?

"Sam, is it okay if I take my lunch at one today? Kelly wants me to meet her at the diner," she asked, as he walked out of the office.

"No, I don't mind. In fact, I've noticed that you haven't been sitting by Joe at church lately, and I thought maybe you two were fussing. So where've you been?" he inquired easily, leaning on the counter.

"Oh, you know how women are. We're always running late for something," she said off-handedly.

"Oh. So why don't you sit by Joe anymore?" He wasn't letting her off the hook.

"Well, I didn't want everyone to think we were an 'item,' so I just figured I'd give Joe a break." She hoped he'd be convinced.

He raised his eyebrows. "Ah, I see. So is that the reason you're always on break when he comes into town?" Luckily, the door opened before she had the chance to answer, and she just gave him a sweet smile.

"Excuse me," someone rasped behind them.

Carly looked toward the door, and her smile faltered. The ugly man. He came in every day, always stared at her, and always bought one box of nails after fifteen minutes of looking at them.

She shuddered and thanked God Sam was still next to her.

"Yes, sir?" asked Sam, standing up and straightening his shirt. "May I help you find something?"

"I was wondering if you could show me where the nails are," he asked Carly, completely ignoring Sam.

"I'll show you where they are, sir," Sam said firmly. He didn't like this guy almost as much as Carly.

"I wasn't talking to you," he snarled.

"Sir," Sam said quietly but firmly, "I have seen you in this establishment for a couple of weeks now, and you've bought enough nails to know where you could find them. My assistant is busy at the moment."

The ugly man stared at Sam and smirked. "Yeah, I know where they're at; I just wanted her to go with me." His grin made her skin crawl.

"I'm sorry, but she's supposed to be doing the accounts in the back right now. If you need any help, you'll have to ask me," Sam said. She walked back to the office, glad to get away from him.

"Sure, I understand. I wouldn't want to stop Carly from doing her job." He laughed as he walked back out the door.

Carly froze. *How does he know my name? Maybe someone told him*, she thought. *Like Ian?* a tiny voice seemed to whisper in her ear. All the other times when Ian found her, he'd sent someone after her right away. She'd been here longer than anywhere else.

Too busy to puzzle over the situation while in the back office, it was soon lost in the glories of accounts payable and accounts receivable, and she was surprised when Sam called her to the front at a quarter to one.

"Carly, Kelly's here, and was hoping that you'd be able to go a little early. You ready?"

"Oh my goodness, I can't believe how fast time flies when you're doing paperwork!" Carly joked. "I'll be back in a minute; I've got to get some money," she called over her shoulder as she went up to her apartment. She was there only a moment when she heard a small knock on the doorjamb. Not having closed the door behind her, she looked up to see Kelly standing in the doorway.

"Kelly, hey there. Come on in," she said kindly. "Welcome to my home." She was a little bashful about her place. She hadn't had anyone in it since she moved in, and she wasn't sure how Kelly would react.

"Wow, you live here?" Kelly asked in amazement. "It's so tiny," she said as she looked around the minuscule apartment.

Carly chuckled at her astonished look. "Yeah, it's small, but it's cozy. I don't have too much to clean up. Sorry it's not as tidy as usual."

"Don't worry about it. I just came up to let you know that you're going to need a coat. It's really kind of chilly out there. I've always loved this time of year, but it really gets cold fast if you're not used to it."

"All right, I'm ready," Carly said, grabbing her denim jacket. They talked about everyday things as they walked to the diner together. Weather. Colleges. Todd. Carly was completely comfortable with her and enjoyed her company.

They seated themselves at a booth in the back of the diner as she looked around. No Joe. Feeling a little silly and a lot disappointed, she turned to Kelly and smiled.

"No, he's not here. I didn't want you to be mad at me," Kelly said, looking at her menu.

"Who?"

"Joe. You know who I mean."

Carly blushed. "Why would I get mad at you if Joe was here? He can come eat here whenever he wants to."

Sandy came and took their order. Burger and soda for Kelly

and soup and water for Carly.

"I must say that I never met anyone who liked soup and water as much as you do. That's all you ever order!" Sandy said, exasperated.

Carly laughed. "It's my favorite."

"Why don't you sit with us anymore?" Kelly asked after Sandy left.

"I've just been running late." She looked down, placing her napkin in her lap, avoiding Kelly's frown.

"I'm not convinced. You live three minutes at the most away from church, and you're late? I don't think so. Are you trying to avoid Joe?"

Sandy brought their food, and there was an awkward pause before Carly could answer.

"Why would I want to avoid Joe?" she asked with a shrug of her shoulders after Sandy had left.

"I don't know. Maybe you're scared of something; maybe you don't like him; maybe you've been abducted by aliens, and I'm just talking to your look-alike. But for whatever reason, I wish you would tell me."

Carly took a deep breath and pushed her soup away.

"Why am I trying to avoid Joe? Where do I begin? Because last time I saw him in church, he was busy with Angie."

Kelly eyes widened. "Are you jealous of Angie?"

"No. Yes. I don't know." She sighed. "All right. I guess I am," she admitted.

"But you don't have to sit in the back. He really wants you to sit by him instead of Angie. He can't stand her. Don't be a noodle."

"That's the problem. Kelly, I can't stay here. I'm going to have to leave again, and I don't want Joe to feel bad. He's too nice to hurt." Carly sighed heavily. "Trust me. It's better for everyone this way."

Kelly was unconvinced. "Why can't you stay? I don't understand."

"I can't stay because I have a problem to deal with," Carly

answered evasively.

"A problem to deal with? Oh my. Oh *wow*," Kelly breathed, her eyes wide, her face pale. "Carly, are you *married*?" She squeaked the last word out.

Carly burst out laughing. "Married? No way, trust me. You should see your face. If you opened your eyes anymore, I think they'd fall right out!"

"Are you sure you're not married?" She eyed her doubtfully.

"Positive. You remember me telling you all at the Bairds' that I was engaged once?" Kelly nodded, not taking her eyes off Carly's face. "Well, when I broke off our engagement, my fiancé was less than pleased. In fact, he was furious."

"So? Why would that make it to where you couldn't stay here?"

"He told me that he would follow me wherever I went, that he wouldn't let anyone else have me, and that he'd kill me if I tried to marry anyone but him. That's pretty much it in a nutshell."

"Are you serious?" Kelly stared. "He loved you a lot then, right?"

"Love? Ian didn't love me. He felt that I was his property, and he can't stand for someone else to have what he wants. It isn't romantic. It's frightening. I've had to keep running, because he keeps finding me and trying to force me to come back to him. I've lost everything I had because of him. When I tried to leave the first time, he took the car he bought me away, and he locked me in my apartment for a while. He's crazy. Obsessed."

They finished their meals, paid their bills, and left without another word. Kelly was quiet until they arrived at the hardware store.

"Carly, I'm sorry you've had it so rough, and I wish you felt safe here. I want you to stay here, and I know Joe wants you to stay."

"I would love to stay, but Ian will find me and will hurt anyone that he thinks I'm interested in. I can't let that happen to Joe. I'll just leave before he likes me too much," Carly said simply, shivering. The wind was cold and whipped through her light jacket.

"I think you should tell Joe and see what he thinks. You should give him that option before you leave," Kelly said stubbornly, refusing to see it Carly's way.

"Thanks for listening. You're the only person I've told, and it feels like a load has been lifted off my shoulders." Carly smiled sadly, giving her friend a hug.

"I'll see you later, girl. If you need anything, let me know," Kelly said, walking away. Carly watched her go, thankful for her friendship.

Todd called Kelly that evening.

"Hey, babe! How are you?" He always acted like it was the best part of his day to call and talk to her.

"I'm good. How was your day?"

Todd told her about his day at the farm as she listened patiently.

"How's Joe been today?" she asked, wanting to tell him about her experience with Carly.

"Joe? Let me see. How can I describe Joe? Hmm. Grouchy? No, too nice. Grumpy? Sounds too much like the Seven Dwarfs. Just plain cantankerous. He's grumpy, grouchy, crabby, irritable, and he's just not happy with anyone or anything. In fact, I'd have to say he's miserable. He spends a lot of time out at the horse corral though, which is good for the rest of us. Makes me feel sorry for the horses. Why do you ask?"

"I had lunch with Carly today."

His curiosity was piqued immediately. "Oh really? Did she have anything interesting to say?"

"Yes, she had some pretty interesting things to say, but I'm not going to tell you everything. Just the important things. It's not my business to tell you the rest; she'll have to do that. Joe doesn't need to be so miserable. She cares for him, but she's really scared, like I thought she was. And tell him that she's jealous when Angie sits next to him at church, that should make him feel better."

"Good. Maybe it'll cheer him up finally. He's been awful to be around." They continued talking for a while, said their good-byes, and hung up.

Todd went to look for Joe. He found him outside at the corral, scratching behind Ashes' ears. He was deep in thought and didn't hear Todd walk up. Todd rested his leg on the bottom rung and leaned his chin on his fist.

"I just got off the phone with Kell," he started. Joe kept scratching Ashes as though he hadn't heard. "I thought you'd want to know that she had lunch with Carly today."

Joe looked over at him. "Really," he said evenly. He waited.

"Kelly said Carly was jealous that Angie sat by you at church."

Joe nodded his head approvingly. "That's very interesting." He was thoughtful. "Thanks," he said finally, turning back to the horse.

"Welcome," Todd answered, walking back toward the house. He stopped and turned back toward Joe. "Oh. I almost forgot. She told Kell that she cares for you, but she admits that she's scared." He turned and left before Joe could reply.

Joe's mood had changed drastically when he finally came into the house. He hugged his mom, punched his dad on the arm, and tousled Todd's hair, which he knew he hated with a passion.

"How do you like that?" Todd asked, looking at his family. "You give the guy some good news, and he comes in and treats you with no respect. That's the last time I tell you good news!" Joe laughed.

"Good news? What good news?" Penny asked, soap bubbles up to her elbows.

"Nothing," Joe said as he walked out of the kitchen whistling.

They looked over at Todd. "What's got him so happy?"

"I just told him that Carly likes him."

"Carly? He's been in a bad mood because of a girl?" Tom looked impressed. "Hmm. I thought he'd never like another one of those after Amy. Well, I guess that's good news after all."

Penny looked at Todd thoughtfully, then went and finished the dishes.

The next morning, Joe got up earlier than usual. He showered, shaved, made coffee, ate some cereal, and waited for Todd to come down to the kitchen.

He had lain awake the night before, wondering what he should do. Should he go talk to her? He didn't want to scare her anymore than she already was, but he had to talk to her. He wanted to know what she was afraid of and how he could help her. She might not even know that Kelly had spoken to Todd and told him any of their conversation and would still avoid him.

Todd came to the breakfast table yawning. "What are you doing up so early?" he asked, stretching. He helped himself to a cup of coffee and sat down opposite Joe. "Mmm. Good coffee."

"I was wondering if Carly knew that Kelly told you about their conversation yesterday."

"Wow, no beating around the bush with you, is there? No. I don't think Carly knows anything. Why?"

Joe's face fell.

"I wanted to go talk to her, but if she didn't know Kelly told you anything, then she'll still avoid me."

"Well, for some reason, I don't think she'd really want to talk to you anyway at five in the morning. Most people don't wake up with the chickens, you know." Todd's large grin suddenly stretched bigger. He had an idea.

"Ashes is looking a little fat, you know. You should exercise her more often. It's supposed to be nice weather today and tomorrow; perfect for riding. Maybe I'll get Kelly out here later and have her help me with the horses. We could take care of Ashes for you if you wanted." He looked at his brother out of the corner of his eye.

"I wonder if Carly would like to ride," Joe mused, taking the hint. "Do you think Kelly could entice her to come out here for a ride?"

"I could have her try, but Carly's probably got to work until five tonight, and by then it'll almost be too dark to ride. Or would you rather have Kelly ask her for tomorrow when you have all day?"

"Try for tomorrow so we won't be so rushed. Thanks for the idea, little brother." Joe smiled, put on his hat, and went out to the barn to start doing his work.

Kelly went to see Carly around lunchtime.

"Hey there, Kell. How's it going today? Any mean people yet?" Carly teased.

"Boy, do I have a story for you! There was a couple in this morning, and all they did was fight, fight, fight. It was embarrassing. Most of the guests were eating in the dining room, and everyone could hear what they were saying, they were so loud. Man, I hope Todd and I never fight that way." Kelly laughed, leaning her elbows on the counter.

"Anyway, on to more important stuff. I was wondering if you would like to go horseback riding tomorrow morning. We would have a picnic in the afternoon, and we could ride all day." Carly was frowning. "Don't you like to ride?" Kelly asked, disappointed. She had hoped their scheme would work.

"Where?" Carly asked bluntly, crossing her arms. She knew Kelly wouldn't lie.

"At the Bairds'," she said quietly. "Come on, Carly, please? You'd have fun," she pleaded when Carly shook her head.

"It's no good, Kelly; I can't go out there when I've been trying so hard to avoid him here. What good would that do?" Carly asked, exasperated.

"All right. I understand. But you know, the Bible says that we're supposed to bear one another's burdens, and you're not letting anyone else help you with yours." Kelly was just warming up.

"Have you even prayed and asked God what he wanted you to do? What if he wants you to stay? Would you? Or would you be too scared? Give God a chance to tell you what he wants, Carly," Kelly ended in a storm. "I've got to get back to work. See you around." She stomped out the door.

"Wait!" Carly called, following her. "Kelly! Stop!" Kelly stopped and turned around. She was furious.

"You know, Carly, you haven't even given God a chance to take care of your needs. You've just kept running and running," she sputtered.

"Kelly." Carly grabbed her by the shoulders. "I'm sorry. I didn't mean to make you so upset. You're right. I've been running so long I think that's the only thing I know how to do. I'm sorry. Please don't be angry with me," she pleaded.

Kelly softened. "Okay. I'm sorry I yelled at you like that. I usually don't do that."

Carly smiled and gave Kelly a hug. "Yeah, but you haven't dealt with a stubborn old mule like me."

"Please say you'll go tomorrow. Please, Carly. Joe's been so miserable and hard to live with," she begged.

"If I say I'll go, are you going to yell at me like that again?"

Kelly smiled. "No, I won't freak out on you again."

"Are you sure he wants me around? I'm not going to be unwelcome, am I?" Her stomach twisted into a knot at the thought of spending the day at the Bairds' farm.

"Of course he wants you around! He's been unbearable! You'll definitely be welcome. I'll pick you up at seven tomorrow, okay? And be sure to bring a jacket."

"All right, sounds good to me. I'll see you then." Carly walked back to the shop, shivering in the brisk wind. She was excited and scared at the same time. She could hardly wait for today to be over so tomorrow could begin.

Lord, please forgive me. I haven't asked you lately what your will is for me, and I've made a mess of things again. Please let me know what to do, and help me not to operate on my emotions. Help me to seek your will in all things, and do it. No matter what. She smiled as the peace that passes all understanding enveloped her.

Just before closing, the short, ugly man came in. Carly was still at peace and felt that nothing this man could do would bother her.

"The nails are in aisle three," she said automatically.

He scowled. "What if I wanted something else?"

"Do you need anything else?" Carly retorted, looking up from the receipts she was tallying.

He leered at her. "Yeah. I need a hammer now."

"You'll find those in aisle three as well. Right next to the nails." She stared steadily back at him.

He dropped his gaze first and went to find the hammer. He came back promptly with a small hammer and set it on the counter.

"Is that all for you?" Carly asked sarcastically. "Seven fifty-eight please." He paid her, walked to the door, and turned around to glare at her one last time before leaving.

"Good-bye," she called sweetly, waving.

The next morning, Carly was up and ready long before Kelly came to get her. Apprehensive about the day, she had been unable to sleep very well the night before. How would Joe treat her? Would his parents act differently toward her?

Finally, she spied Kelly's uncle's truck in the street below. Grabbing her denim jacket, she ran out to meet her. "Good morning," she said as she climbed into the passenger seat.

Kelly backed out and started toward the Bairds' farm. "Good morning! Did you sleep well?"

"I slept like garbage. I just couldn't seem to concentrate on sleeping because I was worrying about what to expect today."

"Everything will be fine. Did you eat breakfast?"

"I had some applesauce." Carly shrugged.

Kelly looked over at her in surprise. "Is that going to be enough? We're going to be out all day."

Carly smiled amiably. "I'll be fine. That's all I usually eat for breakfast. So how did you sleep?"

"I slept wonderful. I love it when Todd asks me to help with the horses. We ride all day, have a picnic by the pond, skip stones, and just talk. Joe usually comes with us, but he's a little quiet and stays to himself quite a bit."

"How come Joe goes?" Carly asked, surprised that Todd would allow a chaperone if he could get away without one.

"I ask him to go. If I'm out alone with Todd, that's just a reason for people to talk, so I always ask Joe to go with us. Todd doesn't mind either. They talk rough to each other sometimes, but they're best friends."

They talked agreeably for the rest of the ride. As they got closer, Carly became more quiet and reserved.

There were lights on in the kitchen when they pulled into the driveway.

"Kelly, why did I let you talk me into this?" Carly whispered, so nervous she could hardly breathe.

"You'll be okay. You're with people who care about you and like you. You're going to have a good day, I promise." She got out of the truck and started walking to the porch before she realized Carly hadn't gotten out yet. She waited for her. Carly opened the door reluctantly and stepped out.

Todd swung the door open, smiling broadly before they had the chance to knock. "Good morning," he called as he gave Kelly a hug. "Carly! I'm glad you could make it. It's been a long time since we've seen you. Come on in."

She muttered a quiet "good morning" and "thanks" as she followed them into the kitchen. She smiled shyly at Joe, who was seated at the breakfast table. He beamed.

"Good morning, girls," called Penny as she prepared dough for biscuits. "How are you this morning?"

"Great!" was Kelly's exuberant reply.

"Here, Carly, have a seat. Sorry we're not ready to go. We got up late, and we haven't had breakfast yet. Would you two like some?" Joe said kindly as he pulled out a chair for her.

"Oh yes please," Kelly cried out. "Carly only had some applesauce this morning. She might get hungry." Carly blushed with embarrassment.

"Only some applesauce?" asked Penny in surprise. "That's why you're so thin, you poor thing. You're staying for breakfast, and that's not a question. That's a command." She laughed, waving a doughy hand at her.

"Thank you, but I'd feel better if I could help you with something," Carly said, putting her jacket on the back of a chair.

"Me too," chimed in Kelly.

"I don't think you should let Carly help, Mom. I remember the last time she was here she said she could only make macaroni and cheese, and that doesn't sound so good for breakfast," Joe teased.

"I said that's about the only thing I've been able to make," she retorted.

"Is there a difference?"

"Yes!" she said playfully. "What can I do to help?" she asked as she washed her hands.

"You're a dear. You can fry the bacon and sausage, and Kelly, you can fry the eggs while I finish up with these biscuits, if you don't mind. The pans are already out," Penny directed them.

Joe came to stand at the counter next to Carly and started cutting potatoes into an electric skillet. Unable to resist a sideways glance at him, he caught her look and grinned back, his eyes twinkling. She turned quickly and started the bacon. She'd always been a sucker for the tall, dark, and handsome sort, and he was definitely all of those.

He finished with the potatoes and started on the onions. They started to cook, and she remembered how much she loved the smell of fried potatoes and onions. He reached over and flipped an onion into her pan and bumped her arm, making her drop her spatula.

"What?" she asked, smiling. She scooped the onion out, tossing it back into the skillet.

He was grinning mischievously. "Nothing."

"Are you purposely trying to aggravate me?" she asked, waving her spatula at him menacingly. "'Cause if you are, I'm going to swat you!"

He laughed and went back to his potatoes and onions. They worked in companionable silence, listening to the conversation around them.

He leaned over toward her and whispered, "I'm glad you came today." It wasn't much, but it made her stomach flip-flop and her face turn red.

Breakfast was ready just as Tom came in.

"Smells good," he bellowed, smacking his lips and holding his stomach. "I'm famished! Good morning, how are you girls doing this fine day?" He grabbed hold of Penny and started dancing around the kitchen.

"Good morning," they said in unison, laughing.

They all sat down amiably in the same spots as before, but this time Carly sat down next to Joe. Todd winked at Joe, and Carly made a face back at him. It was a cheerful breakfast with much talk, laughter, and eating, but it was over so soon. The girls helped Penny clean up while Joe and Todd went to saddle the horses.

"Carly, how have you been? I haven't seen you at church for a while," Penny asked, running the dishwater.

"I've been sitting in the back, but I've been pretty good," she replied. She wasn't too sure of her position with Penny. She was very kind when she spoke to her, but Carly felt that she was reserved and unsure of what to say. "Just keeping to myself pretty much." Carly rinsed the dishes as Kelly dried and stacked them on the counter.

"I've noticed," she said quietly. "I wondered where you were when I saw Angie sitting beside Joe. Have you met Angie?"

"Yes, I have," she answered evenly.

Penny was silent for a moment. "She seems nice, but I think she's jealous of you, you know," she said with a smile. "Do you have any other relatives living?"

"I don't think so. My mom's parents had already passed away

before I was born, and my dad's parents never forgave him for marrying my mom. I guess they had words and split company. The only family I had was my parents. They were everything to me."

"What about your spiritual birth, honey? When were you introduced to Jesus?" Penny couldn't help but feel for this young woman who had lost so much. She had always been a family-oriented person and couldn't imagine what it would have been like to live without them.

"Both my parents were Christians before they met, and we went to church every Sunday and Wednesday. I asked Jesus to be my Savior when I was six, but the reality of heaven didn't hit me until I watched my mom die. I never had a doubt that I wanted to go there and see her again. Now that Dad's gone, it just makes heaven sweeter." Carly's voice broke slightly as she talked, but she held her head up and didn't cry.

"If I lost everyone I loved, I'd go nuts," Kelly said softly.

"Dad used to say, 'If it don't kill ya, it'll just make ya stronger.' And I wasn't really alone. I've had Jesus with me through everything, and he's the greatest friend ever." Carly stopped, catching a movement out of the corner of her eye. Joe and Todd were standing in the doorway, listening. Joe cleared his throat.

"Are you ready? We've got everything ready except the food."

"Oh!" Penny exclaimed. "I almost forgot. Here you are." She had packed a leather backpack full of delicious-looking food. "You have fun and be careful," she called after them as they walked out to the barn. Tom came and put his arm around her shoulder.

"You know what? They're grown up, girl. What do you think of that?" He gave Penny a bear hug.

"I know. It sure didn't take long, did it?" There were tears in her eyes.

Chapter Eight

"Carly, have you ever ridden a horse before?" Joe asked as they walked to the waiting horses.

"Is it legal to live in Texas and not ride a horse?" she teased.

"Good. I want you to ride Ashes because I know she'll behave. Up you go." He helped her into the saddle. He adjusted the stirrups then mounted his own horse.

They rode off down the dirt road single file, then out into an open field. Todd and Kelly raced, galloping across the field, while Joe and Carly followed, cantering at an easy pace.

"We're taking you two up to Wilson's Pond, and then after we eat, we'll follow the creek back down to the farm. It'll take us all day." Joe turned from surveying the land to survey Carly. "How you holding up over there? Are you comfortable? She handling well?"

Carly looked over at him and flashed him one of her best smiles. "She's a magnificent horse, and she rides so well. Thank you for letting me borrow her for the day." She nodded to the Palomino Joe was riding. "How's your horse doing?"

"Chessy? Oh we're doing fine. This is Dad's horse. Kelly is riding Mom's, and Todd is riding his own, of course. He likes them a little more on the wild side. He likes to let them have their head and run. I'd rather take it easy and look at the scenery." He looked at Carly with a twinkle in his eye.

She pretended not to understand his meaning. "Yes, the mountains sure look beautiful, don't they?"

"They're all right I suppose. I've lived here all my life, so I'm used to them."

It was a beautiful fall day to be riding. Not too warm, not too cold, just right. The leaves crunched under the horses feet, the air was fresh and pure, the company wonderful. They came to a trail in a patch of woods. Todd led the way, Kelly was next, Carly, then Joe brought up the rear. Pine trees, maple trees, elms, and oaks lined their path. Carly breathed deeply. She hadn't felt this peaceful since before her dad died. The trees suddenly cleared away to reveal a beautiful lake.

Wilson's Pond.

She hadn't expected it to be this big, she had thought it would be more like a small fishing hole, but this would be more accurately called a lake. She caught her breath at the sight. She'd had no idea that Wilson's Pond would be so beautiful. Snowcapped mountains were off in the distance, pine trees ringed the pond on three sides, and she thought the very air seemed magical and sweet.

"It's beautiful," she breathed, glancing at Joe with amazement as she dismounted.

He grinned and took the lunch pack off Chessy, and Todd spread a blanket on the ground next to a large boulder sitting beside the pond. Carly and Kelly emptied the lunch pack and set the food out. Cold chicken, carrot and celery sticks, ranch dip, potato chips, and freshly baked chocolate chip cookies for dessert. They all sat down, prayed, and ate until they could barely budge.

After lunch, Kelly caught Carly's eye and motioned toward Joe. Carly looked away, pretending not to notice, but Kelly didn't give up. She caught her eye again and motioned toward Joe more aggressively. Carly pursed her lips together and shook her head firmly.

"What in the world are you two up to?" Todd asked, looking from one to the other. "Are you trying to swat something away?"

"No," Kelly answered sweetly. She gave Carly another look, and frowned her displeasure.

Joe had caught the looks as well. Whatever it was that Kelly wanted her to talk about, Carly wasn't going to do it without help.

"So, why have you been avoiding me lately?" He leaned lazily on the boulder behind him, his arms crossed across his broad chest.

"Avoiding you?" She repeated lamely. "Who says I was avoiding you?"

"I say you were."

"So do I," Todd agreed. "And so does Kelly, but she won't say so." Kelly punched his arm. "Come on and tell us. Joe's been miserable these past couple of days, and I don't think I can handle any more of it." Todd rolled his eyes.

Joe threw a handful of grass at him. "I admit, I've been a little short lately, but I wouldn't go so far as to say that I was miserable."

"Of course you wouldn't say it, but I'll admit it for you. You were terrible to live with."

Carly looked over at Joe, and he grinned sheepishly. "I plead the fifth."

"Oh no. Not that again. If you plead the fifth, then I'll plead the fifth, then Kelly will freak out on me again." Carly laughed. "And that was *really* scary."

Todd leaned over to stare into Kelly's red face. "You freaked out on Carly? Wow, I've never seen you freak out. Why do I miss all the good stuff?"

Kelly gave him a playful slap on his leg. "Yes, I freaked out on her. But it worked, because she's here, and she wasn't going to come. Right Carly?"

She batted her eyes innocently. "Can I plead the fifth?"

"No!" they all said firmly.

"Now, honestly. Why have you been avoiding me? Actually, it's not just me, it's been all of us, and we'd really like to know why." Joe spoke for all of them.

"Well, to be honest, I was really trying to avoid just you. Todd and Kelly just always happened to be with you, so I had to avoid them as well," she admitted. "Why isn't so easy to tell. It's a long story, and I wouldn't know where to start." She shrugged her shoulders, looking away at the mountains.

"Start when you moved to Houston," Kelly prompted her.

Carly moaned. "You know too much already. It's not very interesting, and you're going to be bored," she answered, trying to get out of it.

"That's okay. We're country folk. We love stories. Even the boring ones," Joe stretched his legs out in front of him and leaned back on his elbows.

"Don't say I didn't warn you." She sighed expressively. "You all know that my mom died when I was eight, and when I was twelve, my dad and I moved to Houston, Texas, where he got a job transfer. We were pretty happy there, but then he got sick with cancer when I was nineteen. We had a fine church that we belonged to, and a rich businessman went there as well."

"A single, rich business man?" Joe questioned, his eyes dark with suspicion. Carly blushed.

"Yes. A single, rich business man. He offered me a good job in his company as his secretary. I accepted, hoping to be able to help Dad pay some of his medical bills. He paid really well even though I didn't know as much about the job as I should have. I thought he was just trying to help us out, but Dad didn't see things that way. Dad didn't like him from the beginning." She paused and surveyed the distant mountains, collecting her memories.

"Ian was the only thing we disagreed about, really. He kept telling me that he didn't trust him and I should find a new job. I always argued that Ian was a Christian and just wanted to help. The pay was exceptionally good, he said all the right things, did all the right things, and I fell for him hook, line, and sinker." Joe grunted quietly. Carly looked at him and smiled. "He was rich, handsome, and I was only nineteen." He scowled and looked away. "Joe? Is there something wrong?"

"You could probably skip this part," he answered sourly.

"No, if you want to hear my story, you've got to listen to the whole thing, and it's mainly about Ian. If it makes you uncomfortable, I'll stop," Carly answered hopefully.

"Keep going, Carly. He'll just have to get over it." Todd said, elbowing Kelly and nodding toward Joe, who was still sulking. "He was engaged once too, you know."

"Really?" Carly asked, surprised. Now it was her turn to be a little jealous. "Joe, do you have a story to tell after I tell mine?" She gave him a playful smile and tossed a weed his way.

"Nope," he answered shortly.

"Anyway," she resumed, smiling wryly. "I worked for Ian for about six months before he asked me to marry him. I thought the world of him, so of course, I accepted. Dad was shocked. He didn't speak to me for a week after I told him the news." A bitter smile wrapped itself on her lips.

"I was the only thing he had left in the world, and he worried about me." Carly paused, remembering. "He got sicker, and the doctors said they couldn't do anything for him, so I took care of him at home. Ian had given me time off work, and I stayed by his side. I was reading to him one day, and he asked me to stop. I did, and we talked about Ian. He told me again that he didn't trust him, but if I thought that was who the Lord wanted for me, then I should marry him, but to be very sure. I remember watching him labor to talk to me, and I knew it was the end. He told me to give everything to God, including Ian, that he loved me, and that he'd see me in heaven one day. Then he gave me a kiss and died."

Carly wiped tears from her eyes. "The weeks following Dad's death were a whirlwind. Ian took care of everything. I was a robot. I did everything he said without question. I couldn't even think on my own. So Ian had me moved out of Dad's apartment into an expensive place across town in two weeks." Joe looked at her oddly. "No, Ian didn't live there with me, Joe, if that's what you're thinking. He wanted to, but I wouldn't allow it. It would have gone against everything that I'd been taught. I felt that I would be dishonoring my parent's memory, not to mention displeasing God, so that was one thing I stuck to."

"After Dad died, I got to know Ian a lot better. I still worked as his secretary, but now he wanted me to go with him to corporate parties, meet his friends, pretty much everywhere. I was his little prize, and he liked to show off. I didn't mind it at first, but then his real nature started showing. If we went to a party together, he'd leave me alone to 'mingle,' and he'd get furious if a guy came up to talk to me."

"That started happening more and more, until I couldn't do anything to please him, although I tried. I wouldn't talk to anyone at a party, and he'd get mad that I was being a snob. If I talked to someone at a party, he'd accuse me of cheating on him. If it was a woman, he'd accuse me of trashing him behind his back." Carly stopped.

"Is that when you decided to leave him?" Kelly asked, frowning.

"No, I would just make up excuses for him. I'd tell myself that I deserved it, that I was being too friendly or whatever, and I'd try even harder to please him."

"Was he like that everywhere?" Todd asked, amazed.

"At first it was just at the parties. Then it started showing up in other areas. He would take me shopping and insist on buying me anything and everything. He would tell me that he wanted me to look perfect and be happy. I'm ashamed to admit it, but I enjoyed it, and that helped me stay with him longer than I should have." She blushed and tore a piece of weed to shreds.

"I had grown up on the poor side of everything, and Ian was so rich. It was exciting to be able to have everything I wanted. Nothing was too expensive. He bought me a BMW, cell phone, he paid for my apartment, he bought all my clothes and accessories, we went to the most expensive restaurants, everything."

"Well, that doesn't sound too bad. Why didn't you stay with him?" Joe asked a bit too sharply.

"I'm getting there," she answered softly. "I'm not as unworthy as you think. I didn't leave him because one day he wouldn't buy me something I wanted." She looked at him, a mirthless smile on her lips. "He began to get abusive if I didn't do everything he thought I should. If I went shopping without him and I bought something he didn't like, he'd slap me. Just a slap at first. Nothing that would leave bruises so people could see. I told him I wanted to break it off after the first slap, but he was so sorry and kind afterward. He promised that he would never hit me again, and I believed him."

"Gradually it got worse. If I talked to another guy at work, he'd punch me. If I didn't call him right away after I got home, he'd punch me. If I didn't look just right for a party, he'd punch me. Then he'd slap and punch, then he'd add a kick when I fell to the floor. He broke my arm once just because I got a ticket for speeding on the expressway. So I'm not as unworthy as you think, Joe. I didn't use him for what he could buy me. I thought I really loved him. And what's worse, I thought it was just his way of showing me that he loved me."

They were all quiet for a while, scarcely daring to believe that a man would do such things to a woman that he professed to love.

Or that a woman could excuse those actions as *showing* love.

"But I thought he was a Christian, Carly. Christians aren't supposed to do those things," Kelly said in disbelief. Todd hugged her closer to him.

"I just know what he told me. Like I said, he always said the right things, and if he wasn't beating me, he did the right things."

"Is that when you left?" Joe asked quietly.

"No. That was only about six months into our engagement. I didn't even start thinking about leaving until he broke my arm. After my arm healed and I went back to work, I started to hear rumors about him and another secretary that worked in another office. I was stupid enough to ask him about her one day, and he went off like a bomb. We were at my apartment, and we had a terrific screaming match. He was angry that I had the nerve to ask him about the other woman, and he started punching me. I was too mad to back down, and I started punching him back, but he just laughed."

"He was like a crazy man, and he was enjoying himself. Every time I punched him once, he'd punch me three times. The neighbor next to my apartment heard all the fighting and called the police. When I turned my back on him to open the door, he knocked me to the floor and starting kicking me. When he opened the door, he tried to block the doorway and act as if nothing was going on, but it was too late. They saw me, and they took him to jail for domestic abuse while I went to the hospital."

"That's when I decided to leave him, but I had already gotten in over my head. Before I could leave the hospital, Ian had paid his way out of jail, and it was too late for me to get away. He came to the hospital every day, crying in shame, apologizing, bringing me gifts, admitting his guilt, begging me to forgive him, and promising he would get some sort of counseling."

"Did you forgive him?" Kelly interrupted.

"No. I'd heard it all before. It was always the same. He'd be kind and loving for about a week or two, maybe even a month, then it would start all over again. No, my love for him had died, and I knew I couldn't marry him."

"While I was staying in the hospital, I had a lot of time to remember how my dad had acted toward my mom. How much he loved her and cherished her, for better or for worse. They were best friends. The day she died, I was sitting on the end of her bed and Dad was rocking her gently to ease her pain. She died in his arms. Dad had taken Mom and loved her dearly through the worst possible circumstances. That was what marriage should be like, and I knew it wouldn't be that way with Ian. If I stayed with him, he would kill me."

"I bet he took it bad when you told him that," Todd said.

"I didn't tell him that time. If I would have told him, I don't think I would have made it out of the hospital," Carly answered evenly. "No, I had to pretend that I still loved him. He took me back to my apartment and acted like nothing out of the ordinary had happened, but he was different. He was more watchful and suspicious, and he was always around. So now, my problem was even worse. I was becoming panicky, and I knew that I would have to leave everything that he'd bought me or given me. Even the money that I'd earned working for him. If I left him, I'd only have the money in my purse, which was about four hundred dollars."

"Why did you leave the money you made?" Joe asked incredulously. "Didn't you put your money in the bank?"

"Yes, I did have a bank account, but when Ian asked me to marry him, we made it a joint account. He told me it was a start for our future together, and I was so stupid that I believed him. I didn't know until I wanted to leave that it was just another way he could control my actions and keep me with him. I was trapped. He would give me money once a week for gas or other things that I might want, but that stopped after I got out of the hospital. He started to pick me up for work, take me to lunch, drive me home, stay as long as he could, and then the whole process would start the next day. I told him I could drive myself to work and that he didn't need to bother about me so much, but he wouldn't hear any of it. I was locked in some sort of fancy prison. I couldn't get away from him."

"About two months after I got out of the hospital, I was at my apartment and he wasn't there, which was very rare, and the new next-door neighbor came over to introduce himself. We were standing in the hallway talking when the elevator door opened, and there stood Ian. He was furious. I couldn't really tell if he was madder that I was out of my apartment or talking to a strange man. He grabbed my arm and yanked me inside, slamming the door behind us. He beat me up and threatened to kill me if I ever talked to the neighbor again. He left pretty late that night, and the neighbor must have seen him leave. He came over, and I let him in. He saw my black eyes and bloodied lip, and he offered to help me get away. I was desperate now. I knew that I had to run then, I couldn't wait any longer, so I grabbed my denim jacket, two pair of jeans, some shirts, and my purse. I left his engagement ring on the counter, and we snuck out the back of the apartment building."

"He drove me to a battered women's shelter and left me there. I waited until he left, and I got on a bus and headed for a different state. I didn't care which one. Any would work if I could just get away. That was a little over two years ago, and I'm still running because he finds me wherever I go. I don't use credit cards, I don't have a phone, and I live under assumed names. I've tried everything, but he still keeps finding me. It'll never stop. One day he'll catch up to me and kill me and anyone else I may be with."

Carly ended her story with a sigh and a rueful look at Joe. They were all silent for a few minutes. Kelly got up and hugged her tearfully while Todd looked helpless. Joe let out a low whistle.

"Would you two mind if I talked to Carly alone?" He finally

asked. Todd shook his head, took Kelly's hand, and walked toward the pond, leaving them behind.

Joe rubbed his face distractedly, looking toward the mountains. "What do you plan on doing now? Are you planning on just running still?"

"What else is there for me to do? If I stay, he'll find me. I think he already has."

He looked up sharply. "Why? What makes you think that?"

"There's been too many prank calls. One or two, maybe even three isn't anything to worry about, but we get about ten a day. Then there's this weird ugly man that comes into the store every day to buy nails. Nothing else, just nails. Wait, I take that back. One day he bought a hammer. Other than that, I can't explain it to you. It's feelings. I just know. He's found me, and he'll be coming for me if I stay. That's all there is to it. That's why I've been avoiding you. I don't want you to get hurt or take a chance like this. Ian is crazy, and he likes to give people pain, especially me. If he thinks it'll hurt me, he'll do it, and I don't want you to get hurt."

Joe was silent for a moment. Finally, he stood up and helped her to her feet. "Let's go for a walk for a minute." Joe held her hand and led her away from Todd and Kelly, who were coming toward them.

"Carly, what would you say if I told you that I was willing to take that chance? That I was willing to deal with this Ian guy if it meant that you wouldn't go away?" Taking her hands in his own, he looked deep into her eyes. "Would you stay then?"

"I would think you're on drugs," she whispered. He smiled tenderly down at her. Could she trust God enough to stop running away?

"Will you think about staying? I don't want you to leave. I want you to stay here, and I want us to deal with Ian together. Please. Think about it; pray about it. Ask God to lead you, please," he whispered, gently stroking her fingers.

"Joe, I'm afraid. I don't want anything to happen to you. I'd never forgive myself if you got hurt. You'll find someone, and you'll have a wonderful life together. Wait for her. It's not me. God didn't make me for you." Carly felt as if her heart would break.

"Don't say that!" Joe said harshly, grabbing her by the shoulders and peering into her face. Todd and Kelly looked over at them in surprise. They couldn't hear everything that was said, but they knew Joe was upset by his tone. "I don't want to find anyone else! God brought you here for a reason. Me. And I'm not going to give you up without a fight. If it means that I have to fight Ian to keep you, then I will. I want to protect you. Give you a home. Give you what you need the most, but how can I if you run away?" He pulled her close. "Please think about it. Please don't leave. I need you to stay."

"How can you ask me to hurt you? I never wanted to feel this way about you; I tried so hard to stay away. What if things don't work out between us?" Carly tried to pull away, but he wouldn't let her go.

"Carly. I'm not giving up. God made you for me. I know that. I can't explain it; I can't tell you how I know; I just do. I need you, and I will never get tired of you. You are precious to me. I just know that God created you for me." Carly was silent. "Will you please think it over?" Joe asked, pulling away to see her face. She looked at him, troubled, and nodded slightly.

Todd and Kelly had already packed up most of the picnic things and were back down by the pond, talking quietly. Carly shook out the blanket and folded it while Joe bypassed her to join the others.

"Are you all right, Joe? You look a little pale," Kelly asked, concerned.

He tried to smile, but it just wouldn't come. "She said she'll think about not leaving."

Kelly left to help Carly finish packing up, touching Joe sympathetically on the shoulder as she passed.

"She'll come around, she's just scared. Truthfully, I don't blame her a bit for being terrified. I wouldn't put it past that guy to really come out here looking for her. What would you do if he did? She lives in town, and it takes you a half hour to get there. It'd be all over by the time you showed up. She's right to be scared. She's not trying to hurt you, just to protect you. You've got to realize that," Todd said as Joe kicked at the ground. "Why do you want her to stay so bad anyway?"

"Why do I want her stay?" Joe looked up in surprise. "Because I love her, Todd. I want to protect her. Wouldn't you do the same for Kelly? Wouldn't you want to erase every hurt she's had to live with? Wouldn't you want to be the one to make her happy?" Joe picked up some stones and hurled them into the pond.

Todd was quiet. He had known that Joe cared for her, but he was a bit surprised to hear him talk about love. His heart ached and rejoiced for him at the same time.

He had learned to love again.

Chapter Nine

Joe and Carly rode in restrained silence. It was getting much colder, and Carly shivered involuntarily.

"Are you cold?" Joe asked with concern, suddenly noticing her thin jacket.

"Oh no, I'm fine," she answered with a sweet smile. He could tell she was bitterly cold, and his heart ached for her. He took off his heavier jacket and handed it over to her. She blushed but accepted it and put it on. It swallowed her up it was so big. She inhaled deeply. It smelled of him, and she reveled in it.

She giggled. "I guess this means you didn't believe me." Joe smiled at her tensely. "What are you going to wear?" He was wearing a blue flannel shirt, rolled up at the sleeves, and worn blue jeans. She couldn't help but admire his broad shoulders and athletic build.

"I'll be all right. I'm a farm boy, remember?"

He looked at her intently. He hadn't expected her wearing his coat to affect him so deeply. She looked so little and lost inside that huge jacket, he wanted to force her to stay with him forever. He looked away but not before Carly had caught his expression. It told her everything he felt, everything he thought, everything he longed for.

Her.

She suddenly knew she wanted to stay. She loved him with a passion that was so unlike any other she had ever known. She knew now that Ian had played on her emotions and had tried to buy her love by helping her dad and giving her anything she wanted. She had been flattered and delighted that he was interested in her, but it hadn't been love. She had desired to love him, but he wasn't capable of giving her any real emotion except anger and hatred, and she had turned to loathing and terror before any love could form.

Could she stay?

The very wind seemed to breathe, "Stay." The few birds that were left were singing, "Stay." The rustling leaves waved, "Stay." She did the only thing she knew to do. Pray.

Lord, I love Joe. I didn't mean to, and I tried not to, but it happened, and I don't want to give him up now. I'm afraid to stay, but I'm more afraid to leave. Please help me. Let me know what you want me to do. Please lead me in a plain path and guide each step I take. Take care of him, and help us deal with whatever your will might be. She felt a load lift off her shoulders, and she turned to look at Joe. He was looking straight ahead without expression. Carly reined Ashes in so he could ride beside her.

"Are you cold?"

"No," he replied evenly. They were silent for a minute but Carly was determined to make him talk to her.

"Oh yeah, I forgot. You have a story to tell me now, don't you? Let me see. What was it about?" Carly teased, but he was implacable.

"Why do you want to hear my story?"

Carly was silent for a moment then went on. "Don't be angry with me, please," she asked softly.

They were getting near the Bairds' farm now; Todd and Kelly were already there.

Joe stopped his horse and she turned to face him. The sun had gone down, but she could still see his face and was surprised at the pain she saw.

"I don't want to love you more than I do if you're going to leave," he blurted. "I don't want you to know my secrets if you're not going to be here to share them with me. I don't want…" He stopped, trying to control himself. He took a deep breath. "I've been praying since we left Wilson's Pond. Maybe that's too soon for you to have an answer, but I'm asking anyway. I can't wait, and I want to know if you're going to stay where you are." His face looked hard as nails.

Carly sighed and shook her head sadly. He looked away in frustration, angry with her.

"I'm not going to stay where I am," she said softly, directing Ashes in front of Chessy, forcing him to look at her. "I don't want to live in that tiny apartment forever. It's pretty confining."

Joe frowned, not understanding what she meant. She smiled radiantly at him.

"What are you saying?"

"What do you think I'm saying?" she teased. "I'm saying that I'm not going to stay in that apartment forever."

"Carly," he growled.

"What?" she asked innocently, batting her eyes at him.

"Give me a straight answer."

"Do you solemnly swear to tell me your story if I answer you? No matter what my answer is?" She knew she was just aggravating him now, but she was enjoying herself.

"Why is everything so difficult with you? Why can't you just answer a simple question without an argument?"

"Because it's so fun!" She smiled, looking away. "And you better get used to it."

"Are you going to stay?" he asked hopefully. It was getting colder and darker, but neither of them noticed.

"What do you want me to say, Joe?" she asked so softly he had to lean forward to hear her.

"I want you to say yes," he said even softer.

"If you really want me to, then I will," she whispered. She turned Ashes and galloped toward the barn, Joe close behind her.

"Todd!" he yelled as they came into the corral. "Kelly!" They both hurried out of the barn, anxious to see what the fuss was about. Joe hopped down from Chessy and helped Carly down, holding her as if he'd never let her go. "Do you want to tell them?" he asked happily.

She shrugged as if nothing important had happened, but they could tell she was as excited as he was. "I don't have a clue what you're talking about."

"Carly said she's going to stay!" He whooped and swung her around easily, his jacket flapping around her.

"I am so glad!" Kelly cried, breaking in between them. She hugged her tightly, wiping tears from her eyes. "I just knew everything would work out!"

"Kelly, if you knew everything was going to work out all right, why are you crying?" Todd asked in confusion.

"Because I'm so happy, you idiot!" she cried, tears streaming down both girls' faces now.

"I'll never understand why you women cry when you're happy. That's the dumbest thing I ever heard of," he retorted, ducking as a couple of handfuls of hay were thrown at him. "Come on, Kelly; let's see if Mom's got dinner made," he said, grabbing her hand and pulling her toward the house at a run.

Joe continued to stare at Carly as she wiped her eyes. He was looking at her thoughtfully, making her nervous. She took off his coat and handed it to him.

"No, you wear it," he said, putting it around her shoulders, still staring at her oddly.

"What?" She frowned. "Did you change your mind already? If you did, we don't have to tell anyone else, we'll just act like it never happened."

"No. I didn't change my mind, and I want to shout it from the mountain tops that you're staying," he said, putting his arm around her shoulders, hugging her to him. He led her toward the house.

"Well then, what's wrong? You're making me really nervous."

"How much do you weigh?" he asked casually, looking ahead.

But there was nothing casual about it. He was really worried. "When I picked you up, you didn't feel like you could weigh much more than a bag of feed." He stopped and turned her to face him.

"I don't know how much; I don't have a scale." She turned and walked briskly toward the house.

He caught up to her. "Are you eating?"

"Yes, I'm eating," she answered crossly. "I eat fine. Let's go inside before you catch a cold." She tried to turn him toward the house, but he wouldn't budge.

"What did you eat yesterday?"

"Yesterday? I have no idea. I don't remember. Can we talk about this later, Joe? Please? You're standing out here in the cold, I'm wearing your coat, and your mom isn't going to like me very much if you get sick. Please?" she pleaded. He still wasn't budging. "Fine. Take your coat and put it on, or I'm not telling you anything," she said as she handed him his coat.

He put it on silently, watching her. "Okay, I'm ready. What did you eat yesterday?" he asked, hugging her to keep her warm.

"Breakfast, I had juice. Lunch, I had rice; and dinner, I ate leftovers. Is that okay?" she answered, irritated.

"Leftover what?" He wasn't letting her get away with anything.

"Leftover rice," she said quietly, looking down at the ground.

They stood there for a bit. Carly started shivering, and Joe led her into the house without saying another word.

Chapter Ten

"Carly! Joe! We wondered if you were ever going to come on in," bellowed Tom jovially, as they walked into the kitchen.

"I didn't think Joe was going to let me," Carly answered, smiling. Joe pushed her lightly, and Tom laughed.

They were all seated at the table talking animatedly while Penny warmed up some potato soup for everyone. Joe led Carly to a seat and sat beside her, pulling his chair close to hers.

"Is there anything I can do to help?" Carly called from the table.

"You could set the table for me," she answered cheerily. Carly got up to get the dishes, and Joe followed. They set the table as best as they could, Joe bumping Carly every chance he got, and Carly threatening him with the spoons.

They all ate hungrily and teased continually until the end of dinner. They quickly cleaned up the kitchen and went to sit in the living room around the fire. Todd and Kelly sat in the love seat, Tom and Penny sat at one end of the couch, Carly curled up in the recliner, and Joe lay at her feet near the fire.

Todd smiled mischievously as he put his arm around Kelly. "Hey, anyone want to play a game?"

"What game do you want to play?" Tom asked.

"How about Twenty Questions?" Kelly called out.

Joe groaned, rolling his eyes at his parents. "This is a set up. She's been asking me to tell her about Amy all day, and now she'll hear the whole thing." He winked at Carly.

She smiled ominously at him. "Oh yeah. Let's play Twenty Questions. I'm dying to know about the competition." He smiled and took her hand, bringing it down to his chest. Carly was a little nervous that they were holding hands in front of his parents, but no one seemed to mind.

It was settled that they would play the game, and the usual, trivial questions were asked. Then things started getting a little more complicated.

"This one's for Joe," Todd called out for everyone to hear. "Is it true that you sucked your thumb until you were fifteen?" Joe glared at him, and Carly laughed heartily.

"No," he answered, kicking Todd's foot. "I was only fourteen." He grinned.

"Carly," Joe called out. She stopped laughing and tried to hide her smile. "Is it true that you were once engaged to a very rich business man?"

Penny and Tom stared at them both in surprise.

"Yes," she answered, still smiling slightly. "Joe, this question is for you. Were you miserable to live with when you thought I was avoiding you?"

"Yes!" everyone shouted before he had the chance to answer. They all laughed hysterically at the surprise on his face.

"I was a *little* hard to live with," he answered. "Mom. do you like Carly more than you liked Amy?" Carly blushed, embarrassed.

"Yes," she answered, surprised at his question. Joe grinned mischievously, a twinkle in his eye.

"Joe, this is yours," Penny said. "Do you like Carly more than you liked Amy?" Carly squirmed. She didn't like being the center of the attention, especially about something like if Joe liked her or not.

"Yes," he answered, smiling up at her. Carly continued to look away, blushing profusely. "I like her more than I've ever liked any girl. She means the world to me, and I'm glad that she's going to stay."

She stood up hastily. "May I use the ladies room please?"

"Of course, dear. It's down the hallway, second door on the right," Penny answered, surprised by her abruptness.

"Thank you," Carly stayed in the bathroom for a few minutes, trying to still her panicky nerves.

"I hope I didn't offend her," Penny said, worried that they had somehow hurt her feelings.

"I don't think you did, Mom," Joe said, standing up and

stretching. He sat down in the recliner, waiting for her to come back.

"What did you mean about Carly going to stay?" Tom asked. "Was she going somewhere?"

"Yes. She's been running from place to place because she's afraid her ex-fiancé is coming to find her," Joe answered simply. Todd, Kelly, and Joe told them some of the details of Carly's experience with Ian before she got back.

"How awful," Penny whispered.

Tom was thoughtful. "What are you going to do?" he finally asked. "You know, with a man like that, there could be quite a bit of trouble."

"I know, she keeps telling me that there's going to be trouble, but I want her to stay anyway," Joe answered as she came back in.

"And just what do you think you're doing? That's my seat, buddy," she said playfully, sitting down at his feet.

"Watch out, Carly, he's been wearing cowboy boots all day, and those things probably smell awful," Todd teased.

"Here, switch with me. I'll sit on the floor," Joe said, his face bright red.

She laughed, pushing him back into the chair. "No, I'm fine. Really. Just sit. I'm fine."

"Carly, the kids here were telling us about some of your past. I'm awfully sorry to hear about it," Tom said kindly.

"I hope you're not upset with us," Kelly said hastily.

"I'm not upset. It's okay. I don't have anything to be ashamed of," she answered, soothing her friend's fears.

"Is there a possibility that he will come find you?" Penny asked. Carly hesitated. She was afraid that Joe's family would have serious reservations about their relationship if Ian could come back, but she couldn't lie to them.

"Yes," she answered finally. "He's found me everywhere I go."

"Why don't you go to the police?" Tom asked.

"Ian's very rich, and he's got contacts everywhere. Even in the police force. Money talks more than honesty, I'm afraid. I've hidden pretty well before, and it doesn't usually take him long to find me."

"Do you mind talking about it?" Tom asked her quietly.

"It's not my favorite subject, but it feels kind of good to have someone to talk to about it."

"How bad was it? The kids just told us that he beat you. What did he do?" Penny asked sympathetically.

"At first he was afraid of leaving bruises. Then as things got worse, he'd punch, kick, pull my hair, slap. Anything and everything."

Joe leaned forward, putting his hand on her shoulder. "Tell them the worst that he's done to you."

Carly shrugged her shoulders helplessly. "I really can't tell you the worst. I think he was terrible when he broke my arm, when he blackened my eyes, when he'd just scream at me for no reason, when he took over my bank account and wouldn't allow me to have any money unless he gave it to me. I don't know which is worse. I can't answer."

"How did he take over your bank account?" Tom asked incredulously.

"After we were engaged, he said it would be better to build credit with something that had both of our names on it. He said it would be easier to do it right away, but I had no idea that he had it fixed that I couldn't take out any money without his being aware of it. If I went to the bank to withdraw, they would call him before I even left and tell him how much I took and what time I was there. It was eerie. I didn't realize what he was doing until it was too late."

"How have you survived so long without money?" Kelly asked.

"When I left, I had about four hundred dollars that I had squirreled away without him knowing. I took that and saved as much as possible. When I thought I was far enough away, I'd stay a little while, find a job, and save every penny, until he found me. Then it would start all over again."

"What's the longest you've hidden before he found you?" Todd asked. Joe leaned forward to see her face.

"This is definitely the longest I've been able to stay at the same place," she replied.

Joe and Todd looked at each other.

"But," Joe interrupted before she could continue, "she thinks he's found her again."

Penny and Kelly gasped in surprise.

"Why?" asked Tom quietly. He was watching Joe and Todd. He had seen the look that passed between them and he was curious.

"I don't know really. Just some prank calls, a weird customer, but mostly just instinct. I always get a feeling right before someone shows up that Ian has sent."

"What do you mean, that 'Ian has sent'?" Kelly wondered, pulling closer to Todd.

"Ian doesn't come for me himself, he sends someone to bring me back. I've been forced into a strange car twice before I learned to listen to my intuition. Now I try to act first."

They were all quiet. Tom leaned forward speculatively while Penny moved nearer to him, rubbing his back.

"Well, that's good for me then," Joe finally said, trying to lighten the mood. "We don't have to worry about him, just watch out for strange cars and people."

Everyone was apprehensive, and she was sorry for it. Maybe God didn't want her to stay after all. Maybe He wanted her to leave.

"You know what; it's okay." She stood and gave them a bright smile. "This is a lot to deal with, and I completely understand. I tried to tell Joe I was just going to cause trouble. Thank you for being so kind to me. I've got to go." She left so quickly, they didn't realize that she was leaving until they heard the door close. They all sat in bewildered silence. Except Joe.

Joe stood in the cold, dark night, slipping on his coat as he searched for her. Short puffs of frozen air punctuated the blackness, and he saw movement on the gray road.

"Carly!" he shouted, jogging out to the road. "Wait!"

He finally caught up to her and walked beside her for a while, catching his breath. "You got far."

"I'm good at running. It's the only thing I know how to do," she answered flatly.

"Why are you out here?" he asked quietly. "Where are you going?"

"I'm going home," she said tiredly.

"Come back. I'll give you a ride into town," he took her arm. She pulled away from him and kept walking. "Carly, stop it!" he said angrily, grabbing her arm again.

She spun to look at him. "What, Joe? What do you want? I don't want a ride, and I don't want to cause you or your family any more trouble than I already have, okay?" she answered, frustrated.

"What is the matter with you?" he asked, surprised. "Where did you get the idea that you've caused us any trouble? Can't you see that we want to help you?" He took her other arm, pulling her to him. "I'm not the only one here that cares for you. I've seen how my mom and dad talk to you, how they treat you like family. Todd admires you almost as much as he adores Kelly, and let's not forget how much Kelly likes you. Why can't you see that?"

"I'm terrified. Everything that I've cared about is gone. I've got no one. I've been running for so long, I'm afraid that this is some sort of dream, and I'm going to wake up and you'll all be gone and I'll be back to nothing," Carly blurted. "I'm afraid that once I belong somewhere or with someone, I'll lose it all." Joe held her close for a little while, letting her relax against him.

"Come back, and I'll drive you home," he answered quietly. She sighed and allowed him to lead her back to his house. "You know, I can't speak for God, but I can speak for myself and my family. We don't want you to hurt anymore, or be afraid to love somebody again." He stopped, taking her hand. "I'm not planning on going anywhere without you, Carly. If you left, I'd look for you, and I'd hunt for you just like Ian, but with different intents and purposes. I'd find you wherever you went, so you might as well stay and make it easy on me." She could hear the smile in his voice.

They walked the rest of the way in silence, thinking about the uncertain future and praying to God that somehow he'd make it all right.

"Carly!" Tom bellowed good-naturedly as they walked back in. "Where'd you run off to so fast?"

Carly blushed, ashamed. Joe saw her discomfort, and came to the rescue. "She was walking home," he answered lightly.

"What?" Penny asked in surprise. "It's too far for you to walk all that way."

"I'll give you a ride home," Kelly chimed in. "I figured you knew that I would seeing as how I brought you here. Are you ready to go?" she asked, standing up.

"Whenever you are. Don't rush for me," she said hastily, feeling stupid.

"Oh no, I need to be going anyway. I've got Uncle Charlie's truck, and he'll be worried about me if I don't get home soon." Todd helped her on with her coat and walked her to the door, waiting for Carly to say good-bye.

"Well, thanks for the wonderful evening," she said politely.

Tom shook her hand affably, and Penny gave her a hug. "You come back, you hear? Don't you be a stranger. You're always welcome," she said affectionately. "If you need anything, or just need to talk, give me a call, okay?"

"I will. Thank you for being so good to me," Carly said around the lump in her throat.

Joe walked her to the truck and opened the door for her. "Thank you for coming today. I'm really glad you did," he said, leaning on the open door, smiling at her.

"Thank you for letting me," she replied shyly.

There was something different between them now. Something deeper. They had reached a crossroads and had passed it together.

Chapter Eleven

Carly was ready for church early the next morning. She had had terrifying nightmares all night about Ian and had woken up intending to tell Joe that she had changed her mind and couldn't stay. She drank some juice for breakfast, waiting for the clock to tell her it was time to go. The time just crawled along, teasing her. She sat at the small table for what seemed an eternity before she could leave and not be too early. She grabbed her Bible and jacket, ran down the steps, and let herself out, locking up behind her.

"I was wondering when you were going to come out!" a voice called behind her, making her jump. She was surprised to find Joe there, waiting to give her a ride to church. All her plans vanished at the sight of him smiling at her, and she was reassured that God wanted her to stay.

"Good morning," she said cheerily as he opened her door from the inside. She got in and scooted next to him. He put his arm around her shoulders and kissed her gently on her forehead. She cuddled next to him, breathing in his cologne.

"Good morning," he said as he backed up and headed toward the church. "How'd you sleep last night?"

"Not good. I had nightmares about Ian all night. They were so bad that I had made up my mind to tell you that I wasn't going to stay after all," she answered, looking out the window.

"And now?" he asked casually.

"Everything looks better in daytime," she giggled at his frown. "That means yes."

"I was wondering if you ever answer a question directly."

"Not if I can help it." They both laughed as Joe parked the truck. He got out and opened her door for her.

"Don't look now, but I think you're in big trouble," she said. Joe turned around to see Angie glaring at both of them. She stalked into the church, banging the door behind her. "I'm sorry. I didn't mean to get you into trouble with your girlfriend," she teased. He pinched her ear and took her hand.

"It's gotten pretty cold out," he said, looking at her jacket.

"Oh, I don't know." She pretended not to notice the stinging wind in her face.

He held the door open for her. They found their usual spot next to Todd and Kelly and sat down. Angie sat directly behind Joe, pretending to ignore them.

"What did you have for breakfast this morning?" Joe whispered as the music started.

"Shhhh!" Angie said angrily behind them. They both chuckled, making faces at each other.

They behaved themselves during church, knowing that a loud "shhh" would be headed their way if they even dared to sniffle wrong. After church was over, they went and spoke to Joe's parents.

"Good afternoon," Carly said, hugging Penny and shaking Tom's hand.

"Are you coming over for lunch this afternoon? Nothing really big, just sandwiches," Penny invited. Carly was about to accept, but Joe interrupted her.

"Actually, I was thinking about asking Todd, Kelly, and Carly to go with me over to the mall this afternoon. Would you like to go?" he asked Carly.

"Sure, if that's okay with your parents," she answered, blushing with pleasure.

Penny smiled. "Oh, that's all right with us. We'll just take it easy today anyway." Joe went off to ask Todd and Kelly if they would go, leaving Carly alone with Penny.

"Carly, sit and talk to me while you wait." Penny sat down, patting the seat next to her. "Last night when you were telling us about that awful fiancé of yours, I just had some questions I wanted to ask you privately." She looked around discreetly making sure no one was around. "You had an apartment, right?" Carly nodded. Penny looked embarrassed, and then plunged ahead. "Were you two living together?" she whispered.

Carly was so relieved that she almost burst out laughing. "No, ma'am. I wouldn't allow Ian to stay at my apartment before we were married."

"I'm relieved." She sighed, putting her hand to her chest. "I was so afraid that you were."

Carly laughed. "I was afraid that it was going to be a harder question."

"Well, here's a harder one." Penny cleared her throat and looked to see where Joe was. He was still talking to Todd and Kelly. "You do know that Joe was engaged before, right?" Carly nodded. "I was wondering if he's told you about that yet."

"No, he hasn't really said anything about it."

"Please don't take this the wrong way, Carly," Penny said uncomfortably.

Carly's heart was thumping. Was she going to try to stop their relationship?

"I don't want Joe to get hurt again," she said finally. "Do you really care for him?"

"Penny, I would rather die than to see him hurt or to cause him any pain," Carly reassured her. "That's why I avoided him. I was going to leave here, so Ian would never find me, but I couldn't. It broke my heart to think of leaving, but I would have if he wouldn't have cared for me." Penny was silent for a moment. "Does that help you any?"

"Immensely, my dear." Penny smiled, standing up. "I'm glad that he found you, but I'm even happier that you've decided to stay. It would have broken his heart again."

"You're not upset about Ian maybe coming here?" Carly asked hesitantly.

"Upset? No. Worried, yes." she said quietly. Joe was walking toward them. "People always fight harder to keep the things they love safe. He'll take good care of you."

"What are you two talking about?" Joe asked, quizzically.

"You don't need to know everything." She winked at Carly, and walked away.

"Todd and Kelly said they'd go. We've just got to go downstairs and set up some chairs and tables for the deacon's meeting tonight. I'll be right back." He flashed her a smile and was gone, Todd following.

"Well, I guess we're going with you two. I hope you don't mind," Kelly said, coming to talk.

"No way! It makes everything better to have a couple of friends along," Carly replied, smiling warmly.

"Don't look now, but Angie's coming," Kelly whispered, grabbing her arm. They turned to walk away, trying to avoid her.

"Carly!" Angie called, her voice high and false. "It's been some time since you sat next to Joe. I hope everything is okay between you two now. But I must admit, you both were awfully distracting."

"Distracting? What are you talking about?" Carly couldn't help asking.

"Oh don't be coy," she said loudly, wanting to draw attention and embarrass Carly. "I saw you two holding hands during service, and I don't think you could have put a piece of paper between you two. A little close, don't you think?"

People were starting to stare at them, including Tom and Penny, and Carly thought it best to put her in her place once and for all.

"Well, Angie, if you were paying more attention to the service than to us, you probably never would have noticed that we were holding hands," she answered coolly, taking Kelly's arm and turning to go, but Angie stopped them, her voice lower, so only they could hear.

"You know, I really feel sorry for you."

Carly turned around to face her, her anger rising. "Excuse me?"

"Everyone knows that Joe is still madly in love with his ex-fiancée Amy, and it's only a matter of time until they patch things up and get back together. You don't stand a chance. In fact, Amy's my best friend, and she's coming back to town soon. You'll see. He's just using you, and I thought you'd like to know." She smiled cruelly, enjoying Carly's anguish. "Oh, hi, Joe. I was just telling

Kelly and Amy, oh I mean *Carly*, to have a good day." She turned and walked away with a smirk.

"Don't pay her any attention," Kelly urged her, glaring at Angie's back. Joe took her hand protectively.

"Are you two done already?" Carly asked, smiling up at him as if she hadn't heard anything he'd said to her. "I'm ready, are you, Kelly?" she said, turning to her friends and smiling warmly. She wasn't about to let Angie know that she had aggravated her.

"Um," Todd answered, unsure of what he should or shouldn't say. "We're ready to go if you both are."

Joe looked at Carly for a minute then seemed to make up his mind about something.

"Just a minute," he said, walking toward Angie, who was talking with a group of people.

"Angie, what's your problem? You have been nasty to Carly since the day she walked in this church, and I was just curious as to why."

Angie turned almost purple with embarrassment. "What are you talking about?" Angie sputtered, trying to look innocent.

"You know very well what I'm talking about," he said through gritted teeth. "I won't have you treating her like that. Do we understand each other?" He glared at her, making her stare at the floor. She looked like she would have liked to find a hole and crawl into it. Joe nodded his head at the people staring at him, turned, and walked back to his family.

"Bravo, brother," Todd said, clapping him on the back. "You know, I don't think I've ever seen you react like that before."

"Wow," Kelly breathed, stunned.

"Why did you do that, Joe?" Carly asked, distressed at all the people staring at them now.

"I promised that I would take care of you and protect you, and I figured that if I couldn't do it with Angie, then I wasn't going to be able to do it with Ian. Just getting into practice," he said, helping her on with her jacket. "You're not embarrassed are you?"

Carly grimaced. "That's the understatement of the year. But I'm glad that you took care of it. Thank you." She gave him one of her best smiles. His heart flip-flopped, and he took her hand.

"You did what was right son," Tom said, punching his shoulder. "You better be getting along if you're going to be back in time for church tonight. Take care," Penny said, kissing each of her boys.

"We'll see you tonight, Lord willing," Todd called over his shoulder. "Just pray for us. Joe's driving." Joe grabbed him and tousled his hair. Kelly and Carly laughed, and they were gone.

"Well, dear, what do you think of that?" Penny asked quietly.

"I think we'd better really love that girl, 'cause he isn't going to give her up."

"I agree. I'm thinking we're going to have some additions to our family." She smiled contentedly.

"I do believe you're right, sweet-pea," he said fondly, helping her on with her coat.

Chapter Twelve

They stopped to eat at a quaint little restaurant in the next town before they got to the mall.

"You know," Joe said quietly as soon as they were seated. "You still haven't told what you ate this morning."

Carly pretended to be engrossed in the menu and didn't answer. "Don't make me pinch you," he leaned over and whispered in her ear.

"You wouldn't do that in a restaurant," she whispered back mischievously.

He promptly pinched her arm, making her cry out. "Joe!" A few people turned to look at them.

Todd shifted uncomfortably in his seat. "Um, Kelly, maybe we should sit at another table. People are beginning to stare at us."

Carly scooted her chair a little further away from Joe, her face bright red. "I think that's a good idea. We can sit at another table and leave Joe here to himself."

"All I wanted was her to answer my question, and she wouldn't do it, so she got what she deserved."

"What was his question?" Kelly asked curiously.

Carly scowled. "He wants to know what I ate for breakfast." He just grinned, enjoying himself at her expense.

"That's a weird question." Todd nodded his head in agreement.

"It may be a weird question, but I have my reasons." He looked deliberately at Carly.

"If he's got a reason, by all means, let's hear the answer so we can eat in peace," Todd mocked.

"I had …" Carly mumbled into her glass of water.

Todd leaned forward, pulling his ear. "What was that? Didn't catch it."

Carly mumbled unintelligibly into her glass again.

Kelly giggled. "Nope. Didn't get it that time either."

"She said she had some juice," Joe answered for her, unsmiling.

"Juice? That's it?" Todd couldn't fathom not having bacon, eggs, and toast for breakfast, and thought everyone should eat as much as he did.

"You must be starving," Kelly added, looking concerned.

Carly batted her eyes innocently, grabbing her flat stomach for emphasis. "I'm famished."

"Good, because here comes our food," Todd said hungrily.

"You're going to have to eat better than that, you know," Joe said softly into her ear.

"What? And ruin my girlish figure?"

Joe was uncompromising and looked at her sternly. "You know what I mean. You need to eat better."

"I'll work on it," she promised, blushing prettily.

"Good," he said.

"You know," Todd said between bites, "you two never told us what Angie was saying before we came upstairs. You both looked pretty upset."

"Yeah. What did she say?" Joe asked curiously.

Kelly, always loyal, jumped to her friend's defense. "She was being really mean to Carly. She started out by telling her that you two were, what did she say, disgusting? No, that's not right. Carly what did she say?"

"Distracting. We were distracting her because we were holding hands," Carly answered, laughing at Kelly's mistake.

Todd shook his head at his brother. "Holding hands? You two were holding hands? Joe? Come on now, fess up and tell me. Did Carly make you hold her hand?"

"No, actually I took her hand first." Joe smiled mischievously. "She didn't have a choice, and I wasn't giving it back."

Carly laughed. "I did have a choice. I felt sorry for him," she said impishly, winking at Kelly.

"Anyway. Back to the story. Angie said that you two were distracting her during service, and Carly pretty much told her off.

Well, she was really mad, and she started telling Carly that you were just using her, and that you and Amy were going to get back together," Kelly finished the story in a rush, waiting for Joe's reaction.

"Whoa," Todd said, pursing his lips together and leaning back in his chair. "That was cold."

"If Billy Pruit had said that, I would have knocked his teeth down his throat," Joe said furiously. "You wait until I see her again."

"It's okay. Don't let her bother you. So what? She was being a jerk, big deal. I've handled bigger jerks than her before. Just let it go, okay?" Carly coaxed, not wanting him to do anything rash.

"Why? Why should I let her get away with it?" he asked angrily.

She reached over and rubbed his arm soothingly. "Because I asked you to."

He stared down at her, some of the anger leaving his face. "But I don't want anyone to think that I'm just using you," he said slowly. "You do know that I'm not using you, right?"

"I don't think you are," she answered honestly.

"Carly, I love you, and I want you to be sure of that," he said, pulling her closer to him.

"He said the *L* word, Kelly. It must be real," Todd whispered loudly.

"And in front of us," Kelly whispered back. They all laughed, breaking the tension.

"Joe, I'd like to know what happened between you and Amy," Carly said.

"Uh oh. I knew that was coming. Come on, Kell, we'd better go," Todd said, getting up.

"No, you don't have to go," Joe said, laying some bills on the table to pay for their meal. "I'll tell it to her on the way to the mall."

"I met Amy when I was about nineteen, and she was eighteen," he began when they were all situated in the truck and on their way. "I thought she was the closest thing to perfect that God had made, and I thought I loved her. We started dating right away, and I asked her to marry me about seven months after our first date. She said yes, and I thought that was it." He gripped the steering wheel a little harder, and stared at the road.

"But as our wedding date got closer and closer, I began to see that she wasn't nearly as perfect as I had thought. She would lie about little things, and I'd make excuses for her. Then she'd pick on my family, and once again, I made excuses for her. She began to get greedy and whiney, and downright nasty if she didn't get her own way on everything. She expected me to answer her every beck and call, and I usually did. I was her little lap dog, I'm ashamed to say. Todd can testify to that."

Todd nodded vigorously. "It was pitiful."

"Well, I began to build a house for us on some property that I had gotten from dad. I got the foundation finished without telling her. I wanted to surprise her with it on Christmas morning. I took her to see it and she blew up. She started screaming about how inconsiderate I was to not even ask her what she wanted and proceeded to tell me that she could never live that close to my family. So, being the lap dog that I was, I stopped building and started looking to buy a house that she wanted. All the houses she looked at were way too expensive for me, but if I even mentioned looking at smaller homes, she would say I was being a jerk." He paused and swallowed, trying to control his emotions as he remembered the past.

"About two months before our wedding, she left, leaving me a note that said she had made a mistake. She wasn't ready to throw her life away on a piece of trash, and she hoped that she never saw me again. That was six years ago, and I haven't seen her since."

"I'm sorry. I should never have asked you to tell me," Carly said quietly, looking out the window.

Todd added quietly, "And you're the first person he's been

interested in since."

"Don't be sorry for me, Carly. Losing her has been one of the best things God has done for me. I thought at the time that I wouldn't love anyone again, but you've shown me otherwise." He smiled tenderly at her. "I'm glad she's gone, and I'm glad she left the way she did. Now I know what I've got, and I'm not going to lose you."

Kelly bounced excitedly in the backseat, her face beaming. "Here we are!"

Todd groaned, shaking his head. "This is Kelly's favorite place."

"Have you ever been here before, Carly?" she asked gleefully, as they walked inside the huge entrance.

Amused, Carly grinned at her excitement. "No, can't say that I have."

She hugged Todd's arm happily. "I love this place, but I don't get to come here very often, so it's a real treat when Todd takes me. I'm so glad you asked us to come with you, Joe."

As soon as they were inside, Joe steered Carly toward a store. "My pleasure. I'm taking Carly in here for a little while, so you two can go wherever you want." Carly looked at him in surprise.

"Oh, I think we'll come too. I haven't been here in ages, and they have some pretty good sales." Kelly started to follow, but stopped when Todd groaned, holding his stomach.

"What's wrong? Are you sick?" she asked worriedly, putting her hand on his arm.

"I think I ate too much or something. My stomach is killing me." He groaned again, bending over a little bit.

"Are you going to be okay?" Kelly tried to help him stand up. "Joe, I think we'd better take him home."

"Do you want to go, Todd?" Joe asked, his disappointment evident.

Todd stood up still holding his stomach. "No, I don't need to go home yet; I just need to find a men's room. I'll feel better in a little bit. You all just keep shopping, and I'll be back." Kelly looked unconvinced, but he kissed her and left before she could argue.

Kelly watched him leave, her face anxious. "I hope he's going to be okay."

"He'll be okay. Come on, Kelly. Let's look for some of those sales you were telling us about," Joe said, trying to ease her mind. "Really. He'll be okay; he just ate too much at the restaurant. Come with us."

Kelly followed them reluctantly, but sale racks soon put her back into the shopping mood.

"Where exactly did you want to look, Joe?" Carly asked quizzically.

Joe grabbed her hand and pulled her along, not answering. He seemed intent on one purpose. "Where would they be?" he muttered to himself, looking around for something in particular.

She laughed, still trailing behind. "Maybe I could help you find what you're looking for if you just told me what it was." His grip tightened as he turned to smile at her mysteriously. "Now I'm really nervous."

They turned the corner and found themselves in the winter coats. Carly, knowing what he was up to, stopped and pulled her hand out of his.

"What are we doing here?" she asked suspiciously, narrowing her eyes at him.

He grinned at her. "You need a winter coat, and we're going to buy you one."

"I don't think so," she answered with a stubborn shake of her head.

"Why can't I buy you a coat?" he asked in bewilderment.

"Because I don't want people to think that I'm using you," she answered firmly.

"I don't care what people think," he answered mildly, taking her hand again. "I want to take care of you, and you need a coat. Don't take away my blessing of doing this. Please?" he argued. She held back. "I'm not Ian, Carly."

"I know," she answered softly.

"Do you trust me?"

"Yes."

"Then please let me do this for you." He drew her into the leather coats. "Pick one out."

"I don't know," Carly said doubtfully, looking at the price tags.

"Don't worry about the price," he admonished, playfully smacking a tag out of her hand.

"I thought that you said I could pick one out. Doesn't that mean that I can look at the ones that I like, even if they're cheap?" She gave him a pert smile.

"Yeah, you can find whatever you like, but if I think you're picking them because they're cheap, I'll pick one out for you," he said light-heartedly. Carly rolled her eyes and grinned.

"There you two are!" Kelly said, joining them. "I've been looking for you. I thought you left me."

Joe shook his head, grinning. "And have to deal with an irate little brother like Todd? You must be crazy! Hey, will you help Carly pick out a winter coat? She seems to be having trouble finding one."

"Sure! Carly, which ones do you like?" Kelly came over to help her decide. They conspired together quietly for a couple of minutes, then hung three out on the racks.

"These are the ones I like," Carly said self-consciously. Joe examined each one individually, noticing the sales tags. They were the cheapest she could find, but they were durable.

"All right. Which one do you want?" he finally agreed.

"This one," she said immediately, holding up the cheapest of the three.

"Sounds good. You two can go look around while I pay, and I'll meet you," Joe said, giving Carly a hug.

"Thanks, Joe," she whispered, "but you didn't have to."

"I know. I wanted to," he affirmed, still holding her close. She kissed his cheek, blushed, then left quickly, Kelly in pursuit. He watched them go, made sure they weren't coming back, and switched the coat to the most expensive of the three.

He joined them shortly afterward, bag in hand, to find that Todd still hadn't returned. Kelly was beginning to get worried.

"Joe, we've been in here for a while. Do you think we could go look for him?"

"Sure, but I think that's him right there," he said, nodding toward the door his brother had just walked through.

Kelly sighed in relief. "Todd! Are you feeling better?"

Todd hugged her to him. "Sure! I feel great! I don't know what it was, but it's gone now. Where to next?"

"Let's just show Carly around," Joe said quickly, leading the way.

Walking through the expansive hallways and going into various stores, they were rounding the last bend when Todd pulled Kelly ahead, excitement written on his handsome face.

"The Apple Barn! They've got some of the best caramel apples. Do you want one, Kell?" he asked, already pulling his wallet out.

"I thought you weren't feeling well," Kelly asked with a doubtful look.

Panicked, he decided to beg. "But I feel better. Nothing a caramel apple couldn't cure. Joe, help me out here. Tell her I'm feeling better."

Kelly laughed, giving in easily. "Okay. If you say you're feeling better, then go ahead."

"You want one?" Joe asked Carly, already taking some off the shelf.

Carly giggled. "Do I have a choice?"

"You always have a choice. You can say yes or yes!"

They paid for their apples and sat down.

"Well, I guess he's feeling better," Carly said as Todd wolfed his apple down.

"I guess so," Kelly said, eating hers more daintily.

"Which one do you want? Nuts, or no nuts," Joe asked, giving her the choice.

"With nuts, definitely," she answered immediately. Joe took the wrapper off and held it out to her. She reached for it, but he pulled it back before she could get it.

"Hey!" She laughed, reaching for it again.

He grinned as he held it further out of her reach. "Apple for a kiss!"

She shook her head. "I don't know if they're that good."

Stubbornly, Joe repeated his plea as she reached for it again.

"Apple for a kiss."

"I think you better give him that kiss, Carly," Todd said, pointing toward a little girl about five, staring fixedly at the apple. She laughed then gave him a quick kiss on the cheek.

Smiling indulgently, he handed her the apple. "There. Was that so hard?"

"Yeah," Carly said, taking a bite from her apple. "It about killed me!"

Kelly and Todd laughed hysterically, while Joe tapped her head into her apple as she took another bite out of it, causing the caramel and nuts to smear all over her face.

"Oh, I'm so sorry," Joe said with an unapologetic chuckle. "I really didn't mean for that to happen."

"Yeah right. Sure you didn't." Carly laughed, wiping her face with a napkin. "Now I'm all sticky. I better go wash off." She stood up to go to the ladies room.

"I'll walk with you if you want, Carly," Kelly offered, coming with her.

"Thanks. We'll be back," she called over her shoulder.

Kelly showed her to the restroom, and she washed her face the best she could.

"Here," Kelly said, pulling a nut out of her hair.

Carly laughed genially. "That was funny."

"You know, it was rather funny." Kelly giggled. "But I don't think you should let him get away with it."

"I have no intention of letting him get away with that." She winked.

As they walked out of the restroom, a strange man stepped away from the wall he had been leaning against and stopped in front of them, blocking their exit.

Surprised, Carly stepped to the side. "Oh excuse me." He stepped back in front of her, not letting her pass. She stepped the other way, and he blocked her path again.

"Can I help you?" Carly asked, wondering what he was doing.

"Well, now that you ask, yes. You can help me." The man leered at her, looking at her from head to toe approvingly, puffing on a cigarette and dropping ashes onto the ground. "I was just wondering why a Houston woman was so far away from home."

She turned pale. "Do I know you?" Kelly grabbed her arm, scared.

"You *are* from Houston, right?" Carly didn't answer. "I'd know another Texan anywhere. You can't fool me. I was just wondering what you found so interesting way up here." He continued to stand in their way, not allowing them to pass.

"None of your business," Carly said haughtily, hoping to discourage him from any further conversation.

He laughed, blowing smoke into her face, making her cough. "Well now, there's no reason to be rude. I was just wondering when you're going back home." He reached into his pocket. They were both frightened now, but he only pulled out a cell phone and laughed at their terrified faces.

"I don't know what you want, but we've got someone waiting for us, so you'll have to excuse us," Carly said, trying to step around him, but he moved expertly back in the way.

"Hold on, ain't no rush. We're just having ourselves a friendly little chat. Your name wouldn't happen to be Carly Richards, would it?" Carly was silent. "I'll take that to mean yes. I've got a message for you. Ian wants you to come on home now." He leaned forward, smoke hanging heavily in the air. "And leave that pretty boy here. Ian gets a little touchy when his fiancée starts hanging around other men, kissing them and all." He held out his cell phone for them to see a picture of Carly kissing Joe on the cheek. He shut the phone and turned to walk away, throwing his cigarette onto the floor, squashing it.

"I'm not his fiancée!"

He turned around, surprised. "What's that?"

"I said I'm not his fiancée. And you know what? I've got a message for him. I'm not going back to him; I'm staying right here." Carly continued to talk loudly, her face red with anger and fear. "In fact, why don't you just go ahead and send him that picture? Maybe he'll get the idea that I'm not his anymore, I'll never be his, and maybe he'll leave me alone!" she said through gritted teeth, her hands clenched at her sides.

"I'll do that," he said placidly, his grin infuriating. "But for some reason, I don't think things are going to turn out the way you have planned. He's pretty determined when he wants something."

"Tell him to find another secretary!" she cried angrily after him. He walked away, his laughter bouncing off the polished walls.

"Carly, did you know him?" Kelly asked, frightened by the whole ordeal.

She crossed her arms and rubbed them as if she were cold, her voice shaking. "No. I haven't seen him before."

"He had a picture of you kissing Joe," Kelly said pensively. "He called you Carly Richards, though. Is that your real name?"

She shuddered. "Yes. Adams was my mother's maiden name. I had to use a fake name because Ian would find me if I used my real one." They were silent.

"Hey! What are you two doing in here?" Todd said as he and Joe walked down to meet them a few seconds later. They didn't reply.

"What's wrong?" Joe asked, alarmed by their expressions. "What happened?"

"He found me, Joe," Carly said tonelessly. "I knew he would. But I told him off, didn't I, Kelly?" She broke down and cried. Joe rubbed her back soothingly, hugging her tight.

"What happened, Kelly?" Todd asked helplessly, holding her close to his side.

She looked at Joe, shaking. "This guy wouldn't let us pass by him and started talking to Carly. He called her by her real name,

Carly Richards."

"Her real name is Richards?" Joe gave her a blank look.

"Yes. And he had a picture on his cell phone of her kissing you. He said he was going to send it to Ian," Kelly said, her voice trembling.

"Is he still here?" Todd looked around, ready to fight in case he was still watching them.

"No, he left just before you came."

"I think it's time to leave," Joe said compassionately. "Are you ready?"

Carly wiped her eyes and looked at him with a sigh. "I'm ready."

"Well, here. It's cold out, and that jacket isn't going to keep you warm," he said, handing her the bag.

"Joe!" she said, taking the coat out. "This isn't the one I picked."

"Yes, it is. That was one of the three that you hung out for me to look at. Remember?" He gave her an affectionate smile.

"This was the most expensive one I picked out, wasn't it?" She smiled wanly. "Thank you," she whispered, tears welling up again.

"Don't cry. I can't stand to see you cry," he said hoarsely, a lump in his throat. He helped her on with her coat.

They drove home in silence.

Chapter Thirteen

Carly woke up the next morning and looked out her window. It had snowed during the night, blanketing the town and making it look clean and pure. No worries or crime or hate. Only beauty as far as the eye could see. She opened her window just a crack, took a deep breath of the wintry air, and let it out slowly, watching the steam rise toward the sky.

How beautiful, she thought. There was just something special about the first snowfall of the year, stimulating, refreshing. Perfect.

"Thank you, Lord, for letting me live another day," she said out loud, thinking of Joe and smiling to herself. Wonderful Joe. "Thank you for Joe, Lord. Thank you for letting me stay. Please protect him, and give me the strength I need about Ian. Could you make him just leave me alone? "

She remembered the man from the mall the previous afternoon and shivered. Had she been too hasty with what she'd said? Another shiver raced down her spine as she thought of the last time she'd dared challenge Ian. His fury at her had been terrifying and she didn't want to repeat the ordeal. With an enormous amount of effort, she put Ian out of her mind and decided to take one day at a time, and got ready for work.

She sauntered down the stairs, whistling. Sam was already there.

"Good morning," Sam said jovially. "Come into the office with Sue and me and have some doughnuts."

"Good morning," she said cheerily, hugging Sue and helping herself to a doughnut.

"Well, you're awfully chipper this morning." Sue smiled, peering at Sam with an 'I told you so' look. "What's got you in such a happy mood?"

"God is just so good to me. The snow, my job…"

"Joe," Sam said, chuckling.

"And especially Joe." She beamed at them merrily.

"It's about time you admitted you like him you know," Sue said kindly. "Everyone knows you're crazy about each other."

"Everyone except Angie," Sam said. "We heard what she said to you yesterday morning, and we were plum ashamed of her, weren't we, Sue?"

"Yes, we were. I thought she was a nice girl, but the way she treated you was appalling." She poured a cup of coffee for Carly and handed it to her. "She's just jealous. Don't let her upset you. She's liked Joe ever since that good-for-nothing Amy left him, poor boy. But I'm sure glad that you two are working out pretty well. How was your day yesterday?"

Carly told them a little about their excursion to the mall, omitting the episode with the strange man.

"I'm mighty glad to hear it," Sam said warmly. "That Joe is one nice kid, and I wish you both lots of happiness."

"Thank you." Carly blushed. "Well, I better go unlock the store. People are going to be barging in here any moment." She winked.

"Wait a minute on the store, Red. Sue and I have something we need to talk to you about. Pull up a chair."

"Uh oh, this sounds serious. Am I in trouble?" she asked light-heartedly, sitting down.

"No, what could you do to be in trouble?" Sue asked affectionately.

"I might surprise you." Carly laughed, pointing to her red hair.

"Red, Thanksgiving is coming this Thursday, and with it comes the holiday season. It's not much of a time for hardware selling, and most people around here go over to Billings to buy their presents." Sam cleared his throat. "Sue and I were considering taking a vacation to go visit our family."

"I think that'd be wonderful," Carly said, sincerely happy for them.

Sue smiled kindly as she stared at her young friend. "Well, that's a matter of opinion. We're concerned about you."

"Me? Why are you concerned about me?" Carly asked awkwardly.

"We just hate to put you out in the cold with nothing to do. We'd have to close up the store for as long as we're gone, and we didn't want you to be hurting financially, or to be alone over the holidays," Sam said quickly. "You'd still have your apartment though. We wouldn't expect you to move out or anything while we were gone."

"You worry too much. I'll be fine. I think it's great that you want to go visit your family and I wouldn't want to stop you. Don't worry about me. I'll stay here and watch over the store and make sure no one bothers it," Carly said, reassuring them.

"Are you sure, honey? We wouldn't want to inconvenience you or anything," Sue asked compassionately.

"You two? Inconvenience me? Where have you been? It's me that's the inconvenience. You two have been terrific since the minute I stepped foot in this door, and I appreciate every kindness that you've shown me. Take your vacation and enjoy your family. Don't give me a second thought."

"One other thing. We're stopping by Sue's sister's house in Billings for Thanksgiving dinner. If you don't have anything else to do, we'd be glad to have you come with us," Sam said.

"Thank you, that's very nice. But Penny's already asked me over to their house, and I told her I'd be there. How long are you going to be gone for anyway?"

"We've been saving for a vacation like this for about three years, and we're going to make the best of it. We're leaving out Thursday morning, and we don't plan on being back until after the New Year. Will you be able to manage that long?" Sue asked, worried.

"Absolutely!" Carly said brightly. "I've been saving for a while myself. You never know when a rainy day might come." She knew it would be tough financially, but she felt it was her duty to put their fears to rest.

"Oh good! I'm so excited, I think I'll go home and start

packing! See you tonight, dear," Sue said, giving Sam a hug and a kiss. She hugged Carly excitedly and went home to commence packing.

"Well, I better open the store now," Carly said, standing up and stretching. "I hope you two have a great time, Sam."

"We will. It's been hard for Sue with the store and all. I can't just up and leave whenever I want to, and she won't go visit the boys without me, so it's been a while since we've seen them. They come up whenever they can, but it's just not the same. Thanks for being so nice about it all, we appreciate it," Sam said, his eyes twinkling.

"You don't have to thank me. I need to thank you for taking me in like you both did. I really don't know where I'd be if you hadn't," Carly said, a lump forming in her throat. "I'm going to open up if that's all you need." Sam nodded, and she went to unlock the door.

It was a slow morning, as not too many people seemed to want to be outside with the snow. The phone rang about ten thirty. Reluctantly, Carly picked it up, Sam not being available.

"S&S Hardware, may I help you?" she asked quickly, not daring to breathe.

"Yes. I was wondering if you have any beautiful, good-natured, wonderful, happy young ladies in stock?"

It was Joe. Carly smiled, happy to hear his voice.

"No, I'm sorry sir. We sold out of those Saturday. We do have the cantankerous, annoying, cry baby, whiny know-it-alls left if you're interested."

Joe laughed. "Good morning. I just wanted to call you and make sure you didn't pack up and leave in the middle of the night," he said half-seriously.

She paused for a slight moment, wanting to give him a hard time.

"Of course I didn't pack up and leave last night."

"I'm glad to hear it." She thought she could hear relief in his voice.

"I was going to wait until this afternoon when it warms up a little."

"You cat." He laughed. "I wanted to come into town to see you, but I've got a lot of work to do over this way, so I probably won't make it."

"Really?" Carly said, her voice thick with disappointment. "That's too bad. I was hoping to get to see you today, but I understand. It's okay."

"You really did want to see me? Or are you being sarcastic?" Joe asked, his voice hopeful.

"Of course I want to see you. I've missed you," she said warmly. "But you stay and do what you've got to do, and maybe you could call me again around closing time?" she said, playing with the phone cord distractedly.

"I never thought I'd hear you say that you missed me."

"Why wouldn't I? You're the best you know."

"Maybe I should come into town this afternoon, to make sure that this is really Carly speaking," he said in mock astonishment.

"That's it. I'm hanging up. Try to let a guy know that you care for him and he treats you like this. Good-bye," she said teasing as she hit a button on the handset.

"Don't you hang up on me!" Joe said gruffly. "I've finally got you to talk to me like this and now you threaten to hang up? I don't think so!" Carly laughed, enjoying their playful banter.

"Listen. I've got to go, and I just wanted to make sure you were still here. I'll try to call you back around five." Joe hesitated then said quietly, "I love you, Carly."

Her heart flip-flopped, and she blushed even though no one was around. "I love you too. Have a good day, okay?" she whispered happily, her face hot.

"Without seeing you? Impossible, but I'll try. Bye!" She smiled faintly to herself and hung up the phone. She blushed when she saw Sam standing behind her grinning.

"I just wanted to let you know that while we're gone, you can call us if you need anything, I'll post the numbers up in the office." Sam turned to go. "But for some reason, I think you'll be taken care of pretty good."

She smiled. "Thanks, Sam. I'll call if I need anything."

Carly had trouble finding things to do to keep busy the rest of the day. She swept the floor, mopped, straightened shelves, dusted, everything she could think of, and still the day seemed to drag slowly by. Afternoon came and went with unhurried nonchalance, and Carly was bored almost out of her mind.

"Sam, is there anything I can do to help you back here?" she asked, finding him in the stock room, taking inventory. She glanced at her watch. Two more hours before closing, and consequently, Joe's phone call.

"Sorry, Red, but you've just about done everything there is to do already." Sam grinned. "It's been pretty slow today, hasn't it? Is Joe going to come by later tonight?"

She sighed. "No, he's not going to be able to make it, and that makes it worse."

The bell above the door tinkled and her heart leapt with joy.

Joe!

She dashed out of the room, leaving a laughing Sam behind her, and stopped short when she found the ugly man searching for something behind the counter.

"May I help you?" she asked stonily, crossing her arms.

He jumped, nervously stuffing his hands in his pocket as he slunk away from the counter. "I was just looking for a tissue."

It's a good thing that cash register stays locked! she thought angrily to herself, tapping her foot.

"Uh huh," she said, unconvinced. She stared at him for a moment, when she was suddenly struck with an unappealing thought.

"Do you know a man named Ian?" she asked impulsively, watching for some sort of reaction.

He stared at her for a moment, his face expressionless but for a slight twitch at the corner of his mouth. "I know lots of people. One of them may be named Ian. Why do you ask?" he said evenly, the nervous twitch worse.

"How about an Ian Lane?" she asked, her eyes narrowing suspiciously.

"Ian Lane. Hmm." He pretended to think, his face contorted. "Maybe I do, and maybe I don't."

"I was just wondering," she said sweetly. "I've got a message for him, and I was hoping you could give it to him." She walked behind the counter indifferently. "But I guess you can't help me if you don't know him." She started cleaning off the spotless counter, waiting for his reaction. He hesitated, considering his options.

"Well, maybe I could look him up for you," he said, leaning on the counter toward her.

"That's okay. If you don't know him, it's not going to help me any." She turned away and started sweeping.

"Suit yourself," he said gruffly, shrugging his shoulders. He left the store, slamming the door behind him.

Carly leaned the broom up behind the counter and went to find Sam. She needed some company to calm her shaking nerves. She found him emptying some boxes in the storeroom.

"Well, who was our first customer of the day?" he asked as Carly leaned against the wall next to him.

"Just the 'nail' man," she said. Sam chuckled. It was a joke they had shared for a couple of weeks.

"Well, what nails did he buy today?"

"Actually, none."

Sam raised his eyebrows in surprise. "None?"

She picked at her fingernails distractedly, keeping her eyes averted from his gaze. "Nope. I think I scared him."

"Scared him?" Sam looked at her in surprise. "How'd you do that?"

She was cornered. She hadn't meant to tell him what was said, but it was too late to worry about it now.

"I caught him behind the counter. He said he needed a tissue, and I asked him if he knew a guy named Ian Lane," she said as nonchalantly as she could manage.

"Ian Lane? Who's that?"

"My ex-fiancé."

He stopped and peered at her over his bifocals, quiet for a moment.

"No kidding. Now why would he know your ex?"

"Ian didn't take it very well when I broke off our engagement," she said quietly, squatting down and cutting open a box to sort out the contents, trying to act normal.

"Hmm. So he sends people to find you," Sam said flatly, going back to work.

"Something like that. There's the phone! I'll get it!" She jumped up and ran to answer the phone, glad for a reason to get away and not answer any more questions.

"S&S Hardware, may I help you?" she asked into the phone.

Silence. "Hello?" Nothing. She hung up the receiver, frustrated.

"Steve!" Chuck said softly, knocking on his buddy's door.

Steve yanked the door open abruptly, and soft sounds from the television drifted into the hall. He glared angrily at him. "What do you want?"

"She knows. Our cover is blown," Chuck said hoarsely, beads of sweat standing out on his thick forehead.

Steve glared at him then stepped aside to allow him to enter, closing the door behind him. "How could she know? Did you slip and say something?"

"No, I swear I didn't. She caught me getting the number and asked me if I knew a guy named Ian Lane. I'm telling you, she knows."

"What did you say when she asked you if you knew Ian?" Steve said through gritted teeth.

"I said I know lots of people, and one of them might be named

Ian." Steve shook his head disgustedly. "Well, what was I supposed to say?"

"You could have tried 'no.' That might have worked really well, you idiot! What else did she say?"

"She said that she wanted to get a message to him."

Steve sat down on the bed, running his fingers through his thinning hair. "What was the message?"

"She wouldn't give it to me. Maybe she doesn't really know anyway. Maybe I'm just overreacting," Chuck said hopefully.

Steve shook his head. "If she had the nerve to ask, she knows we're connected with him."

"What're we gonna do?" Chuck asked tensely.

Steve glowered at him. "I'll have to call him," he spat out, pulling the phone toward him. "You watch the store to make sure she doesn't leave." Chuck left quickly, thankful that he didn't have to deal with Ian. Steve watched him go, muttered something under his breath, and dialed Ian's number. It rang once before Ian's secretary answered.

"Ian Lane please." He waited.

"Ian here," was the usual curt reply not a second later.

"This is Steve. I've got bad news. She knows we're watching her." He winced, waiting for him to blow up.

"Good. I'm glad she knows," was the unruffled reply.

"You are?" Steve asked in shock.

"Has she run yet?"

"No," he said cautiously, wondering if that was soft laughter he heard or if he was going nuts.

"She's getting tired of running. She's going to be easy to get back home now." He was still calm.

"What do you want us to do? You want us to force her in the car and bring her back?"

"No. I want you both to stay there and make sure she doesn't run until I get there. I'm going to come and get her this time." Pause. "I want the number to the store." Steve read it off the paper Chuck had given him.

"When do you think you'll be up here?"

"I can't come right away. Sometime over the holidays," he said noncommittally. "I'm going to take care of this whole business once and for all. She's either coming home with me willingly, or I'll have to persuade her. Keep an eye on her." He hung up.

Steve hung up the phone, sweating. He'd never heard Ian so calm before. It was like the calm before the storm, and it gave him the creeps.

Carly looked at the clock. Five. *Finally*, she thought, standing next to the phone, anxiously waiting for Joe's call.

"Red," Sam called, "I'm leaving. Will you lock up please? I'm going out the back door to throw away some boxes before I go home. I'll see you in the morning."

"Good night, Sam," she called, leaning over the counter to wave. "See you in the morning." She heard him leave, shutting the door behind him. She locked the front door, pulled up the mat, and started to mop up the wet footprints left by the few customers they'd had. The phone rang and she ran to pick it up, dropping the mop.

"You're late. I've missed you," she said, unable to stop smiling.

"How sweet, I've missed you too," a voice said. She caught her breath, her heart thumping with horror.

"*Ian.*"

"Of course. Who else did you expect?" He waited for an answer.

She didn't give him one. He went on, "You know if you missed me so badly, you could have come home anytime you wanted to. You don't have to do this cat and mouse thing anymore."

Silence.

"Carly," he said in a singsong tone. "What's the matter? Cat got your tongue? I know you're still there. You wouldn't dare hang up on me; you've missed me too much. Why don't you just come home now?"

"Why won't you leave me alone?" Carly said helplessly, her hands shaking.

"Because I love you, dear," he said slowly, enunciating every syllable.

"You don't love me," she said vehemently. "You hate me!"

"Hate you?" he asked, his voice rising. "If I hated you, why would I buy you everything you ever wanted? Why would I have paid you so well? Why would I have taken such good care of you? Why would I still want you to come home?"

"*You?* Take good care of me?" She laughed scornfully. "If I recall, I don't think beating me was taking very good care of me, but I may be a little biased."

"You have to admit that you deserved it. If you wouldn't have provoked me, I wouldn't have beaten you."

She gave a short bitter laugh. "All I had to do was breathe to provoke you."

"You're starting to provoke me now, Carly, and I don't think you want to do that. All I've got to do is make a phone call, and you're on your way back down here," he said through gritted teeth. "Besides, I wouldn't want to force you to come home; I want you to decide to come back of your own free will because you love me. We'll start all over, and it'll all be better. You'll see," he said, forcing himself to be calm.

"Why are you doing this to me?" she said quietly, starting to cry. "You don't need me, you don't even want me, so why won't you just leave me alone?"

"You belong to me," he said menacingly. "I bought and paid for you, and you owe me."

"How do I owe you?" she asked angrily. "I left everything you bought me. I didn't take one thing of yours, or anything you gave me. I left it all for you to do whatever you wanted to with it. Even the engagement ring, which I could have very well kept and pawned, seeing as how you've stopped me from being able to get any money of my own." She paused. "You know, I have an idea. Why don't you give everything that you gave to me to your new secretary? I know how you are with secretaries. I'm sure she'd be happy with it all," she said bitterly, remembering how humiliated she had been.

"Yes, I think my secretary would like to belong to me, she's made it very obvious. But I don't want her. She's too easy. I need a challenge," he said with a cruel laugh.

"So that's it? That's why you keep hunting me like a wild animal? Because I'm a challenge?" Her voice rose as she endeavored to control herself.

"Every man loves a good chase, and you've given me a good chase," he said coldly. "But, I'm ready for you to come back now. My patience is running out. Just tell me you're coming home, I'll send you a first-class ticket, and we'll be married immediately."

His calmness of manner infuriated her. "I'm not ever coming back," she said through clenched teeth. "I'm staying here, and I don't ever want to see you again. We're through, so leave me alone."

It was his turn to get angry.

"Why? So you can waste your life in that filthy little town? What could you possibly want to stay there for? Oh yes." He laughed sardonically. "You've found yourself a little farm boy who can't offer you anything, not even a place to stay."

The color drained out of Carly's face.

"I know all about him. I've had you watched since the first week you arrived, you and that backwards hick that you're so fond of. I won't let him have you. You're mine, and I don't share, so if you really care for him, stay away from him. I don't like to see my future wife kissing anyone but me, understand? We'd hate to see anything bad happen to him, now wouldn't we?"

"I'm staying here, and that's it!" Slamming the phone down, she sank to the floor, her knees unable to keep her shaking body erect any longer.

The insistent phone rang several times, but she refused to answer, knowing it was Ian. After a little while, it stopped, and she gave a sigh of relief.

She was still there when she heard a knock on the door. She was afraid to look and see who it was, sure that it was one of the people Ian had alluded to. They knocked again, this time more loudly.

She peeked around the corner of the counter, relief spilling over her in torrents. It was Joe. She ran to open the door and flung herself at him.

"Carly!" he said, surprised. "Are you okay? Why were you on the floor?" He walked her back inside, trying to keep her warm.

"Oh Joe, I'm so glad you're here," she cried fervently, not letting go of him for a moment. "I thought it was you calling, so I answered the phone, and it ended up being Ian, and..."

"Shh, shh," Joe said, putting his finger to her lips. "I can't understand what you're saying. Slow down. Shh."

She took a deep breath and started again. Slowly. "I was waiting for you to call me. When the phone rang, I answered it, thinking it was you, and it was Ian instead. He knows all about you, and he threatened to hurt you if I stayed with you. He told me to come back, and we'd get married right away, and things would be fine." She looked up at him, upset. "I can't let him hurt you, but I can't go back there and marry him. He's a monster." Her voice caught with emotion. "He said that he's had me watched since the first week I was here." She leaned her head against Joe's chest. He held her close and rubbed her back soothingly. "What are we going to do?"

"I don't know anything we can do except pray. Why don't we do that right now?"

They bowed their heads and pleaded for God's protection for both of them, for wisdom and guidance in what to do, and for the peace that only God can give.

She sighed sadly when their prayer was finished. "Do you want me to go? I would understand if you did. I wouldn't blame you."

His arms tightened around her. "I wouldn't want you to go for anything in the world. You are a part of me, and if you left, I think I'd die of a broken heart. Your leaving would hurt me more than anything Ian could possibly do," he said lovingly. "But the real question is, what do you think God wants you to do? It really doesn't matter what I want if it's not the Lord's will."

"I'm terrified of Ian, but staying here is the one thing I know God wants me to do. I don't understand it, but I've got peace. I know God is able to take care of the whole situation. My place is here beside you, if you want me."

"I love you, Carly Richards," he said, kissing the top of her head.

"I love you too, Joe," she said softly, laying her hand on his chest. They leaned on each other for a few minutes, gaining comfort from one another.

"Why do you always kiss the top of my head?" she asked after a few moments. He had never really kissed her yet, and she was a little confused.

"Because I'm afraid that I wouldn't be able to stop kissing you, and then I'd be in trouble. I try to keep my distance, but it's getting difficult."

"In that case, I'd better stop letting you hug me," she said, blushing, stepping away from him.

"Oh no. I can't give that up now." He pulled her close again.

She leaned on him for a little while then stepped back again so she could look up at him. "I thought you weren't going to come to town today," she asked. "Don't get me wrong, I'm very grateful that you did come, but I was just curious."

"I came into town to plow the church parking lot, and I had to see you. If you'll go get your coat on, you can come with me while I plow."

"Sounds good to me," she said thankfully, hurrying to get her old jacket on as she didn't want to mess up her new one.

"You're going to plow with that?" she asked quizzically, looking at the snowplow attached to the front of his truck as he helped her inside. "How in the world do you get it to work?"

He and got in before he answered her question. "I've got it hooked up in here. This toggle switch turns it on and off, and I can turn the plow with this little control box," he said, backing out and driving to the church.

She watched him control the plow once they were in the parking lot. "I've never seen anything like that before!" He glanced at her, laughing at her delight. "Do you do this every time it snows?"

"Not every time. Dad, Todd, and I take turns. I volunteered to do it tonight, the next time will be Todd's turn, then Dad's. It doesn't take too long, and I enjoy doing it. Want to try to control it?" he asked, eyes twinkling.

She shook her head vigorously. "Oh no, I wouldn't want to break it."

"Come on and try. If you break it, I'll fix it. Here..." He took her hand and showed her how the controls worked, allowing her to try. He drove slowly, giving her plenty of time to figure out the turns. She squealed in delight.

"Are we done?" she asked, disappointed when all the snow was cleared in the parking area a little later.

"Yep. I'll shovel the walkway, and we'll be out of here in ten minutes," he answered, opening the door and grabbing a snow shovel out of the back of the truck. "Stay here. I'll be right back." He grinned, winking at her.

She watched him start shoveling the walkway and quietly opened the door, closing it behind her. She bent down, made a few snowballs, and snuck up behind him. When she was close enough to hit him, she hurled a couple at his back, enjoying the smacking sound as it hit him. Surprised, he turned around as she ducked behind one of the bushes, laughing hysterically.

"That's it! You're going down," he hollered, grabbing snow and making a gigantic snowball. He ran toward her, dodging the barrage of snowballs she hurled at him. She ran toward the truck as he got closer, slipping and falling on the freshly plowed parking lot, tripping him as well. They were both laughing uncontrollably as they continued to pummel each other with snow.

"Uncle! Uncle!" he shouted, falling back to the ground out of breath. She tossed more snow on him, then gave up and lay down next to him, giggling.

"That felt good," she said breathlessly, watching her breath float up to the stars.

He chuckled, reaching over and punching her arm lightly. "You cheated."

She grinned, her eyes twinkling. "There's no such thing as a fair fight."

"Let me help you up," Joe said, standing and offering her his hand.

"Thank you," she said. "You aren't done with that walkway yet? I thought you said it would take you about ten minutes." She grinned impishly, walking with him.

"I was attacked by a runaway snowball," he said, putting his arm around her waist.

"I hate to argue with you, but you're wrong." She batted her eyes innocently. "It wasn't a runaway. It hit exactly where I wanted it to!"

He scooped up some snow and tossed it on her playfully. "You're soaking," he said, looking at her in amusement. "Don't you have any gloves or boots?"

"Gloves? Boots? I had a pair once when I was young."

"You sit here on the porch while I finish up the walkway, and we'll go. This way, I can watch you and make sure you don't attack me again." He grinned. "Here, wear my gloves."

"Thank you," she said, taking them gratefully, rubbing her hands together and stomping her feet to get warm. She watched him admiringly as he quickly finished up.

"Done," he said, offering her his arm. "Are you ready, or do you want to stay and have another snowball fight?"

"Do I get to keep your gloves?" she asked mischievously, stooping down to gather more snow.

He laughed. "No way!" He opened the door for her, put the shovel in the back, got in, and started the truck. "Thanks for coming with me. That's the most fun I've had shoveling snow in a long time."

"Thank you for coming into town." He turned to her. "Are you hungry?"

"Mmm," she said, evading his question.

"Sure you are. You're starved," he said, driving past her apartment and taking her to the diner.

"Joe, I can't go in there! I look awful." She ran her fingers through her wet hair.

"You look great," he said, pulling into a parking spot and turning the truck off.

"Do you have a comb or anything?" she asked anxiously.

He grinned at her discomfort. "Sure don't."

She grumbled as she got out of the truck resignedly. "That's just mean." He laughed and held the door open for her.

They picked an empty booth in the back and sat down across from each other, looking over the menu. Sandy came up to take their drink order.

"Sandy, do you ever go home?" Carly asked pleasantly.

"Me? Oh yeah, I'll be off in about an hour. I'm working the evening shift for someone else. So, Joe," she asked, looking at him with raised eyebrows. "I haven't seen you in here in a long time." She looked over at Carly and winked. "I see you're keeping Carly company."

He grinned while Carly blushed. "And enjoying every minute of it."

"Oh really? Sounds fascinating. Carly, we'll have to get together sometime so you can tell me all the juicy details," Sandy said with a wink.

"What's there to tell?" Carly asked naïvely.

Sandy snorted. "Are you two a couple?" she asked pointedly.

Carly gave Joe an awkward look. He just smiled in return, waiting for her answer. "Uh, well, I guess it depends on what you mean by 'couple,'" she said feebly.

"How many different things can the word 'couple' mean?" she asked.

"Joe?" She kicked him lightly under the table.

He looked up from his menu, amusement plastered on his handsome face. "What?"

"Do you want to answer her?" she asked, looking at him intently.

"She asked you, not me."

Sandy stood by the table with her hands on her hips, waiting inflexibly for a reply.

"You want to know if we're a couple," she said, tearing tiny strips off her napkin.

"That's all I want to know."

She looked down at her menu, refusing to meet her gaze. "Yes. We are a couple." Joe laughed quietly, his head down, his shoulders heaving.

"Well finally! You would've thought I'd asked if you were getting married." Sandy grinned mercilessly. "I don't think I'd get much of an answer to that one, but it would be a very interesting question to ask, don't you think?" she said, while Joe laughed heartily at Carly's red face. "But I'll just stick to taking your orders. What'll you have?"

Carly managed to squeak out her order, while Joe had no trouble at all telling her his.

"I can't believe you did that to me," she said, flustered as Sandy walked away to fill their order.

"What?" Joe tried to look innocent. "I didn't do anything."

"You could have stepped in anytime you know. It would have been okay. I'm going to need a new napkin. Mine looks shredded." She looked forlornly at her pile of napkin pieces. Joe passed her his, trying hard to suppress his smile. It didn't work.

"How else am I supposed to know what you think?" His eyes twinkled wickedly.

She glared, resisting the urge to smile. "You could try asking next time."

"I'm sorry." He tried to look penitent. She threw her straw wrapper at him.

"Well, well, well. Lookee what we got here," a voice sneered.

Randy and Billy Pruit had come in unnoticed while they were talking and sauntered up to their table.

"Billy. Randy," Joe said, nodding at them curtly, all humor gone.

"Joe," Billy said quietly, staring at Carly, some sort of emotion clouding his face.

"Red, we haven't seen you in quite a while. Where've you been?" Randy asked, laying a filthy hand on her side of the table.

She looked at Joe. "Just working," she answered as politely as she could.

"We need to go to the hardware store more often, huh, Billy?" he said, jabbing Billy's side with his elbow.

"Is there something we can do for you two?" Joe asked coldly.

"I'm sure there's nothing you can do, but I was talking to Red, if you don't mind," Randy answered dismissively.

"Knock it off, Randy," Billy said, suddenly coming out of his musing. "Come on, let's eat. Carly." He nodded at her and walked away, seating himself at the counter.

Randy scowled. "Red, I'll be seeing you. That's a promise." He laughed derisively and went to join his brother.

Carly watched them for a moment. "What was that all about?" she whispered, looking warily at Joe.

"I'm not sure," he answered thoughtfully. "But my guess is that Billy's a little jealous."

"What?" she asked incredulously. "Why would he be jealous?"

"Maybe he wishes it was him with you and not me." He looked at her peculiarly. "You know, you are quite pretty and any guy would like to be with you."

She blushed profusely. "I don't know why he would be jealous. I never led him to believe that I was interested in him," she said quietly, looking at her plate as Sandy placed it in front of her.

"A guy can still like a girl even if he knows she doesn't care for him," he answered after Sandy left. "I feel a little sorry for him, myself. He seems to make a lot of bad choices, but I don't think he's got much of a role model at home."

"I do too," she answered slowly, after a long pause. "You know, that's the first time he's used my real name."

"Now don't go feeling too sorry for him, you hear?" he answered, shaking his fork at her. "Let's pray." He reached over to hold her hand.

"Joe, can we pray for Billy and Randy too?" she asked hesitantly. "I just kind of feel bad for them, especially Billy. Do you mind?"

"Mind that you want to pray for another man? It depends on why you want me to pray for him." He grinned. She threw some napkin shreds at him. "Okay, okay. No need to get violent."

They prayed quietly. When they were through, Carly glanced toward Billy to find him watching her, his face gloomy. She smiled kindly at him. He looked away.

"Do you want some dessert?" Joe asked hopefully after they had finished their meal.

Carly laughed, holding her stomach. "Oh my goodness, I ate too much as it is!"

"Good! Sandy. We'd like two pieces of pecan pie."

"Sure thing, Joe," Sandy said, fixing their plates and bringing it to them right away.

"You didn't tell me anything about your day today," he said, starting to eat his pie.

"There's really not much to tell you. I don't think I'm going to be able to eat the whole thing," she said, eyeing the large slice in front of her.

"Sure you can. I have faith in you!"

"Well,"—she took a bite—"I think I made a guy nervous today. This is really good." She was a little surprised.

"Really? How'd you do that?"

"Well, this guy's been coming into the store for a while now, and all he ever buys is a box of nails. I've told you about him," she said between mouthfuls.

"Yeah, go on."

"Well, today I caught him behind the counter, and he said he was looking for a tissue. I thought that was a little weird, so I asked if he knew a guy named Ian Lane."

"What did he say?" Joe asked, fork poised over his remaining pie.

"Nothing really. He just got this nervous twitch. You should have seen the look on his face. It was funny." She paused to take a sip of water. "This is really good. Thank you," she said, wiping her mouth.

"My pleasure," he answered, polishing off his pie and leaning back in his seat. "Are you ready to go?"

She reached into her pocket for her money. "Whenever you are. I've just got to pay."

"Are you trying to pick a fight?" He glared at her. "You aren't paying."

"Me? Pick a fight with you? Why would I want to do that?" she asked, batting her eyes innocently.

He chuckled as he picked up the bill. "That's what I thought. Let's go." He led her past Billy and Randy, and over to the cash register.

"Bye, Red," Randy said tauntingly, his eyes fixed on her chest.

"Bye," she said uncomfortably.

Joe held open the door for her, staring coldly at Randy and Billy as she walked out to the truck.

"Joe," she asked as soon as they were both inside. "Let's pray for Billy every day and see what the Lord does, okay?"

"Well, it couldn't hurt him any," he said, putting his arm around her shoulders. "Do I need to be worried?" She elbowed him hard in the ribs.

"Ow!" he exclaimed, pulling into a parking spot in front of the hardware store. "I've had a good time tonight," he said softly, his arm still around her shoulders. "Even though I'm going to have a bruised shin and side."

"Me too." She leaned her head on his arm comfortably. "Thanks for coming to see me today."

"My pleasure. I can hardly wait for Thursday."

"Why? Do you like turkey that much?" she said, snuggling as close as she could to him.

He squeezed her tightly. "I like this turkey that much! Then I'll be able to have you all day long."

"What time did your mom want me to be over there? I don't think she told me," she asked, scooting toward the door to leave.

"The earlier the better," he said, holding her hand for a moment. "What time do you want me to pick you up?"

"Is Kelly going to be there?"

"I think so. I'm pretty sure Mom asked her to come. Why?"

"I was just wondering," she said mysteriously. She squeezed his hand tightly then got out of the truck.

"So what time do you want me to pick you up?"

She stamped her feet to keep warm. "Well, what time do you get up and start doing your work?"

"I get up at five. Why?" he asked, puzzled.

"I just thought that maybe you could show me what you do on a farm. I'd like to help," she said awkwardly, looking at the snowy sidewalk.

"You want to help me with my chores?" he asked, taken by surprise.

She looked at him a little defiantly. "I'd like to help if it's okay. Plus I want to be there to help your mom with dinner."

"All right," he said after a slight hesitation. "I'll pick you up at six."

"I thought you said you started at five."

He grinned. "That's only if I don't take a shower before I start. But seeing as how you're going to help me, I've got to take my shower and look good for my girl before she gets there."

"You don't have to do that," she said, embarrassed. "Don't worry about it; you just come get me when you're done."

"Oh no. You're not getting out of the work that easily. You're committed to help me now." He chuckled. "Get inside before you freeze to death."

"Bye," she said, starting to close the door.

"Wait! You never answered my question!" he said before she could shut it all the way.

"What question?"

He grinned. "Do I need to be worried about you and Billy Pruit?"

She slammed the door, and went inside without waving.

Chapter Fourteen

The next day was much busier for Carly and Sam. Everyone seemed to need something from the hardware store, and there was a steady stream of customers almost all morning. She didn't get a break until almost lunchtime when Kelly came to see her.

"Hi, Carly," she said as soon as she came in. "I just wanted to see if you want to go get something to eat."

"Hey, Kelly." Carly looked up from her receipts. "I don't think I'm going to be able to go today. We've been pretty busy, and I'd hate to leave Sam if he needs me. But thanks for asking." Kelly sighed her disappointment and drummed her fingers on the countertop.

"Wait, I have an idea. Do you just want to come up to my apartment and have lunch there? I can whip up some macaroni and cheese really quick."

She brightened up considerably at the suggestion. "That would be fun."

"Let me see if Sam will be okay for a half hour. I'll be right back," she said over her shoulder, walking back to the office to find Sam. She came back quickly, smiling.

"You ready?" she said, leading Kelly to the stairs. "You'll have to forgive the mess. I've been doing laundry, and it's hanging everywhere." She laughed and opened the door.

"I can't get over how small this place is," Kelly said, amused, taking off her coat as she stepped in. "Not very many people would be able to handle it."

"You can hang your coat here." Carly pointed to a small hook on the wall beside the door. "If you think this is bad, you should have seen the last place I lived at. This is the Hilton compared to that!" She laughed. "Do you like macaroni and cheese?"

"Love it. That's all I would eat when I was little." Kelly sat down on one of the tiny kitchen chairs and looked around at the clothes hanging from clotheslines stretched from the bathroom to the opposite wall that was supposed to be a small living area. Carly was at the sink, putting water into a small pan.

"Why are all these clothes hanging here?"

"Oh, I was just doing laundry yesterday evening, and they won't dry until probably tomorrow night. I've only got that little wall heater over there, so it takes things longer to dry when it's cold." She set the covered pan on the stove and turned on the fire.

"Why don't you just dry your laundry at the coin place down the street?"

"It saves me quite a bit of money if I do it this way," Carly said. "Would you like some water, juice, or milk?" She took two mismatched glasses out of the tiny cupboard hanging on the wall next to the tiny refrigerator.

"Juice please," Kelly said politely, watching Carly pour two glasses of juice, check the water in the pot on the stove, add some salt, and return to the table with their drinks.

"Here you go."

Kelly took a sip. "I'd think that it'd be a lot less of a hassle to just dry the clothes while you were at the Laundromat instead of hauling wet clothes home."

"I don't go to the Laundromat." Carly blushed but looked steadily at her. "I wash them in the tub."

Kelly colored with embarrassment. "I'm sorry. I didn't mean to pry."

"It doesn't bother me, Kelly," Carly said kindly. "I've had to work hard to save every penny I've made since I left Ian, and when I see something that would save me money, I do it. I have to."

"But not anymore," Kelly said firmly. "You don't have to live this way anymore. Joe will take care of you now."

Carly smiled at her naivety. She wasn't offended at her friend's reaction to her living conditions. She hadn't had to live like Carly had had to, just to survive. Carly reached across and squeezed her hand.

"I can't ask Joe to take my problems and make them his. I've got to take care of myself the best that I can."

"But he loves you," she said, arguing. "It wouldn't be a burden to him."

Carly stood and went to the stove, adding the macaroni to the boiling water. "I can't ask Joe to pay my way, Kelly. That wouldn't be right." She stirred the pasta, put the lid on, and sat down before continuing.

"Well, when he asks you to marry him, he'll be taking care of you then." Kelly was not going to be convinced easily.

"He hasn't asked me to marry him. And what if he doesn't? It might not work out between us, or," she looked at her friend firmly, "he may change his mind about me after all."

"But he will. I know he'll ask. And I know he isn't going to change his mind, either!" Kelly sighed heavily, wishing she could help make her friend's life easier.

"If he asks, then we'll see." Carly smiled. "Don't worry about me. God knows what he's doing. I had everything the world has to offer when I was with Ian, and now it's my time to struggle. Truthfully, I enjoy my life a lot better now, even though I have to struggle and depend on God to survive. I'm happier now than I ever was with him. Don't feel bad for me. I'm very happy."

"How do you do it?" Kelly asked quietly.

"Do what?" Carly asked, getting up to strain the pasta.

"Be so calm and peaceful when you had everything, and now you've got nothing," she said compassionately.

"Nothing? I've got everything now, and I had nothing then! I've got God, good friends that really care about me, a job that I love doing and don't have to feel guilty about, I've got a good church home." She paused, getting the butter and cheese slices out of the refrigerator. "And I've got a man that I love. What's better than all that?" She turned to look at Kelly, smiling. "Do you like your macaroni really cheesy, or just a little cheesy?"

Kelly grinned. "Really cheesy."

Carly finished making their lunch, piled two heaping helpings on two mismatched plates, and brought them to the table.

"This is the best macaroni and cheese I've ever had," Kelly said, taking a bite after they prayed.

"I'm glad you like it." Carly smiled. "I eat this almost every day."

"Every day?"

"Oh yeah," she said, helping herself to another bite, smiling.

"Is this another way for you to save money?" Kelly asked.

"Yep. I eat this, rice, and juice, and sometimes I pull all the stops out and go over to the diner and have a bowl of soup." She laughed.

"Well, whatever you do, please don't ever make it for Todd. He'll like it too much, and then I'll have to figure out how to make it. I'm a terrible cook. I try really hard, but I'm no good at it." Kelly sighed.

"I bet you're a good cook," Carly said, smiling.

"No. I'm not. Just ask Todd Thursday. He'll tell you the truth."

"Speaking of Thursday. Are you going over there for Thanksgiving?"

"Yes, why?"

"There's some more if you want it," she said when she was finished. Kelly helped herself to another helping and sat back down. "I was wondering what time you were going out there."

"I really hadn't thought about a time, why?"

She grinned mischievously. "Well, I was wondering how early you wanted to be there."

Kelly leaned forward, interested. "Ooh, you have an idea."

"I just thought it would be nice to get there early and surprise the guys. Then we could help them with their chores, and help Penny with the dinner. After that, we'd have the rest of the day."

"I think that's a great idea. Then we could show them that we know how to work hard too," Kelly said excitedly. "What time were you thinking?"

"Well, Joe said he'd be here at six to pick me up, so if we showed up there before five thirty, we'll probably surprise them pretty good," Carly said eagerly.

"We'd have to leave here at five," Kelly said, her spirits dampened slightly. She thought a moment. "I still think it's a great idea. Let's do it," she said, regaining her enthusiasm. "I'd like to show Todd that I can do it. He thinks I can't get up before eight. Won't he be surprised?" She grinned gleefully at Carly. "I'll go to bed early, and I'll be here by five. I'm so excited!"

They finished their lunch, planning what they would do and wear on Thursday, talked a little about Joe and Todd, and went back downstairs after they had cleaned up.

"Kelly, if it'll make it easier for you, I can just meet you at the bed and breakfast, then you won't have to come here to get me. What do you think?" Carly said, walking Kelly to the door.

"Okay, that sounds good. I'll meet you there," she said, excitedly giving Carly a hug before she left.

Carly went back to work in a cheerful mood. She was thinking about Thursday when the bell above the door tinkled. She looked up to see Billy Pruit walking in. Her heart sank a little before she remembered that she and Joe were praying diligently for him. She forced a bright, sunny smile onto her face.

"Hi, Billy. Is there something I can do for you?" she asked cheerfully.

"Uh, no," he answered, embarrassed, walking past her. She stared after him and helped some other customers that had walked in after him.

She didn't see Billy again until everyone else had left, and she had almost forgotten him when he came up to the counter with a socket set in his hands. He set it on the counter hesitantly, shuffling his feet.

"Are you ready?" She asked kindly, wondering at his discomfort. She wondered fleetingly if he had stolen anything, but decided to give him the benefit of the doubt. He mumbled something incoherently, still shuffling his feet.

"Billy, are you okay?"

"I'm fine," he snapped. "Just ring me up."

"Sorry," she said, irritated. "I was just trying to be friendly."

"I know," he said, less snappish, but still not pleasant. She rang him up quickly, offering up a hurried prayer for him, half-wishing he were gone. He gave her the money. She counted out his change and handed it to him.

"There you go," she said as pleasantly as she could, wanting him to leave so she could resume her daydreaming.

He just stood there, holding his change, his face cloudy. "Do you need something else?" she asked, perplexed.

"I want to know why you won't go out with me, but you'll go out with Joe," he blurted furiously, stuffing his change into his pocket.

"What?" Carly asked, taken by surprise.

"Yeah. I want to know why you wouldn't give me the time of day, but you're always with Joe. What's he got that I don't?" he asked angrily. Carly took a deep breath and swallowed her irritation.

"He's treated me with respect ever since I met him, while you try to irritate and show nothing but disrespect," she answered shakily. She had never expected Billy to even care for her that much, let alone be jealous. "More importantly, I'm a Christian. Are you?"

Billy looked at her exasperatedly. "What does that have to do with anything?"

"It has everything to do with it," she said quietly. "I try to please God with everything I do, and it's wrong for a Christian to date a person who isn't one."

"I've always heard from Pops that Christians are the worst people there are," he said, sneering.

She stared at him fixedly, refusing to be intimidated. "Well, you heard wrong."

"How do people get to be Christians?"

"You have to ask Jesus to forgive you and to save you," she said.

Before he could answer, more customers walked in, eyeing them curiously. She blushed, wondering what they could be thinking.

"Why don't you come to church with us tomorrow?" she asked after the customers had walked by.

"Church?" He frowned, curling his lip. "I wouldn't be welcome."

"Yes, you would. You could come by and sit with Joe and me," she said, trying to encourage him. "The people are very friendly, Billy."

"I don't know," he said, hurrying out.

"I hope to see you there," she said, hoping he heard her as the door closed behind him. She watched him leave and prayed fervently that he would come hear the gospel and be saved.

Carly was locking the front door when the phone rang. She walked slowly toward it, afraid it might be Ian. She knew she'd still stand up to him if it was, but she didn't like confrontations, and with Ian, she dreaded them.

She picked it up. Her voice cracked as she answered. "Hello?"

"Carly?" It was Joe.

"Hi, Joe." She breathed a sigh of relief. "How are you?"

"Good, I just wanted to talk to you for a little bit before going back out to work. How was your day?"

"It was pretty good. No ugly little men who only buy nails today." She laughed. "But I did get to talk to Billy today. Are you still praying for him?"

"Yes," he said slowly. "I knew it. You didn't answer me last night, and now I've got to worry." She could hear his grin.

"Joe, if you keep that up, I'm going to hang up on you, and I won't answer the phone again," she said huffily.

He laughed. "Okay, I'm sorry. I was just kidding. Go on, what were you going to say?"

"Well, I invited him to church."

"That's great!" he said warmly.

"And I told him that he could sit with you and me," she said apprehensively. He was quiet for a minute.

"You told him that he could sit with me and you. Hmm. That'll be fine. But I want to ask you again. Carly, do I need to be worried?" He sounded more serious this time.

"That's it. Good-bye," she said, getting ready to hang up.

"Don't hang up. I was just wondering, nothing to get so huffy about."

"Let me ask you a question. If Amy were to come back like Angie said, would I have anything to worry about?" she asked, half-dreading the answer he might give.

"That's silly. You wouldn't have anything to worry about for anybody," he said softly.

She felt the tension easing away. "Are you sure?" she asked, trying to irritate him a little.

"Yes, I'm sure. Don't you trust me?" he said, a little hurt by her doubt.

"There you go. Don't you trust me, Joe?" she asked softly, using his own words against him. "I would hope that you could find someone more worthy of being jealous over than Billy."

"All right. You win. I won't mention it again." He laughed. "But seriously. Do you think he'll really come?"

"I don't know, he didn't answer. So what have you been up to?" she asked, desiring to change the subject.

He told her the things he'd been doing during the day. He was a part owner of his dad's farm, and taking care of the farm was his main job, but he was a top mechanic when it came to fixing farm equipment and vehicles, so they had renovated the back of the barn for a garage for him and Todd when they took on side jobs. People knew of the quality of their work from miles around and trusted them implicitly. She admired his mechanical ability tremendously, and was really proud of him. He was also a skilled woodworker; if it needed to be built, he could build it cheaper and better than anywhere else.

"That's amazing," she said admiringly when he paused for

breath.

"What?" he asked, puzzled.

"How you can do anything and everything. I just never knew anyone like that. How did you learn so much?"

"I don't know, I guess I just like doing things with my hands, so I do the best I can possibly do." He sounded a little self-conscious.

"Oh, I almost forgot," she said suddenly. "You don't have to pick me up Thursday. Kelly and I are going to ride out together."

"I don't mind picking you up," he said, disappointed. "I thought you were going to come out here to learn how to be a country girl."

"I'll still be there," she said, smiling. "And you can still show me the farm. You'll just have to wait until I get there."

"You were afraid that I was going to work you too hard, weren't you? Uh huh, I see exactly how you are. Shirker." He teased relentlessly.

"Shirker? Did you just call me a shirker?" she asked humorously. "You don't want to get along. Maybe you should be worried about Billy after all!"

He laughed. "And you say I'm the one that doesn't want to get along! Hey, I've got to let you go. I'll see you tomorrow night, okay?"

"Maybe," she said. "I might just have to avoid you again if you're going to try to pick fights."

"No, please don't do that," he said sourly. "That was awful. I couldn't handle that again. Really. That was rough."

"I'm just teasing. I'll see you tomorrow night."

"Good night, Carly," he said softly.

"Good night Joe," she said, hanging up before he could say anything else, smiling to herself. She waited by the phone for a minute. It rang. She picked it up quickly.

"Wanda's Waffle House," she said, in a high nasally voice. "May I help you?"

"You hung up before I could finish." Joe said. "I was going to say I love you." He hung up on her. She giggled and put the phone back on the cradle.

After she had mopped up the floor, dusted the shelves, and wiped the counter, she put the broom and mop away in the back room and went upstairs to her apartment. Sam had left hours ago, trusting her to keep the place in order. She was going to miss them terribly when they were gone. She sighed. It was going to be a long month and a half.

She was daydreaming about Joe while she was folding her laundry when she heard someone banging on the front door of the store. Apprehensively, she turned off her light and crept over to her window to look outside. She peered around the curtain and saw a man walking quickly across the street. She waited for him to turn the corner before she unlocked her door and went downstairs to make sure the store was fine.

At first, she didn't see anything out of the ordinary, but as she tiptoed closer to the counter, she saw another man come to a halt at the doors. She froze in terror. He glanced inside quickly, not seeing her, and turned around swiftly, as if watching for someone. She dove behind the counter and grabbed the phone.

Who am I going to call? she thought to herself. *If I call Joe, he'll come into town, and I'll feel terrible if it's just a drunk. If I call the police, I'll look like an idiot if it's just a prank. Maybe Sam, but he and Sue are probably getting ready to go to bed.* So she did the only thing she knew to do. She prayed.

Lord, I'm all alone here, and I'm pretty scared. I don't know who to call, or what to do. Could you please take care of this situation for me?

She peeked around the corner to see if the man was still standing outside the door. He wasn't. Relief flooded over her. She watched a little while longer and saw a police cruiser go slowly by with his spotlight on the store.

She was about to go back upstairs when she noticed an

envelope caught under the rubber mat just inside the door. Cautiously, she ran to the door, grabbed the envelope, and ran back upstairs. After double checking to make sure it was locked behind her, she leaned her back on the door, her heart beating fast. Calmed down a bit, she went into the bathroom, shut the door, turned on the light, and slowly opened the envelope.

Chapter Fifteen

The next day went fast for Carly and Sam. They had posted a sign on the door at the beginning of the week and had spread the word to everyone that had come by about the coming hiatus at the hardware store. At lunchtime, Sam and Carly closed the shop and went to eat lunch with Sue.

"I'm so glad that you could come, Carly!" she said, giving her a hug. "I was afraid that all these leftovers would spoil while we were gone. Here you go." She took Carly's coat and hung it up. "What a nice coat! It's so pretty!"

"Thank you," Carly said with a huge smile. "Joe bought it for me."

Sue smiled knowingly at Sam, and they sat down to eat.

"Whatever we don't eat, I want you to take back to the apartment and eat it while we're gone," she said cheerily. "Unless you don't like leftovers." She looked alarmed.

"Love them," Carly said reassuringly. "It doesn't take as long to get them ready!"

"Now, Sam posted all the numbers up in the office," Sue said after Sam asked the blessing. "If you need anything, just give us a call. But"—she looked slyly at Sam—"you'll be pretty well taken care of I'm sure."

"Yes, I will," Carly said good-naturedly. "I'll make Joe pay attention to me."

"I don't think you have to worry about making Joe pay attention, Red. He lights up like a firefly whenever you're around." Sam winked at her.

"Is there anything you need while we're gone?" Sue asked.

"Yes." Carly wiped her mouth with a napkin. "I need you to pray specifically for something for me."

"Well sure, honey, whatever you need us to pray for, we'll do it," Sue said, piling delicious smelling food onto their plates. Carly looked at her plate with relish.

"It's going to sound kind of odd, but would you please pray for Billy Pruit?" They stopped eating and stared at her, their surprise evident.

"Joe and I are praying for him to come to church tonight. Will you pray that the Lord deals with him?" Carly said hurriedly, making sure they understood Joe was praying with her as well. She didn't want them to think that she was interested in Billy.

"Sure," Sam said, recovering first.

"That's so sweet of you two. Praying together already. You know," Sue waved her fork in Carly's direction, "they say those that pray together stay together. That's what's kept us so long, isn't it, Sam?"

"Among other things," he said jovially with a wink at his wife. "Anything else, Red?"

"Um, yes," she said hesitantly. "Would you please pray that the Lord will guide and direct me and Joe, and give us wisdom to deal with things?"

"Things?" Sue asked, raising her eyebrows. "There isn't trouble with you two, is there? I knew as soon as I first saw you that you were made for Joe."

Carly shook her head expressively. "No, no. Everything's fine with us. So far. I just want to do God's will, no matter what." She thought instinctively about the envelope in her coat pocket. She had put it there, wanting to show Joe as soon as she saw him at church that night.

"Good girl." Sue beamed happily. "There's more if you want it." Carly helped herself to some small helpings to please her.

"While we're gone, could you please look in at the house every once in a while? You don't really have to do anything, just make sure that everything's okay. Sam will give you a house key before we leave." Sue paused to eye Carly's clean plate. "Have some pie."

"Sure, I'd be glad to," Carly said pleasantly, wondering how she was going to eat the huge piece of pie she dished out. Somehow she finished it and stood up before Sue could feed her any more.

"Can I help you with the clean up?" she asked, taking her plate to the sink.

"Oh no, sweetie. I need something to keep me busy for the rest of the day, seeing as how I've got all the packing done." Sue grinned, clearing off the table. "You go ahead and get back to work. I'll send Sam over later with the leftovers if you don't mind."

"Thanks for lunch," she said, putting on her coat. "It was delicious. I'll see you in a little bit, Sam."

"You're welcome, dear." Sue gave her a big hug, her eyes moist. "I'm going to miss you."

"I'm going to miss you too, but I hope you both have a great time. Don't worry about anything while you're gone," Carly said, trying to swallow the lump in her throat, knowing she was going to miss them both terribly.

Sam came to work about an hour later, bringing a large basket full of Tupperware bowls for Carly. "I hope you like to eat." Sam laughed and handed her the basket. "Do you have room for all of this in your little refrigerator upstairs?"

She eyed the basket, laughing. "Wow. I thought we made a pretty good dent in the leftovers for lunch!"

"She made you some special treats for taking care of things for us, so it's not all leftovers," he said as she lugged the basket up the stairs.

She struggled to find room in her refrigerator, but she finally stuffed the last bowl into the last tiny space and went back downstairs.

"Well, did you get it all in there?" Sam asked, giving a customer some change. "You have a good day." He called after them, "Remember, Mike. We're going to be closed until January fifteenth, so you'll have to go to Billings if you need anything." Mike nodded and left the store.

"I didn't think that refrigerator could hold so much!" Carly laughed, leaning on the counter.

"There's one other thing we forgot to mention to you." Sam pulled a set of keys out of his pocket and handed them to her.

She looked at them curiously. "Are these all for the house?"

"This is for the house; this is for the garage door if you need anything." He paused, showing her each key. "And these two are for my truck in the garage," he said, smiling at her significantly. She was speechless for a moment.

"Sam, I can't use your truck," she said softly, handing the keys back to him.

Everyone knew that Sam's truck was his baby since his boys had left home, and he took care of it like a young schoolboy. It was a dark blue, 1970 Ford Bronco in perfect condition. If he wasn't at work or with Sue, he was tinkering under the hood or waxing or just admiring it. Joe and Todd had helped him work on it, and they often talked about its excellent condition.

"Red, take the keys," he said, pushing them into her hand. "We're not going to leave you here without a way to get around."

"Sam, there's no way I can possibly use that truck. What if something happened to it? I'd never be able to forgive myself." She pushed the keys back to him, shaking her head. "Besides, if I need anything, I'll ask Joe to help me out. He won't mind."

"It's just a truck, Red," he said, putting the keys into her hand and closing her fingers over them. "Joe's a great guy, and I'm sure he'd do anything for you, but what if something happened and he couldn't come help you? I want you to use it, in fact, I expect you to use it. If you don't, I'm going to be upset when I get home." He winked at her. FShe took the keys reluctantly.

"Why have you been so nice to me?" she asked softly, looking at him.

"You needed a friend," he said with a simple shrug. "You're like a granddaughter to us now, and we love having you around." She gave him a hug, tears stinging her eyes. "Promise that you'll use the truck; it'd make me proud to have Joe see you in it. He helped me restore it you know."

"He told me about that," Carly said, smiling. "And he enjoyed every minute of it. Thank you Sam." She wiped a tear from her eye. "I thank the Lord for you and Sue every day."

"All right, all right. Enough mush. Let's get to work," he said, turning away abruptly, but not before Carly saw that his eyes were red.

Carly was ready for church early that night. She checked her coat pocket to make sure she still had the envelope, locked the front doors behind her, and set out, putting the key ring in her pocket. She was so engrossed in her thoughts, she didn't hear Joe calling her. He beeped the horn, causing her to jump.

"Where are you going?" Joe said, getting out of the truck and walking toward her.

"Joe!" she said, smiling weakly, her hand on her chest.

"Don't you want a ride?" he asked, taking her hand and leading her back to the truck. He opened the door and helped her in.

"I didn't know if you were going to come here or not, so I wanted to start out and not be late," she said after he got in next to her.

"It's cold and snowy, and you have no boots or gloves. What kind of guy do you think I am? Of course I'm coming to get you, silly!" He looked at her, surprised. "How was your night?" he asked, pulling out and driving slowly toward the church.

"Not too good. Are you getting tired of me telling you all about my troubles?" she asked, giving him a pensive glance.

"No," he said, concerned. "I think of your problems as my problems. What happened?" He pulled into a parking space, shut off the truck, and turned to her.

She told him quickly about what had happened and handed him the envelope, her face grave.

"What's this?" he asked grimly.

"Open it," she said quietly.

He opened the envelope, letting two pictures slide out onto his lap. He picked one up. It was a picture of him and Carly at the diner the night before, laughing. Someone had circled his face, and put an

X over it, with the words, "Better get rid of the farm boy before he gets hurt!" written above his head.

He picked up the next picture. It was a picture of Carly and Ian eating at an expensive restaurant. The same person had drawn a heart around both of them.

"Turn it over," Carly said quietly. The slight tremor in her voice didn't escape his notice.

He turned it over. Someone had written in all capital letters:

YOU'LL ALWAYS BE MINE! I'M COMING TO GET YOU. SEE YOU SOON!

"Do you think Ian slid this under the doors?" he questioned, looking at her uneasily.

"No." She sighed. "I think it was someone Ian sent to scare me. I think if he were here, he would have shown himself by now. He's not the very patient type." She smiled wryly.

"Why would he tell you that he's coming to get you? That doesn't make sense," he said musingly, scratching his chin. "You could just run again."

"He sees you as a threat. Ian hated to see me by other men, especially the handsome ones. That was what my first beating was about." She looked out the window, shivering involuntarily. "So, he probably wants me to run. He'd just have me followed again, and you'd be out of the way."

He put his arm around her shoulders and drew her closer. "Are you cold?"

"No." She smiled up at him. "I was just remembering. We should probably go in now."

"We're okay for a couple of minutes." He refused to let her go. "Carly, why didn't you call me last night?"

She shrugged her shoulders. "I didn't want to seem like an idiot calling you that late. What if it was just a drunk?"

He frowned at her. "But what if whoever it was had broken into the store?" He hugged her tightly. "What if you'd gotten hurt? Don't be so stubborn next time, do you hear?"

"I'm sorry," she said meekly. "I just didn't want to bother you for something that could have been silly." He glared and yanked a piece of her hair.

"Ow!" she said, rubbing her head.

"That's what you get," he said, getting out of the truck.

She got out on her side, opening the door before he could do it for her, smiling at him obstinately. He grabbed her hand and held it tightly, not letting go when she tried to pull it back. They walked in silence to the church door. He stopped, turning her toward him.

"Carly. Promise me that if something like this happens again, you'll call me," he said urgently. "Even if you just have a feeling. I'd rather come and make sure you're okay than to have something happen to you." He took her other hand, his eyes pleading.

"I promise," she said, smiling tenderly at him.

"I worry about you." His expression softened. "And I want you to be safe."

"Guess what?" she said, looking over his shoulder. "Billy Pruit just pulled up. Look." She nodded her head in Billy's direction. He turned and stared, letting go of Carly's hand as Billy came sauntering up to them, a scowl on his face.

"Hi, Billy," she said kindly. "Glad you could make it."

"Yeah, well, I just didn't have nothing else to do tonight," he said moodily.

"Billy," Joe said, holding his hand out to shake. Billy hesitated, took his hand quickly, and let it go as if he'd been burned. He turned toward Carly, dismissing Joe.

"Are you two ready to go in?" she asked nervously, trying to ease the tension between them.

"Yep," Joe answered tersely as Billy pushed between them into the church, making Joe drop Carly's other hand. He glared at Billy's back as Carly grabbed his hand again, smiling anxiously at him.

If there was a difference in the attitude of the church people when they saw Billy Pruit walk inside, it was very slight. They were very friendly to him, shaking hands and trying to make him feel welcome. There were a few stares of disbelief, Angie being one of them, and it was obvious that he felt uncomfortable.

"Hello there, Billy." Sam and Sue came over, shaking his hand kindly and nodding at Joe and Carly. "We're glad you could make it here tonight."

"Red invited me," he said almost defiantly, daring anyone to make fun of him for being there. Carly hoped Sam wouldn't be offended and gave an anxious glance toward Sue.

"Yeah, she told us that. We think it's great you're here," Sam answered mildly. "You're welcome to sit with Sue and me if you want to." Sue nodded, mustering a smile.

"She said I could sit with her," Billy said loudly, jerking his thumb toward Carly. She turned beet red with embarrassment. She saw Angie looking triumphantly at Joe with a smirk on her face as if to say 'I told you so'.

She took a deep breath, squeezed Joe's hand, and said loudly, "I sure did. Joe and I would love to have him sit with us, wouldn't we, Joe?"

"Yep. He's going to sit with us," Joe said politely. Carly looked over at Angie and smiled at her. She turned and stalked to her seat, looking as if she had just eaten a lemon.

Joe led Carly to their usual place next to Todd and Kelly, who were watching them in amazement. Carly and Kelly always sat next to each other in the middle of the bench, but Todd had made her sit at the very end of the pew, making it impossible for anyone but him to sit next to her.

"Go ahead, Billy," Joe offered politely, intending to sit next to Billy himself with Carly safely on his other side.

"I'll sit by her," he said roughly, looking at Carly.

"Okay," she said, smiling sweetly. "You go ahead." Joe glowered at him as he walked past. Carly sat next to Billy, with Joe sitting very close on her other side. He put his arm around her shoulders, pulling her slightly away from Billy. She found the whole situation amusing and grinned brightly up at Joe.

The service went pretty well. The pastor preached a wonderful salvation message, and Carly managed not to glance over at Billy, praying fervently for the Holy Spirit to deal with him instead. She did look over at Joe, who looked grave and serious. He was paying a great deal of attention to the message, and she hoped he was praying for Billy as well. He glanced at her, winked, and pulled her a little more toward him and away from Billy. She felt a little thrill run through her and gave a contented sigh.

As soon as the service was over, and he could get away, Billy shot out of the church like a bullet without a word to anyone.

Angie snorted behind them. "Well, I don't think he liked his first church experience."

Carly turned and glared. "Maybe the Lord was dealing with him," she said hotly, her face burning.

"Oh I'm sorry," she said mockingly, putting her hand to her mouth. "I didn't know he was that important to you. Better watch out, Joe."

"He's so important," Carly said before Joe could respond, "that Jesus died for him, Angie. Maybe you should try to remember that and have a little compassion." She stalked away, leaving Joe, Todd, and Kelly staring after her.

"What's your problem? Why are you so nasty?" Joe asked contemptuously, turning to glare at Angie.

She batted her eyes innocently. "I just don't want to see you hurt again."

"You're just jealous," Kelly said angrily, turning to follow after Carly.

"Jealous? Of Carly?" She laughed derisively after her. "Why would I be jealous of that ugly redhead?" Kelly turned and walked back to her, her face dark red with anger.

"You're jealous of her because she's got something you want," she said quietly, looking over at Joe. "And you know what, I think you'd better get used to seeing them together."

She glared hatefully at her. "What are you talking about?" Kelly shrugged her shoulders as she took Todd's hand and walked away.

Angie turned to Joe, her face red with anger and jealousy. "What's she talking about?"

He looked at her without pity. "That was Kelly's way of telling you that I love Carly and that we're going to be together for a long time."

"Are you going to marry her?"

Joe's face was as dark as Angie's was now pale. "I'm not going to answer that."

"Why not if you love her?" she said spitefully, her face contorted.

"Because I don't want you to know before her," he said quietly, walking away. She stood motionless for a minute, staring after him in dismay.

"Are you still coming over tomorrow morning?" Joe asked, driving Carly home after church.

"Yes." She tried to hide her mischievous smile and looked out her window. "You know the worst thing about you driving me home?"

Pulling into a parking spot, he turned off the truck before answering. "It's too short."

"What do you think Billy thought tonight? Do you think he was offended?"

"I don't know," he said thoughtfully, playing with her hair. "He left so fast, I didn't have a chance to see his face or talk to him."

"That Angie. She makes me so mad. I can't believe she tried to make it sound like I was interested in him. I hope no one took her seriously."

"Everyone knows that she's jealous of you, even if they did hear her, which I doubt."

"Did you take her seriously?" she asked anxiously. "Because if it's going to affect our relationship, I'll avoid him and just pray for him."

"Our relationship? It's about time you admitted we have a relationship," he said, tugging on a piece of her hair lovingly.

She made a face at him. "Well, we don't have to have a relationship if you don't want one," she retorted, scooting away.

"Come back here!" He laughed, pulling her back. "Of course I want a relationship with you, you turkey! Anyway, what I was going to say before you interrupted me,"—she punched his arm— "I'm glad that you had the nerve to invite him to church. But I didn't like how close he sat to you."

"He didn't sit close to me! You kept pulling me away!" Carly giggled.

He laughed heartily. "Well, I had to make sure he didn't put the moves on my girlfriend, didn't I?"

She looked at him with a wicked twinkle in her eyes. "Your girlfriend? You've never asked me to be your girlfriend."

"Don't you think we're too old for all that?"

"Too old?!" She huffed, trying to look offended.

He looked adoringly at her, taking her hands in his. "Yes, too old. 'girlfriend' and 'boyfriend' just seem so high schoolish. Don't you think we're old enough to know what we want?"

Her stomach flipped at the look he gave her. "I don't know what you're talking about."

"I don't want you for my girlfriend," he said quietly, leaning closer to her.

"Oh my. Well. Um, I've got to go," she said uneasily, scooting out of the truck before he could stop her. "Bye! I'll see you tomorrow!" she said as she ran to the door.

"Carly! Come here!"

She pretended not to hear him as she unlocked the door and quickly ran inside. She locked the door behind her, waved, and was gone, leaving him to look after her, astonished.

He watched for the light in her apartment to come on before he started the truck again, thinking about what had just happened. Grinning, he sat for a moment longer, looking at her window, hoping she would look out and wave.

There she was! His heart beat faster. She waved, smiled, and let the curtain fall back into place.

He whistled happily all the way home.

Chapter Sixteen

The alarm went off the next morning at 4:00 a.m. Carly sat up in bed, rubbing her eyes tiredly, wondering why it went off so early. Joe! She jumped up out of bed excitedly, remembering that she was going to surprise him. She showered and dressed quickly, put her hair up, ate an apple turnover that Sue had sent over, and finished getting ready. She put on her coat and shoes, picked up her keys, and ran to meet Kelly at the bed and breakfast.

She locked the doors to the store and started walking. It was bitterly cold out, and she walked fast to keep warm, enjoying the scenery as much as she possibly could. She walked quietly up the porch steps, not wanting to disturb anyone, and peeked in the front window.

Kelly opened the door. "Come in," she said quietly. "I'm almost ready. Is it cold?"

"It's freezing out!" Carly said, shivering, following her into the kitchen.

"Did you have anything to eat? My aunt left us some doughnuts if we want them," Kelly said quietly. "Do you want some coffee?" she asked, sipping from a steaming mug.

"Thank you," Carly whispered gratefully. Kelly handed her a doughnut and poured her a cup of coffee.

Carly looked admiringly around the cozy kitchen. From the blue and white china plates that adorned a huge hutch, the blue gingham-check curtains that dressed each of the windows and the bay window with a table for that two overlooked the flower garden, everything had a homey, country look to it. But what drew her attention, and admiration, the most, was a beautiful fieldstone fireplace that sat in the middle of the room, beckoning to her to sit on its low stone wall and warm herself.

"What a beautiful kitchen!"

"Thank you. I've always liked this kitchen myself. Whenever

you're ready," Kelly said, putting on her coat. Carly swallowed the rest of her coffee, put the cup in the sink, and followed her out to the car.

"Do you think we'll surprise them?" Carly asked, rubbing her hands together as Kelly headed toward the Bairds' farm.

"I think we will. Like I said, Todd doesn't think I can handle getting up before eight in the morning. He'll be shocked to see me up and alert at this hour!" She laughed.

An easy, comfortable conversation made the half-hour drive slip by quickly, and before either of them had run out of things to say they were pulling into the driveway.

"There's a light on in the kitchen," Carly said, disappointed. "I was hoping to catch them off guard."

"We might surprise them yet," Kelly said, turning off the lights before anyone could notice them. She drove the car noiselessly to the barn, and turned the engine off. They shut their doors quietly and, making as little noise as possible, tiptoed softly up the porch steps by the kitchen.

Kelly peered quietly into the bright kitchen window.

"It's Joe!" She motioned for Carly to come look, moving over to give her room.

Joe was wearing a pair of old jeans, no shirt, and standing barefoot at the open refrigerator, drinking milk straight from the carton. His hair wet and tousled, a towel draped across his broad shoulders as if he had just stepped out of the shower.

"That's gonna have to stop," Carly said, laughing softly.

"Oh that's funny." Kelly giggled. "I hope Todd doesn't do that!"

"Shh! Someone else is coming!" They both ducked instinctively. They waited a moment and peered inside again. Joe had sat down at the table, and Todd had shuffled into the kitchen, pajamas flapping, hair stuck out everywhere, eyes half closed, yawning. He opened the door to the refrigerator, pulled out the milk, and to Kelly's dismay, drank right from the carton.

"That's so disgusting," Kelly said, trying unsuccessfully to stop laughing.

Carly snorted and wiped tears from her eyes. "Shh, they're talking. Maybe we can hear them."

"Are you going to let Kelly see you like that?" Joe asked, laughing as Todd shuffled to the table and plopped down.

"I don't have to worry about Kelly. She can't get up out of bed before eight." He grinned sleepily. "You're up early." He laid his head down on his hands.

"I couldn't sleep," Joe said simply, leaning lazily back in his chair.

"Are you going to let Carly see you like that?" Todd asked, yawning. "If you wait much longer, your hair is going to dry like that. You should leave it. She might like the sticking-up-everywhere hairstyle."

"I'm almost ready." He grinned. "Anyway, I guess I won't have to worry about it until about eight. They're riding in together, remember?"

"You stay here and watch their reaction while I knock on the door," Carly said quietly. Kelly nodded, grinning.

Carly tiptoed to the door and knocked softly, watching Kelly. Kelly shook her head. Carly knocked a little louder. She heard a chair scrape across the floor as someone stood up. Kelly came and stood next to her. Joe opened the door slowly, looking out.

"Good morning," Carly and Kelly said cheerily, walking quickly into the room before either of them could get away. Todd saw Kelly, jumped up, and bolted upstairs without saying a word.

"Uh, good morning," Joe said in astonishment, still holding the door open.

Carly giggled. "Nice hair." Kelly doubled over with quiet laughter.

"Thanks," he said, his face turning bright red. "I'll be right back." He slammed the door shut and hurried out of the kitchen, bounding up the stairs, taking two at a time.

"Oh, my side hurts." Kelly gasped, sitting down to the table. "That was worth getting up early for." She wiped tears from her eyes, still laughing quietly.

Carly sat down next to her. "Do you think we surprised them? The look on Todd's face when we walked in was priceless. Looks like you're going to have to keep him away from the milk jug too!" They laughed quietly, waiting for the men to return.

"That was mean," Joe said walking into the kitchen and causing a fresh burst of quiet laughter. He grinned, buttoning the cuffs of his flannel shirt. His hair was still wet, but combed into place, and he had put his socks on. "Do I look better?" he asked, posing in front of Carly.

She looked up at him, her eyes twinkling merrily. "I thought you looked great before."

"Especially with the milk carton stuck to your lips," Kelly said, burying her head in her arms, Carly quietly laughing with her.

"You saw that." Joe grinned sheepishly. "By the way, Kelly. I think you've scarred Todd for life, so he's going to be a while." He pulled up a chair next to Carly and sat down, watching her try to control herself.

"Did we surprise you?" she asked with an impish grin.

"To put it mildly, yes. We were surprised." He chuckled and stared admiringly at Carly, enjoying the brightness of her eyes, and the flush in her cheeks.

"What?" Carly asked, wiping tears from her eyes.

"Sneak."

"Do you want some coffee?" She walked over to the counter to start the coffee, suddenly uncomfortable with his nearness.

"Well, good morning!" Todd said jovially, walking into the kitchen as if nothing had happened. He had showered, shaved, combed his hair, and changed his clothes.

"Wow, that was fast," Joe said, amused. "You just set a new record." He grinned and winked at Kelly. "Usually when he knows you're going to be around, it takes him at least an hour to get ready." He came over to the counter and stood next to Carly on the pretense of helping.

"That's nice." Kelly giggled as Todd gave her a hug. "Are you surprised?"

"Undoubtedly." He grinned, his face flushed. "I thought I had plenty of time, but you proved me wrong."

"You should have seen your face." She laughed. "It was priceless. I wish we had a camera. Carly, don't you?"

"Oh yeah." Carly grinned, looking at the happy couple. She turned to Joe. "Where are the coffee filters?" she asked, agitated by his close presence.

"They're in the cabinet beside the stove," he said mildly, leaning on the counter.

"Could you please get one for me?" Carly asked, flustered, trying to maneuver around him. He was standing in front of the cabinet she needed, in her way on purpose.

"Nope," he said, his eyes twinkling mischievously.

She gave him a withering look and pushed him gently out of her way. "Thank you," she said saucily, getting the filter herself.

"Not a problem. Anything I can do to help you." He leaned back on the counter, making sure he was in her way again. She bustled around him, trying to ignore him. He moved closer and turned off the coffee pot when she wasn't looking.

"Where does your mom keep the coffee grounds?" she asked, filling the pot with water, still not paying him any attention. He leaned over her to open the door where she could find the coffee grounds.

"So..." He leaned closer. "You thought I looked pretty good this morning."

She grinned and caught a whiff of his cologne. "Man," she exclaimed, giving him an intense look. "What kind of cologne do you wear?" She took another deep breath. Joe grinned, moving a little closer. She backed up slightly.

Kelly elbowed Todd in the ribs, nodding significantly at Carly and Joe.

"Do you like it?" he asked playfully.

"I love it." She breathed heavily, blushing. "That's what you wore the first time I came over here."

"Really?" he said softly, brushing a piece of hair from her

forehead. He put his hand on her waist, pulling her a little closer. "I didn't get a good morning hug yet."

She placed a hand on his chest as if to ward him off. "I didn't know you wanted one."

"Yes, you did." He grinned wickedly, pulling her a little closer.

"Good morning!" Tom bellowed, standing behind Todd's chair and grinning at them. Carly jumped away from Joe as if she'd been burned, causing everyone to laugh. They hadn't heard him come in.

Carly turned beet red with embarrassment, barely managing to eke out a reply. "Good morning." She turned away quickly and fumbled with the coffee pot, not looking at anyone, especially Joe. He hadn't moved away when Tom had come in.

"You two sure are early," he said jovially. "Is that coffee ready yet?" he asked, pulling up a chair to the table. Carly turned the coffee pot back on, glancing distractedly at Joe. He was grinning at her. She punched him in the arm, mortified.

"We were here before five thirty," Kelly said proudly. "We sure surprised the guys this morning, didn't we, Carly?"

She mumbled a vague yes, trying to find something to occupy her at the counter so she wouldn't have to face Tom. Joe reached over and took her hand, leading her to the table.

They talked quietly for a little while, waiting for the coffee to brew. Carly grew more comfortable with time, joining in the conversation every once in a while. When the coffee was done, she got up to serve it, Joe getting up to help her.

"Who wants coffee?" Joe asked, reaching beside her to get the cups.

"I would like some," Tom said cheerfully. "But I don't think it's a good idea to have you two over by the counter without a chaperone." He winked at Carly. She turned bright red but laughed good-naturedly, bringing the pot to the table.

"All I wanted was a good morning hug, but she wouldn't give me one," Joe whined, putting the cups on the table.

"Looked more like you were putting the moves on her. Was he bothering you, Carly?" Tom asked, grinning at her red face as he took a sip of hot coffee.

"It didn't look like she minded to me," Todd said, receiving a swift jab in the ribs from Kelly. "Well, it didn't!" He laughed, holding his side.

"Kelly, do you want some coffee?" Carly asked, trying to change the subject. Kelly nodded, handing her a cup. "Todd?" she questioned, holding up the coffee pot.

"No way! That stuff stunts your growth. Just look at Kelly!" he said, earning another jab to the ribs. "I better stop, or my ribs are going to be bruised." He pulled Kelly to him, putting his arm around her shoulders.

"Don't try to change the subject, girl," Joe said, grinning. "You haven't given me a good morning hug yet!"

She smiled playfully at him as she poured his coffee, staying out of his reach. "The best things in life are worth waiting for."

"Ouch!" he said, grabbing his heart as if in pain. "That was cold."

"Well, we'd better get moving." Tom stood up, finishing his coffee in one big gulp. "The cows are getting anxious. Are you girls staying here?" he asked, putting on his coat.

"Nope, we're here to help," Carly said, grabbing her coat.

Joe looked doubtfully at her jeans and thin flannel shirt. "Is that what you're wearing?"

She looked down at her clothes self-consciously. "Yes. It was either these jeans or my jean skirt."

"Wait here a minute," Joe said, running upstairs. He came back quickly, holding some clothes in his hands. "Here, you'll be warmer in these," he said, handing the clothes to her.

"Hey, that's a good idea! I'll be right back," Todd said, going to find some warm clothes for Kelly. "Don't mess these up, these are my favorite pair of overalls." He grinned as Kelly apprehensively took them.

"You two can change in the boys' rooms while I keep them occupied down here," Tom said kindly.

"No!" Both Joe and Todd answered simultaneously. Tom and

the girls looked at them in surprise.

Todd looked at Joe for help, his eyes wide with panic. "Our rooms aren't clean."

"Clean-shmean. They don't care if your rooms are clean or not. All they want to do is change, right?" He turned a questioning eye to Kelly and Carly.

With smiles too wide to be innocent, they answered, "No, we don't mind."

"Just a minute!" Joe bolted up the stairs before anything else could be said. He came sauntering back downstairs a moment later, hands in his pockets.

"That was fast," Tom said, looking at him curiously.

"My room isn't that bad. It's Todd's that's really dirty." He grinned. "Go ahead."

"I gotta see this!" Kelly said, running up the stairs before anyone could stop her. Carly laughed at Todd's horror-stricken face.

"Joe? Where's your room?" she asked politely.

"Upstairs, first door on the right." He smiled, watching her go.

"What was that all about?" Tom asked suspiciously, after they heard Joe's door close.

"What?" they asked, smiling a little too broadly.

Tom folded his arms across his chest and leaned his back on the door, watching them expectantly.

"Did you get it?" Todd asked quietly, holding out his hand. Joe nodded and pulled something out of his pocket, handing it to him with a grin.

Todd put something into his hand. "Look."

Carly looked around at Joe's room curiously. It was a nice-sized room, not too dirty, but not clean. An unmade bed stood under the window, an oak night table beside the bed with a small reading lamp on it, a desk with papers scattered all over, an oak dresser, and a mid-sized closet, with the door standing open.

She laid the clothes on the bed and walked toward the desk curiously. Something caught her eye and she pulled a paper out from underneath a large messy pile. It was her name, written over and over again, filling up both sides of the sheet. She smiled sweetly, putting the paper on top of the desk conspicuously.

She pulled the overalls on over her jeans, rolling up the pant legs so she could walk. Next she pulled on the flannel shirt over the overalls and her shirt, rolling up the sleeves so she could use her hands. She giggled, feeling ridiculous.

"Carly?" Kelly's muffled voice came through the door.

"Come in."

"Is there a mirror in here?" Kelly asked, pushing it open. "Wow, this is a lot cleaner than Todd's room!"

"No mirror." Carly laughed. "How do I look?" She swung around for Kelly to see.

Kelly laughed. "Probably as funny as I look!"

They did look interesting with clothes that were way too big, cuffs rolled up like doughnuts around their ankles and wrists, with tiny feet and hands sticking out. They laughed heartily at each other.

"You ready?" Kelly asked, heading out the door.

"Not yet. I'm going to make Joe's bed for him," Carly said, pulling the sheet and blankets up.

"I should do that for Todd too, but I can't find the bed!" Kelly giggled.

Carly finished tucking and straightening, put the pillows where they should go, and stood up. She took the paper with her name on it and placed it on top of his pillows, where he would be sure to find it.

"I'm ready!" She followed Kelly down the stairs and into the kitchen.

"Oh!" Kelly said softly, stopping so suddenly that Carly ran into her. Surprised, Carly looked over her shoulder in time to see Tom giving both Joe and Todd a tremendous bear hug. Seeing the girls in the doorway, he let them go, and walked outside hurriedly, his face flushed.

"Well, how do we look?" Kelly asked, turning around as she walked toward Todd.

Todd cupped his mouth with his hand and poked Joe in the side with his elbow. "I think a circus has lost their clowns." Kelly put her hands on her hips and frowned.

"You look fantastic," Joe said to Carly as she walked over to him. "In fact, I've never seen my clothes look so good!" He grabbed her and gave her a bear hug. "That's my good morning hug," he said in her ear.

"We better go." She smiled. "The cows are anxious." He let her go reluctantly.

"You can wear this and these." He handed her his work coat, a pair of thick gloves, and a hat. He looked at her tiny feet. "I don't have any boots that will fit you though. It can get pretty cold out there, but you'll warm up in the barn once you get working. If you get cold and can't get warm, let me know." He slipped a coat on, pulled on a hat, tied his boots, and held the door open for her.

They were halfway to the barn when Carly realized something. "Aren't you going to eat anything for breakfast?" she asked, her voice muffled.

"I had a bowl of cereal before you and Kelly got there. I was washing it down with the milk you caught me drinking." He grinned, holding her hand. "Why?"

"Because you're always fussing at me to eat, and I thought I was going to have the chance to fuss back at you." She laughed, swinging his hand.

Todd, Kelly, and Tom were already in the barn when Joe and Carly opened the door. Joe took off his gloves and led her to a small room in the back where they kept supplies.

"What do you want to learn to do first?" he asked, smiling.

"I'll just follow you around, and you can show me what you do," she said, wondering where they would begin.

"Sounds good to me." He led her to a stall with a huge cow inside. He put some feed in the trough, washed her, and sat down on a stool, explaining what he was doing and why. Carly watched fascinated as a stream of warm milk spurted deftly into the pail by Joe's feet.

"Could I try it?" she asked, pulling off her gloves. Joe laughed, allowing her to sit on the stool. He showed her what to do, holding her hands so she could get the feel first. She squeezed. Nothing.

"What did I do wrong?" Carly asked, disappointed.

"Just relax," he said, taking her hands and showing her what to do again. She relaxed, squirting some milk into the pail. She yelped gleefully; Joe laughed heartily.

"Do you think you've got it?" he asked, standing up.

She beamed up at him. "I think I can handle it."

"We've got three more cows to milk, so I'm going to get started on the others. When you're done, just bring the pail over to me, and I'll show you what to do with it." He started to leave.

Carly looked up anxiously. "Wait! How do I know when I'm done?"

"You'll know," he said cryptically, leaving her alone.

Carly continued milking until she thought her arms couldn't possibly do any more, and the milk came slower and slower until finally there wasn't a stream. Thankfully, she patted the cow, stood up, and arched her back. She grabbed the pail and took it to Joe, who was milking a cow in the next stall. Her heart sank. He had filled up two and a half pails with milk while she had done only one. He looked up and smiled.

"Done already?"

"Already? It took me forever!" She laughed, setting her pail next to the others. "Are you almost done?"

"Almost," he said, winking at her. "What'd you think of milking your first cow?"

She stretched, rolling her head to get the kinks out. "It was really neat, but my arms feel tired."

"You'll get used to it." He grinned, finishing. He stood up, took his pail, and reached over to take hers.

"Nope," she stopped him. "I'm going to help," she said,

stubbornly taking her own pail plus another one.

"You're going to be sore," he said playfully, taking the rest. "They're pretty heavy."

"It'll be okay. I wanted to help you, not make you carry all my stuff." She followed him to a small chilly room in the back of the barn. He showed her how to separate the milk from the cream, and where to put the pails when they were finished.

"This is where Mom comes in to make butter and cheese, and where we keep our eggs," he said, putting the pails in a large refrigerator.

"You make your own butter and cheese?" she asked, impressed. "What do you do with it all?"

"Our neighbors buy a lot of it, along with some milk and eggs. It's a good business I suppose. Keeps Mom pretty busy sometimes."

"Where is your mom?" Carly asked wonderingly.

"She doesn't come in here until later. She says it's too cold early in the morning, but I think she just wants to sleep in." He winked, joking.

"Do you think she'd mind if I asked her to show me how to do all that stuff?" Carly asked, following him around like a devoted puppy.

"I don't think she'd mind. She'd probably like the help!"

He showed her around, both of them doing his chores together, as he explained and showed her how to do things. He found her to be an avid learner and enjoyed her enthusiasm about whatever he showed her. It was obvious to him that she tried to please him in everything she did, and she grew confident as he praised her.

"That's it," he said after all the work was done. "You were a big help, thank you."

"Really?" she asked enthusiastically. "That went by fast!"

"There's always less work to be done in the winter," he answered simply.

"What do you usually do when you're done?" She leaned over one of the horse stalls, trying to get Ashes' attention.

"Well," he hesitated, "mostly we work on the equipment for the farm, or on a car someone has asked us to fix. Sometimes neighbors bring their tractors over for us to work on. Sometimes if I have time, I do a little bit of woodworking."

"Are you working on anything now?" she asked, looking around at him.

He gave her a strange look before answering. "I've got a little project I'm working on."

"What is it?" she asked after a little pause, her heart fluttering a little.

"I'll show you later today if you want to see it," he said softly, smiling.

She smiled shyly, looking away. "I'd like that."

"You all done?" Todd asked, walking toward them, holding Kelly's hand.

"Yep," Joe said casually. "Are you?"

"Just got done. Kelly's been a big help!" He hugged her. "I don't think I'm going to let her go now. She knows how to run a farm."

Joe chuckled. "After seeing your room this morning, she may decide she doesn't want you!"

"A woman loves to be needed," Todd said. "And I definitely need someone to clean up after me, right, Kelly?"

"I agree that you need someone to clean up after you." She laughed. "I couldn't even find your bed!"

Todd smiled guiltily. "Job security, my dear, just think of it as job security." She smacked him playfully. "Are you two ready to go in? Maybe Mom's got something for us to eat!" He smacked his lips hungrily, rubbing his stomach.

"We're ready," Joe said, taking Carly's hand. "Where's Dad?"

"He went in about half an hour ago. He said we didn't leave anything for him to do." Todd grinned, pulling Kelly toward the door.

Chapter Seventeen

"That was the best Thanksgiving dinner I've had in a long time!" Carly said later that afternoon, leaning back in her chair contentedly. "Thank you."

"You're welcome and thanks for your help." Penny smiled. "We're glad you could come. Did you do anything special for Thanksgiving with your dad?"

Everyone except Todd was done eating, just relaxing in their chairs talking. Joe leaned back, bringing his chair closer and resting his arm on the back of her chair. He watched her closely, enjoying the flush of her cheeks and the sparkle of her eyes as she talked.

She smiled, glancing at him. "Well, we didn't cook much seeing as how it was just dad and me. Just a turkey and stuffing, mashed potatoes and biscuits. That was pretty much it. Then we'd spend the day watching a movie or playing a board game. He had only two days off a year, Thanksgiving and Christmas, but we sure did enjoy them."

"Who did the cooking?" Todd asked, finally done eating.

"It was Dad at first after Mom died, but I always helped in the kitchen, so I took over the cooking when he thought he could trust me to run the stove and oven." She grinned. "I started doing all the cooking when we moved out to Houston. Dad worked all the time, so I had to learn really fast."

"I thought you didn't know how to cook," Joe said, leaning up to see her face.

"I know how to cook; it's just that lately I've just been cooking macaroni and cheese." She laughed, looking at Kelly.

"You should try some," Kelly said cheerily. "It's the best I've ever tasted, and that's saying a lot. I'm difficult to please when it comes to macaroni and cheese!"

"You cooked for Kelly?" Joe asked, surprised. "I'm jealous. You haven't cooked for me yet."

"Yes, she did," Penny said gaily. "She cooked the sweet potatoes and took care of all the mashed potatoes for me. This was the easiest Thanksgiving I've ever had! I couldn't have done it without you, Carly." She smiled warmly.

"Oh no, you had it almost finished when we came in."

"Did Kelly cook anything?" Todd asked, a wary look on his handsome face.

Penny laughed good-naturedly. "She watched the pies and set the table."

"I told you I wasn't a good cook." Kelly laughed, looking at Carly. "I try really hard, but I'm just no good at it."

"So when do I get to try some of your famous macaroni and cheese?" Joe asked.

"Oh, I don't know, maybe never. I've had it almost every day for about two years, and I'm getting a little tired of it. Especially after eating your mom's and Sue's good cooking. They've spoiled me!"

"Speaking of Sue, Sam told me that they were going to be gone until after the New Year. What are you going to do while they're gone?" Tom asked lazily, rubbing his stomach.

"I really don't know. I thought I'd wax the floors, straighten the shelves, dust, and just try to keep myself busy. I really hadn't thought too much about it though," she said thoughtfully, picking at her napkin.

"You were such a good help here this morning, you could always come out and help us. I'm sure Joe wouldn't mind," Tom said, watching for her reaction.

She blushed. "I'd be glad to help. I was wondering if Penny could teach me how to make butter and cheese."

"Nothing to it. I'd love to show you. Why don't you come on out while Sue and Sam are gone. We'll find lots for you to do."

"I wouldn't want to be a bother though," Carly said awkwardly, not sure if they really wanted her to come out or were just being nice.

"You wouldn't be a bother," Joe said quickly, grinning widely at her.

"All right. I'd like that." She looked at Joe warmly, not dropping her gaze.

"Well, let's clean up, and we can go in and sit by the fireplace and talk," Penny said, getting up to clear off the table. They all got up to help her, taking the food and dishes to the counter to be cleaned off and washed.

"I'll do the washing," Joe said, pulling Carly's arm.

Penny laughed, knowing what he was up to. "Oh no, I don't want another episode like the last time! I'll wash, Carly can dry, and you can put them away. Todd, would you and Kelly mind clearing off the rest of the table and sweeping the floor?"

"Sure thing, Mom," Todd said for them both.

They cleaned up the kitchen quickly with no messes, only slight attempts from Joe to get Carly's attention. After they were finished and the kitchen tidy again, they went into the living room by the fireplace.

"Carly, we have a tradition here for Thanksgiving," Penny began as soon as they were all seated. "After dinner, we always come in here and tell what we're thankful for. Kelly, you did this with us last year, so you know how it goes. Whose turn is it to start first?"

"I went first last year," Joe said quickly, taking Carly's hand in his. "So, I think it's Dad's turn this year."

"Are you sure?" Tom asked sleepily. "I suppose it is. Okay, let me see. What am I thankful for?" He rubbed his chin, thoughtfully. "I'm thankful for a lot of things. First, my salvation. I praise the Lord every day for saving me. Next, I'm thankful for my beautiful wife, who is also my soul mate. I couldn't live without you." He gave her a kiss. "Then there's my two boys. I'm proud of you both, and I'm thankful that you love the Lord and are willing to serve him. Now, I'm thankful that my turn is over so I can go to sleep!" He laughed as Penny playfully punched him on the arm.

"Don't go to sleep until you hear what we're all thankful for," she admonished. "It's my turn. I'm thankful for my salvation too, of course. And I'm thankful for my wonderful husband and my two fantastic boys, who have grown into fine young men." Todd bowed self-importantly. "And now, I'm thankful to have gotten to know two of the most amazing young women God could have brought into our lives." She smiled kindly at Carly and Kelly. "Todd, I do believe it's your turn."

"Okay." He moaned playfully. He sat on the floor in front of Kelly's chair, his back leaning on her knees. "I'm thankful for my Christian parents, who loved me enough to teach me the difference between right and wrong, and who led me to the Lord. I'm thankful that when I asked Jesus to forgive me of my sins, he did. I'm thankful for my big brother, who has borne with me through thick and thin, and who has always done everything with me"—he nodded meaningfully at Joe—"and"—he turned toward Kelly—"I would be extremely thankful right now if this beautiful young woman would consent to be my wife." Kelly gasped, her hand on her chest.

He knelt on his knees, pulled a velvet pouch out of his pocket, and handed it to her. "Kelly, I love you with all my heart and soul, and I want to spend the rest of my life with you."

Kelly was speechless, tears welling up in her eyes. She picked up the pouch and dropped it, her hands shaking. Todd took it from her and pulled out a diamond ring, taking her left hand in his.

"Will you marry me?" he asked quietly. She nodded immediately, still not able to talk. Todd put the ring on her finger tenderly. She threw her arms around him, laughing and crying at the same time.

Carly glanced over at Tom and Penny, who were both smiling, but teary eyed. Tom pulled Penny close and gave her a tremendous hug, kissing her soundly on the lips. Carly wiped tears from her eyes, overjoyed for her friend.

"Kelly, I think you should probably go next," Joe said quietly, grinning broadly.

Kelly sniffed, wiped her eyes, and said, "I'm thankful for everything!" More tears. "Especially that he finally got around to asking me! When did you get this?" she asked, looking at the beautiful ring.

"Remember when we went to Billings to the mall with Joe and Carly?" he said, nodding toward them. "I got sick and had to go to the bathroom? Well, I did go to the bathroom, but I stopped at a little jewelry store first."

Kelly hugged him again. "You sneak!"

"Me? Sneak? Who was it sneaking around the porch this morning, Joe?" he asked with a hearty laugh. "And by the way. You all are witnesses that she said she would marry me, even after she saw my room!" They laughed, congratulating the happy young couple.

"Joe, it's your turn," Todd said, grinning.

"That one is going to be hard to beat, little brother," Joe said, smiling happily. "Let me see. I'm thankful that Jesus saved me as well and gave me two of the best parents a kid could possibly have. I love you, Mom and Dad. Don't faint. I know I don't say it enough, but I really do love you both, and I appreciate all you've done for me." He paused and cleared his throat.

"I'm tremendously thankful that God didn't allow me to marry Amy, which would have been the biggest mistake of my life. I'm thankful that he brought Carly into my life, and I don't intend to let her get away from me." He squeezed her hand tightly. She smiled gently and rubbed his hand with her fingers. Todd looked at him a little perplexed but didn't say anything.

"It's your turn, Carly," Tom said kindly.

"I've got so much to be thankful for, I don't know where to start," she said softly, feeling a little out of place. "I'm thankful that for the first time in quite a few years, I've been able to have a real Thanksgiving dinner with people that I care deeply for. I'm thankful for my salvation, just like all of you, and I'm thankful that God has taken care of my every need, and led me to this little town, where I could meet you all. He's given me some of the best friends I could ever wish for, which I haven't had since my dad died, and"—she paused, taking a deep breath—"I'm very thankful for you letting me milk your cow!" They all laughed heartily.

"Anyone want to watch a movie?" Todd asked, wanting a reason to cuddle with Kelly when they were done.

"Sure!" Tom and Penny said merrily. "Joe, Carly, what do you want to watch?"

"Well, I thought Carly and I would exercise some of the horses for a little bit if she wants to." Joe gave her a hopeful look.

"Why not just let them out in the pasture for a little while," Penny said helpfully. Tom cleared his throat, trying to get her attention. "Besides—"

Tom squeezed her hand, smiling. "Let them go, dear. They'll be back soon."

"Oh." She looked at him, confused. "Okay, have fun."

"I want to show Carly the project I've been working on before it gets dark," Joe said gently, hoping to ease his mom's bewilderment. "We'll be back." He led Carly out by the hand.

"Project?" Penny asked after they left. "What project?"

Todd and Tom smiled knowingly at her, Tom squeezing her to him.

"Oh! That project!" She smiled, relaxing considerably.

Joe and Carly rode in comfortable silence for a little while, listening to the snow crunching under the horse's hooves.

"I want to show you this place first," he said, leading her up an old, overgrown driveway she'd never noticed before.

"What a neat place!" she exclaimed as they came to an old but well kept, two-story farmhouse in the middle of a pine clearing.

"This is Todd and Kelly's place," Joe said confidentially, reining in his horse so she could look around.

"Todd's?" Carly asked, looking at him questioningly.

"It used to be my grandparents' house. When Grandpa died, he left it to my dad along with all the property he owned. When Todd turned twenty-one, Dad split all the property he had three ways, giving one piece to Todd, and one to me, letting us choose which we wanted," he explained, walking his horse around the place. Carly followed. "Dad, of course, kept the place he's got now, Todd really wanted this one, because of Kelly I assume, and I took the piece of property on the other side of Mom and Dad's."

"Oh," Carly said thoughtfully, admiring the beautiful old house. "It's in pretty good shape."

"We've kept it up pretty well, and we've remodeled a few things inside that Todd wanted done. All it needs now is a good painting, and it's ready to live in."

She could just imagine how it would look after Todd and Kelly were married. The picket fence painted white to match the house, flowers blooming profusely in the flowerbeds along the front, two rocking chairs looking inviting on the front porch.

"You're awfully quiet," Joe said softly, turning to go. He looked at her compassionately, walking next to her back to the road.

"I was just imagining what it's going to look like when they're living here," she said sadly. "I'm happy for them, but it's kind of bittersweet, you know?"

"What do you mean?" he asked, going back the way they had come. They had passed his parents house before she continued.

"Things just won't be the same," she said sadly. "They'll be married, and Kelly and I won't be able to visit like we do now, nothing against Todd, of course," she added quickly with a quick smile.

"And you feel a little alone," he said, understanding what she was feeling. She nodded slightly. "When he asked her to marry him today, it brought back all kinds of memories of Amy and me. And," he said slowly, "I suppose it did the same for you with Ian."

"Yes," she said quietly, looking ahead of her. "Do you miss Amy?" She couldn't help asking, her curiosity burning.

"Miss Amy?" He laughed incredulously. "Why would I miss her? She was awful. I couldn't possibly miss her. You don't have anything to worry about with her. Why? Do you miss Ian?" he asked, glancing at her sideways. "He could afford to give you everything."

"If I missed Ian, I could go back to him anytime I wanted to." She smiled wryly. "And I don't want everything, never did."

They were silent as Joe led them down a tractor path lined by trees on both sides.

"Here we are," he said, coming into a gently sloping meadow, mountains towering big and black in the setting sun.

Carly caught her breath, looking around her in amazement. "This is gorgeous," she said quietly, gazing at the scenery.

"There's more," he said, walking his horse toward the back of the meadow.

Just inside the tree line, Carly saw an unfinished house emerge. "Is this the project you've been working on?" she asked breathlessly, awed by the beauty of the scene before her.

"Yep. This is it." He slid off his horse, tying the reins to a tree. He helped her down, tied her horse next to his, and took her hand protectively, leading her toward the house.

It was much more than a foundation now. The outside walls and roof were done, the porch and front steps almost finished. He had already put in the windows and front door. She looked at him in amazement.

"This is the one you were building for Amy," she said with a pang of envy. "She was a stupid woman," she said softly, looking steadily at him.

His face lit up with hope.

"It was just a foundation when I showed it to Amy," he said, leading her up the front steps. "I stopped working on it for a while because I didn't have any hopes or dreams," he said, turning to her. "But when I met you, I came alive again. I knew that God had meant you for me, and I started building again. Dad and Todd have helped me a lot, and it'll be done soon. I've just got to do the inside and finish some things outside."

"You've been busy," she said, her heart beating madly, butterflies in her stomach.

"Do you want to see the inside?" he asked softly, pulling her

187

after him. He unlocked the door, stepped aside to let her in, and followed after her. He left the door open behind them to let in some of the remaining light.

"This is the living room," he said, pointing to his left. "That frame on the floor there is going to be the fireplace. It's going to separate the kitchen from the living room, and it'll be open on all four sides so we can enjoy it everywhere."

Her heart skipped a beat at the word 'we.'

"Over here to my right, is going to be the master bedroom and bathroom, two more bedrooms will be down on the other end of the house, and the guest bathroom will be right here." He stopped, pointing each of the rooms out for her to envision.

"Well? What do you think?" he asked, heart in his eyes.

She looked down at her feet, not meeting his gaze. "What can I say?" she said, shrugging her shoulders. "I think Amy was the stupidest woman in the world."

"Is it too close to my parents?"

"Too close?" She remembered that was one argument he'd had with Amy. She smiled gently. "No, it's not too close."

"Does that mean you like it?" he asked quietly, walking toward her.

"Do you want me to like it?" she said shyly as he took her in his arms.

"No." He paused, kissing her forehead. "I want you to love it." He kissed her cheek. "In fact, I want you to want it." He kissed her other cheek.

"Why do you want me to want it?" she asked, breathing fast.

"Because I want to give it to you," he whispered, pulling her to him tighter. He kissed her right hand. "I love you with all my heart, Carly." He kissed her right palm. "I'm asking you to be my wife." He looked at her keenly. "Will you?"

"Can I think about it?" she asked slyly, relishing the power she had over him.

He grinned, his eyes flashing. "No."

"Yes!" she threw her arms around him and hugged him fiercly.

He stepped back slightly and slipped a diamond ring on her finger. "I know it's not much…" he began.

"I don't want to hear it," she said lovingly, gazing at the ring. "I love you more than words can say, Joe. I just want you." She threw her arms around his neck, laughing.

He pulled her close, kissing her on the mouth, taking her by surprise. He stepped back, passion smoldering in his eyes. She looked at him, touching her mouth where his kiss still burned.

"I'm sorry," he said thickly, afraid that he had offended her.

"No. It just took me by surprise, that's all." She smiled, placed her hands on his cheeks, brought his face down to hers, and kissed him boldly on the lips.

He let out a whoop of excitement, picked her up, and swung her around as if she weighed nothing. He set her down gently, kissing her again.

"I hope you'll marry me soon," he said seriously, still holding her fast. "I can't take too many of those." He kissed her again. "I love you."

"I love you too," she said, resting her head on his chest. They stood for a moment, savoring the newness of their relationship, confident in each other's love and affection.

"Let's go back and tell everybody," Joe whispered in her ear.

"I don't think we should," Carly said anxiously. Joe stepped away, perplexed. "It's Todd and Kelly's day. We can tell them another time," she said hurriedly, trying to soothe his fears.

"Todd and Kelly's day?" Joe smiled, visibly relieved. "Todd wanted me to ask you after he asked Kelly, but I needed to show you this place first. I wanted to know if you'd like it."

"I love it, just like I love you." She smiled. "Truthfully, I'm glad Amy's so stupid, or I wouldn't have had a chance!"

"I thank God every day for taking her away from me." He gave her an affectionate kiss. "Let's get married tomorrow," he said mischievously, grinning.

She laughed, delighted. "Tomorrow! You sure don't give a girl much time! Where would we live?"

"Nuts," he said with a gloomy look. "If I work on this place every day from now until Christmas, will you marry me on New Year's?"

"I'll marry you when it's time, Joe Baird!" She laughed, kissing him happily.

"What's that supposed to mean?" he asked, following her out of the house. He locked the door behind them and helped her up onto her horse.

She looked down at him, her eyes twinkling merrily. "That means when the time is ready, we'll get married!"

"Let's get one thing straight right now, Carly Richards," he took her reins so she couldn't start without him. "I'm not going to wait four or five months to marry you."

"Really. And what do you think you're going to do to change my mind?"

He swung up onto his horse easily, still holding her reins. "I'll kidnap you and force you to marry me!" he said triumphantly, relinquishing the reins.

"What if I refuse to say 'I do'?"

"You won't," he said confidently, leading the way back to the house.

They teased and taunted and finally talked about their future together, walking the horses very slowly, not wanting it to end.

"Thank you, Joe," Carly said as they finally came up onto the porch together.

"Why are you thanking me?" he asked in surprise.

"Because you love me."

"I love you so much it hurts," he said, kissing her earnestly.

Suddenly, the porch light came on and the door was thrown open wide. Todd, Kelly, Tom, and Penny were all there staring at them knowingly.

"Uh huh," Todd said, nodding his head. "I told you they were back." He grinned wickedly at them.

"I tell you, you've got to watch those two," Tom said. "If he isn't putting the moves on her in the kitchen by the counter, he's out here on the porch!"

"Joe! What are you doing?" Penny asked sharply, pretending to be upset.

Joe pulled Carly close to him, his arm around her shoulders. "Mom, Dad, I'd like to introduce your future daughter-in-law to you," he said, showing them Carly's ring finger, grinning from ear to ear.

"Oh my goodness!" Penny said, coming out onto the porch and giving Carly a tremendous hug. "I'm so happy for you both!" She wiped a tear from her eye. "But you know what, I knew the first time I saw you two together that God intended you for each other."

"Congratulations, Son," Tom said, clapping him on the shoulder.

"I thought you were going to ask her after I asked Kelly," Todd said, tousling his hair. "Chicken!" Joe punched him playfully in the stomach.

"Carly, this is so wonderful!" Kelly said, giving her a hug.

"Are you sure?" Carly asked, looking doubtfully at her. "I didn't want you to feel badly because it's really your day."

"Nonsense! It's our day, and I'm thrilled to share it with you!" She hugged her effusively, rubbing her back. "What could be better than your fiancé's brother asking your best friend to marry him? It's wonderful!" She giggled, taking Todd's hand.

"Well, Ma," Tom said, his voice booming over the rest of them, "what do you have to celebrate with?"

"Just the thing. Pumpkin, apple, and lemon meringue!" She laughed merrily.

"Oh yeah!" Todd said enthusiastically, rubbing his stomach. "I'm starving!"

"Did Joe show you the house?" Tom asked with a smile, sitting down to the table as Penny served everyone pie.

Carly beamed, looking adoringly at Joe. "Yes, he did."

"What do you think of it?"

"I think it's the most beautiful house I've ever seen."

"You're just biased," Todd said, helping himself to another

piece of pumpkin pie. "She's just saying that to make Joe feel good."

Carly grinned. "I *am* biased." Joe looked up, startled. "I'm biased because I think Joe's the greatest, and I think you all have done a wonderful job." Joe squeezed her hand lovingly.

"Did he tell you that was the house he was building for Amy?" Todd asked, regretting the words as soon as they left his mouth. "I'm sorry. I didn't mean anything by it," he apologized quickly, shaking his head. Joe frowned at him.

"Yes, he did." Carly smiled, understanding that Todd had meant it to be a joke. "And I told him that I was thankful."

Kelly looked at her, surprised. "Thankful? I don't understand why you would be thankful for that."

"I'm thankful that Amy was so stupid." She looked steadily at Joe. "Stupid that she rejected that house, and stupid that she threw a man as wonderful as Joe away." He relaxed perceptibly, but still frowned slightly at Todd.

"To tell you the truth, Carly," Penny began. "I'm quite thankful for those same things! But I'm even more thankful now that he's got a girl like you." She smiled sweetly. "And I'm thankful that Todd has finally asked you to marry him, Kelly. He's made us wait too long!" Kelly nodded her head in agreement.

Todd tried to look hurt. "Too long? It hasn't been too long! I've intended to marry her for a long time. I was just waiting for Joe to catch up. I didn't want to leave him behind you know. He'd miss me too much!" Joe threw his napkin at Todd, while the others laughed.

They talked companionably for the rest of the evening, laughing and teasing one another until they were interrupted by an enormous yawn from Kelly.

"Oh my goodness," she apologized. "I hate to admit it, but I'm really tired!" She rested her head in her arms.

"Are you ready to go?" Carly asked, trying to hide her yawn.

"I saw that," Joe said, teasing.

She smacked him on the arm playfully. "I don't know what you're talking about."

"I'm ready to go if you are," Kelly said, dragging herself out of her chair. "I've got to go to work tomorrow. This time of year is one of the busiest for us," she said, yawning again.

Todd laughed, walking with her to get her coat. "I don't think I should let you drive."

"I'll drive if she's too tired," Carly said, setting her dirty plate in the sink. "Thank you for a wonderful Thanksgiving dinner, Penny." She gave her a huge hug and shook Tom's hand. "Thank you both for everything. I really enjoyed myself."

"Well, of course you did!" Tom said jovially, winking meaningfully at her and Joe. "We're glad you could come, and we're especially glad that you're going to be part of our family. How long are we going to have to wait for the weddings?"

"Not long!" both boys answered at the same time, making everyone laugh.

"What do you think of that, Kelly?" Penny asked merrily, giving her a hug as well.

"Sounds good to me!" She took Todd's arm.

"How about you, Carly?" Tom asked, eyes twinkling.

Carly shrugged her shoulders nonchalantly in an effort to irritate Joe. "Oh, I don't know, I was thinking about a year from now."

"A year from now?" Joe said hotly, pulling her to him. "I'm not waiting that long! I'll kidnap you and make you elope before a year's through!"

"I was just joking." Carly laughed, trying to breathe.

"I'm not waiting longer than three months at the most," he said, looking stubbornly at her.

"But where will we live?" she asked coyly, batting her eyes at him.

"She's got a point, Joe," Penny said. "You've got to have somewhere to live when you get married. You can't live with us. Two women in one kitchen never works." She winked at Carly, making her laugh.

"I'll start working on the house non-stop after my work here is done, and I'll have it close to being finished when we're married."

"Non-stop?" Carly said in mock disappointment. "That means I'll never see you. How will I remember what you look like? What if I marry the wrong guy by mistake?"

"You better watch out, or we're going to have a Christmas Eve wedding," he said good-naturedly, giving her a kiss on her cheek.

"Well, I guess I better hush up. Good-bye!" she said, shrugging on her coat as Joe walked her out the door with Todd and Kelly.

Penny followed them out onto the porch. "Oh, Carly! If you really want to learn how to make butter and cheese, come by Saturday, and I'll show you."

"Okay, sounds great. What time do you want me here?" Carly asked, opening the door to the car. Kelly was already in saying a quiet good-bye to Todd.

"I can come get you before I do my chores!" Joe said hopefully.

"No way. If I came to help you with chores again, you'll be spoiled and expect me to come help every day." Carly said saucily, giving him a hug.

Penny stomped her feet and hugged herself to keep warm in the frigid air. "Why don't you come by around ten? That's usually the time I start."

"I'll see you Saturday at ten then," Carly said, closing the car door behind her and giving Joe a lingering final kiss good-bye through the open window.

"We're down to three weeks," he said softly, laughing.

"I love you, Joe Baird."

He jogged a little way beside the car as they drove down the drive. "I love you too, Carly Richards! Be careful and call me if you need anything."

Chapter Eighteen

Carly woke up early Saturday morning, stretched happily, and admired her ring. She'd slept more peacefully than she had in a long time.

Carly Baird.

It just didn't seem possible. She didn't deserve him, but she loved him and he loved her. God had brought them together, and somehow she knew God would keep them together.

She showered and dressed lazily, having quite a bit of time before she had to leave to go to Joe's house. She ate some of Sue's delicious leftovers that she had sent over for her, reading her Bible as she ate.

Lord, she prayed silently. *I love you and thank you for Joe. He's wonderful. Thank you for bringing me here to meet him. Please keep us safe from Ian, and keep him safe as he does all that he needs to do today.*

She sighed happily, cleaned up after breakfast, and decided to go and check on Sam and Sue's place early. She was just putting on her coat when the phone rang downstairs. She ran to get it.

"Hello?" she asked breathlessly, leaning on the counter.

"Happy Thanksgiving, Carly," Ian said, his voice icy.

"Thanks," she said flatly, disappointed.

"Not much of a greeting," Ian said, irritated. "I was calling to be nice, and you can't even be polite."

"Happy Thanksgiving, Ian," Carly said unenthusiastically. "Is there something that you needed? I've got somewhere to go."

"I need you, of course. Where were you Thursday? I tried to call all day, and no one answered," he said evenly as shivers went down Carly's spine.

She knew that tone. He always used that tone when he was really angry with her for something. She'd have to be careful.

"I was with some friends."

"With that farm boy again, I presume," he said coldly. "I thought I told you to stay away from him."

Wearily, she sat down on the floor and hugged her knees. "Ian, what will it take for you to realize that we are no longer together, that I don't want to marry you, and that I want you to leave me alone?"

"What will it take to convince you that I want you to come home?" he asked edgily.

"I'm not coming back," she said softly. "It's over, Ian. Please. Just let it go."

"I'm not going to let you go." He was silent for a moment. "Carly," he said gently. "Remember when we were first engaged?"

Silence.

"I haven't forgotten our conversation. I remember you telling me that you wanted to go to the Bahamas for our honeymoon. Do you remember?"

Carly closed her eyes, chilled to the bone.

"I want to take you there," he went on gently. "Come home, and we'll leave right away."

"Are you telling me that you're sorry for all the things you've done to me?" she asked scornfully, knowing that he was just trying to buy her.

"I haven't done anything to you that you haven't deserved," he said, not quite as calmly as before. "Look at what you're doing to me now. You're costing me a lot of money."

"I know how to save you some money," she said bitterly. "You can call off all those people you hired to find me and harass me. I'm sure that'll save you a lot."

"You will be home with me by the New Year, even if I have to come there to get you myself. You will not belong to anyone but me, and you might want to remember that and stay away from your little farm boy before he gets hurt. Do you understand me?" She could imagine the spittle flying from his pursed lips as he shouted into the phone.

"Don't you even think of bringing him into this mess!" Carly said, her voice rising. "He has nothing to do with this!"

"Really," he said, dangerously calm. "I think I've just hit a nerve. I'm not the one who brought him into this, remember? You did when you went out with him the first time. How much do you care for him, Carly?"

Silence.

"Do you love him, Carly?" he asked, agitated.

More silence.

"Answer me!" he said through gritted teeth, making her jump.

"Please," she begged, dangerously close to tears. Crying was the last thing she wanted him to hear as it would only please him. "Please, Ian. Just leave me alone."

"You belong to me! If you get involved with him anymore than you already are, you will regret it!"

"Do you know why I left, Ian? I was tired of being bullied and beaten by you. And now that I'm free, I'm not going to let you tell me who I can and cannot be with. You don't own me, you aren't my husband, and I'm not going to listen to you. Do you understand what I'm saying? I'm not going to be your little robot anymore, and I'm not leaving here!"

He sneered contemptuously. "Can he give you all the things I can give you? Can he afford to take you to the Bahamas or anywhere for that matter? Can he give you the cars, money, clothes, and homes I can?"

"No, he can't," she said softly. "And I'm happier now than I ever was with you."

"What can he give you that I can't?" Ian asked coldly.

"Love," she whispered. "He can give me the one thing you never could. Love."

"Love?" he asked scornfully. "I loved you and I still do. I'm not going to let you throw yourself away like this, Carly."

"You don't have to call me anymore, Ian."

"Wait!" he said quickly before she could hang up. "All right. Maybe there were a few times I was a little too hard on you, and maybe things moved too fast after your dad died, but we can make this work, Carly, I know we can. Give us another try," he said, changing tactics.

"It's too late. I don't want to give us another try. We're over. Please don't call me again."

She could just imagine his furious countenance as he bellowed into the phone. "You and I are not over! I will come and get you, and bring you back!"

She hung up in the middle of his tirade, shaking. She sat on the floor for a little while, calming her nerves. The phone rang. She didn't pick it up, knowing it was Ian. Instead, she got up, buttoned her coat, grabbed her keys, and headed out the door, the phone still ringing insistently behind her.

She walked to Sam and Sue's house quickly, thinking of her conversation with Ian. Would he hurt Joe? Would he really come up there and force her to go back? She shuddered at the thought. She had been afraid to talk to him so boldly after he'd beaten her when she'd confronted him about the other women. She trembled to think what he might do to them both if he came to get her. He didn't forgive and forget. She knew that she'd hear from him again and was worried that it might be face to face.

She watered Sue's plants quickly, checked for any messages, and locked the doors behind her, walking tentatively to the garage, unsure if she should drive the truck or not.

Sam had insisted and made her promise that she would drive it, but she was still nervous. She wouldn't be able to forgive herself if something happened to it while they were gone. She opened the garage door, got inside the cozy truck, and turned the key, wincing.

The truck roared into life, seemingly anxious to get out onto the road. She eased it out of the garage, closed the door, and carefully headed out toward Joe's. She became more confident as she drove, taking extra precautions not to damage it.

She drove into their driveway at exactly ten and parked next to Joe's truck, thrilled to see Joe coming out of the barn to meet her.

"Good morning!" He kissed her. "Sam let you drive his truck? He must really like you." He grinned, checking out the truck admiringly. "That's a nice piece of work there, but I've got to admit, you sure do make it look a lot better!"

She smiled wanly, taking comfort from his hug. "Good morning. I'm so glad to see you."

"I missed you," he said softly into her hair.

"Guess what I got this morning?" she asked, stepping back to look up at him.

He smiled lazily. "What?"

"I got a phone call," she said grimly. "From Ian."

"What did he have to say?" he asked, his face tight with concern.

"He told me to stay away from you again, and he asked me if I love you."

"What did you say?"

"I told him that I wasn't going to be pushed around anymore and that he could stop calling me. But I didn't tell him that we're going to get married," she said awkwardly.

"Why didn't you tell him? Maybe he would have left you alone," he asked, upset.

"I didn't tell him because I was afraid that he'd come here and try to hurt you," she said, noticing Joe's hurt expression.

"Ah." He nodded his head knowingly, refusing to meet her gaze. "I see. Well, Mom's over there in the cheese room as we call it, waiting for you." He cleared his throat. "I've got to finish my work here, so I'll see you later." He walked away quickly.

She followed after him, catching his arm and turning him around to look at her. "Are you mad?"

"Why would I be mad?" he said evasively, shrugging off her hand and walking into the barn. She followed him, grabbing his hand tightly.

"Will you talk to me?" she pleaded. Tom and Todd turned to look at them in surprise. "I can't fix it if you don't talk to me," she said, fighting back tears.

"Okay," he said, nodding his head impatiently. "Why didn't you tell him we were getting married? Are you ashamed that I can't afford to buy you everything he could?" His face was red with jealousy and anger.

Penny came out of her room, wondering what the commotion was all about.

She lowered her voice, embarrassed that his family was watching them argue. "I told you why I didn't tell him. And I don't want all those things he gave me. I want you. That's it. Nothing else."

Joe looked at her silently, unconvinced.

"I just don't want him to hurt you," she said, tears starting to streak down her face. "I want you to be happy. I'll do anything to make you happy." She looked at his family, watching them silently. "Do you want me to leave?" she asked sadly, wiping her tears away, afraid he would want her to go.

"I don't want you to be ashamed of me!" he said fiercely.

"How could I ever be ashamed of you? I love you, Joe," she said as he turned away.

She looked at Penny helplessly. "I'm sorry, Penny. I can't stay and help." She turned away, her voice breaking.

"Nonsense!" Penny said, taking her hand quickly. "You came to help me, and I'm not letting you leave." She cast a bewildered look at Tom, ignoring Joe completely. She led Carly to the back room and closed the door quietly behind them.

"You can sit here until you feel better," Penny said kindly, offering her a chair. She busied herself, giving Carly time to calm down.

She covered her mouth and sobbed involuntarily, feeling as if her heart would break. Penny hugged her fiercely, rubbing her back and rocking her gently.

"Shh," she whispered comfortingly. "It's okay. It'll all turn out right. He'll come to his senses. He may get upset quick, but he's even quicker to forgive. He doesn't hold grudges. Shh."

She looked at her desperately, anguish written across her face. "It's all my fault. What if he doesn't want me anymore?"

"Joe? Not want you?" Penny smiled incredulously. "Joe

wouldn't throw you away if his life depended on it. Anyway, if he stopped loving you because of a misunderstanding, then it wasn't worth much. You just give him some time to think about things. Right now he's jealous and hurt, and if I don't miss my guess, he's more afraid of losing you!" She smiled comfortingly.

Carly sighed, wiping her eyes. "I love him so much, Penny. I don't want to lose him for anything or anybody. Especially Ian."

"You won't. Trust me," Penny said, tying her apron and handing one to Carly. "Here, you're going to need this."

"Thank you, Penny," she said with a small smile as she tied her apron around her waist. "I feel better."

Penny hugged her again, smiling. "Hey, what are future mothers-in-law for?"

They worked well together, Penny explaining what she was doing and what Carly needed to do. They finished quickly, enjoying the time they spent together.

"That seemed to go by quick," Penny said, her face flushed. She sat down, fanning herself.

"Are you okay?" Carly asked, concerned.

She leaned over in her chair and grimaced. "I don't feel too well."

"I'll help you to the house." Carly helped her up, wrapped her in her coat, and led her out of the room. She looked hastily for Joe or the others. Not finding anyone, she helped Penny to the house, holding her securely so she wouldn't fall.

"Where do you want to go?" Carly asked, taking her inside the kitchen. She sat her down in a chair, helping her off with her coat and boots.

"I'll just go lie down on the couch," Penny said weakly, trying to stand up on her own. "On second thought," she whispered, holding her stomach. "I think I need to go to our bedroom. I think I need to rest for a while."

Carly led her into her bedroom and helped her lie down.

"Is there anything I can do for you?" she asked anxiously, sitting on the edge of the bed.

"Will you make the men's lunch? I was just going to make sandwiches from leftovers."

"I would love to. Don't worry about a thing. If you need anything, let me know." Penny nodded feebly.

Carly went to the kitchen to prepare lunch. She was just finishing up when Tom and Todd came in, stamping their feet and rubbing their hands expectantly.

"Where's Mom?" Todd asked curiously, washing his hands in the sink.

"She's sick," Carly said uneasily, looking for Joe.

"Sick?" Tom asked in surprise, going to their bedroom to check on her. Carly avoided Todd while she quickly set the table, unsure of how he would react to her after seeing them argue.

He sat down at the table and smiled at her. She finished setting the table, not meeting his eyes.

"Joe won't be here for lunch," he said calmly as she set out enough plates for all four of them. She looked up in surprise and sat down across from him. "He's out at the house if you wanted to know," he said casually, fixing his plate.

Carly looked down at her fingernails, fighting back the urge to cry. "Well, I guess I should go home now," she said finally, getting up to leave.

"He's miserable, you know," he said, looking at her seriously. "Do you want my advice?"

"Yes." She sat back down across from him.

"Go over there and talk to him. He'll forgive you as soon as he sees you." He winked, taking a big bite out of his sandwich.

"Thanks." Carly smiled. "I appreciate it." She got up and quickly packed a lunch for her and Joe.

"Where are you off too?" Tom asked, coming back into the kitchen.

She shrugged on her coat, her back to him. "I was going to take Joe's lunch to him."

"Good girl," Tom said proudly. "Here." He handed her a set of keys. "You can't take Sam's truck out there, so take mine."

"Thank you. I'll be careful," she said, hurrying out the door.

She drove to the house and turned off the truck, her heart beating in her throat. A thousand worries accosted her mind as she slowly walked up to the porch, carrying their lunches. She knocked softly on the front door and waited, unsure if she should walk in uninvited or not.

Joe opened the door, surprised. "You don't have to knock, Carly," he said, turning and walking away from her. "This isn't the fanciest place, but it's yours if you still want it," he said gloomily.

Aggravated, Carly put his lunch down on the fireplace frame and walked back outside to the truck, intending to leave. She was just starting the truck when Joe came out to stop her.

"Where are you going?" he said, opening her door.

"I'm going to take your dad's truck back, and I'm going home."

She put the truck in reverse.

"No, you're not," he said, grabbing her left arm. "Don't, Carly." She stepped on the brake, looking at him.

"Why should I stay so you can ignore me and make me feel terrible about Ian? I can stay home and do that."

"Because," he said with difficulty. "I need you to stay."

Slowly, she put the truck in park and scooted over to let him climb in.

"Joe," she said quietly. "I didn't tell Ian about us because I am afraid that he will come here and hurt you. You don't understand how mean he is." She put her hand on his arm imploringly. "I could never be ashamed of you. I love you with all my heart, and I want to be the best wife I can possibly be for you."

Joe looked out the front window, ill at ease. "I know I can't afford to buy you everything I want to, and it bothers me that Ian can."

She looked at him tenderly. "If I wanted the things Ian could buy me, I'd still be with him. You've got to believe me, Joe. I want you and that's all I need."

"And it bothers me that you were engaged to him," he said sullenly, taking her hand in his.

"I hate to bring it to your attention, but you were engaged once before too, you know." She smiled, leaning to look into his face. "I don't like it either, but God stopped both of us before we married the wrong person."

He grimaced in disgust. "You don't have to remind me. I would rather forget that I ever knew her."

"Now you know how I feel about Ian."

"I'm sorry I was such a jerk," he said suddenly, pulling her close to him.

"I'm sorry I made you feel bad," she said simply, kissing him lightly. "I love you."

"I love you so much," he said, taking her face in his hands and kissing her. "I don't want to lose you." He hugged her tightly, taking a deep breath. "I don't want to wait to get married. Let's just run off somewhere."

Carly giggled, pulling away from him. "Where would we live?"

"We could live at your apartment until the house was finished," he said reaching for her.

She scooted out of his reach playfully. "My place? It would drive you crazy, it's so small." He scooted closer to her, forcing her back against the door. "Be reasonable, Joe," she said, putting her hand on his chest.

"You're the one being unreasonable," he said, taking her hand and kissing it. He scooted closer.

"Me?" She opened her door and stepped out quickly, laughing at the surprised look on his face.

"Come here!" He laughed, getting out after her. She smiled impishly, backing slowly toward the porch. She turned and ran up the steps, Joe in close pursuit. He caught her arm as she fumbled with the doorknob and turned her around, kissing her firmly, oblivious to everything around them.

"Did you two make up yet, or are we too early?" Todd called out, opening the door to his truck and getting out.

Joe groaned, leaning his chin on top of Carly's head.

"Are we interrupting anything?" Tom asked, getting his tools.

"No." Carly laughed merrily as Joe reluctantly let her go. "We were just getting ready to eat lunch."

Todd shook his head, shocked. "You haven't eaten yet? That must've been some argument to keep you from eating. I don't think there's a fight out there that would keep me away from food!"

"Get on in there and eat while we bring the tools in," Tom said, bringing his tools up to the porch.

Joe took Carly's hand and led her inside, pulling her down next to him on the fireplace frame. Quietly he kissed her and prayed for their food. They ate in silence, watching Tom and Todd set up the tools on the porch.

"Carly," Joe said, turning to her after he was finished eating, "I can't wait long to be married. Do you think you could live here if I finish our bedroom, bathroom, and part of the kitchen? I can't stand it when you're not with me, and I don't like you living so far away. I need you here." He kissed her quickly, putting his arms around her waist.

"Joe..." she began softly.

"It's either that or your apartment," he said, interrupting her. "I'm not giving in."

"How long will it take you to finish our room and the kitchen?" she asked, shivers of anticipation running up and down her spine.

"I figure it'll be right before New Year's if I work at it every day." He kissed her ear. "Could you live like that?"

"Hmm." She grinned playfully. "I think we could make it work." He hugged her, grinning.

"Where do we start today, Joe?" Tom asked merrily. "You are finished eating, right?"

"By the look of things, he just started on dessert!" Todd said, coming in behind Tom.

"Well, I'm going to go," Carly said, disentangling herself from Joe's grasp.

"Are you going back to our house?" he asked, letting her go reluctantly. He helped her pack the lunch things.

She grinned saucily. "I have to if I'm going to drive Sam's truck back."

"Cat," he said, pinching her arm and making her jump. "You really don't have to go."

"Yes, she does if we're going to get you to do anything around here!" Todd said, one eyebrow arched.

"I'll probably check on your mom before I go home," she said, putting on her coat.

"What's wrong with Mom?" Joe asked, following her onto the porch.

"She started feeling bad just as we finished this morning. Bye, Tom; good-bye, Todd!" she said just as Joe closed the door.

"Oh wait!" She turned to go back inside. "I need to know if I can drive your dad's truck back."

"Take mine instead. I've already got all the things I needed out, and I don't know if Dad will need anything." He reached into his pocket and handed her his keys.

"Okay." She smiled, exchanging keys. She gave him a kiss and climbed into his truck. "I love you, Joe."

"I love you too," he said, closing her door. He watched her leave and walked back into their house, whistling.

"I'm glad to see you two made up," Tom said approvingly. "Holding a grudge isn't good for marriages. Where do you want to start?"

Joe grinned, tossing his keys to him. "Well, I need the fireplace, the bedroom and bathroom, and some of the kitchen done before the New Year."

"Why before the New Year?" Todd asked curiously.

"Because she promised to marry me when I get those things done," he said, putting on his tool belt.

"You two are going to live here without the house being done?" Todd asked, dumbfounded.

"Why not?" Tom said, coming to Joe's rescue. "That's the way your mom and I did it." He clapped Joe on the back. "We've got a lot to do, and just a little time to do it in, so let's get started."

Chapter Nineteen

Carly parked Joe's truck and quietly went inside, setting the lunch stuff on the counter.

"Penny?" she whispered, peeking in the bedroom. "How are you feeling?" She sat on the edge of the bed next to her.

She opened one of her red-rimmed eyes. "Not too good."

Carly felt her head and went into the bathroom, wetting a washcloth.

"You've got a fever," she said, putting the cool washcloth on Penny's burning forehead. She went back into the bathroom, filled a glass with water, and brought it back, helping Penny sit up to take a sip.

"Thank you," she said weakly, lying back down. Carly tucked her in gently, and got up to leave.

"I'll go make some soup for you to eat," she said quietly.

She managed a smile, closing her eyes. "I'll be fine. Tom will be back soon."

"I'm not going to leave you alone here by yourself, so if you need anything, call me," Carly said, leaving the door open in case Penny needed her.

She went into the kitchen and started some broth for Penny, cleaning up the kitchen while she waited for it to be done.

"Here you go," she said a little while later as she brought the warm soup in for her. She set it on the nightstand and propped her up on some soft pillows.

"You don't have to eat much," she said, spooning some broth into her mouth. "Just enough to keep you from getting dehydrated."

She smiled weakly, swallowing the soup slowly. She leaned back into the pillows after a few more spoonfuls and shook her head. "I'm done," she said softly. "What kind was it?" she asked quietly, closing her eyes.

"Turkey broth," Carly said, setting the bowl back on the

nightstand. She got up and rewet the washcloth, wiping Penny's flushed face. She smoothed some hair away from her face, tucked her in, and left quietly.

She sat down at the table, drumming her fingers, wondering what she could find to do. She looked at the clock, knowing it would be a while before the men got back. Bored, she got up and checked in on Penny, who was sleeping fitfully.

She went into the living room and turned on the television, turning it off a moment later. She tidied up some newspapers that Tom had left by his recliner, straightened up some knick-knacks, and re-fluffed the throw pillows on the couch. Sighing, she walked upstairs to Joe's room and stood in his doorway, undecided as to what she should do. She glanced around, noticing his dirty laundry and unmade bed.

Smiling to herself, she quickly gathered up his dirty clothes, put them in the hallway, and made his bed, lovingly patting his pillows into place. She stood over his desk, straightened up a few loose papers, and left the rest for him to deal with. She picked up the dirty clothes and carried them down to the laundry room, emptied the laundry hamper, and started a load of jeans. Opening the dryer, she found some towels Penny had washed that morning, and folded and stacked them neatly into a laundry basket. She was about to put them away when she heard Penny calling for her.

Hurriedly, she put down the basket and went to find Penny crouched on the floor in the bathroom, shaking uncontrollably.

"Penny!" she said, helping her up and leading her to the bed. "Here you go." She tucked her in, wiping her face gently. "Are you okay?"

"Did I make it?" she asked, shivering.

Carly looked around. "I don't see any messes. Were you sick?" Penny nodded feebly, pulling the blankets tighter around her. "Here," she said, bringing the water glass to her lips.

Penny took a small sip and lay back down. "I'm sorry," she said, closing her eyes.

She wiped her forehead comfortingly. "Don't be sorry. I helped my dad take care of my mom when she was sick, and I took care of Dad when he got sick, so it's nothing to be sorry about. You just rest and feel better." When she was sure Penny was resting, she got up and checked the laundry, putting the jeans into the dryer.

She kept herself busy with laundry, dinner, and Penny until the men came back later that night. She was sitting at the table resting her head in her arms when they came in.

"What's that smell?" Todd asked, grinning hungrily. "Dinner," she said, getting up from the table.

"I didn't think you'd still be here," Joe said, coming and putting his arms around her.

She smiled, kissing him tenderly. "Who else is going to make sure you guys get to eat?"

"How's Penny?" Tom asked coming inside, rubbing his hands together.

She pulled herself away from Joe and started to set the table. "She's got the flu."

Todd groaned and slumped into a chair. "The flu? You know what that means, Joe."

"What?" Carly asked anxiously, looking at them both.

"We always share the flu," Joe said miserably, sitting next to Todd.

"And those things you wanted to finish in your house won't get done," Tom said ruefully, going in to check on his wife.

Joe groaned, putting his head down.

"That's okay," Carly said, trying not to be disappointed. "It'll get done." She sat next to him, rubbing his back.

"It's not just that," he said, looking at her. "It's always harder to do the farm work when one of us is sick. It takes us twice as long to do it all, and by the time the work is finished, there won't be much light left to work on the house."

"So we have to wait longer to be married; it'll be okay," she said, squeezing his arm.

"I don't want to wait longer to get married. I want to get married right now." He pulled her over to him and set her on his lap.

"Neither do I, but sometimes we have to," she said softly, tracing his jaw with her finger.

"You don't want to wait to get married?" he asked, grinning wickedly.

She shook her head earnestly. "No. I want to be married just as much as you, but we just have to have somewhere to live."

"We always have your apartment," he said, winking mischievously. She smacked him playfully on the chest and stood up, finishing the table.

"Her apartment?" Todd asked skeptically, one eyebrow raised. "Kelly told me how tiny that thing is. You wouldn't last a day there, Joe."

Carly set dinner on the table, staying out of Joe's reach. "That's what I've been trying to tell him."

"I could handle it for a little while," he protested, getting up to wash and be in Carly's way. She giggled and pushed him away lightly, bringing the forks to the table.

Todd shook his head doubtfully. "I don't think so."

"What's for dinner?" Tom asked, coming out of their bedroom and closing the door softly.

"Turkey pot pie," Carly said, cutting the steaming pastry into servings.

"I thought you didn't know how to cook," Todd asked suspiciously, his eyes narrowed.

"I said I didn't get the practice."

"Turkey pot pie?" Joe asked doubtfully, sitting down. "Where did you learn to make that?"

"Sounds great to me," Tom said, rubbing his stomach.

"Well," Tom said after praying, helping himself to dinner. "I think your house isn't going to be done before the New Year."

Joe scowled with disappointment. "I know."

"What can I do to help you guys?" Carly asked.

"You know, we might not even catch it," Todd said optimistically before anyone could answer. He cautiously tasted a small bite of food. "This is really good, Carly," he said, surprised, taking a more generous bite. "You really need to teach Kelly how to cook."

Joe laughed. "I think it's funny that you asked a girl that couldn't cook to marry you."

"Not bad," Tom said approvingly. "Thank you, by the way, for taking care of Penny today."

"You're welcome," Carly said, blushing with pleasure. "I wasn't able to do much to help her though."

"What did you do then?" Joe said, teasing.

Her eyes twinkled mischievously at him. "Well, I didn't do much, just cleaned up your room."

Joe looked mortified.

"You cleaned his room?" Todd asked incredulously. "That must've taken you all day!" Joe shot him a withering look.

"It was tough." Carly laughed, rolling her eyes. "I didn't know it would be such hard work."

"Better get used to it." Tom laughed heartily, enjoying the playful banter. "He's notorious for not keeping things neat."

Joe turned crimson. "Hey now, I've had other things on my mind lately."

"Uh huh," Todd muttered skeptically, keeping his head down.

"Back to our other conversation," Carly said, anxious to be of help to them.

"Well now," Tom said kindly, leaning back in his chair. "We appreciate your help, and I'm sure we'll be able to find something for you to do, right?" He winked at Joe, who gave an enthusiastic nod of his head.

Todd snickered. "Yeah, she could keep his room clean."

"That would work pretty good for me," he said, unruffled.

"How are you going to let me know if you need my help or not?"

"I'll call you at five every day and let you know," he said simply, finishing his dinner. "That was good, babe." He winked, leaning his arm on the back of her chair.

"Babe? Is this something new?" Todd asked, raising his eyebrows. Joe grinned, shrugging his shoulders. "I think I'm going to be sick." Todd groaned and held his stomach.

"I think I'll start cleaning up now," Carly said, blushing charmingly.

She cleared off the table, washed the dishes, and finished the laundry she had started while the men sat at the table drinking coffee and discussing how they were going to divide the work.

"Carly," Tom said, standing up and stretching. "Thank you for dinner, it was good. I'm going in to check on Penny, so I'll see you three later."

"You're welcome," Carly said kindly as he walked out of the kitchen.

"Well, I'm not staying in here. You two make me sick," Todd said, going into the living room and turning on the TV.

Joe got up and silently helped Carly finish the dishes. Carly folded her towel and hung it up on the oven handle.

"Well," she said awkwardly, aware that she was alone with Joe. "I guess I'll get on out of here."

"You don't have to," Joe said quietly, walking toward her.

"I've been here all day," she stammered, backing toward the door.

He caught her arm and drew her to him, kissing her lightly. "And I like it. You have to get used to it, you know," he whispered in her ear.

"I know," she said breathlessly. "But I've really got to go," she said, pushing him away.

He pulled her back to him. "Why? What are you going to do? Don't you want to stay a little longer?" He kissed her ear.

"Yes, but I don't think that would be a good idea," she said, placing her hand on his chest.

"Why wouldn't it be a good idea?" He caressed her cheek tenderly, holding her face in his hand, looking longingly into her eyes.

"Because I don't want any regrets."

"Ah," he said softly, after a short silence. "I understand. I'll see you at church then, Lord willing." He walked her to the door, helping her on with her coat.

"I love you," she said quietly, standing on her tiptoes to give him a kiss. "I'll see you later." She walked away quickly before she could change her mind.

"Drive careful," he called as he watched her drive slowly away.

Chapter Twenty

Sunday morning Carly waited as long as she could for Joe to pick her up for church. Checking her watch one last time, she sighed, wrapped her scarf around her, and started to walk briskly, jamming her hands deep into her pockets. She bent her head down, trying to shield her face from the icy wind, too preoccupied with her thoughts to notice a truck was pulling over to the curb.

"Hey!" Billy called, rolling his window down.

Startled, Carly looked up and stepped into a large snow drift

"You want a ride?" he asked, pointing to the empty seat next to him.

"Oh, no." Carly hesitated, trying to think of an excuse. "I'm fine. Thanks anyway." She smiled politely, starting to walk again after she shook the snow out of her shoe.

"You don't have to worry. I'm sure Joe won't get upset," Billy said sarcastically. "Come on, you're turning blue."

"I'm on my way to church," she said awkwardly, unsure of what to do. It was a bitterly cold morning, her feet were wet, and she was sure she was about to freeze.

"That's where I'm heading," he said easily, leaning over to open the passenger door for her.

She hesitated a moment longer, smiled pensively, and walked to the other side of the truck.

"Thanks," she said, climbing inside and closing the door behind her. "It's good to feel heat again."

"Sure," Billy said, spinning away from the curb. He looked at her curiously. "Where's Joe? I thought he'd pick you up on such a cold day."

She turned red, embarrassed. "I don't know."

He pulled into a parking space and turned off the truck. "You two didn't break up, did you?" he asked hopefully, trying to hide a smile. She opened the door and got out, not wanting anyone to get the wrong idea.

"No," she said, hurt at his obvious enjoyment of their possible breakup. "We didn't break up. In fact, we're engaged." She held up her ring for him to see.

Billy stood next to the truck in stunned silence, an angry scowl on his face.

Somehow, in spite of all his rudeness, unpleasantness, and obnoxious behavior toward her, she suddenly felt extremely sorry for him.

"Billy," she started, wanting to comfort him in some way. "I'm sorry."

"Sorry? For what?" he said in disgust. "I don't care anyway." He looked away, his face turning red.

"Billy."

"I hope he'll make you happy," he spat, getting back in the truck.

"Aren't you coming in?" she asked in surprise.

"What for?" He slammed the door and started the engine, revving it up.

"Please?"

He glared at her.

"Can't we be friends?" she asked softly.

"Not with Joe in the way," he said bitterly, leaning over to close the door and quickly driving away, leaving Carly to stare after him.

"What was that all about?" Kelly asked, joining her as Billy sped off.

"He's mad at me," she said sadly.

"Why would Billy be mad?" she asked as they walked into the church together.

"I told him Joe and I are engaged."

Kelly nodded. "Oh."

"I feel terrible," Carly said as they sat in their usual places.

"Terrible? Why?" Kelly asked in surprise.

"Because I hurt his feelings, and now he isn't in church." She smiled ruefully. "I feel responsible."

Kelly squeezed her hand reassuringly. "He's a big boy, Carly, and he can make those decisions on his own. You can't make his problems yours. Pray about it."

"Where are Joe and Todd?" She asked, desiring to change the subject.

"Was that Billy Pruit I saw you with, Carly?" Angie said nastily behind them before Kelly could answer.

Carly tried to ignore her, knowing that she was just trying to bother her.

"Did you and Joe break up or something? I would have thought that you'd find someone a little better than Billy to hang out with. Oh, you must be desperate," she said sarcastically, leaning forward on the back of their seats. "You'll never be able to replace Joe, he's irreplaceable. You wouldn't mind if he and I went out, would you?" She smiled hatefully.

She turned to look at her, eyes flashing. "We didn't break up."

"Are you two-timing him? He better not find out; he's kind of funny about things like that," Angie said maliciously.

Carly was about to reply when she spotted Joe and Todd coming toward them.

"Good morning." She beamed, ignoring Angie. "I'm glad you could make it! How's your mom doing?" she asked, noticing that neither of the elder Baird's were there.

"Good morning." Joe smiled, giving her a quick hug. "Sorry I couldn't pick you up this morning. We were trying to hurry, but we weren't fast enough. Mom seems to be getting over it, but Dad stayed home anyway to help her."

Angie leaned over, putting her hand on his arm. "Don't worry, she got a ride with Billy Pruit."

"With Billy? Well, that was nice of him," Joe said, unperturbed, his look cold. Carly squeezed his hand, relieved that he wasn't upset.

"Where is Billy anyway?" he asked, smiling at Carly.

"He left like he was mad," Angie said in a last attempt to make

Joe jealous.

"Mad?"

Carly nodded, blushing. "I made him mad."

Angie sneered, rolling her eyes contemptuously. "What did you do? Tell him you were afraid Joe was going to catch you two?"

"Angie." Joe sighed, tired of her nastiness. He put his arm around Carly's shoulders and smiled. "I've got some news for you." He smiled at Carly tenderly. "I'd like you to meet my fiancée."

"Fiancée?" Angie choked, her face turning pale. "Well, I guess if that's what you want," she said, turning and leaving abruptly.

"That's pretty much how Billy reacted when I told him," Carly said softly, watching her go.

"So that's why he was mad," Joe said, giving her one last squeeze as the music started. She smiled up at him, thankful that the Lord had brought them together.

"Joe! Todd was just telling me that he and Kelly are engaged!" The pastor greeted them, shaking their hands after the services. "When's he going to ask you, Carly?" He winked amiably.

Joe beamed, holding up Carly's hand to show him her ring. "I already did!"

"Whew!" He whistled, impressed. "I'm blind!" He put his hand over his eyes, teasing. "Congratulations! When's the wedding?"

"We haven't agreed on that yet," Carly said hurriedly, noticing a small crowd gathering around them.

He flashed her a happy smile. "I'd like to get married today, but she seems to feel that we need somewhere to live first."

"Oh yeah? Aren't you staying at the apartment up top of Sam's store? Why couldn't you live there for a while?" he asked good-naturedly.

"That's what I keep telling her, but she just won't listen."

She laughed, elbowing him in the ribs. "I'd do it in a heartbeat if I thought Joe could handle it, but I just don't think he's got what it takes."

"I could handle it. How bad can it be?"

"Not bad if you're a sardine." Kelly laughed, coming to Carly's rescue. "It's okay for one person, but I couldn't imagine Joe living there. Not a doubt in my mind that he couldn't handle it."

"Is it really that small?" the pastor asked, amused.

"Yes." Carly sighed, nodding her head. "It's perfect for me because I just go to work in the morning anyway, and I don't spend a lot of time there. But Joe's a different story."

Joe hung his head dejectedly, trying to look pitiful. "She doesn't think I'm capable."

"Whatever happened to that place you were building for Amy?" Angie asked contemptuously, joining the group around the two new couples.

Joe looked at her evenly. "We're working on it. We're hoping to have it done before the New Year." He turned his attention to the pastor.

"I don't think I would want a house that a guy was building for someone else he used to be engaged to," she said, trying to pass her remark off as a joke. Joe turned red with fury, and a silent hush fell on the crowd around them, as everyone was curious to hear what he would say.

"Well, she didn't want it and," Carly said, coming to Joe's defense, "she didn't want him either, so I guess he can build it for anyone he wants to build it for."

"Well," the pastor cleared his throat, embarrassed, "I'm sure there's quite a few young women around here that are jealous of you, Carly. Joe's quite a catch. The same goes for you two." He turned to Todd and Kelly. "I think everyone here has known that you would get married, we just didn't know when it would be. Congratulations to both of you." The people around them offered their congratulations as Angie slunk away sullenly, unable to be happy for the two couples.

"Do you have to hurry home?" Carly asked, walking with Joe to the truck and getting in as he opened her door.

"I'm afraid so," he said glumly, driving her home. "I need to make out a materials list for the house and help Dad with the rest of the work that we didn't get to this morning." He parked the truck in front of the store, leaving the engine running. "I'm not even sure I'll be able to make it to church tonight."

"Well, I hope you can make it. I'll miss you if you don't." She kissed him lightly, opening her door. "Are you going to call me tonight to let me know if you need my help in the morning?"

"I'll try to call you by five and let you know. I love you." He leaned across the seat to give her another kiss.

Smiling, she closed the door gently and waved as he pulled out of the parking spot and drove away. She watched him as long as she could and let herself into the store, wondering what she was going to do with herself for the rest of the day.

After she ate, she changed into some grubby work clothes, mopped and waxed the entire store floor, straightened the stockroom shelves, labeled boxes, scrubbed the downstairs' bathroom, dusted, washed the windows, and was just finishing scrubbing her bathroom floor when the phone rang downstairs. She ran to answer it.

"Hello?" she asked hesitantly, hoping it wasn't Ian.

Kelly's voice floated over the line. "Hi, Carly."

"Kelly! Hi!" She leaned on the counter and wrapped the cord around her fingers.

"Todd just called and asked me to let you know that Joe won't be able to make it to church tonight. He thinks Joe might be getting the flu now."

"Oh," Carly said, disappointed. "Well, I guess that means that they'll need my help in the morning then."

"I'm not sure about that. Todd did say that Penny was feeling a bit better tonight, but he wasn't sure if she would be able to do much tomorrow. Who knows? Penny might be the only one that feels well tomorrow!" Kelly laughed. "Are you going to church tonight?"

"I was just about to get ready when you called. Are you?" Carly asked pleasantly.

"Yes. I'll come pick you up so you won't have to walk, and we can chit chat on our way."

"Isn't Todd going to church tonight? I thought he'd pick you up," Carly said.

"No, he's going to stay home and help out there. He figures he'll be sick before the weeks out, so there's really no use in him trying to avoid it. I'll be over in a few minutes."

Joe and Todd weren't the only ones to miss evening services that night, as there were only a faithful few in attendance. The pastor preached a short message and dismissed early on account of the weather getting worse, and Kelly drove Carly back to her place.

"Do you want to come up for a little hot chocolate? It's the least I can do for you giving me a ride."

Kelly smiled, turning off the car. "Okay, that sounds nice."

Carly let them in, locking the doors behind them, and led the way upstairs. Just as she unlocked her apartment door, the phone rang.

"Maybe that's Joe," she said breathlessly, pushing the door open. "Make yourself comfortable. I'll be right back," she said, hurrying back downstairs.

"Hello?" she asked, trying to keep her voice steady and not sound as though she had been running.

"Good evening, Carly. I'm so glad I finally got a hold of you," Ian said softly.

"Stop calling me, Ian. I don't have anything to say to you," Carly said after a moment's hesitation, trying to sound braver than she felt.

"Where've you been? I've tried to call you for a while now," he asked calmly, ignoring her request.

"I've been at church if you want to know," she answered tersely, as Kelly came and stood beside her with a questioning look. Carly shook her head, indicating that it wasn't Joe.

Ian sneered, mocking her. "You still go to church?"

"Of course I still go to church."

"It's nice to see that you're dedicated," he said disdainfully. "I didn't think you'd go without Joe."

Carly's blood froze.

She looked helplessly at Kelly, her face pale. "What are you talking about? How did you know Joe wasn't at church?"

He laughed heartlessly, enjoying her panic. "I'm watching everything you do."

"Is it Ian?" Kelly whispered anxiously. Carly nodded her head, squeezing her eyes shut, trying to concentrate.

"I also remember that when I was sick, you wouldn't go to church without me. You were more dedicated to me than you are to him."

"That's because you wouldn't let me. I couldn't go anywhere if you weren't right there to keep an eye on me," she said, her voice rising. "At least Joe trusts me."

"He shouldn't," Ian spat. "I couldn't trust you."

"You never tried!" Anger rose up in her throat making it difficult to talk. Kelly put a comforting hand on her arm.

"You definitely didn't make it easy to trust you," Ian said angrily.

"How did I make it difficult?" she asked, unable to think of a time when he couldn't trust her. "I did everything I could to make you happy, and nothing worked. You were the one that couldn't be trusted if I remember correctly. Or did you forget that you were the one cheating on me?"

"A man has needs, and you weren't meeting them," he said unrepentantly.

"We weren't married, Ian. If you had needs, why didn't you move up the wedding date?" Carly asked softly, remembering the humiliation she felt when she found out the truth about him.

"You weren't supposed to find out," he said through clenched teeth.

"It wasn't right, even if I wouldn't have found out. I felt so stupid when I found out that everybody knew except me. I was humiliated. You were the one that couldn't be trusted."

"And you think I wasn't humiliated when I came back to your apartment and found that you had left without a word? You think it was right of you to leave everything without even explaining why?"

he asked fiercely. "I think you owe me an apology, Carly."

"Then I'm sorry, Ian. I apologize. But if I would have told you what I was going to do, would you have let me go?" she asked quietly, leaning her head in her hand, waiting for him to answer.

"Of course I would have."

"If you would have let me go, then why won't you leave me alone now?"

"Because it's not over," Ian answered, his voice cracking.

"I'm being honest with you. It's over. I'm not coming back to you, and I will not marry you. I'm going to marry Joe." She regretted the words as soon as they left her mouth. She hadn't intended to tell him about her engagement to Joe.

"No, you won't! I will come up there and stop you, do you hear me?"

Carly held the phone away from her ear until he was finished spewing his hateful speech.

"Ian," she said quietly, praying silently for strength. "I'd rather die than go back to you."

"Be careful what you ask for," Ian said furiously. "You may get what you want."

"I'm not going to let you hurt me anymore, Ian. Don't call me again," she said, putting the phone back on the cradle before he could answer. She looked up at Kelly and gave her a thin smile.

"I think that went well," she said sarcastically, rolling her eyes ruefully. "No one seems to be very happy about us getting married. It's made a few people mad. Billy. Angie. Ian."

"I'm sorry, Carly," Kelly said softly, giving her a comforting hug. "They'll get used to the idea. What did he say when you told him that you'd rather die than go back to him?"

Carly sighed, running her fingers nervously through her hair. "He said that I might get what I wish for."

"What do you think he'll do?" she asked, worried for her friend.

"I don't know. Honestly, I really don't want to think about it either. Come on. We never did get that cup of hot chocolate." They were silent, preoccupied with their own thoughts as they walked upstairs.

"Have a seat," Carly offered, getting the cups and starting the kettle once they were in the room.

"Are you okay?" Kelly asked quietly. "Is there anything I can do for you?"

Wearily, she sat down across from her, leaning her head in her hand. "I'll be fine. I just wish he'd leave me alone."

"Too bad Joe was sick," Kelly said thoughtfully.

"What do you mean?"

"If Joe wasn't sick, you two could get married right away. Then maybe Ian would leave you alone."

"I don't think it would be that simple," she said unhappily, getting up to get the singing teakettle.

"You don't think he'd realize that you didn't love him if you were married to someone else?" she asked, perplexed by Carly's pessimism.

Carly set her lips into a thin line, set their cups gently on the table, and sat down before she answered her friend. "With Ian, it's not about love. It's about winning and losing. I was Ian's little trophy that got away, and he's mad. He doesn't like to lose, and he'll win anyway he can." She took a cautious sip of her hot chocolate.

"Do you think he'll kill you?" Kelly asked anxiously, looking scared.

She shook her head. "No. I don't think even Ian would go that far. I think he'd try to scare me and force me to come back to him, but I don't think he would try to kill me for revenge or anything. I'd probably get the beating of my life, though! Whatever happens, Kelly, I just want you to know I am grateful that you are my friend." Carly patted her hand and smile wanly.

"Soon to be your sister-in-law as well," Kelly said dreamily. "I'm so excited I can hardly wait."

"I know what you mean." Carly smiled knowingly. "I'm kind of disappointed that Joe isn't going to be able to work on the house. It'll be longer before we can get married."

Kelly put her cup down and looked around at the apartment.

"You know, Joe would probably do okay here for a while. He'd be out at the farm everyday and then working on your house when he wasn't there, so he wouldn't be stuck here without anything to do. He might manage."

She frowned. "I don't know. He's got to get up so early as it is, I'd hate for him to have to get up even earlier and have to drive. Plus, I don't know what Sam would say."

"Sam?" Kelly looked at her in surprise. "I don't think he'd have a problem if you two were married. Do they know about you two yet?"

"I haven't talked to them since they left. I don't really expect to. They just asked me to keep an eye on their house, water the flowers, and drive the Bronco while they were gone. It was kind of like a second honeymoon for them." Carly smiled gently, remembering how excited they were. "I've got the numbers where I could reach them if I needed to, but I really hate to bother them."

"There you go!" Kelly said, excited. "Give them a call and tell them about you and Joe. Ask Sam if it would be okay for you two to live here until your house gets done."

Carly shook her head. "I don't know. I'll think about it," she said, seeing Kelly's disappointed look.

"What are you going to do tonight?" Kelly asked, finishing up her chocolate and putting her cup in the sink.

"I just thought I'd get to bed so I could get up and out to the farm early to help them." Carly stood up and stretched before taking care of her cup as well. "Is Joe the only one sick?" she asked, walking Kelly to the door.

She shrugged her coat on. "Todd didn't say. I wish I could go out there with you tomorrow, but I've got to work."

"I know. Don't worry about it. We can handle it. Here." Carly handed her gloves to her and walked her downstairs.

"What are you going to do if you get sick?"

She shrugged her shoulders as she unlocked the doors. "I haven't thought about it. I guess I'll just rest and relax until I get better."

"If you gave me a set of keys, I could come check on you," Kelly said kindly. "I'll be careful."

"Don't worry, I should be fine."

"I really think you should let someone help you every once in a while," Kelly said, a little hurt. "I've known Sam and Sue all my life, and I know they'd be worried to death if you were sick and didn't let anyone check up on you."

"I'll be fine. Really," Carly said, trying to soothe her friend's hurt feelings.

"All right. If you're sure." Kelly smiled. "Thanks again for the hot chocolate. It was great." She gave Carly a hug.

"Thank you for giving me a ride home! Drive careful!" Carly smiled, holding the door open for her. She waved as Kelly backed out and drove away.

Sighing, she locked the door behind her. She turned, silence all about her. Loneliness washed over her like a tidal wave. She walked to the counter, picked up the phone, and dialed Joe's number, anxious to hear his reassuring voice.

"Hello?" Tom said with his usual booming voice.

Carly smiled in amusement. "Hello, Tom. This is Carly. I was wondering if I could speak to Joe."

"Joe? Sure. Just a moment." She waited for what seemed like an hour before he picked it up.

"Hello?" he asked groggily as if he had been sleeping.

"Did I wake you up?" she asked, embarrassed. "I'm sorry."

"No," he answered quietly. "I was just lying down, trying to get my stomach to relax. How are you?"

"I'm okay," she said, trying to sound happy. "I just wanted to talk to you, but if you're not feeling well, I'll let you go."

"No. I want to talk to you." She could hear a faint smile in his voice. "This is the first time you've called me, and I want to make the most of it. What's up?"

"Ian called, and I told him we were getting married," she blurted, unable to keep it to herself.

"Good," he said. Another smile. "What did he do?"

"Just threatened. Kelly was here and heard almost the whole thing. I think it might have scared her a little."

"What do you mean 'threatened'?" She could hear the kitchen chair scraping across the floor as if he were pulling up a seat.

"I told him I'd rather die than go back to him, and he said to watch what I wish for because I might get it." She sighed, wishing he were there to comfort her.

"That's not good," he said quietly. "I don't think you should answer your phone anymore."

"How will I talk to you?" she asked miserably.

"I'll call you at five o'clock every day that I can," he said simply, sounding groggy again. "If the phone rings before or after that time, don't answer it."

"Okay," she said softly. "You sound awful, so I'm going to let you go. I'll see you when I see you, all right?"

"Sounds good to me. I'll see you later, babe. Love you."

"I love you too. Bye." She hung up and walked quickly upstairs, making as much noise as she possibly could, and locked herself into her apartment.

Chapter Twenty-One

$\mathcal{S}$he woke early the next morning to a freezing apartment, seeing her breath as she exhaled. Getting up, she checked her little space heater and found that the pilot light had gone out in the night.

Rubbing her arms and stamping her feet on the floor to get warm, she relit it as quickly as her shaking fingers could function and jumped back into her bed, pulling the warm covers around her. She waited a little while, hoping the tiny room would heat up a little before she had to get up. She looked at her clock, 5:27. She groaned and waited for the alarm to sound, trying to get warm in the three minutes she had remaining.

She jumped out of bed as soon as the alarm went off and ran to the bathroom, turning the hot water on in the shower. She ran in place until it was warm enough to get in and showered as quickly as she could, thankful for hot water. She got ready quickly, drank a cup of juice, and ran out the door, anxious to get to the farm and see Joe.

She ran down the slippery sidewalks to Sam and Sue's house, letting herself in and locking the door behind her. She watered the flowers, checked the messages, let herself back out, and carefully drove the truck out to the Bairds' place, heat going full blast. She was almost warm when she pulled into their driveway. She pulled up next to the porch and turned off the truck, noticing a light on in the kitchen. Quietly she stepped up to the porch and glanced inside to see Tom in the kitchen, pouring himself a cup of coffee. The door opened quickly at the sound of her soft knock.

"Carly!" Tom said in surprise. "Come in, come in," he said, stepping aside to let her in.

"Good morning," she said shyly, looking around for Joe.

"I didn't know you were going to be here today," Tom said, closing the door behind her.

"Yeah, when I talked to Joe last night, he didn't sound like he felt well, so I thought I'd come by and see if there was anything I could do to help out," she said quietly, glancing around the kitchen.

"You were right. I woke up this morning, and both Joe and Todd are down." He smiled wryly. "When one of us gets sick, we all pass it around. We're a sharing family." He winked at her and sat down at the table. "Help yourself to some coffee."

"Thank you," Carly said gratefully, pouring herself a cup and sitting across from him. "That's good," she said, taking a sip and wrapping her cold fingers around the steaming cup.

"Cold outside, huh?" Tom asked, amused.

"Extremely. They definitely picked a great time to be sick." She grinned. "How's Penny feeling?"

"She's doing all right, but I asked her to take it easy today. I can't afford any of us to have relapses! You're going to need something warm to put on. You can wear Joe's old overalls and coat, and these are his gloves and hat," he said helpfully, handing her the gloves and hat. "I believe the overalls are in the laundry room on the dryer, and that's his work coat." He gulped down the rest of his coffee and put on his coat and boots. "I'll be out in the barn," he said, closing the door behind him, leaving her to finish her coffee alone.

She watched him thoughtfully for a moment, finished off her coffee, and got ready to help him outside. She was about to go outside when she heard a sound behind her. She turned to see Penny shuffling sleepily into the kitchen.

"Good morning," Carly said quietly, smiling. "I hope you're feeling better."

She jumped, putting her hand to her chest. "Oh my goodness! I thought you were Joe!" She grinned. "Good morning, Carly. I'm feeling much better. I just hate getting the flu; it wears me out so much," she said tiredly, getting a cup of coffee. "I didn't get a chance to thank you for being such a big help to me the other day." Wearily, she sat down at the table.

"I'm glad you're better," Carly said honestly. "I'm going to go help Tom now, so I'll see you later." She started out the door.

"I'll be out in just a minute."

"Don't rush. We'll be okay," Carly said gently. "You need to take it easy. See you in a little while." Carly left her and joined Tom, who was already milking a cow. He smiled as he looked up at her.

"You remember how to milk?" he asked.

She hesitated. "I think I do. You want me to start in the next stall?"

"Just remember their food, wash 'em, and you'll do just fine," he said, milking away.

Carly was just beginning to milk when Tom finished and went to the next stall. It wasn't as hard this time as it had been the first. She finished quickly and set to work feeding the other animals. She was just about to muck out Ashes' stall when Tom spoke to her, making her jump.

"You did pretty good there with the cows. I appreciate your help."

"Thanks." She blushed with the praise. "I'm glad to help. Just let me know what I can do."

"Sure thing." He nodded approvingly, and walked away.

She finished Ashes' stall and went to start the other horses before Penny came out.

"You've gotten far," she said, surprised. "I didn't know you knew how to do so much on a farm."

"Last time I was here, Joe showed me a lot of what needs to be done."

"It's a good thing he did." Penny laughed quietly. "I guess God knew we were going to need some help around here."

Carly smiled warmly. "I guess he did." She finished cleaning out the stalls and was kept pretty busy with whatever Tom and Penny needed her to do. She was helping Tom work on the tractor when Penny called them both inside for lunch.

"Here," Tom said, handing her a grease rag. "Wipe your hands on that." He grinned as he looked at her greasy hands and smeared face.

"What?" she asked, puzzled.

"You've got grease everywhere. Reminds me of the first time Joe helped me fix a car." He laughed and helped her wipe the grease off her face.

"Thanks," she said self-consciously.

"No problem," he said. "You were a lot of help today. Thanks."

"Anytime." She smiled, following him out of the barn and into the house, where Penny had a delicious lunch ready for them. They sat and ate together companionably, getting to know each other a great deal.

"That was great, Ma," Tom said to Penny affectionately, pushing his chair away from the table. "Just like always. You need to take it easy now." He kissed her gently and stood up. "I'm about finished in the barn, so you can check in on Joe if you want to," he said to Carly, who had started to get up and follow him back outside.

"Are you sure?" Carly asked doubtfully. "I'm pretty sure I could get a little more grease everywhere." They laughed, as she started to clean off the table.

"Just leave those, Carly." Penny started to protest. "I'll pick up in a minute."

Stubbornly, she continued. "I don't mind. You just go ahead and take it easy while I do the clean up. Besides"—she winked— "I've got to have something to do seeing as how Tom won't let me play in the grease anymore!"

"That's it. I'm leaving before I get into anymore trouble!" Tom laughed, closing the door as he went outside.

"Carly, what would I do without you?" Penny sighed, leaning her head down on her arms. "I just don't seem to be able to get the energy that I used to have."

"Why don't you go ahead and lie down? I'll finish up here and go up to check on Joe if you don't mind."

"I think I will," Penny said gratefully as she got up from the table.

Carly finished cleaning up and went upstairs to check on Joe.

Noticing Todd's door was open, she glanced in and saw Penny sitting by his bed taking his temperature.

"Do you need anything?" Carly asked quietly.

"No, I think they'll be fine," she said, getting up and closing the door partway behind her. "I'll be downstairs in the living room, so when you're done, come on down."

"I'll be down in a little bit."

She tapped gently on Joe's slightly open door and tiptoed in when there was no answer. Joe was lying on his side, sleeping fitfully. She moved the desk chair over to the bed and sat down quietly, brushing a lock of hair out of his face. He woke.

"Carly," he said softly, trying to smile. "I didn't know you were going to be here this early."

"It's past one in the afternoon." Carly smiled, running her finger down his jaw. "How are you feeling?"

"Not too well," he mumbled, closing his eyes and rolling onto his back.

"Do you want me to leave you alone?" Carly asked quietly, getting up to leave.

He reached for her hand. "No."

She massaged his hand and sat back down. "Can I get you anything?"

He moaned, clutching his stomach. "No, I'm fine."

Carly sat next to him, wiping his forehead periodically with a damp cloth she had gotten from the bathroom. She waited until she was sure he was sleeping before she got up and went downstairs in search of Penny.

"There you are," Penny said kindly. "Come have a seat for a little while." She patted the couch beside her. Carly sat down where she indicated and pulled a throw pillow onto her lap.

"Well, how's Joe doing?" Penny asked, seeming to feel much better.

"He doesn't look so good." Carly grimaced, pulling distractedly at the tassel on the pillow. "I just wish there was something I could do for him."

She patted her hand. "He'll be fine."

"I just remember my dad and how he took care of my mom in her last days, and I feel that I should be doing something to make him feel better."

"You being here will make him feel better than anything else right now. He'll be up before you know it, wait and see. Do you want to watch a movie? I've got a little time before I start dinner," she asked hopefully.

"I haven't watched a movie in a really long time; I'm not sure if I know how to sit through one!" Carly laughed.

Penny went over to the movie cabinet and opened the doors. "What do you want to see?" She poked her head up, looking expectantly at Carly.

"You pick," she said, unsure of what Penny liked.

"The men all hate it when I pick movies," she said apologetically. "I like the old movies the best."

"So do I!" Carly said excitedly. "Bing Crosby, Audrey Hepburn…"

"Fred Astaire, Ginger Rogers!" Penny finished, laughing. "We'll get along great then. Let me see; are you in the mood for a Christmas movie?" She asked hopefully. Carly nodded, grinning from ear to ear.

"*White Christmas* sound good to you?" Carly beamed with pleasure. "That was the one my dad and I watched every year after Mom died. It's one of my favorites!"

"Good!" Penny popped the movie into the DVD player and started it, sitting down eagerly. They were completely absorbed with the movie when they heard a commotion in the bathroom. They jumped up simultaneously and ran to help whoever it was. They arrived just in time to see Joe emerge, grabbing onto the doorframe to support himself.

"Joe!" Penny said, surprised.

"Let us help you," Carly said softly, helping him on one side while Penny helped him on the other. They managed to help him slowly up the stairs to his bedroom, sitting him down on his bed.

"Will you stay with me?" he asked Carly, lying down, shivering as though he were about to freeze to death.

She pulled the covers up to his chin and gave him a sweet smile. "Of course I'll stay," she whispered, running her fingers through his hair.

"It's about time to start dinner anyway," Penny said, checking the clock. "You're more than welcome to stay and eat."

"Thank you," Carly said thankfully, pulling the chair close to the bed.

"I'll let you know when dinner's done." Carly heard her check on Todd just before she went downstairs, closing his door softly. She turned her attention back to Joe.

"I'm glad you came by today," he said weakly, watching her. "I'm sorry you have to see me like this."

"I'm glad I was able to be here. Try to go to sleep."

"Talk to me," he whispered, closing his eyes. "I like to hear you talk."

"Well, let me see," she said, trying to think of something to say. "What do you want to hear about?"

"You and your parents," he said softly, eyes still closed.

"Well, before my mom died," she began, running her fingers through his hair again. "She would talk to me and tell me how wonderful God was, and that even if I didn't understand why he allowed bad things to happen to me, that I could always trust him to do what was best. At first I didn't want to believe her. Don't get me wrong, I was saved when I was young, but I couldn't understand why he was taking my mom away from me."

She stopped and took his hand in hers, tracing his fingers with her own. "But I loved him because she had taught me to love him, even though it was tough sometimes. I remember I would lie on the end of her bed right before she died and listen to my dad read the Bible to her. She loved to hear the Psalms, and he never seemed to get tired of reading them to her." She smiled sadly, wishing she could have spent just a little more time with both of them. "When she'd get really bad pains, Dad would take her into his arms and rock her gently and sing to her until she'd go to sleep. He was holding her and singing to her the night she died.

"That was the only time I remember seeing him cry. I asked him once why he didn't cry at the funeral, and he told me that even though he missed her so much, he was happy for her because all of her pain was gone, and one day, he'd get to see her again. I think that's when heaven became a real place to me. When Dad showed me in the Bible what God had to say about one of his children dying, how the angels rejoice, I was finally at peace, knowing that she was where she had longed to go." She paused, wondering if she should stop talking and leave him alone.

"Keep going," he said faintly, keeping his eyes closed.

"After she died, I was afraid to trust God to take care of me. I was afraid that he was going to take everyone I cared about away. So I clung to my dad, not liking to let him out of my sight. Poor Dad." She sighed. "He didn't really have a clue how to raise a daughter, but we sure were close. We did everything together. After Dad got sick and I started dating Ian, I clung to Ian for my security instead of trusting in the Lord. You know, it's a whole lot easier to say that I need to trust in him than to actually do it. I didn't want to be alone, so I thought Ian was the one God wanted me to be with for the rest of my life. But looking back, I can see that all the real trouble started when I depended on a person instead of God."

She stopped, listening to his even breathing, and watched him sleep for a little while, loving him all the more for needing her. She bent down and softly kissed his cheek. She pulled up his covers and turned off his light, leaving him to rest.

"Dinner's ready," Penny said cheerfully as Carly came into the kitchen.

Carly took a deep breath, appreciating the enticing aroma. "Smells wonderful!"

Penny placed the steaming pan on the table. "Have a seat. Tom and Kelly will be here any minute."

"Kelly's here?" Carly asked in surprise. "I didn't hear her come in."

"She came over after she got out of work to check on Todd. Here." Penny handed her a plate piled high with delicious roast and vegetables.

"Hello," Kelly said happily, seating herself next to Carly.

She smiled brightly at her friend. "Hi. I didn't hear you come in."

"You and Joe were talking, so I didn't want to disturb you. Boy, does Todd look rough!" she said, shaking her head. "I didn't know the flu could be that bad. He looks almost green. How's Joe look?" she asked, turning to Carly.

"He looks a little green too." Carly chuckled. "I thought he'd probably be better off sleeping, but he wanted me to talk to him. I was lucky to get out of there to eat!"

"Well, this is odd. I know we had two boys, but there are two girls here instead!" said Tom as he came into the kitchen and sat down. "Glad you both are here. Makes it a little easier on Penny." He winked at her as she sat next to him. "She doesn't have to do as much babysitting."

"Babysitting is right!" Penny laughed. "I always thought men were supposed to be big and strong, but when they get a little case of the flu, they're nothing but big babies."

Tom laughed heartily. "That's right! And if you have helpers, you can spend all your time babysitting me when I catch it!" He took her hand and blessed the food before continuing. "That's our job. We need to be babied every once in a while. Just think when those two boys are out, you can give me all your attention."

"I'll miss them when they're gone." Penny sighed wistfully. "When you two start having kids, be sure to enjoy every minute you've got with them, because they grow up way too fast! There are too many people out there that just don't take the time to enjoy their kids until it's too late. You blink, and wham. They're getting married and moving out."

"Uh oh, I think I hit a sore spot!"

Penny elbowed him in the ribs. "I just meant to enjoy them while you've got them." She smiled weakly, her eyes wet with unshed tears.

"What are you planning on doing tomorrow, Carly?" Tom asked, changing the subject so Penny could regain her self-control.

"I'm planning on coming back out here in the morning to check on Joe and help you both if you need me to," she said helpfully.

"I'm sure we'll find you something to do." Penny winked at her. "Joe will be glad to see you. I'm pretty sure he'll be feeling a lot better in the morning though, so if something comes up and you can't make it, don't worry about it."

"I hope he's feeling better." Carly sighed. "I miss him."

Tom laughed. "What do you mean you miss him? You've been with him almost all afternoon."

"I know what you mean," Kelly interjected, patting Carly's hand. "It's just not the same without them joking around and fussing like they do. I'll be glad when Todd's up and doing better too."

Penny started clearing away dishes. "You're both welcome to come over tomorrow and see them."

"I'll help," Carly said, getting up.

She smiled warmly at Carly. "No, you go on up and see Joe for a little while. I can handle the clean up tonight."

"Are you sure?" she asked doubtfully. "I don't mind helping."

"I've noticed, but you go on. You've done enough for one day," she said, taking the dishes out of Carly's hands.

"Thanks," she said gratefully, dashing up the stairs to Joe's room. She poked her head quietly around his door, checking to see if he was awake. He hadn't moved since she'd left for dinner. She sat down at his desk and rested her head on her arms, watching him sleep for a few minutes.

"Carly," Kelly whispered loudly, shaking her shoulder.

She woke with a start. "Was I sleeping?" she mumbled, rubbing her eyes and trying to focus on the clock.

"You were snoring." Kelly giggled. "I could hear you all the way in Todd's room."

"What time is it?"

Kelly smiled. "It's eleven. I'm getting ready to leave, so I just came in to say good-bye."

"Eleven?" Carly said, surprised. "I better leave too, or they're going to think that I moved in." She stood up, stretched, and kissed Joe's cheek. "Do you mind if I follow you into town? I got kind of tired sitting here."

Kelly grinned as she got her coat. "Sounds great. I'll keep an eye on you to make sure you're not driving erratically."

"Are you leaving already?" Tom asked as they walked into the living room.

Kelly gave Penny a good-bye hug. "Yes, we're going to get on home before it gets late. Thanks for dinner."

"You leaving too?" Penny asked Carly as she shrugged on her coat.

She laughed. "I figured I better or you were going to think I moved in."

"By the way," Tom asked as he and Penny walked them to the door. "Who was that snoring upstairs?"

Carly gave him and innocent look. "Snoring? I didn't hear any snoring. Penny, I think you need to have his hearing checked."

"There's not a thing wrong with my hearing!" Tom said, grinning.

"You know, I've thought his hearing must be going. He says I snore too. I've tried and tried to tell him that ladies don't snore, but he doesn't believe me." Penny shrugged helplessly as Tom grabbed her to him in a bear hug. "You two be careful driving home, you hear?"

"We will," they said over their shoulders as they hurried out the door into the icy night.

Chapter Twenty-Two

Carly was miserable the next morning. She pulled the blankets around her tightly, trying to warm up, while every muscle protested loudly with even the smallest movement. She pulled her knees up closer to her chin and started rocking herself slightly. The pain in her stomach was almost unbearable.

"Oh," she groaned miserably as she looked at the clock. She shut her eyes tightly and concentrated on feeling better. Finally, she gave up. There was no way she was going to make it out to Joe's house that day. She had the flu. She knew she should probably call and let Penny and Tom know that she wasn't going to be able to make it, but the mere thought of getting out of bed and walking somewhere other than her bathroom was too overwhelming. The pain in her stomach worsened.

"Oh," she moaned again, clutching her stomach in misery. She jumped out of bed and ran to the bathroom, reaching the toilet just in time. When she was finished, she sat shaking on the cold floor, unable to stand up. She lay her feverish forehead against the cool porcelain sink pedestal, tears streaming down her face, wishing she had someone to take care of her.

She sat for a moment longer, waiting to make sure the worst was over, washed her face, clumsily brushed her teeth, and wobbled back to her bed on legs that felt like rubber. She fell into bed and pulled the covers up to her chin, anxious for the day to be over.

"I thought Carly was supposed to be here this morning," Penny said as she and Tom sat at the breakfast table, sipping their coffee and preparing to start the day.

"Maybe she's sick."

"I hope not. Who's going to take care of her?" Penny asked

with concern. "I wish I had a key. Maybe I should call," she said, going toward the phone.

"Call who?" Joe asked faintly as he walked into the kitchen.

"Joe! What are you doing up?" Penny asked, holding the phone in mid-air.

He sank slowly into a chair. "I'm getting ready to help with the chores."

"Are you feeling better already?" Tom asked with a doubtful glance.

"I'm feeling better," he said a little shakily. "I'm a little weak, but I'm good to go. Really."

"I don't think so," Penny said, hanging the phone back up to take care of the situation at hand. "I think you should take at least another day to rest. What do you think?" she asked, looking at Tom for his approval.

He finished his coffee and stood to his feet. "I think it's really up to Joe."

"I'll help as much as I can today, and if I start to feel worse, I'll stop and rest, okay?" he said soothingly. "I'm doing pretty good actually. Todd's still up in his room moaning."

"Maybe Carly's just late," Tom said, putting his arms around Penny and giving her a kiss. "She'll be all right."

"I hope so," she murmured, kissing him back.

"Where's Carly?" Joe asked as he, Tom, and Penny took care of the chores together. "I thought she was here yesterday, but I was so out of it, I can't really be sure."

"She sat by your side almost all day after she helped us around the farm. We didn't think we were going to get her to eat without you, but we managed," Tom said heartily, slapping him on the back.

Penny grinned broadly at him. "She's a good girl. I'm glad that you two met."

"I know. I can't even think of why I was ever interested in Amy now," he said, shaking his head in bewilderment. "I hope she's okay."

"Maybe you should go give her a call," Tom said, noticing his worried expression.

"I think I will," he said gratefully, setting down the brimming milk pails he was carrying. "I'll be right back," he said, jogging up to the house. He was back in just a few minutes, his expression glum.

"I take it she didn't answer," Penny asked kindly.

"No," he answered miserably, going about his work with much less vigor than usual.

"She'll be okay, son," Tom said, trying to make him feel better. "She knows how to take care of herself. She's had to for a few years now."

"I know, I just don't like her being by herself all the time. I'm afraid for her. I wish that house was done so we could get married. Then I wouldn't have so much to worry about."

"Are you worried about that Ian guy?" Penny asked, concerned. "Do you think he'll come all the way out here?"

"I hope he doesn't," Joe said anxiously. "I don't know what would happen if he did."

"Well, whatever does happen, we'll be right there with you," Tom said confidently. "I'll take you into town later on to check on her, if you want."

"I'd appreciate it," Joe said thankfully, glad he had such understanding parents.

Carly tossed and turned, trying to get as comfortable as possible. Between her frequent bathroom trips and her bed sheets getting all tangled up, she hadn't been able to get to sleep. The phone rang downstairs. Moaning, she pulled the blankets up over her head, trying to drown out the offending noise. Whoever it was didn't give up easily, the reverberations going around and around in her head. Resolutely, Carly flung the blankets off and slowly made her way downstairs to the offending instrument. Restraining an urge to throw it across the room, she picked up the receiver.

"Hello?" she whispered feverishly, trying to keep her voice steady.

Dial tone.

Unsteadily, she punched in Joe's home number and waited for someone to answer.

Penny answered after a few rings. "Hello?"

"Hi, Penny," Carly said shakily, her stomach doing a flip-flop.

"Carly! How are you? We were worried about you when you didn't show up this morning!"

"I'm sorry, I was going to call earlier, but I couldn't make it. I had a pretty hard time making it to the bathroom," she said, holding her head up with her hand.

"You've got the flu," Penny said matter-of-factly. "I knew it when you didn't make it this morning. Oh, honey, do you need anything?" she asked kindly.

"No, I'll be fine," she said quickly, not wanting to put Penny out. "The phone was ringing, so I thought it might be Joe."

"No, Joe and Tom are gone. I thought they were coming into town to check on you. Are you sure you don't need me to come help you?" Penny asked, concerned.

"I'll be all right. I'm going to let you go now. I've got a date with the bathroom," Carly said miserably, clutching her stomach.

"Good-bye! Hurry!" Penny said quickly so Carly could leave. Slamming the phone down, Carly rushed as fast as she could to the bathroom at the back of the store. She wasn't a minute too soon.

She was shuffling out of the bathroom when she heard a knock on the door. Cautiously, she peered around the corner to see who it was.

Joe. Her knees buckling and wobbly, she walked as quickly as she could to unlock the door and let him in.

"Carly!" he said anxiously, peering at her face. "You look

terrible! Here, let me help you up to your apartment." He gently took her arm and led her upstairs and into her bed. He tucked her in and took a look around.

"This is the first time I've ever been up here," he said quietly, trying not to disturb her. "It's small, but I think I could handle it for a little while," he said, grinning.

Carly moaned, drawing her legs up to her chin to get more comfortable. "Yeah right. There's no way you could handle this," she said quietly, closing her eyes. "I'm glad you're here."

"Me too," he said, sitting next to the bed, brushing her hair away from her face. "We kind of figured you were sick when you didn't show up this morning, so Dad brought me into town. Dad! I forgot he was waiting! I'll be right back," he said, jumping up and hurrying downstairs to let his dad know she was all right. He was back up in a few minutes, breathing hard as if he had run all the way.

"He's going to do some things in town for a little while, then he's going to come back by and pick me up, so I don't know how long I'll be here," he said, pulling up a chair and sitting beside the bed.

"Thanks," Carly said quietly, rocking slightly on her side to ease her pain. "How are you feeling?"

He grinned. "A lot better than you by the looks of it."

"You know, if we ever get married, you don't have to share your illnesses."

"If? What do you mean 'if we get married'?" Joe asked, his eyes wide. "Are you trying to pick a fight with me?" He glared at her.

"Yes," Carly said, smiling faintly.

"You're lucky you're sick, or I'd get you back for that one," he said saucily.

"Oh really? And what do you think you'd do?" she asked faintly, squeezing her eyes shut.

"I'd kidnap you and take you to the pastor's house and get married right away." He laughed. Carly moaned. "Can I get you something?" He asked anxiously, ready to do whatever was helpful.

"I think…never mind," Carly said hastily, jumping up and running to the bathroom, slamming the door shut behind her.

"Carly," Joe said through the closed door, trying to ignore the sounds coming from inside. "How can I help you if you shut the door? Come on, let me in. I can handle it."

"No way," Carly said weakly. "You're not supposed to see me like this until after we're married."

"Okay, I'll shut my eyes then. Come on, let me in," he coaxed, leaning on the door.

"Nope. You'll have to wait," she said, flushing the toilet.

"Are you okay?" he asked, listening for her to be finished. "Carly?"

She sat on the floor for a moment, too miserable and weak to move.

"Are you all right?" Joe asked, wiggling the doorknob impatiently. "Can I come in?"

"Yes." She sniffled, wiping her face with a cool washcloth. She leaned her head against the wall.

"Come on," Joe said, taking her arm and supporting her back to her bed. He helped her lie down, tucking the blankets in around her.

"Thank you," she said softly, trying to smile at him. He sat down next to her, smoothing her hair away from her face. "What are you going to do now?" she asked, curious to see how he would handle the tiny space. He fidgeted a moment before answering.

"Well." He hesitated. "I thought I'd just sit with you until Dad came back for me. Unless you needed me to stay with you longer." He looked around, stood up and went to the window, peered outside, shuffled back to his seat and sat down. "Honestly, I really don't know what to do now that I'm here." He grinned sheepishly. "What did you do while you were sitting with me?"

"I fell asleep." She smiled thinly, enjoying his discomfort. "Admit it. This place would drive you batty in fifteen minutes."

"Fifteen minutes?" he asked in mock indignation. "At least give me the benefit of the doubt. Make it twenty." He grinned and took her hand in his. "But if I could marry you right now, I'd make myself endure this place." He rubbed her fingers tenderly. "Why don't you go ahead and go to sleep. I'll wake you up when Dad gets back."

"And miss seeing you so uncomfortable? No way, buddy. I'm enjoying this."

He leaned down and kissed her on her forehead. "You're rotten, you know that?"

"Hey, I'm good at it; what can I say? Are you hungry? You'll find some fruit in the kitchen if you want any. Just help yourself."

"I am getting a little hungry. Do you think you could tell me the way? This place is so huge I might get lost," he said as he walked to the kitchen and helped himself to an apple. "I'd ask if you wanted anything, but I'd be afraid that I'd have to clean it all back up!"

"Ha ha." Carly groaned, trying to glare at him. "What are you going to do today?"

"I think Dad and I were going over to the city to pick up some things for the house, but he might have changed his mind. It's pretty cold out today, so I don't know if he'd want to help me work on it. If we go, is there anything that you might need me to pick up for you?" he asked as he walked over to the window to check for Tom.

"Can't think of anything."

He sat back down next to her, petting her forehead. "I guess Kelly's pretty sick too," he said, trying to take her mind off her stomach. "Mom called her this morning, and her aunt told her about it. Is that the phone?" he asked, surprised. He stood up to go answer it.

"Don't answer it, Joe. The only phone calls I've been getting have been from Ian, and I have no desire to talk to him."

He stopped at the door to look at her. "Maybe I *should* answer it then," he said heatedly, opening the door and taking the steps two at a time.

Carly struggled to get out of bed to follow him, praying he wouldn't make things worse than what they already were.

"Who is this?" she heard him ask as she came to the bottom of the stairs. "Ian, she doesn't want to talk to you, so just let her alone."

Silence.

Carly stood next to him now, watching his face anxiously. "Oh really? Well, I don't think that's going to happen. Thanks for calling." He hung up quickly, his face red with anger.

"Well?" Carly asked nervously. "What did he have to say?" He stared at her blankly as if he didn't see her. "Joe?" She shook his arm.

"What?" he asked, shaking his head as if to clear his thoughts. "What are you doing out of bed?" He took her arm as if to help her back upstairs, but she shook it off.

"What did he say?" she said, extremely agitated.

"He said a lot of things," he answered evasively, trying to help her back upstairs.

"I'm not going back up there until you tell me what he said," she said, crossing her arms. "Just tell me."

"Well, he knew that you're sick, that I was here, and that he really wanted to talk to me." He stared at her oddly for a second. "He said that you told him that our wedding was off and you two had patched things up. He also said that you knew now that I couldn't ever give you the things he could or take you the places he could and that you didn't think you could live on a farm with a hick like me."

"Do you believe him?" she asked weakly, her face pale.

"Should I?" he asked, looking at her squarely.

"No." She groaned, afraid that he wouldn't believe her. "He's just trying to break us up and make you think that I don't love you." She looked at him helplessly. "Please, Joe. You've got to believe me." Weakly, she put her hands on his chest, desperate to know what he was thinking.

He pulled her gently into his arms. "Will you do me a favor?" he asked, gazing down at her. She nodded. "Don't answer this phone anymore. Don't even call out on it. I want him to wonder if you're gone, okay? Will you promise that?"

"Okay," she said shakily. "But..."

He put his finger over her mouth, hushing her. "I'll take care of it," he said quietly, hugging her. "I'll buy you a cell phone when I'm in the city today. That's the only phone I want you to use for now, okay?"

"Joe, I can't ask you to do that for me. It's not right."

"For what? Taking care of you? You better get used to it, dear. That's my job now, and I'm going to do the best I can."

"Joe," she began.

"I'm not going to change my mind, so you might as well get used to the idea. You already promised, remember?" he said, teasing her.

"What did I promise?" she asked innocently. "I don't remember a thing. It must have been the flu talking."

He led her toward the stairs to her apartment. "Yes you do and you know it. You might as well get used to it."

"I know. I just don't feel right letting you do this. Are you sure it's the right thing to do?" she asked, stopping stubbornly in front of the stairs.

"Would you rather keep getting phone calls and take a chance that it might be Ian, or would you like to know exactly who is calling?"

"There's your dad," Carly said, interrupting him. She walked with him to the front door.

"Don't try to change the subject, girl," he said, allowing her to lead him. "And you're not really 'letting' me do anything. If I remember correctly, you're arguing with me as much as you possibly can." He pulled her close and kissed her forehead. "Now, get back upstairs. You're burning up."

"Tell your parents I said hi. Thanks for coming by," she called weakly as he walked out the door. She locked the door behind him, waved good-bye, and shuffled back upstairs, feeling better just because he had been there with her.

246

"Well, did I give you enough time?" Tom asked jovially, waving to Carly as Joe shut the door behind him. "How's she doing?"

"Yeah, you gave me enough time. She's pretty sick, but she's handling it well. She doesn't complain and cry, but I can tell she's not doing too well. Thanks for stopping by today," Joe said, preoccupied with his thoughts.

"You're welcome," Tom replied. He glanced at Joe. "Everything okay? You seem a little worried over there."

"Are we going to Billings today?" Joe asked suddenly, taking Tom by surprise.

"I thought we were heading that way, unless you've changed your mind."

"No, I really need to go. I've got to make a stop at the mall though if you don't mind."

"Sure," Tom said simply, knowing Joe would tell him what was bothering him when he was ready. It wasn't long.

"She got a phone call today," Joe began a few minutes later, looking out at the frozen world. Tom looked at him in surprise. He hadn't expected that to be the problem. "It was Ian. He said that he wanted to talk to me, not Carly." He turned his attention to Tom. "Dad, he knew I was there. He knew that you dropped me off and that Carly was sick. How does he know so much?"

"Sounds to me like he's either having her watched, or he's here in town."

"I thought the same thing. He told me that they had patched things up and gotten back together, but she just hadn't told me yet," he said glumly, looking out his window again. "And that I could never afford to give her everything she wanted."

Tom let out a low whistle. "So that's what's bothering you. Well, that might be partly true."

Joe looked at him in surprise, a scowl firmly in place. "You think they got back together?"

"No, I don't think she's like that. She loves you, and she's very happy with you. What I meant was that I don't think you'll be able to give her everything that he could. Did you tell Carly what Ian had to say?"

He looked uncomfortable for a moment before answering. "I didn't tell her exactly what he said, no."

"Why not?" Tom asked gently, keeping his eyes fixed on the road.

Joe turned his attention back to the window. "I was afraid of her answer."

"You were afraid that she was going to tell you that everything was all over?" Joe nodded silently. "Why do you think she'd go back to a guy that beat her and controlled her every movement? Do you think she liked that kind of attention?"

"No," he answered after a slight pause. "I'm afraid that it's just too good to be true."

"What's too good to be true? Your relationship with Carly? Do you think that God, the Creator of the universe, can't make a woman that will love you with all her heart? Do you think that God can't make a woman that's happier with her soul mate than with material things that the world has to offer?" Tom asked kindly.

Joe was silent.

"Joe, when Amy treated you the way she did, she hurt you so deeply that you seem to think that all women are like her. That's just not true."

Tom glanced sideways at him and clapped him on the shoulder.

"You've got to let Amy go. Get her out of your mind. Forget her and ask God to help you trust Carly and give you two the best marriage possible. He can do it, but you've got to ask first. Just look at your mother and me. We weren't always as happy as we are now. In fact, we were headed for a divorce, but then we got saved and gave it all to God. He turned everything around and did a better job than I ever thought possible. Now I couldn't live without your mother, and she feels the same about me. We're best friends. God's just waiting for you to ask and believe him, but you have to make that choice first."

"I never knew you and mom had marital problems," Joe said softly, looking at him. "You both always seemed so happy together."

"Every marriage has problems; it's just how those problems are dealt with. If you try to take care of everything on your own, you're going to lose. You've got to give it to God and ask him to help you both be who he wants you to be. I wasn't always worried about being a good husband, in fact, I was pretty selfish. But after I got saved, there was a big difference in the way I handled things and in who I was, but I still had to give all my problems to him. Just because I got saved, all my difficulties didn't just magically disappear. In fact, some of them got worse."

Tom smiled ruefully at the memories. "Not everyone was happy that we got saved. Most of your mom's family accused us of becoming 'Jesus freaks,' and my parents weren't too happy about it either, but when they saw the difference in our lives, they wanted to know more about God. They both received Jesus as their Savior before they died."

"I'm afraid," Joe said honestly. "Amy was sneaky at the beginning of our relationship, and I don't want to make the same mistake."

"Do you think Carly's not afraid of you?" Tom asked simply. "She's been through quite a bit with this guy Ian. He's treated her very badly, and she's probably wondering if you're going to end up like him. But she seems to be willing to take that chance. She knows that God can and will take care of everything. Now it's your turn."

"I never thought of it that way," Joe said thoughtfully. "You're right. I love her too much not to trust her."

Tom smiled. "It'll make your marriage a whole lot better too."

Chapter Twenty-Three

"Carly!" Joe shouted desperately, shaking her vigorously as she lay motionless on the bathroom floor. "Carly! Can you hear me? Wake up!"

He tried to pick her up and carry her to her bed, but she was too heavy. No matter how much he strained, he couldn't seem to even lift her arm. What was wrong with her?

He looked around wildly at the apartment, noticing for the first time that it wasn't the same neat and tidy apartment he had left earlier. This place was trashed. The refrigerator door hung on one hinge, the oven door was cracked, and the kitchen table had been broken in two. The door to the apartment looked as if someone had kicked it in. Why hadn't he noticed that when he came in?

"What happened in here?" he asked, still trying to shake her awake. Frantically he felt for a pulse. Not finding one, he ran downstairs looking for the telephone. Someone had ripped it off the wall, leaving just a wire hanging where it should have been.

Why hadn't he brought the cell phone to her earlier? Why had he waited? He ran to Sam's office, hoping to find a phone in there. It too had been smashed into tiny pieces. He had to get help for her, but everything seemed to go in slow motion. He couldn't run fast enough, he couldn't find a phone, he couldn't help Carly. What was wrong?

"Joe!" Todd said loudly, shaking him awake. "Joe! Wake up! You're having a nightmare!"

Joe sat up, scanning the room for Carly's lifeless body. Instead, he saw his own disheveled room, the blankets and sheets strewn on the floor, his pillow beside them.

"What? What are you doing in here?" he asked dazedly, still trying to get his bearings.

"You were having a nightmare," Todd said shakily. "You were hollering and yelling, nearly scared me to death. I'm surprised Mom and Dad didn't hear you." Todd sat down next to him. "What was it about?"

"Carly was dead." Joe shuddered involuntarily. "Her apartment was all tore up like someone had broken in. I've never been so glad to be awake before," he said thankfully. "What time is it?"

"Twelve thirty," Todd said. "Sounds like a pretty bad dream. You okay?"

"Yeah," he said quietly, rubbing his eyes. "I hope she's okay."

"It was just a dream. She's fine; you'll see. Try to get back to sleep," Todd said, getting up to go back to bed.

"Todd," Joe said before he left. "Do you believe that dreams have meanings?"

"Well," he said thoughtfully. "I suppose I do. When I dream about food, I'm hungry."

"I'm serious. Do you think that something bad could have happened to her tonight?"

"You just had a bad dream. She's fine, just go back to sleep. Good night," he said from across the hall.

"Sorry I woke you up," Joe said, unable to shake the helplessness he felt.

He lay back in bed and tried to relax. He tossed and turned, plumped up his pillow, willing himself to think of something else.

Nothing worked. He was wide awake. He got up and went downstairs into the dark kitchen, leaving the lights off so he wouldn't disturb his parents. He helped himself to some milk and sat down at the table, allowing himself to think about the nightmare he'd had. Was it a sign? Was God trying to tell him something? Was Carly in some danger? Worry gnawed at him. Doing the only thing he could, he lay his head down in his arms and prayed.

Lord, I don't know if this dream means anything, but I feel a strange uneasiness. I'm afraid for Carly. Will you please keep her safe and let me know what I can do to protect her? I love her so much Lord. I don't want to lose her. Please keep her safe.

He fell asleep, the unfinished prayer dying on his lips, his milk untouched. But God is faithful, even to the unfinished prayers of his people.

"Why in the world are you sleeping at the table instead of in your bed?" Tom said loudly the next morning, scaring the wits out of Joe and making him jump. He rubbed his eyes and looked at the kitchen clock.

"Is it really five forty-five?" he asked groggily. "I didn't think I fell asleep."

"I guess you did." Tom laughed. "What, were you afraid we would eat breakfast without you?" He slapped him on the shoulder and started some coffee. Soon, the welcoming aroma filtered through the air.

Joe inhaled deeply. "No." Joe grinned, feeling a little foolish. "I had a nightmare." He stood up and stretched, trying to work out the kinks in his back and neck.

"A nightmare? Oh I know. You were dreaming about all the outrageous cell phone bills you're going to receive." He winked as he poured himself a cup of coffee. "Want some?" he asked, offering a cup to Joe.

"Not yet." He smiled, thankful for the peace God had given him. "I'm just a little anxious for Carly, that's all. I'm going to run up and get ready to do my chores," he said as he trotted up the stairs to his room, passing Todd, who was just coming into the kitchen.

"Joe's up early," he remarked, opening the refrigerator door and helping himself to a glass of orange juice. "I thought he'd sleep in this morning." He took a big swallow.

"Yeah, I heard," Tom said thoughtfully, sitting at the table. "I guess he had some sort of nightmare."

Todd sat down across from him. "That's an understatement. I had to go in and wake him up. I'm surprised you and mom didn't hear him. He was loud. Kicking and yelling. About scared me to death. He dreamed that Carly was dead. It was pretty weird." He took another swallow of his orange juice, emptying his glass and pouring more.

"That doesn't sound too good. Did he tell you anything else?"

"Just that someone broke into her apartment and trashed it," he said simply. "But I was too tired to talk much about it, so I told him she was fine and that he needed to go back to sleep. Why?"

"Yesterday, when he was at Carly's place, that Ian guy called and talked to him. I think it shook him up more than I thought."

"Ian called and talked to Joe? Why?" Todd asked, dumbfounded.

"I guess to try and cause problems is all I can figure. He succeeded too. He seemed to know an awful lot about what goes on with Carly. I don't know if he's having her watched or not, but Joe's afraid that she won't be safe where she's at."

"I don't blame him," Todd said uneasily. "What's he going to do?"

"I don't know. I haven't got that far," Joe answered from the doorway. Tom and Todd looked at each other, embarrassed. Joe poured himself some coffee and sat at the table with them. "What do you two think I should do?"

"Do you think he's here?" Todd asked.

"No. If he were in town, he would have caused a lot more problems than he has. I think he's having her watched." Joe took a cautious sip of the hot liquid.

"Well, if he's not here, you don't have much to worry about. I'd worry when he was here, if he even comes out this way. I think he's just trying to scare you and Carly. He's all hot air," Todd said confidently, leaning his chair back on two legs.

"I don't know," Tom shook his head. "I think you're right to be concerned. This guy knows too much to just be hot air. If he wasn't interested in her anymore, he wouldn't have her watched. No, I think he's a threat. Maybe you two should get married right away."

Joe shook his head, discouraged. "She doesn't want to get married without having a place to stay. I thought I could stay at her place for a little while, but to be honest, it would drive me crazy. Anyway, she'd be left alone in town while I came out to work on the house. I need to get more of that house done so we can get married and move in, then he won't know where she is."

"Why is this guy so obsessed? I'm not trying to be mean or anything"—Todd looked apologetically at Joe—"but she isn't the only woman in the world. I'm sure he could find another woman, especially one that likes his money."

"That's probably why he wants her so bad," Tom interjected. "Carly's the only one that doesn't want him, and that bothers him. It's like a hunt. It's not necessarily that he loves her; it's just that she got away. In fact, if she would have stayed and married him, they would probably be divorced right now. Sounds to me like nobody's ever said no to him before."

"That's pretty much what Carly said," Joe said, finishing his coffee. "He doesn't like to lose. She's pretty sure that he's got another girlfriend, but he just won't give her up and leave her alone."

"So that's it then. Your plan is to just work on the house," Todd said flatly, looking him squarely in the face.

Joe set his mouth in a grim line. "No, I'm going to work my butt off on that house. She said she'd marry me when the bedroom, bathroom, and part of the kitchen were done, so that's where I'm concentrating."

"I'll help," Tom said, standing up and taking his coffee mug to the sink. "I'm ready whenever you are."

"I'll help as much as I can too," Todd said. "As much as you've helped me get my place ready, I figure I owe you at least an hour's worth of work." He laughed as Joe punched him in the arm.

Joe swallowed the lump that was in his throat and grinned.

"Thanks. I appreciate it."

"Dad, I'm finished! I'm going to run into town to check on Carly," Joe said, wiping his hands on his overalls when the chores were finished. "Do you need anything?"

Tom glanced up from the horse he was brushing. "I don't, but you might want to check to see if your mom does. Drive careful, the roads are pretty slick."

"I will," he said, heading out the door.

"Joe!" Todd said, following close behind him. "Can I hitch a ride with you so I can see how Kelly's doing?"

"Sure, just be quick," he said shortly, trying to hurry. As much as he tried to hide it, he was still pretty worried about Carly and could hardly wait to see her.

"I will," Todd said, hurrying to his room to change his clothes.

Joe hung up his overalls, washed his face and hands, put on his baseball cap, and waited impatiently for Todd to reappear.

"Hi, Mom," he said, sitting down at the table. "I'm going into town today, so if you need anything, let me know."

"I can't think of anything really. Well—oh, never mind. Are you going to eat lunch here, or in town?" she asked kindly, busy about the kitchen.

"I was thinking about eating in town, but I don't know now. Todd's coming along, so I don't know what he had planned." He drummed his fingers on the table.

"We'll eat in town," Todd said quickly, coming into the kitchen and grabbing his coat. "See you later, Mom." He kissed her on the cheek and followed Joe out the door.

They rode into town in silence, Joe preoccupied with his worries, and Todd was unwilling to interrupt.

"Do you want me to drop you off at Kelly's?" Joe asked edgily. He wasn't sure which he wanted to do first. He really was anxious about Carly, but he also knew that Todd wanted to see Kelly.

"I'll go with you," Todd said simply. "If she's feeling better, we can all go to get Kelly and then to lunch, if that's okay with you."

"Sounds good," Joe said, grateful for Todd's concern and loyalty. He pulled into a parking space and turned off the truck. He grabbed the cell phone he had bought for her and climbed out of the cab. Todd got out on his side, ready for anything that Joe might need him to do. Joe knocked on the door and peered inside, covering his forehead to cut the glare on the glass. Irritated, he knocked on the door a little harder.

"I will be so glad when we don't have to do this anymore," he said crossly as Todd took a step back to look up at her window.

"Carly," he called, cupping his mouth. Looking at Joe, he said, "Maybe she's still sick and can't hear us."

Joe's face was gray with worry and frustration. He walked around to the back of the store to check the back door. Locked. He banged on the back door, knowing that would get her attention if she were able to hear him. After a few minutes, he walked back to the front where Todd was continuing to knock.

"Nothing?" Todd asked, trying to keep the worry out of his voice. Joe shook his head grimly, getting back inside the truck.

"I think I'll take you over to Kelly's now." Starting the truck, he backed out and turned toward Kelly's place, throwing slush and muck up like a rooster's tail behind them as the tires spun.

They were just passing Sam and Sue's house when Joe had an idea. Hastily, he pulled into their driveway, put the truck in park, and jumped out before Todd could ask what he was doing.

He stalked up to the side door and knocked. Almost immediately the door opened and Carly walked out, wrapped in her heavy winter coat. Todd breathed a sigh of relief. Without a word, Joe grabbed her hand and pulled her into the truck, placing her between him and Todd.

"Hi, Todd," Carly said, a bewildered look on her face. She looked at him questioningly. He shrugged, not wanting any part of the situation.

"What's wrong, Joe?" she asked, turning to look at him.

He didn't answer.

"Joe!" she said, tugging a hand away from the steering wheel as he drove over to Kelly's place. Still no answer. "Are you okay?"

"Yes," he answered evenly, not looking away from the road.

"Okay," Carly said uneasily. "So how are you today, Todd?" she asked, her voice catching.

"I'm good," he said kindly, wishing to ease the tension in the truck. "How are you feeling?"

"Better," she said quietly as they pulled into Kelly's driveway. Joe turned off the truck.

"Uh, I'll go on in and check on Kelly if you don't mind," Todd said, already out the door, closing it hastily.

They sat in silence, unsure of what to say. Carly sighed and scooted over to Todd's side, opening the door.

"Where are you going?" Joe asked roughly, grabbing her arm. She pulled her arm away from him.

"I'm going to see Kelly."

"You can stay with me," he said hotly, grabbing her arm again and pulling her to him tightly.

Angrily, she resisted and tried to pull away from him. "Joe, let me go!" she said furiously, straining against him. "You're hurting me!" Immediately he relaxed his grip on her, giving her enough room to breathe but not letting go of her entirely. "What is wrong with you?" she asked, her face red with anger.

"What's wrong with you? You can't stand to be with me now, is that it?" he said bitterly, letting go of her completely.

She sat next to him in stunned silence. "What are you talking about?" she asked, all the anger gone out of her. "What is bothering you?"

Silently, Joe looked out the window. Gently, she put her hand on his arm. "Joe, what is it?" She leaned over to look at him, trying to catch his gaze.

"Are you going to stay with me even though I can't afford to buy you everything?" he said suddenly, taking her by surprise. All the jealousy and anger and helplessness he had felt came rushing out in a torrent of emotion.

"Joe, what did Ian say to you yesterday on the phone?" Carly asked gently, turning his face toward her. "Did he tell you that I wouldn't be happy with you?" He nodded, unwilling to talk. "You don't need to be afraid. You can give me everything I've ever wanted. I love you with every fiber of my being. Other than Jesus, you are the best thing that's ever happened to me. I don't ever want to lose you." She kissed him. He pulled her to him, hugging her tightly.

"Are you okay now?" she asked quietly, stroking his face tenderly.

"Yes," he said, still holding her close. He kissed her palm.

She grinned, pulling away slightly. "Good, because you really had me worried!"

"Worried? Do you want to talk about worried?" he said, grimacing as he pushed some hair out of her face.

He proceeded to tell her all that had happened to him the night before, starting with his conversation with Ian and finishing with the panic that had overtaken him when she didn't answer her door. "That's about it. How was your day?"

"Better than yours." She smiled regretfully. "I'm sorry that you couldn't find me, but I didn't think you'd be in town. I thought for sure that you'd still be doing your work."

"Can we come out now, or are you two still fighting?" Todd asked, opening the door and leaning inside the truck.

"Fighting?" they both said innocently."We don't know what you're talking about," Joe said, his arm snugly around Carly's shoulders.

"Good. We're hungry," Todd said, motioning toward Kelly, who was waiting patiently at the front of the truck. Kelly climbed in behind Carly, giving her an awkward hug and smiling from ear to ear, Todd getting in beside her.

"Ready?" Joe asked happily, pulling out of the driveway.

"I sure am glad you two made up. I wouldn't want to ride home with Joe if you hadn't worked everything out," Todd said, leaning forward to glance at his brother. Joe laughed, unruffled.

"It's good to have a little fight before you get married," Kelly said, smiling wickedly at Todd.

He frowned. "No way! I don't like fights, so don't pick any."

Carly laughed, snuggling closer to Joe. "But it keeps things in perspective."

They talked amiably on the way to the diner, halting only to find a seat together.

"I hear congratulations are in order for both of you!" Sandy said loudly as she came to take their orders. "When y'all getting married?"

Carly and Kelly looked at each other and giggled, unsure of how the men would answer.

"We haven't picked a date yet," Joe said finally, trying to stall for time. Todd laughed. "How about you, Todd?" he asked, putting Todd on the hot seat.

Todd turned red. "I'm not really sure either."

"You mean to tell me that you're engaged and you don't even have a date picked out yet?" She laughed brashly, causing quite a few of the customers to turn around and stare. "I wouldn't let them get away with that if I were you two," she said to the girls, who were trying heroically to hide their faces in their menus, not coming out until she had gone to get their drinks.

"That was embarrassing," Todd said, his face still pink.

"Are you embarrassed about getting married to me?" Kelly asked petulantly, winking at Carly. "I see how it is. I'm supposed to be your little lap dog now, is that it?" She turned away, lifting her chin toward the ceiling. Carly giggled while Joe pretended not to hear a word.

"What are you talking about?" Todd asked, trying unsuccessfully to get her to look at him. "Did I say I wanted a lap dog?"

She ignored him.

"If you hold your nose a little higher, you'll scrape the ceiling." Nothing.

"Kelly," he whispered, nudging her in the side. Kelly continued to ignore him, perusing her menu with dedication.

"Do you see what you got me into?" he asked, frustrated. "If you two wouldn't have been fussing, she wouldn't think it was all right to fuss with me now. Kelly," he took her hand in his. "I'm not embarrassed of you. I was embarrassed that she was being so loud."

"Okay," Kelly said happily, grinning. "That's all the fussing I want to do."

"Praise the Lord," he said morosely as Sandy brought their drinks. She took their food orders without further embarrassment, and they went back to their playful banter.

"Hey, Sandy," a gruff voice called, the door jangling open. "Got anything good to eat here?" Randy Pruitt said as he, Billy, and their father came inside. Randy and his dad guffawed as if that were the funniest thing in the whole world, Billy standing quietly beside them, his eyes riveted on Joe and Carly.

"Wassa matter wit you?" Randy said, elbowing him in the side.

Carly looked up, catching Billy's intense gaze. She smiled and waved at him, trying to be friendly. He stared at her without smiling for a moment, then turned his back on her, making it known that he still wasn't happy about their engagement.

Joe leaned over to whisper in her ear. "Darlin', I believe you've just been snubbed."

"Did it just get really cold in here?" Todd asked sarcastically, rubbing his arms. "What'd you do to him?"

"I guess he's just not in the mood to wave," Carly said flippantly, trying not to be annoyed.

"He's just jealous," Kelly said softly, squeezing her arm affectionately. "He'll get over it."

"Why does he always come in here when we're here?" Joe asked thoughtfully, glancing at Todd.

"Yeah, it's almost like he knows where you're at," Todd said, catching Joe's meaning. "Like he's watching you." He winked meaningfully at Carly, who stuck her tongue out at him. They joked around for the rest of their meal, not noticing when Billy left the diner.

Joe leaned back and patted his full stomach. "Sandy, we're ready for our bills."

"Y'all don't have any bills," she said, walking toward them. "They've already been paid."

"Paid?" Todd and Joe said simultaneously. "Who paid them?"

"New guy I've never seen before. He's gone now, but he was

sitting right over there next to where Billy sat," she said, sticking her thumb in the general direction of the counter.

"You've never seen him before?" Joe asked, immediately suspicious.

"Nope, but I wouldn't mind if I did see him again. Good-lookin' fella. You don't see the likes of his type in out-of-the-way diners like this one. Good tipper too." She grinned, picking up the tip Joe and Todd left for her, counting it expertly and slipping it into her apron pocket, all within a matter of seconds. "Y'all have a good night."

Joe was quiet on the drive back to Kelly's place, deep in his thoughts as the rest were talking and laughing. He pulled into the driveway and turned off the truck.

"Kelly," he said suddenly, taking them all by surprise. "Has there been anyone new that checked in since yesterday?" He took Carly's hand in his, holding onto it as if for dear life.

"Not that I know of, but I was sick yesterday, and Auntie gave me the morning off today. Why?" she asked, her curiosity aroused.

He scratched his chin. "Just wondering."

"What are you thinking?" Todd asked, watching his brother closely.

"Nothing really. Something's just not right. It doesn't add up. Why would someone we didn't even know want to buy our lunch? Doesn't that seem odd to you?"

Carly watched him uneasily, a chill running up her spine. When she had those feelings in the past, she had never ignored them, knowing that an unpleasant surprise always followed. Joe squeezed her to him, giving her comfort.

"Do you want me to check before you leave?" Kelly asked, getting out. "It won't take me long."

"No, that's okay. I'm sure it's nothing. Thanks," he said quickly, not wanting to put her through any trouble.

"Well, I better get inside. Thanks," Kelly said, giving Carly a quick hug. Todd walked her to the front door, hugged her, and whispered in her ear, making her giggle. Running, he jumped back into his seat, slamming the door shut behind him. He waved as Joe started down the road to Carly's place.

"So are you going to tell me what you're thinking?" Todd asked quizzically, leaning forward to see Joe's face.

"What are you talking about?"

"Don't even try it," Todd groaned. "I know you too well. I know when something's bothering you. Spill it." He waited patiently.

"I just have a feeling, that's all," he said, shrugging his shoulders.

"What does the feeling have to do with?" Carly asked as he pulled into a parking space in front of her apartment.

"It's just a feeling, nothing to worry about," he said, not meeting her gaze.

"Todd," she said, turning to his brother for support. "We may have to hurt him. Will you help me?"

"Of course." Todd gleefully rubbed his hands together. "I would love to." He laughed madly, making Carly giggle. Joe smiled, drumming his fingers on the steering wheel.

"Joe, please. Just tell me," Carly said, placing her hand on his arm. "I know it's about Ian."

"It just doesn't make sense," he said quickly, turning to face them both. "I don't even remember seeing anyone sitting at the counter, do you?"

"No, but we were all laughing and having a good time," Todd said for them both. "So, you think Ian's in town?"

Joe frowned, irritated that he hadn't paid better attention. "I don't know."

"Is that who you think paid for our lunches? Why would he do that if he hates you so much?" Todd asked skeptically.

"I don't know. Did you notice anyone at the counter when we walked in?" Joe asked Carly.

"No. I didn't pay attention to anyone except for us," she said forlornly, looking down at her hands, which were clasped tightly in Joe's.

"I'm sure it's nothing," he said hurriedly, noticing Carly's distraught expression.

"Every time I've felt uneasy, there has always been a nasty little surprise behind it, so I can't just dismiss it like you can. What am I going to do?" she asked, tears forming in her eyes.

"Pray," Todd said decisively. "That's the only thing I can think of."

Joe nodded, pulling her close and giving her a quick kiss on the top of her head.

"I don't like leaving you alone here," he said after they had finished praying. "Maybe we could have you stay with Kelly tonight," he said hopefully, looking at Todd for agreement.

Carly shook her head. "I wouldn't feel right doing that. Besides, what would I do in the morning when she had to work? I don't like putting people on the spot like that."

"Well, we could see if Mom and Dad would let her stay in the spare room at our place," Todd said halfheartedly.

"No, they wouldn't allow that before we were married. Too tempting." Joe grinned mischievously at Carly. She blushed and punched him in the arm. "The only thing I can think of is get married right away. Like this weekend. Then we could stay together in the apartment, and you could come with me when I went to work in the mornings and spend the day with Mom."

"Don't you think she'd get tired of me?" Carly asked, wrinkling her nose doubtfully.

"It wouldn't be very long," he said excitedly. "Just until I got some more of the house finished. What do you think?" He looked at her hopefully, squeezing her hand expectantly.

"Well," she said slowly. "It sounds okay to me, but I think we should definitely ask God's will to be done. I wouldn't want to drive your mom crazy too fast." Joe hugged her so tightly she thought she was about to burst.

"All right." He grinned, glancing at Todd. "You heard her. She said we could get married this weekend." Todd laughed.

"I said we need to ask God's will to be done. And if he leads us to this weekend, then okay," she said, smiling broadly.

"Sounds fair to me," he said, bursting with joy, kissing her. "We'll both pray about it, okay?"

"Okay, okay, okay. Knock it off," Todd said disgustedly, trying to hide his smile. "Don't you think we should be getting home now?"

"He's right," Carly said, pushing away from Joe for a moment. "I'll see you later." She waved to Todd as Joe walked her to her door.

"I'll call you tomorrow. Early," he said, kissing her before he ran back to the truck.

Carly watched them leave before she went inside, locking the door behind her.

Chapter Twenty-Four

"What in the world?!" Carly exclaimed, sitting up in bed in fright. She listened fervently for the sound that had awakened her. Unsteadily, she squinted at her alarm clock, trying to make out the time.

Almost 2:30 a.m.

She lay back in bed, listening for creaks and groans that weren't usual in the old apartment.

There it was again! *What is that? Is someone trying to drill the lock in my door?* she thought.

Terrified, she flew out of bed and ran to the kitchen, grabbing the first weapon she laid her hands on. Her frying pan. Holding it like a baseball bat, she tiptoed cautiously to her front door, ready to throttle anyone who stepped through. She waited, holding her breath, her heart pumping wildly.

The sound came again, this time directly behind her. Screaming loudly, she turned around and smashed the frying pan down onto the terrifying noise. Shaking uncontrollably, she sat limply on the floor, trying to regain her composure so she could see what had caused her so much alarm. After a moment, she switched on the light and glanced under the pan.

"Oh my goodness," she said, laughing hysterically as she picked up her cell phone. Somehow it had been switched to vibrate and had caused the awful sound she had mistaken for a drill. Wiping tears from her eyes, she switched it on to see if she had broken it.

No dial tone.

"Hello?" she heard a voice say faintly.

"Hello?" she said, surprised to hear someone talking, and even more surprised that it still worked.

"Carly," Joe said, sounding relieved. "What happened? I didn't think you were ever going to answer."

"It's a long story." Carly laughed shakily. "I know you said you would call me early, but don't you think this is taking it a little too far?"

"I'm sorry. I know it's early, but I've got bad news."

"What is it?" she answered, knots in her stomach. "Did you change your mind about getting married?"

"No way. You're not going to get out of it that easily. No, we got a call that my aunt Ruth is really sick and they don't expect her to last past the weekend."

"I'm sorry. Is there anything I can do?" she asked, concerned.

"Well, that's why I'm calling. We won't be able to get married this weekend like I was hoping." Her heart plummeted, matching the disappointment in his voice.

"That's okay. There's always next month," Carly said, turning off her lights and lying back down.

"I don't think so," Joe replied firmly. "Next weekend, Lord willing. Anyway, I was thinking that maybe you and Kelly could stay out here while we're gone."

"Sure, I don't mind, but does Kelly know?"

"Todd's talking to her right now. I'd feel a lot better if you were out here rather than in town."

"Are you still worried?"

"Just uneasy, that's all. Would you mind taking care of the animals and house for us?" he asked hesitantly.

"No, I wouldn't mind a bit. I'd be glad to help out. It's a good thing you taught us what to do!" Carly laughed, putting him at ease. "I'll miss you though."

"I'll miss you too, babe. I know this is going to sound mean, but I'm really disappointed about this weekend. I can hardly wait to be married."

"Me too, but I guess this is God's will in the matter, right?"

"Yeah," he said, his voice low. "I wish you could go with us."

"I wouldn't feel right doing that. This is good the way it is. What time do you plan on leaving?" she asked.

"We were going to leave around six thirty in the morning."

"Okay. I'll see you when you come back."

"When I come back? You're not going to see me off?" he asked, pretending to be hurt.

"I'm teasing." She laughed quietly. "How's Kelly going to get there?"

Joe was silent for a moment. "I hadn't thought of that. Let me see if Todd is still talking to her. Just a minute." Carly heard a muffled conversation as if Joe had put his hand over the mouthpiece of the phone. "Carly," he said, coming back on the line. "He's still talking to her. They haven't gotten that far yet."

"Tell her she can ride with me if she wants. I'll come pick her up at five." Muffled conversation again.

"She said that sounded good. She'll be ready." Joe sighed. "I'm sorry to put you through so much trouble."

Carly yawned. "It's no trouble. I don't mind. I'll see you in the morning, okay?"

"Thank you. I love you," Joe said softly. "Sorry I woke you up."

"I love you too. By the way. This phone is pretty tough. It can really handle abuse."

"Abuse?" She could tell he was confused.

"I'll tell you about it later. I just wanted you to know that you paid for a pretty good phone!" She laughed. "I love you, and I'll see you in a few hours. Good-bye."

"Good-bye. I love you too," he said, hanging up.

She pulled into Kelly's driveway promptly at five the next morning. She leaned over to open the passenger door. "Hey, girl, how are you this morning?"

"Extremely tired." She smiled, putting her suitcase next to Carly's in the back seat. "How are you?"

"Same here. Are you ready?" she asked, putting the truck in reverse.

"Yep, let's go. Todd scared me out of my wits when he called so early. How about you?" Kelly asked, leaning back in her seat.

"That's putting it mildly." Carly smiled ruefully, relating the story of someone drilling her lock to Kelly while driving to the farm. They were still giggling hysterically when they pulled into the driveway and parked.

Joe and Todd came out to help them with their suitcases.

"What are you laughing at?" Todd asked, ready for something to smile about.

Kelly laughed, wiping tears from her face. "You have to tell them, Carly."

Carly groaned good-naturedly.

"Sounds like a good one already." Joe laughed quietly, setting her suitcase down on the kitchen floor.

"It is." Kelly giggled, hanging up her coat.

"What's good?" Penny asked, filling Tom's cup with coffee. Her face was red and blotchy, like she had just gotten done crying.

"Good morning," Carly said quietly, unsure of how to act.

"Good morning. We didn't expect you two here so early." Tom's boom was softer than usual as he greeted the two girls.

Carly smiled, winking at Joe. "Joe made it sound like it would be a capital offence if I didn't see him before you all left."

"It would have been," he said, wrapping his arms around her from behind. "How do you think I would have survived?" He kissed her ear.

"Oh I don't know. Food. Water. Sleep. Just to name a few of the essentials." She giggled as he pinched her arm.

Penny continued bustling around the kitchen, making sure the last minute items were taken care of. "Have a seat, girls. Would you like some coffee or breakfast?"

"No thank you," Carly said quickly, not wanting to be a bother. "Is there anything I could do to help you?"

"No, I've pretty much got everything taken care of. Anyway, you're both doing us a huge favor by staying here and taking care of the animals. It's a load off our minds, and we really appreciate it,"

Penny said softly.

Tom got up and went over to her, giving her a big bear hug to comfort her. Carly, Joe, Kelly, and Todd were all silent.

"Here," Joe said, getting to his feet. "I'll take your suitcase to my room if you want." He quickly grabbed her suitcase and walked upstairs before she could say anything. She looked over at Todd, who was holding Kelly's hand so tight his fingers were turning white.

"He'll be okay," he said more confidently than he felt. "We just don't know what to expect when we get over there to see Aunt Ruth."

"How far away is it?" Kelly asked quietly.

"It'll take us about three hours to get over there if traffic is good. Lord willing, there won't be any traffic jams or road construction in our way."

Carly stood up to follow after him. "Excuse me." Quietly, she walked upstairs into Joe's bedroom and found him sitting at his desk, his head in his hands, her suitcase beside his dresser. She stood behind him and rubbed his back, trying to console him. He took her hand in his, not turning to face her.

"Are you all right?" she asked, leaning her chin on the top of his head.

"Yes," he said, his voice muffled. "I just hate doing this."

"Doing what?" she asked, hugging him to her.

"Dealing with the memories. The pain of losing someone. Leaving you behind. I wish you could go with me and at least meet her. She was a great person."

"Is," Carly corrected softly. "She's still here. Who knows? Maybe she'll get well. God still performs miracles, you know." Joe was silent.

"Look at us."

"What do you mean 'us'?" he asked, turning around to face her. He pulled her onto his lap.

"Joe, I had no intention of getting to know you better. I didn't want to. I was so afraid. I tried to keep myself from liking you, but

God made it impossible. I couldn't help but love you," she said, looking into his weary face. "And now, for the first time in a long time, I'm not even considering running away if Ian shows up. I'm happy and content and I don't want to be anywhere but with you."

"And now I'm going away," he said regretfully, kissing her hand.

"But you'll be back," she said confidently. "And when you're back, we might actually have a wedding." She smiled and kissed him lightly, as he pulled her into a hug.

"Joe," Tom said, his voice travelling up the stairs. "It's time to go." Joe sighed resignedly, burying his face in her neck.

"I'll walk you down," Carly said, pulling him out of his seat.

"There's really nothing that you have to worry about today. The animals are all fed, watered, and milked. The chickens may lay a few more eggs during the day. Just keep an eye on them, and there's nothing else really to do," Penny said, as they walked into the kitchen.

"Mom, they'll be okay," Todd said, giving Kelly one last kiss.

"Help yourself to whatever you want. I didn't have time to make any casseroles or dinners, but there's plenty to eat," she said as if she didn't hear him.

"We'll be okay," Kelly said reassuringly.

"Everything will be fine," Carly said, letting go of Joe's hand as he put on his coat.

"Do you have your cell phone?" he asked. She nodded, trying to smile. "Good. I'll be calling you."

She winked, trying to ignore the hollow feeling in her heart. "Maybe you could make it a little later than two in the morning this time."

"Maybe." He smiled sadly, wrapping a lock of her hair around his finger. "I love you, Carly."

"Lord willing, we'll be back in no time," Tom said, trying to lighten the atmosphere.

The girls walked them to the door and stood on the porch, waving until they couldn't see the truck anymore. Hurrying inside from the cold, they walked listlessly to the table and sat down.

"Well," Kelly said resignedly. "They're gone."

"Mm-hmm," Carly said sadly. "It's not nearly as nice with them gone, is it?"

"No, it's not. I miss them."

"Me too." They were silent for a while, preoccupied with their own thoughts. Kelly broke the silence first.

"Is there anything you want to do?"

"I hadn't really thought of anything, to tell you the truth. I'll probably go out to the barn and check on the animals, then come back in and work on Joe's room. How about you?" Carly said, getting up to pour herself a cup of coffee. "Would you like some?"

Kelly nodded. "What about going shopping later?" she asked, accepting the cup with a grateful smile. "Thanks."

"That sounds like fun. We could shop for our weddings!"

"Yeah! When do you want to go?" Kelly asked excitedly.

"It's way too early now, so what about after lunch?"

"That'll give me plenty of time to work on Todd's room. Goodness knows it needs it!"

"Well, if you need any help, let me know. I'll be right across the hall."

A few hours later, Carly stepped into Todd's room to see how Kelly was getting along.

"Wow!" she said, looking around the immaculate room. "You've done a lot!"

"Thanks," Kelly smiled, blushing from the praise. "I may not be a good cook, but I definitely know how to clean. That was my first job at the hotel, and boy was Auntie fussy." She grinned at the memories. "I didn't appreciate it then, but I sure do now!"

"It's so clean; he isn't going to be able to function!" Carly said, impressed.

"Truthfully, I couldn't have slept in here if I hadn't cleaned it. I would have had nightmares about Godzilla-sized dust bunnies!"

"Are you ready to take a break now, or do you need some more time?" Carly asked.

"Just let me finish up with the book case, and I'll be right down."

They spent the rest of the day at the mall, trying on clothes, dreaming about their futures with their husbands, and buying some needful things for their homes. They were about to leave when they ran into Angie and another girl Carly had never seen before.

"Hi, Kelly! Hi, Carly!" Angie said sarcastically, elbowing her friend in the side.

"Hi," they both said coolly, exchanging glances.

"What are you two doing here?" she said, trying to peer inside their bags. Instinctively, Carly pulled her bag closer to her side, making it difficult for her to see anything.

"Just shopping," Kelly answered, eyebrows raised.

"Kelly, you remember Amy, don't you?" Angie said, a malicious glint in her eyes.

"Amy," Kelly said coolly, nodding her head in greeting. "This is Carly." She introduced them, obviously uncomfortable.

"Hello," Carly said calmly, knowing that Angie was watching for any adverse reaction she might have.

"You're Carly. I've heard so much about you," Amy said, her voice sugary. "We were just going to sit down and have dinner. Would you two like to join us?" She smirked.

"We were just leaving. Thanks anyway," Kelly said quickly before Carly could answer.

Angie stepped in her way, sneering. "What are you afraid of, Kelly?"

"Nothing," she said disdainfully. "We have nothing to be afraid of."

Angie smiled contemptuously. "Oh really. Well, if you weren't afraid, you would have dinner with us."

"Angie, leave them alone," Amy interrupted, looking at Carly, her blue eyes glittering with hatred. "I don't blame you. I wouldn't want to eat dinner with my fiancé's ex-girlfriend either. Actually, I was almost his wife." She winked knowingly at her. Carly just smiled in return.

"So how is Joe?" she asked, changing the subject.

Carly held her gaze, carefully hiding all emotion. "Good, thanks."

"I bet he's still as handsome as ever. He always was a good-looking guy. I could kick myself for letting him slip away." She laughed, trying to goad Carly into getting angry.

"I'm sure you could. But that's all in the past now, isn't it?" She smiled sweetly at her rival.

Amy glared at her, smiling thinly. "Perhaps. Then again, maybe not. I could come back and take him away from you in a heartbeat. It would be so very easy."

"Are you trying to threaten me?" Carly asked calmly, unperturbed. "You don't worry me."

"Let's go," Kelly said, taking Carly by the arm and pulling her toward the door.

"You *should* be worried," Angie said after them.

"Oh that's right," Carly said, turning around to face them. "I almost forgot. Have a good dinner, and a great night! Good-bye!" she said, waving to them as if they were the best of friends.

"I can't believe they did that," Kelly said angrily, climbing into the passenger seat of the truck. "I didn't think Angie would go that low. Are you okay?" she asked, worried.

Carly sat quietly in the driver's seat, leaning her head on the steering wheel. Kelly put her hand on her arm, hoping to comfort her. Carly looked up laughing merrily.

"That was funny! Did you see their faces? That was priceless!"

Kelly stared at her friend, dumbfounded. "Aren't you mad?" she asked, bewildered.

"Mad? Why would I be mad? I know what Joe really thinks of Amy, so no. I'm not in the least bit mad."

Kelly smiled, visibly relaxing. "Come to think of it, it was pretty funny. Angie thought she was going to hurt you, and you took it all so well. I'm so proud of you! I bet she's so mad she could spit nails!"

"You know," Carly said, her eyes twinkling merrily. "I have half a mind to go back in there and give Amy Ian's phone number!"

"You couldn't do that." Kelly said, surprised. "I'd have to feel sorry for him."

"Let's go home before we get ourselves into more trouble." Carly laughed, expertly driving toward the farm.

"Carly!" Kelly called over her shoulder as she walked into the kitchen. "Your phone is ringing!"

"Oh my word, I forgot to take it with me!" Carly said, dropping her bags and running to the table where she had left it. "Hello?" she said breathlessly.

"Hello!" Joe answered, sounding surprised. "I was just going to hang up."

"I'm sorry. Kelly and I went to the mall, and I forgot to take the phone with me. I'm still getting used to having one. How are you?" she asked tenderly, walking upstairs into his room.

"Better now that I'm talking to you. I was getting worried."

"I'll remember to take it with me next time. Did you have a good trip?" she asked, sitting down at his desk.

"Yeah, I guess it was all right. We're at Aunt Ruth's house right now with a bunch of people I haven't seen in ages, so we're doing a lot of catching up on family things. I just stepped outside to call you. Did you have a good time at the mall?" he said, sounding much more relaxed now.

"Let's say it was interesting. Angie was there," she said, listening to his groan. "And I met Amy."

Silence.

"Amy," he said stiffly. Pause. "Did you talk to her?" His voice was tight.

"Yes, actually I did." Carly waited.

"And?" he prompted.

"And what?"

"What did you say?"

"You never told me how pretty she was. She's about my height, blond hair, blue eyes. Small and thin. You know." She paused.

"She's only pretty on the outside, Carly," he said huffily. "Are you jealous?"

"Should I be?"

"As jealous as I should be of Ian."

"Okay then. I was so jealous that I had to wave desperately at Billy Pruit when we came back through town." She paused for effect. "Maybe I still have a chance with him!"

"Carly," he said, his tone threatening.

"What?" she asked innocently. "I'm just joking. You know, she really is very pretty until she opens her mouth and talks." Joe breathed a sigh of relief. "She said that she could come take you away from me any time she wanted to."

Joe snorted in disgust. "Did you tell her to drop dead?"

"No, actually I wished her a good night. I was very nice to her, and it drove her nuts. It was great. How's your aunt Ruth?" she asked, tired of talking about Amy.

"Actually, she's doing better than we all thought. I don't know when Mom and Dad are planning on coming home, but I know Todd and I are anxious. We should have driven separately, but we didn't think about it. Hey, is Kelly around? Todd would like to speak to her for a minute."

"Sure, I'll go get her," Carly said, jumping up and walking into Todd's room. "Kelly, Todd's on the phone. Do you want to talk to him?" She winked at Kelly.

Kelly grinned, tapping her finger on her chin. "I don't know."

"Here, he says you have no choice in the matter." Carly laughed, handing the phone to her.

She walked back into Joe's room, giving them some time to talk alone. In Joe's room, she wandered around aimlessly, opening and closing his closet doors, looking listlessly through his drawers, pulling out one of his favorite shirts and caressing it lovingly, just trying to be as near him as possible under the circumstances. Finally, she sat on his bed, sighing heavily. Kelly came in, still talking to Todd.

"Here you go. Sorry we talked so long," she said, handing the phone to Carly.

She reached out, grateful for another chance to talk to Joe.

"Hi, it's me again. I guess I better let you go; you've got an early day tomorrow. I miss you and love you with all my heart," he said softly.

"I love you too and hope your aunt Ruth will be okay. I'll be praying for you all. Please tell your parents I said hi. I'll see you when I see you." Carly attempted to sound cheerful, but didn't quite succeed, and hung up.

"Well. I guess that's it then," Kelly said, coming into the room. "I really miss Todd."

She placed the phone on his desk, running her hand over the smooth finish. "I know what you mean."

Chapter Twenty-Five

The next couple of days went by slowly for the two girls, but they kept busy so they wouldn't have as much time to be dreary and feel sorry for themselves. When they weren't out in the barn, cleaning up the house, or doing laundry, Carly helped Kelly work on her cooking, and Kelly kept Carly laughing.

"When do you think they're coming back?" Kelly asked one morning after all the chores were finished. She pulled a perfect cherry pie out of the oven and set it on top of the counter.

"That looks awesome!" Carly said excitedly. "I can't wait for you to make one for Todd!"

"Me neither." She sighed, sitting down at the table. Carly's cell phone rang. They both dove for it, Kelly answering it first.

"Hello!" she said, laughing as Carly stuck her tongue out at her. "Carly? Do you want to speak to her? Okay. I'll tell her. Good-bye!" Kelly said, pretending to hang up the phone.

Carly grabbed it out of her hand. "Don't you dare hang up, Joe!" she said quickly. "Hello? Hello?"

Joe laughed heartily. "Hi, babe. I'm just teasing you."

"You better not hang up on me! I'd have to declare war on you! How are you? I've missed you so much! It's been ages since you called me."

"Ages? It's been only about twelve hours. Anyway, I was hoping you'd rather see me in person than talk to me on the phone."

Carly squealed with delight. "Are you coming home? How's your aunt Ruth? Is she better?" she asked, jumping up and down excitedly.

"No, Aunt Ruth isn't any better. We're still at her house, Mom's going to stay with her for a little while longer, and the rest of us are coming home. Lord willing, we should be home this afternoon, unless of course, you'd rather us stay another week," he said jovially.

"At the peril of your life, you stay another week!" she said, trying to sound threatening but not quite making it.

"Well, give the phone to Kelly, and we'll let her and Todd talk for a bit. I'm coming home, babe, and I can't wait to see you! I love you!"

"I love you too! Drive careful." Carly said before handing the phone to Kelly, unable to stop smiling.

"They're coming home! They're coming home!" They danced around the room after Kelly hung up, giggling like schoolgirls and flopping down into chairs, breathless with excitement.

"I can hardly believe it!" Kelly said dreamily, fanning herself. "Hey! What about making them a special dinner tonight? What do you think? Then I could show Todd how much you've helped me with my cooking."

"Sounds great. What do you want to make? Something easy, or something really difficult?"

"It can't be too difficult, or Todd will never believe that I did it. No, I think something easy but spectacular. Any ideas?" she asked, her face beaming.

"We could make some country fried chicken, mashed potatoes, and green beans. Or we could make some omelets with bacon, cheese, ham, onions, and tomatoes with some homemade bread? What do you think?" she said, blushing with excitement.

Kelly clapped her hands, her eyes twinkling. "Omelets are my favorite! Let's do that. First, I'm going to go over Todd's room with a fine tooth comb and make it perfect."

"Yeah, I'll tidy up Joe's room, then I'll go check on the animals and make sure that the barn is nice and clean and they don't need anything. Come on, I'll race you!" They both jumped up, and raced upstairs, both hoping to get finished before the other.

A few hours later, Carly was in the barn, making sure all the animals were taken care of, when she heard a car driving slowly down the road. She looked out the door window to see a dark green BMW stopping in front of the house. The windows were tinted black, making it impossible for her to see the driver. But she knew beyond a shadow of a doubt who was driving that car.

"Ian!" she breathed, her heart skipping a beat. Frantically she watched the house, hoping Kelly wouldn't come out until the car had gone.

Slowly the car began its crawl down the road, the occupant watching the house incessantly. An eternity passed before the car had completely gone by, enabling her to open the door of the barn a little to listen. Satisfied that they weren't parked just on the other side of the tree line, she raced as quickly as she could, bursting through the kitchen door, locking it behind her.

"Carly!" Kelly exclaimed, dropping the broom she was using. "You sc—"

Terrified, Carly grabbed her by the hand and yanked her upstairs.

"We've got to hide!"

"The attic!" Kelly shrieked, petrified. Quickly she led the way to a door at the end of the hallway and flung it open, taking two steps at a time. "Hurry!"

"Wait!" Carly said, grabbing her cell phone out of Joe's room, and dashed into the attic. Slamming the door behind her, she fumbled with the lock, her fingers stiff from terror.

Joe woke with a start, his heart pounding. "Where are we?" he asked groggily, trying to get his bearings.

Tom smiled, glancing at him in the rearview mirror. "We're a little less than an hour away from home. I've got to stop and get some gas," he said as he pulled into a service station. Todd was in the front seat, snoring loudly. None of them had slept well since they had left home.

"I'll be glad to get back," Joe said out loud, adrenaline

pumping. "I've got to get out of here," he said, grabbing the door handle and jumping out of the truck, trying to calm his nerves.

"You all right?" Tom asked, looking at him doubtfully. "You look a little pale. You're not getting sick are you?"

Joe bent over, gasping for air. "I don't think so. My heart is beating really fast, and I can hardly catch my breath. Dad, something's wrong."

"What?" he asked, coming over to him to help. "Should I take you to the hospital?"

He looked up, his eyes wild with panic. "It's not me. We've got to get home. I think there's something wrong at home."

"Now calm down, Son. Why do you think there's something wrong at home?" Tom looked skeptical.

"I don't know. It's a feeling. I think the girls are in trouble."

"What's going on?" Todd asked, climbing out of the truck, blinking in the bright sunlight.

"He thinks the girls are in trouble, but I think he's not feeling too well," Tom said, putting the cap on the gas tank. "I'll be right back."

"I've got a feeling that something's not right at home," Joe said, still trying to calm himself down.

"You have your cell phone. Call them," Todd said easily.

He punched in Carly's number and listened apprehensively.

"Well?" Todd asked after a moment, reaching for the phone. Joe shook his head and handed it over to him. Todd listened, waiting impatiently. "Are you sure you dialed the right number?"

"Yes," he replied shortly. Tom came back out, carrying a bottle of soda for each of them.

"Here. Maybe this will help," he said, giving Joe the bottle. Silently, Todd handed the phone over to Tom. He listened, shrugging his shoulders. "They're probably outside. Let's go," he said, trying to sound casual, but he climbed hastily into the truck.

Carly snatched up her phone the minute it started to ring and turned it to vibrate, hoping it hadn't been loud. They could hear someone on the porch, shaking the door handles and rattling the windows trying to get in.

Silently, she motioned for Kelly to hide behind a large assortment of old steamer trunks and barrels and handed her the cell phone.

"Shh. Whatever happens, stay hidden. *No matter what!*" she said, tiptoeing toward an antique roll-top desk. She jumped at the sound of glass breaking in the kitchen, her whole body shaking with terror.

Please God, she prayed silently, squeezing her eyes shut. *Please keep Kelly safe. Don't let Ian find her. Please God, please God, please God,* she continued, unable to think of anything else to say, trying to stay as calm as she could.

They heard someone in the kitchen, opening and closing the doors. Giving up, the person went into the living room, checking the closets in there.

"Carly." Ian's singsong tone floated up the stairs. "I know you're here. I saw you run in here from the barn."

Looking up at Kelly, she squeezed her eyes shut, wishing she was having a nightmare. She started to cry, unable to stop herself.

They heard him walking up the stairs, still calling out her name. "Don't be scared, Carly," he called soothingly. "I've come to take you home with me. We'll be married and live happily ever after. Isn't that what you've always wanted?" He threw open the door to Todd's room, carelessly hitting the wall.

He opened the closet doors. "I'm getting closer. There can't be many other places to hide. Come out, come out wherever you are," he sang, walking into Joe's room.

"Well, look what I found. What a nice picture of you, but you look so much better with me. Oops. Look what I just did. I'm so sorry I tore your picture. But no matter. This will soon be just a memory." The sound of Joe's bed being turned over and smacking the wall made Carly cringe.

She held her breath, as if she were afraid that he would hear her breathing.

"I wonder whose suitcase this could be." He flung it across the room, breaking the window. "After all I've done for you, this is the way you treat me? I bought you everything, I gave you everything. And yet you treat me like I'm the enemy. In fact"—he kicked the closet doors and she shuddered at the sound of splintering wood—"I'm the one who bought you and your friends' lunches the other day. Now do you think an enemy would treat you so well?"

Kelly shrank back as far into the wall as she possibly could, both hands over her mouth, smothering her terror.

"You think you would be happy with Joe, but you wouldn't. He can't give you the things I can," he said, flinging the papers on his desk everywhere. Next he pulled out all the desk drawers, throwing them into the wall, smashing them. They heard him trashing his room like a madman.

"You belong to me," he said, unsuccessfully twisting the doorknob to the attic. "Open the door, Carly," he sang, jiggling the old knob, trying to force it open. "You're not playing very fair. You're supposed to come out when you're found!"

He began kicking the doorknob over and over again as Carly cringed further behind her hiding spot, praying for a miracle.

"Hello?" Joe said into his phone after the first ring, expecting to hear Carly. Nothing. "Hello?" he said louder, listening a moment. Todd turned to look at him apprehensively. "There's nobody there. Wait," he said, straining, plugging his other ear. He heard something in the background. "Todd. What is that?" he asked thinly, handing the phone over to Todd. Todd listened intently, his face going pale.

"It's someone calling Carly's name," he said quietly, handing the phone back to Joe. He looked helplessly at Tom. "We've got to go faster," he said thickly, barely able to talk around the lump in his throat.

Without saying a word, Tom pushed the gas pedal down as far as it could possibly go.

"I know you're in here. Why don't you come out, and we'll talk about this like the adults we are," Ian said, stepping slowly up the stairs, the broken door swinging back and hitting the wall.

"Carly. You know I don't like games like these. They make me a little angry. Come out, Carly."

He stepped up another stair.

"You know you love me and not this country hick."

Another step.

"I've got the plane tickets ready and waiting."

Another step.

"We can get married and be on our way to the Bahamas."

At the top of the stairs.

"Come out now. Your little game is over. I've won. You've lost," he said, starting toward the pile of trunks Kelly was hiding behind. Carly stifled a cry, afraid that he would find and hurt Kelly. Immediately he was at the roll-top desk.

"Get up," he said, grabbing her roughly by the arm, glaring at her.

"We've got trouble," Tom said, pulling the truck over to the side of the highway. Todd and Joe groaned as they saw flashing blue lights behind them, unable to believe they were getting pulled over at a time like this. Tom rolled down his window.

"Hello, officer—"

The officer interrupted him impatiently. "Do you know how fast you were going?"

"Yes, sir, I do. But we've got—" Tom said as calmly as he

possibly could.

"May I see your license and registration," he said again, obviously aggravated. "What's the rush?"

"Here," Joe said tersely, pushing the cell phone toward him. "Listen for a minute."

"I don't want to hear any of your excuses…" the officer started, then listened for a second. He glared at them. "Is this some sort of prank?"

"No. My fiancée is in trouble," Joe said with difficulty. "Her ex-boyfriend has been stalking her for years, and I'm afraid he's going to hurt her." The officer looked from Joe to Todd to Tom and back again, unwilling to believe their story. "Just listen!" Joe demanded impatiently, wanting to jump out and run the rest of the way. "If you don't believe us, then follow us home and give us the ticket there! Please! I'm begging you. We're almost there," he said, trying not to give in to the urge to curse.

Todd looked helplessly at him, his eyes begging him to believe them. "Please."

"Let me see that again," he said, reaching for the cell phone.

Carly rose to her feet reluctantly, shaking uncontrollably, knowing a beating was about to happen. She looked at Ian as steadily as she could.

Ian grinned. "It's nice to see you again, Carly."

She was silent.

"Aren't you happy to see me?"

Silence.

"We've got a lot to talk about you know," he said, gripping her arm tighter. "Why don't you just come with me, and there will be no trouble."

"What do you want?" she asked, yanking her arm away.

He reached out a hand to her face, she drew away, wincing as if he'd already hit her. "I told you what I wanted," he said, grinning at her coldly, taking her arm again, his fingers biting into her arm like steel. "I want to take you with me. We're going to get married. Remember?" He leaned down toward her, intending to kiss her. She pulled away, repulsed.

"Don't you ever pull away from me!" he spat, slapping her across the face. Carly cried out, holding her stinging cheek.

"You know," he said, softly. "If you would just do as I say, I wouldn't have to hurt you." Grabbing her to him, he kissed her hard, crushing her lips against her teeth.

She tasted blood. "Stop it! You're hurting me!" she said, trying to wriggle away.

He grinned with pleasure, tightening his grip on her arms. "You haven't seen anything yet, my love."

"Please," she whimpered, blood starting to ooze out of the corner of her mouth. "You're really hurting me."

He yanked her arm and slapped her across the other side of her face, enjoying himself. "Then come nicely, and you won't have to get hurt."

"I don't want to go anywhere with you," she said, freeing her arm from his grasp. Roughly, he grabbed her by the hair, pulling her face close to his. "No matter what you do to me," she said bravely, "I will not go with you or marry you. It's over."

"Sounds like this could be fun," he said mockingly, jerking her to him, kissing her bruised mouth again.

"Stop it!" she said, kicking him as hard as she could in the shin. Yelling in pain, he momentarily let go of her and clutched his leg.

As soon as she was free, she rushed toward the steps. Seeing she was about to escape, he reached out and shoved her as hard as he could, sending her sprawling down the narrow steps. Screaming, she tried to catch herself as she fell, pain shooting through her wrists as she came crashing down to the floor. He limped down the stairs, fury contorting his features. He stood over her a moment, watching her try to crawl away from him, tears streaming down her face.

"It didn't have to be this way," he said, squatting down next to her. Smiling tenderly, he brushed hair out of her face. "Are you hurt?"

Carly gasped for air, still trying to crawl away from him.

"Your nose is bleeding," he said, reaching toward her bruised and bloody face. She pulled away. Angrily, he punched her in the eye, making it swell shut. "I told you to never pull away from me again. When are you going to learn that I'll always win. No matter what." He stared at her thoughtfully for a moment. "It'll all be better when we're married. You'll see."

"No," Carly wheezed, starting to cry. "I'm going to marry Joe."

Infuriated, Ian stood up and kicked her, causing her to roll toward the steps leading down to the kitchen.

"No…" he said through gritted teeth, kicking her again.

"You're…" another kick to the ribs; she screamed in agony.

"Not!" He finished with a tremendous kick to the small of her back, sending her sliding head first down the stairs.

"Beg me for mercy," he said, coming down the steps. "If you beg, I might stop." He grinned, his cold blue eyes glittering. "But then again, I might not."

He looked into her unconscious face, picked up her hand and rudely yanked off the ring Joe had given her, leaving a welt behind. "You won't need this anymore," he said, stuffing it into his pocket. "It's a good thing I love you so much. You've really put me through quite a bit of trouble. But, to show you what a good guy I am, I'll forgive you and act like it never happened. Let's go for a ride, darling."

He picked up her limp arm and dragged her across the floor to the door, out to the porch, down the steps, and into the snow, uncaring that she was without coat or shoes. They were halfway to his car when Carly came to and started struggling, trying to get away.

Letting her go, he kicked her again and again, his face red with rage, unaware that a truck had pulled into the driveway, skidding to a halt just a few feet away from where they were. A police car followed, lights flashing.

"Carly!" Joe shouted, jumping out of the truck before Tom could stop him. He tackled Ian, taking him by surprise and sending him sprawling headfirst into a snowdrift. Tom slammed the truck into park while Todd jumped out to help Joe, who was grappling with Ian in the snow.

The police officer jumped out of his car and ran over to pull Joe off Ian. "Stop!" He yanked Joe up to his feet and shoved him toward Tom, who grabbed his arms, trying to restrain him. He roughly pulled Ian to his feet, put him in handcuffs, and marched him over to the squad car, shoving him in the back seat.

"Kelly!" Todd yelled, running panic-stricken into the house, afraid of what might have happened to her.

Joe jerked his arms away from Tom and kneeled down next to Carly, cradling her in his arms. "What did you do to her?" he screamed at Ian, who just smiled coldly and winked through the frosty glass.

"Carly," Joe said, rocking back and forth, trying to wake her.

"I'll call an ambulance," the trooper said with concern, reaching for his walkie-talkie.

"I already did," Kelly said, running out, Todd close behind.

"Were you here the whole time?" the trooper asked, surprised.

Sobbing, she knelt next to Joe petting Carly's bloody hair. "Yes, I was."

"I'll need you to give a report then," he said, opening his notebook.

"Can I give it at the hospital?" she pleaded. Todd lay a comforting arm around her.

"That'll be fine," he said kindly.

"Joe," Tom said, coming into Carly's hospital room. "Have some coffee." Joe took the cup gratefully, rubbing his red eyes distractedly.

"Did you see her? Did you see how frail and…and broken she

looked, lying there in the snow?" Joe stood up and walked around the room, stopping beside her bed and taking her hand lovingly. "How could a man do that to a woman? How could he do this to her?" he whispered, his voice breaking. "What if she dies? What will I do without her? How will I survive?" He broke down, his shoulders heaving.

"She'll be okay," Tom said, coming around the bed and hugging his son tightly, his voice wavering. "All we can do is pray and trust."

"How is she?" Kelly asked, walking into the room, clutching Todd's hand as if for dear life. "Has she woken up yet?"

"Not yet," Joe said, breaking away and walking over to the window, wiping his eyes.

"Mr. Baird?" the doctor said, walking into the room, unannounced.

"Yes?" Tom, Joe, and Todd all said at once.

"I need the one that's engaged to Miss Richards," he said kindly.

"That's me," Joe said nervously, shaking his hand.

"The x-rays show that she's got four broken ribs, two on the right and two on the left. Her nose is broken, her left arm is fractured, her left wrist is broken, her right kidney is bruised, and she has a complex concussion. We don't know when she'll wake up, but when she does, we'll have to watch for dizziness, nausea, blurred vision, and disorientation among other things. Her spleen and liver aren't punctured, which is a miracle in itself. She took a pretty rough beating. You're lucky that you got there when you did, or he would have killed her."

"Luck had nothing to do with it," Tom said quickly. "God got us there just in time."

"Yes, sir," the doctor said with disinterested compassion. Turning to Joe, he said, "I assume the person who did this is in jail?" Joe nodded, not trusting himself to speak. "Good. After she wakes up, we'll run more tests."

"May I stay with her?" Joe asked, his voice thick with emotion.

"Of course. The couch pulls down to make a bed. The nurse will show you how it works, and she'll bring you sheets and blankets. I'm sure we'll be seeing each other quite a bit." He shook Joe's hand and left the room to see his other patients.

Joe leaned over her bed, watching her anxiously for some sort of movement. "How did he know where to find her? How did he know she was there?"

"You can't blame yourself, Joe," Todd said quietly, understanding what he was thinking. "We all did what we thought was the best thing for her. Just think what could have happened if she had been at the store."

Joe stayed by her bedside, leaving only to shower for the next two days, waiting fretfully for her to wake up. No one could prevail upon him to leave for any reason, or any cost. Tom, Todd, Kelly, and various friends visited often throughout the days, bringing him meals, mail, and news to try to take his mind off his worries.

"Joe," Kelly said softly the third day, laying her hand on his back as he slept fitfully in the chair.

"Hmm?" he murmured, his voice gravelly from exhaustion.

"Why don't you go home for a little while? You haven't shaved for the past three days, and I'm pretty sure that you haven't slept too well either," Kelly said kindly, sitting down in the chair opposite him, setting a book on the small table beside her.

Tiredly, he rubbed his whiskered cheeks, his eyes bloodshot. "I'm all right."

"You need a break," she said, not letting him off the hook too easily.

He stood up and stretched, groaning from the stiffness before he answered her. "I want to be here if she wakes up," he said stubbornly.

"Well, she's going to need you to take care of her, and if you're too tired you won't be able to do it. At least take a short walk outside and get some fresh air."

"Kelly..." he said, his bloodshot eyes restlessly roved around the room as he argued.

"Please," she interrupted before he could finish. "If she wakes up, I'll send someone out to get you. She needs you to be ready to help her."

Joe went to the window and looked outside at the gray, forlorn world. A world that seemed destitute of all hope.

"All right," he relented, knowing she was right. "But just for a minute. I won't be gone long. If she wakes up," he said, turning at the door, "don't let her go back to sleep until I get back. Tell her I love her," he said, his voice cracking.

"I will," she said, settling back into her chair and opening her book.

She was deep into her book when she heard a soft, almost inaudible groan. Surprised, she looked up to see Billy Pruit standing beside Carly's bed, trying to choke back tears but not quite managing. He was holding onto the railing to steady himself, his face ashen gray.

He stared at her bruised and beaten face. "Is she going to be okay?" He asked, not looking away from Carly.

"I don't know," Kelly said quietly, amazed at his reaction. She had never seen Billy so tenderhearted or worried about someone else before, not even his own family. "The doctors are concerned about her not waking up yet, but they're doing the best they can. All we can do now is pray."

"Pray!" he spat. "What good will that do?"

"All the good in the world," she said simply. "God still performs miracles, Billy."

"God?" he asked incredulously. "God didn't protect her, did he? What kind of God is that?"

"What Satan intends for evil, God can use it for good," she said calmly. "Carly loves God, and God always knows what's best."

"Billy," Joe said, coming into the room, breathing heavily as if he had been running. Billy snorted hatefully and stalked out, muttering under his breath. Joe and Kelly looked at each other, astounded.

"Well. That was interesting," Joe said, sitting down in his chair beside Carly, taking her hand. "Did she wake up?" he asked, hoping to see any sign of movement or evidence of consciousness.

"Nothing." Kelly sighed, sitting back in her chair and picking her book back up. Joe lay his head on the side of her bed, needing to be as close to her as possible.

"I'd do anything for her," he said softly, waiting for sleep to claim him and take him to a happier time in the not-too-distant past.

He lay sleeping until someone rubbing his head startled him awake. Sitting up, he looked around the room to see who was there.

No one else was in the room.

He looked at his watch, wondering how long he had been asleep—6:30 p.m. Three and a half hours. Had he been dreaming? Standing up and stretching, he tried to get some feeling back into his legs and arms.

"Joe."

He whirled around from the window, his heart skipping a beat.

"Carly?" he asked, hurrying to her side. "Are you awake?" She nodded as he brushed her hair back, tears welling up in his eyes. "I didn't think you were going to make it." He leaned down and kissed her tenderly.

"No such luck," she said thickly. "What happened?" she said, looking confusedly around her. "Am I in the hospital?"

"You don't remember?"

"Not really. I remember being out in the barn and hearing a car. I watched it drive by, and then I ran into the house thinking it was Ian. We hid in the attic and..." she trailed off, wincing. "My head hurts."

Gingerly, he rubbed her hair. "Stop then. It's all over now. We don't have to worry about it."

"Was I in some sort of an accident?" she asked sleepily, her eyelids drooping.

"Kind of. Don't go to sleep yet, babe. I need to call the doctor so he can come look at you, okay? Can you stay awake?" he asked rubbing her hand, worried that if she fell asleep she might not wake up again. She nodded.

"We're glad you're awake," the doctor said, responding quickly to Joe's call. "How are you feeling?"

She tried to smile, her swollen lips making it impossible.

"Okay."

"Does anything hurt?" he asked, looking at his chart.

"It feels like I've been run over by a semi-truck. My sides, head, arm, nose. Body. Take your pick."

"Do you remember why you're here?" he asked, taking her pulse. She shook her head. "Can you see well?"

"It's blurry."

"Does the light bother you?" She shook her head. "Are you tired?"

She nodded, smiling up at Joe. The doctor nodded, pleased. "Why don't you go back to sleep then."

"Will she wake up though?" Joe asked anxiously, still rubbing her hand.

"She'll probably wake up quite a bit now that she's got the hang of it." The doctor winked, making Carly smile. "I think she's going to be just fine. I'll leave you two alone."

"I'm so glad you're all right," Joe breathed, holding her hand tightly.

"Why wouldn't I be? I've got God and you looking after me," she said drowsily.

Carly woke later that evening still holding Joe's hand. He had fallen asleep, his head resting on his arm. She disentangled herself from his grip and tried to get as comfortable as possible.

She lay trying to remember what had happened, memories flooding back and fading away before she could make much sense of them. She was still preoccupied with her thoughts when the door opened and Billy snuck into the room. He stopped short, amazed to see her awake. She lay a finger on her lips, pointing toward Joe. Billy stood rooted to the spot, unwilling to move and break the spell.

"You're awake," he finally said softly, walking hesitantly toward the bed. She nodded, smiling. Billy stood next to her awkwardly for a few minutes before speaking. "Are you okay?"

"I'm going to be fine," she said. They stared at one another for a few uncomfortable seconds until Carly broke the silence. "What brings you here so late?" her voice barely above a whisper.

Billy looked down and shuffled his feet broodingly. "I just wanted to see how you were doing," he answered abruptly, looking her in the face.

"I'm good, Billy. Good," she said tiredly, leaning her throbbing head back onto her pillow.

"Good?" He scowled. "How can you say you're good? Don't you know you're in the hospital because some guy beat you up?"

She looked at him, her eyes thoughtful. "Actually, I didn't know that I was here because I was beat up. But I guessed as much."

"Guessed? You forgot?"

"I guess he knocked it right out of me." She smiled ruefully, trying to lighten the mood. "I'm glad God took care of me."

He shook his head, frowning. "God? How can you thank God for this?"

"How?" She looked at him kindly, praying for the right words to say. "Because he took care of me. He didn't allow Ian to kill me, that's one thing."

"Fine. What else can you thank God for?" he said earnestly, looking at her.

"For the friends he's given me. For giving me a home. For allowing me to live another day. For my health. For forgiving me.

293

For my salvation," she said softly, praying that God would use her to be a witness for him.

"Forgiving you? What do you need to be forgiven for?" Billy asked suspiciously.

"Because I'm a sinner, that's what I needed to be forgiven for."

"A sinner? What's the big deal about being a sinner?"

"It's a very big deal, Billy. If I didn't ask Jesus to forgive me of my sins, I wouldn't be able to go to heaven when I die," she said, watching his face for some sign of understanding.

"This is all about being a Christian again, isn't it?" he said, eyeing her skeptically.

"I suppose it is." She grinned then grimaced at the pain in her mouth.

"You sure are religious, ain't ya?" He snorted rudely, rolling his eyes. "My dad always said there were people like you, but I'd never met one before."

"It's not that I'm religious," she said quietly but firmly. "My religion isn't what's going to get me to heaven."

"Yeah, I know," he said, interrupting her before she could finish. "That's why you wouldn't date me, because you were afraid that you wouldn't go to heaven." He looked contemptuously at Joe, who was still laying with his head resting on his arm on her bedside.

"You know, there ain't nothing but a bunch of hypocrites at churches, that's one of the reasons I don't like to go to church." He glared at her, daring her to disagree with him.

"I'm sure there are hypocrites in churches, but that isn't all there is," she said, trying to be kind. "But you know, I sure have met a lot more hypocrites out of the churches than in them. They're in the stores, at the restaurants, anywhere you go, but that doesn't stop you from going to those places, does it?" she asked gently, her eyes not leaving his face. He glared at her for a little longer, not saying anything.

"Billy," she said softly, "Don't you want to go to heaven when you die? If you were to die today, where would you spend eternity?"

He blinked, taken by surprise. His mouth opened as if he wanted to say something, then he shut it quickly, watching her to see if she were serious. Emotions rushed through his eyes and face, a mile a minute.

"I can't." Suddenly very anxious to leave, he edged toward the door.

She watched him, wincing as she turned her head. "Why can't you? Don't leave yet. Please."

He turned to stare at her, not wanting to leave, yet not wanting to stay. "Why do you want me to stay? So you can save my soul?" he said, trying to sound tough but unable to hide his true feelings. "I'm unforgivable."

"No one is unforgivable. All you have to do is ask him Billy. Just ask."

"I told you I'm unforgivable!" he said bitterly, misery contorting his face. Shocked, Carly looked over at Joe, surprised that Billy hadn't woken him.

"I'm sorry," Billy said wretchedly, but quieter. "If you really knew me, you wouldn't have anything to do with me."

"Billy, I don't care what you've done. Nothing is so big that God can't forgive it. Please. Won't you just ask him?"

Irresolutely, he stood at the door, unsure of what he should do. "Ian knew where you were because of me," he finally blurted, staring at the floor. He looked up at her battered face and continued. "I met him at the diner, and I was really mad that you were going to marry Joe and wouldn't give me a chance, and I told him everything I knew, including where Joe lived."

Carly lay in stunned silence.

"Now do you see why I'm unforgivable? I haven't cared about anyone but myself for as long as I can remember, then you came into town and changed all that. I cared more for you than anything, and I'm the one who put you here. It's because of me," he said, his voice cracking with emotion. "I better go."

"Wait!" Carly said urgently before he could get all the way out the door. "Let me ask you a question." He nodded for her to go on. "You say that you're unforgivable, right?" He nodded again. "Did you want Ian to hurt me?"

Anguish flooded his face as he looked at her bruised face. "No! I just thought he'd take you away from Joe. I didn't know he was going to beat you up."

"Ask me to forgive you," she said simply.

"What?"

"Ask me to forgive you," she said kindly. He hesitated, a confused frown on his face. "Why did you come here? Wasn't it to ask me to forgive you? Were you sorry for what happened?"

"Yes," he said slowly, looking at her doubtfully.

She looked at him stubbornly, her chin jutting out defiantly. "Then ask me to forgive you. You came all the way here to do it, so go ahead."

"Will you forgive me?" he said uncertainly.

"Okay. I forgive you." She smiled her sweetest smile at him. "Doesn't that feel good?"

He looked at her as if she had two heads. "Doesn't what feel good?"

"That you're forgiven." She smiled happily at him. "See. You're not unforgivable."

"How can you forgive me?" he asked pitifully. "I don't deserve it."

"Don't you get it yet?" She laughed quietly, then winced from pain. "Not one of us deserves to be forgiven, but God gives us mercy and forgives us anyway. Freely, in fact. We don't have to do a thing to earn it. All we have to do is ask. Don't you want him to forgive you? Don't you want to be free from your sins and sorrows and know that whatever happens to you he's going to be right there with you, guiding you and taking care of you? Don't you want peace in times of trouble and heartache? I couldn't have lived through both of my parent's deaths and this situation with Ian without God. Don't you want that? Let go of your hate and rebellion. Ask him to forgive you," she said softly, reaching a hand out to him.

Quietly, he shut the door and walked over to the bed, took her hand gently, and with tears in his eyes, bowed his head and asked God to save him.

"Congratulations, Billy," Carly said, tears streaming down her cheeks after he was finished. "I'm so happy for you."

"Thank you," he whispered, looking at her warmly and brushing her hair away from her face. "I wish I could hug you."

"Right now, that would hurt." She laughed softly, brushing the tears away from her eyes.

"Congratulations," Joe said, yawning loudly, looking at them both.

"How long were you awake?" Carly asked in surprise.

"Just about the whole time." He stood up and offered his hand to Billy. "I'm glad for you."

"I owe you an apology as well, Joe," Billy said, accepting his hand. "I've been a jerk to you ever since we were kids, and I'm sorry. I'm sorry that I was jealous and told Ian where Carly was." His voice broke with emotion. Recovering himself, he added, "But if you change your mind about marrying her, I'm still available." He winked at her, half-joking, half-serious.

Joe took her hand, squeezing it as tightly as he dared. "I don't think you'll have the chance, buddy. I'm going to marry her right here in the hospital while she can't get away. She has no choice."

"Joe…" she said, starting to argue.

"I'm not taking any other answer," he said firmly, not giving in. "We're getting married as soon as I pick up the license. That's it."

"But…"

"Nope. There's no arguing. When you get out of this hospital, you're going to be my wife, and I'm going to take care of you."

"That's not very romantic," she said softly, her eyes shimmering with unshed tears. "But to be honest, I'd love to become your wife as soon as possible." She squeezed Joe's hand affectionately, smiling up at him.

"Congratulations to you both then." Billy cleared his throat, embarrassed. He tried to be as happy for them as he could be. "I should get going and let you two work it all out." Quickly, he started for the door, anxious to be gone.

"Billy," Joe said. He stopped and turned around, still edging toward the door. "You're always welcome at our place, and we'd both like to invite you to the wedding." Carly nodded emphatically. "Will you come?"

"I'll try," he said. "I've got to go." He closed the door and was gone before anything else could be said.

Carly and Joe were married two days later in a crowded hospital room, surrounded by their family and friends (Billy included), doctors and nurses, in a very untypical wedding ceremony. Carly sat up in bed, still unable to get up and walk around, but was beautiful and resplendent, eyes sparkling joyously.

Joe stood tall and protective over her, promising to hold and cherish, love and care for her till death parted them. When the pastor gave him permission to kiss the bride, he kissed her tenderly and softly, not wanting to hurt her bruised mouth, never wanting to let her go.

One Year Later

⌒

"Mail call, Carly," Penny called, letting herself into Carly and Joe's house. "How are you doing?" She went to the kitchen and started some coffee for herself.

"Hi, Mom," Carly said, waddling into the kitchen to join her at the table. "Thanks for bringing the mail." She sat down heavily, leaning her cane on her chair. "What'd we get?"

"Just a bunch of junk, looks like to me. Except for this one," Penny said, handing her an official-looking envelope. "How's the baby?" she asked, patting Carly's enlarged stomach affectionately.

"She's doing well." She grinned, rubbing her belly. "I can't believe I've still got two months to go." She breathed deeply, opening the envelope. "It feels like she's sitting on my ribs swinging from one side to the other. And the heartburn could kill ya! I feel like a dragon."

"I remember exactly." Penny laughed. "Here's some juice," she said, setting a mug of cider on the table for her. Carly sat still, frowning at the letter she held in her hand, her face pale.

"What's wrong?" She laid a hand on her shoulder, her heart skipping a beat. "Is it the baby? Do you want me to get Joe?" she asked, shrugging her coat on.

"Ian's dead," she said flatly after a moment.

Penny gasped, sitting back down. "When? What happened?"

"His plane crashed, killing everyone on board." Carly passed the letter to her to read. Absentmindedly, she got up and walked over to the sink, looking out the window.

"Why does this guy," she paused, reading the letter, "Jed, want you to come out there?"

"The only thing I can figure is that maybe I'll get the money Ian took from me. I don't really know." She paused, her shoulders stooped as if a heavy weight hung on her.

"Are you going to go?" Penny asked gently.

"I've got to talk to Joe about it first, but I was thinking I might."

"Why?" she asked incredulously.

"I need to forgive him," Carly said softly, her eyes begging Penny to try to understand. "I've been trying to ignore the whole situation and just forget it, but it's eating me up inside, making me bitter and hard-hearted. Maybe if I go, it'll be easier, and it'll bring closure."

Penny reached over and gave her a quick hug. "If that's the way you feel about it, then I'd say go."

"Carly!" Jed exclaimed, putting his pen down and coming over to greet her as she walked into his office. "You look great!" He eyed her full stomach and rosy cheeks, his admiration evident.

"Hi, I'm Jed Wilson," he said, offering his hand to Joe, who followed close behind her.

"Jed, this is my husband, Joe Baird. Joe, this is Jed," Carly said, introducing them, proud of her handsome husband. Joe shook his hand, unsmiling.

"Have a seat," Jed said, walking back to his chair. "I know that it wasn't a pleasant surprise when you received my letter, but I'm glad you came," he went on, casting sidelong glances at Carly as they made themselves comfortable. "I must say that you look beautiful, Carly," he said approvingly. "Marriage must agree with you!"

She blushed and shot a quick glance toward Joe.

"To tell you the truth, it wasn't a pleasant surprise," Joe said, irritated with the way Jed kept looking at her and the way he was talking to her.

"It *was* a surprise," Carly interjected, trying to ease the tension.

Jed looked from one to the other, his fingers drumming a quick staccato on his desk.

"First, let me say that I'm really sorry about what happened last year," he began. "Ian told me that you and he were going to be married. I had no idea what he really intended."

Joe cleared his throat, annoyed. Jed glanced at him and went on.

"When he came back though, he was different. He just dove into his work and would hardly talk to anyone. It was like he was possessed. Insane almost."

"What is your purpose for bringing Carly here?" Joe said angrily. He stood up to leave. "Is it to try to make her feel sorry for the man who intended to kill her?"

"I have no intention of trying to make her or you feel sorry for Ian," Jed said, raising his hands in defense. "Please. Sit and listen for a moment. I have some things you both need to hear."

Carly took his hand in hers, her eyes pleading. "Please, Joe." Reluctantly, he sat back down and edged his chair closer to hers.

"Thank you." Jed cleared his throat. "Then, this past October, Ian changed. He was happy, almost jolly. Joking, flirting. Once again, he asked me to watch the business while he was away. I didn't ask questions. Ian hates it when people pry." Jed looked embarrassed. "I just figured that he was going on vacation or something. To tell the truth, I didn't really care. The office is so much more relaxed when he's not here."

He colored, thinking he may have said too much. "Anyway. He left last week and his plane crashed. That part you both know from my letter. Now for what I didn't tell you. He left me as executor of his will. After I read it, I believe it was his intention of kidnapping you and forcing you to divorce Joe and stay with him," he said quietly.

Carly gasped her face pale.

"Why do you think that?" Joe asked, holding her hand firmly in his own.

"To put it bluntly," Jed said, clearing his throat, "he left her everything he owns. Including his shares in this company. Plus, when I went into his apartment, I found these." He lay two one-way tickets on an airplane headed to Mexico. He leaned back in his chair, allowing them to take the information in. Carly picked up the tickets then put them down as if she had been burned.

"Why would that make you think he planned on kidnapping her? He might have been intending on taking someone else. You said that he was flirting again," Joe asked, bewildered.

"Because Ian never gave anything away," Carly said before Jed could answer. "He was a very calculating person, and he didn't like doing something for someone if it didn't benefit him in some way."

She stood up, laying her hand on her stomach absently, and walked about the room. She stopped at the window and turned to face Jed. "So why did you want me to come here? So you could tell me this, or is there something else you wanted?"

Jed opened a file and laid it on the desk in front of him. "That's pretty much it, except you have to sign some papers to claim all the things he left you."

"What if I refuse?" she asked, leaning on the windowsill, looking at Joe.

"I guess it would go to the government, but I wouldn't advise you to let it go," Jed said, perplexed. "I don't think you understand how much you would be getting."

She shook her head stubbornly, her jaw set. "All I want is what he owes me from stealing my wages."

"Okay," he said slowly, drumming his fingers on his desk absently.

He stared at her for a moment, perplexed. Then his face brightened. "When are you due?"

"Two months," Joe answered proudly.

"Were you planning on having a baby so soon after your wedding?"

"Jed." Carly gripped her cane tightly, knowing what he was thinking.

"Not really," Joe said honestly. "We were going to wait a little longer, but it didn't happen that way."

"Don't you think this money could help your family?" Jed asked gently. "Are your medical bills all paid for? That can't be cheap." He stood and walked over to Carly, taking her hands in his, gazing at her face.

"Look. After all the things Ian did to you, he owes you more than just back pay. Don't be so stubborn. Listen to reason."

Carly stepped away, turning her back on both of them. "Joe, what do you think?"

Joe leaned back in his chair, arms crossed. "I think whatever you decide will be just fine."

"Everything, Carly," Jed said. "A major part of this company's shares, which would keep you both nicely for the rest of your lives. All the money that's in the bank, stocks, bonds, his apartment, cars, belongings. Everything."

Carly was silent for a while, contemplating what to do. "Not everything, Jed," she said finally, turning and walking back to Joe. "I think this is what I'll do." She took a deep breath. "I'll take my back pay and enough of the money to pay off all the medical bills, plus what it's going to cost to have this baby. I'll keep the shares of the company, stocks, and bonds. But for the rest, I don't want it. I don't want him having a hold over me. I want this whole thing to be done and over. You take the rest that's left over and keep it for yourself. You've always been kind to me, and he's been rotten to you as well. I've seen it, so you deserve it."

"Don't you think you're being stubborn?" Jed said, confused. "Joe. Make her listen. You both could be living the high life. You can have everything you've ever wanted, and she's just going to throw it away. Don't let her do this."

"Don't you see, Jed?" Carly asked compassionately, taking Joe's hand in hers. "Money can't buy happiness or peace and security. All I ever wanted I've got right here. God's already given it to me."

READING GROUP GUIDE

1. In the opening chapter, we see Carly about to stall out on the expressway and she begins praying for God to take her just one more mile. What insight does this give you about Carly? Is it a reasonable assumption? Why or why not?

2. Throughout this book, we see Carly praying often in various situations - even about little, seemingly meaningless things. Do you think this gives a taste of her relationship with God? When do you find yourself praying the most? After a difficult time or all the time?

3. Is a prayer life important? Why or why not? Would you change your prayer life? In what way?

4. After a time, we see Carly and Joe falling in love. Do you think this was an easy thing for Carly, or difficult? Why? Is it possible for an abused woman to overcome the pain of her past and learn to trust someone again enough to love them? How did Carly's relationship with Christ help her with this?

5. Why would Joe be so willing to take care of Carly and what showed you, the reader, that he was concerned for her?

6. Billy Pruit was the typical, unsaved, from the wrong side of the tracks character. What was your first reaction to his character? Why did you feel this way? After you were finished with the book, did you feel differently about him? What made you change your mind?

7. Joe has been hurt in an emotional way, while Carly has been hurt in a physical way. How do both these situations influence the way they handle life? In what ways are these two similar? Different? What is it about their past that bring them together?

8. Is it believable for Billy's character to readily accept Carly's forgiveness? Why? What about Billy's conversion? Is that possible and what makes you think that?

9. Have you ever done something that someone wouldn't forgive you for? How did that make you feel? If you could do something--anything--about it, what would it be? Does your reaction fit with Scripture?

10. Which character did you find yourself drawn to the most? Why? The least?

11. If you could change one thing about the book, what would it be and why?

12. Is there anything in this book to which you personally can relate? Is there any advice or ideas you can take and apply to your own life?

About the Author

Amanda Stephan is just a normal, everyday country girl. Residing in Middle, TN with her husband and children who closely resemble several of the seven dwarfs, (Sleepy, Sneezy, Grumpy, and Happy), three cats, (only because hubby refuses to get one of his own so she must share,) one dog, and multiple roosters that love to roost under their bedroom windows. She loves to laugh and have a good time, and loves to read a good book.

You can meet up with Amanda at these places -
Facebook www.facebook.com/creativehomemomma
Twitter www.twitter.com/amandastephan
Website www.booksbyamanda.com
Pinterest http://pinterest.com/homemomma4
or her collective blog www.thepriceoftrust.com